CHAPTER

One

The memory of blood is seared into my mind.

It stains the grass in the courtyard of Ivystone Citadel, even if only in my mind's recollection. From the balcony of my room, I have a clear view of where the attack occurred. The battle has scarred the pristine courtyard of the castle with blood of both human and beast. Obstinate, dark patches on the flagstones refuse to be scrubbed away, and the broken lanterns, glinting like jagged teeth in the daylight, remain unfixed. The wind, sharp and cool, brushes against my face, tangling strands of my long, dark hair and carrying with it the faint scent of lingering smoke from the fires that had ravaged the grounds. Not long ago, this same wind carried the haunting cries of the carnoraxis who attacked us. Now, it is eerily quiet, as if the castle itself holds its breath.

"Celeste." Nadya's gentle voice pulls me from my thoughts. I turn to find her standing in the doorway, her usual cheer dimmed, replaced by a seriousness I rarely see in my best friend. Her hands are clasped in front of her, fingers twitching slightly, betraying her unease. Her ebony curls frame her face like a crown, and her deep-brown eyes, accentuated by thick, long lashes, are pools of quiet intensity against her smooth, dark

 1

skin. I can see the turmoil behind them, the weight of so much unsaid, and it mirrors the unsettling storm I feel brewing within myself. "The court is gathering," she says. "The king is about to speak."

My chest tightens. I can guess what the ruler of Hedera will say, but that doesn't make it any easier to face. He's about to lie to the court. He's about to convince them of a story in order to cover up a much more sinister scandal. Still, I nod and smooth my hands over the silk of my onyx-black dress.

I almost falter, my head swimming with doubt and worry. But I release a sigh and gather my strength. I'm the commander of Delasurvia's Royal Regiment, after all, and I'm accustomed to pushing my feelings aside for the sake of duty. "All right. Let's get this shit show over with."

I take the thin, black coronet from atop my bed covers and place it on my head. A wisp of black tulle flows from its edges, covering most of my hair but leaving my face visible. I'm not always expected to wear it, but today I'll be standing on the dais with the king and queen, so I need to dress for the occasion.

Nadya and I exit my room to find Sir Holden, my faithful Royal Ward, waiting in the corridor to escort us. It seems he hasn't bothered to keep his hair cropped short since the attack, and the same goes for his beard. I can't blame him. It's been hard to return to "normal" when it feels like life has been stuck in limbo.

The king's announcement today will no doubt change that, but I'm not positive it will be a change for the better.

"Have you spoken with Dante?" Nadya whispers, leaning close to me.

"No." I swallow down the trepidation in my throat. "The king has doubled the guards since... well, you know. And after what happened to Torbin, there's no way he'll allow me anyway near his only remaining son. Especially not alone."

But the king doesn't fear that I'll hurt Dante. Because I would never do that. The king is keeping us apart as part of his ploy to retain control of my homeland of Delasurvia. He laid his entire plan out to both Dante and me weeks ago. First, he will announce Torbin's death. Then he will

 2

A
SABRE
IN THE
HEMLOCK

A
SABRE
IN THE
HEMLOCK

Blade Bound
Book Two

DOROTHY DREYER

A SABRE IN THE HEMLOCK: BLADE BOUND, BOOK TWO
Copyright © 2025 by Dorothy Dreyer
Published by Crimson Fox Publishing
crimsonfoxpublishing.com

Crimson Fox
PUBLISHING

Cover by Christian Bentulan
Interior Format by Dorothy Dreyer
World Map by Mad Maps

Paperback ISBN: 978-1-963870-23-7
Hardcover ISBN: 978-1-963870-22-0

Other Books by Dorothy Dreyer

Awards for
A DAGGER IN THE IVY

Book one in the Blade Bound Saga

Winner of the 2025 Next Generation
Indie Book Award
for Romantasy

Gold Medal Winner of the
2025 Readers' Favorite Book Award
For Romance – Fantasy/Sci-Fi

First Place Winner of the
Spring 2025 BookFest Award
in the category Romance – Fantasy

Best Book Winner of the
Spring 2025 PenCraft Award
in the category Romance – Fantasy/Sci-Fi

Yes, there's more spice in this one

DULCAMAR

MESSANYA
ISLANDS

KINGDOM
OF
BASTOS

PODROSAN
REPUBLIC

DEADLANDS

MERSOS

legitimize Dante. And finally, once the mourning period for Torbin is over, he will announce that Dante and I are to be betrothed. Because if his new prince marries me—the heir to the Delasurvia throne—then King Silas could essentially keep a foothold on both our lands.

In the corridor, Sir Holden Hale strides ahead of us, his posture rigid with the disciplined air of a man who takes his obligations seriously. His polished armor shines across his broad shoulders in contrast to the shadows of growing scruff outlining the sharp angles of his square jaw. He isn't as massive as Mylo—my fierce lieutenant—but the muscle beneath his uniform suggests strength that could snap a man's neck without much effort. Despite the weight of his sword at his side, he moves with ease, every step deliberate. Though his face remains impassive, I catch the occasional flick of his gaze. Always watching, always assessing, and ready to defend me at a moment's notice.

The hallway feels longer than usual, its high ceilings pressing down on me. The golden sconces that once gave the castle a sense of grandeur now seem to cast long, ominous shadows that taunt me. The soles of my ankle boots echo against the polished floors, the sound too loud in the heavy silence.

Nadya must feel it, too, because she reaches out and gives my hand a squeeze.

As we descend the grand staircase, the slight, almost undetectable limp in Sir Holden's gait is a reminder of the injury he sustained during the carnoraxis attack. I'd healed the injury as much as I could with my fae magic, and to an onlooker, one would never know the tall, muscular guard's flesh had been torn into by the creature's unforgiving claws, but I see it. I know the damage is there, beneath the surface. A shudder rushes through me at the thought of the countless lives I hadn't been able to save, the injuries I wasn't able to heal.

All because of the fucking Shadow Tsar.

On the main floor of the castle, I catch glimpses of servants darting in and out of rooms, their faces pale and drawn. The mourning ribbons draped along the walls seem to mock me with their emptiness. They are

 3

for a prince whose body was never found, the king's son, whom I don't believe is truly gone.

The doors of the great hall are already open as we approach, and the room is overflowing with the presence of Hedera's courtiers. Sir Holden nods to the guards on the far wall and leads me through the crowd toward the dais. I spare a glance over my shoulder at Nadya, who keeps close to the edge of the room. She offers a small smile to let me know she's there for me.

King Silas Copperhammer sits rigid on his throne, his tall frame casting an imposing silhouette against the stained-glass windows that stretch behind him. Soft, colored light filters through in fractured beams, but it does nothing to soften the harshness in his face. His white hair, as pristine as freshly fallen snow, is perfectly groomed, but there's a stiffness to the line of his jaw that wasn't there before. The weight of loss pushes down on him, heavy and inescapable, yet he holds himself with the same unwavering authority—a man who expects the world to bend to his will.

His piercing, blue eyes sweep the hall, cold and calculating, missing nothing and forgiving even less. When his gaze falls on me, it lingers a breath too long, and beneath the surface of his grief, I catch the faintest flicker of something darker. Distrust. Blame. The accusation is clear: I'm the reason his son is gone.

The emerald-green robes he wears are darker today, almost black in the dim light, as if even his finery must bear the weight of his mourning. Gold embroidery traces the edges in delicate ivy patterns, a reminder to all of the wealth and power Hedera commands. But it's not the grandeur that unsettles me. It's the stillness in him, the calculated control, as though if he lets any emotion slip free, the façade will shatter.

His hand tightens on the carved armrest, the only sign of the tension coiled beneath his outward composure. Whatever he's about to say, I know it won't be the whole truth. King Silas does nothing without purpose, and whatever that purpose is, I have no doubt it doesn't favor me.

 4

To his left, Queen Eleanor clutches her linen handkerchief like a lifeline, her red-rimmed eyes belying the grief she struggles to contain. Her posture is as poised and graceful as ever, but the woman before me is not the goddess I first met when I arrived in Hedera. Her pale-blonde hair, once a cascade of shimmering waves down her back, is now cut blunt at her shoulders. I have no doubt the chopping of her hair was an order from King Silas meant to humble her after she received flirtatious compliments from one of Hedera's lords—a lord whom Torbin beat to death in front of the entire court. But to me, the style only makes her look more fragile. Her light-blue eyes, far softer than her husband's unyielding gaze, stare out over the hall, distant and hollow. It's the look of a mother in mourning, yet even in her sorrow, she holds herself with the dignity of a queen.

Her gown, a deep shade of amethyst, hugs her slender frame, the high neckline and long sleeves hiding her from view as if armor could protect her from grief. Silver embroidery winds along the bodice in delicate patterns, and diamonds sparkle at her ears. I can't help but think the jewels serve to draw attention from the pallor of her complexion or the ruddy skin around her eyes.

Her hands, perpetually gloved in velvet, rest motionless in her lap. Aside from her personal servant and her husband, I may be the only one who knows the real reason she hides her limbs and neck from curious eyes. The king doesn't limit his heavy hand to ruling over his realm. I notice the tightness of her grip—a small betrayal of the pain she works so hard to conceal. When her gaze drifts to me, it lingers with something I can't quite place. Not malice, not blame, but a kind of quiet understanding. And yet, like her husband, she does not acknowledge me. Whatever compassion she once showed me is buried beneath the crushing weight of her son's demise—and the king who will not let her forget it.

I step toward my place on the dais, three steps behind the thrones and one step to the left of the queen. My back is bone straight, my face set in the calm mask I've learned to wear.

Then *he* enters the hall, and the air shifts.

 5

My breath catches, just for a moment, as if my body recognizes him before my mind does. It's been days since Dante and I have had a moment alone together, but seeing him now makes me realize the memories I've clung to haven't done him justice.

His wavy, black hair falls just above his high collar, a little more unruly than usual, as if he's run his fingers through his hair one too many times. The smooth, black jacket he wears fits his tall, agile frame perfectly, the tailored lines emphasizing the power in his shoulders and the sharp angles of his body. Beneath it, a dark shirt peeks through, maintaining the sleek, monochromatic style that always makes him seem both elegant and dangerous.

But it's his eyes that hold me—the storm-grey depths I know too well. They sweep across the hall, distant and unreadable, until they meet mine. And when they do, the world around us seems to blur. There's no trace of the sharp-tongued rogue who once mocked me and told me I don't belong here. Instead, there's something deeper, something that makes warmth caress its way up my neck despite the chill lingering in the hall.

He schools his expression, as I'm sure he's been instructed to. But the tension crackling between us is enough to make my heart thrum painfully against my ribs. And as much as I know I should look away, I can't. Not when he holds my gaze like that. Like I'm the only thing anchoring him in a room full of strangers.

Dante takes his place, standing to the side of the king's throne, and though he faces the crowd, I can tell he's not really seeing them. There's a quiet strength about him, though shadows of weariness linger in his posture. I wonder what he's thinking, what he's feeling, but I can't even get close enough to him to ask. Not without the king punishing me—or rather, punishing Delasurvia—for disobeying his command.

King Silas has concocted a distinct plan, and we are expected to abide by it.

I finally tear my gaze from Dante, but everywhere I look, everything I see sours my stomach. The mourning ribbons, the fog of sadness in the air, this fucking mourning gown—it all feels like a farce. Torbin is not

dead. I know it in my bones. But here in the great hall, under the weight of the court's collective grief and suspicion, I cannot say it aloud.

When the king lifts his hand, a somber silence ripples through the great hall. Every inch of the place is occupied, and the crowd spills into the open corridors beyond. The weight of what has happened seems to press down on all of us, making the air thick and difficult to breathe.

The only thing breaking the stillness is my pulse pounding in my ears.

"People of Hedera," the king begins, his voice carrying over the gathered crowd like the heavy toll of a bell. "Today, we gather to mourn those we have lost. The attack on our citadel was a tragedy, and my heart grieves for every life stolen and every family left broken." He pauses, his hands gripping the arms of his throne. "I have ordered my men to assist with the proper burials and cremations of the victims. No family will bear this burden alone."

I keep my gaze fixed on the polished stone floor, resisting the urge to flinch at his words. His tone is measured, his delivery flawless, carefully calculated to project compassion. But I know better. He's not grieving for the citizens lost. They are merely collateral damage, pawns in his larger game.

The king shifts his gaze to the floor, his expression somber, the perfect picture of a grieving father. "It is with the heaviest of hearts that I must confirm the loss of my son, Prince Torbin. Though no body was recovered, the circumstances leave no room for hope. And I cannot dismiss what I've witnessed with my own eyes. The plummet from the castle tower broke his body. And the carnoraxis carried his lifeless form away, leaving behind only the blood that marked their violent path."

Gasps swell through the hall. The faint sound of muffled sobs echoes from the back of the room. The queen lowers her head, shadows masking her expression, but the slight tremble of her chin and in her shoulders betrays her grief. She lost her only son. Even if he is not dead, Torbin had become something else. Something to which even a mother could not devote her love.

The words scrape against me like a violent rash. The people of the court have no idea what actually transpired. They don't know that Prince Torbin had hurt the king, might have even killed him if Dante and I hadn't interfered. The nightmarish memory plays out in my head, causing my heart rate to elevate. Torbin had become a dangerous threat. And I can't bring myself to believe he's truly dead. The people of Hedera are being lied to by their own king.

I lift my gaze, unable to stop myself, and my eyes meet Dante's across the dais. For a moment, I forget how to breathe. His jaw is tight, and his fists are clenched at his sides, but his expression softens as he looks at me. It's fleeting—a brief flicker of understanding and solidarity—but it's enough to steady me.

The king clears his throat, pulling my attention back to him. "Princess Celeste was promised to my son, and as her guardian in these uncertain times, I will honor that promise. Hedera will look after her, as a tribute to Torbin's memory and as a continuation of the bond between our two realms. This is what my son would have wanted, and what I shall ensure as her king."

A murmur of approval ripples through the crowd, and I tighten my grip on my skirts to keep my hands steady. The weight of their stares is unbearable. They don't know the truth. They don't know that their king is spinning a tale to mask his own ambitions. They only see him as a hero. A man worth his word who cares for his people. It's so fucking far from the truth, I could vomit.

I bow my head, though every word from the king grates against me. I don't need his guardianship—I never did. I should be returning to Delasurvia, leading my regiment, defending my own land. But I can't. Not when Hedera has struck a deal with the agriculturally prosperous realm of Mersos to reopen the trade routes that will keep my people fed. If I leave, if I defy Silas, he would see it as a slight against his generosity, a betrayal of our arrangement, and Delasurvia would suffer for it. So I remain, bound not by duty to him, but by necessity—for my kingdom, for my people.

 8

The speech continues, but I stop listening. My thoughts are a whirlwind of anger, guilt, and helplessness. The king's words are daggers wrapped in velvet, and I feel their sting with every passing moment.

And this is only the first part of his plan. The entire reason I am in Hedera is to provide an heir to the Copperhammer bloodline. And now that Torbin is gone, King Silas intends to replace him with Dante, his bastard son. In order for the realms to accept this measure, Silas purports he intends to first legitimize Dante. I'm still unclear how he's going to accomplish this. I can't remember reading or hearing about any legitimization taking place in Terre Ferique in the last hundred years, but then again, until my classes with my magister, Ezra, I always did tend to skip out on history lessons.

All I know is that after Dante is legitimized, the king will announce our engagement, so his plan to acquire an heir can go forward. Until then, I have to play my part as the mourning princess who lost her betrothed to tragedy. Which means I cannot be seen in the company of any man or woman who might be speculated as a love interest. And that, unfortunately, includes Dante.

The hall empties in a slow, solemn procession, black-clad courtiers murmuring quiet condolences to one another as they slip through the towering doors. But I barely hear them. My gaze is locked across the room, past the flickering torchlight and the thinning crowd, to where Dante is being escorted out of the room.

His shoulders are squared, his expression unreadable, but there's something in his stance that betrays him. A hesitation, a reluctance to move even as those around him disperse. His storm-grey eyes catch mine, holding me captive in a silent exchange neither of us can afford to have. There are no words spoken, no gestures made, yet the weight of everything left unsaid coils between us, as thick as the tension that has followed us since Torbin fell from the balcony.

Nadya says something, suddenly present at my side, but I don't catch it. Her voice is distant, muffled by the rush of blood in my ears.

Dante shifts, his fingers flexing at his sides like he wants to reach for me but knows he can't. I want to cross the room, want to tell him that I

 9

hate this—that the only thing I want right now is to speak to him, to hear his voice without the weight of eyes upon us. To feel the warmth of his arms. But the space between us is insurmountable. And before I can find the courage to move, a firm hand grips my arm.

I start, snapping my gaze away as Indira, my feisty maidservant, steps close, her expression carefully composed but firm. "It's time to go, Your Highness." Her grip is not unkind, but it leaves no room for argument. "The mourning period must be observed, and I have been entrusted with ensuring your virtue remains intact."

Nadya, who has been uncharacteristically quiet, gives a dry, unimpressed snort. "Oh, yes, because sneaking off to defile herself is clearly at the top of her priorities today."

Indira barely spares her a glance. "Rules are rules. There will be no room for indiscretions. And you can't argue with me because I'm only following orders from the king."

I set my jaw, forcing my expression to remain impassive even as frustration prickles at my skin. I know what's expected of me. I know the pretense I must uphold. But to have it spoken aloud, to be reduced to nothing more than a delicate thing in need of guarding, grates against me like a dull blade.

"Of course," I say, my voice level, disguising the heat simmering beneath my skin. "Lead the way."

Indira nods, seemingly satisfied, and releases my arm, turning toward the grand doors. I follow, Nadya at my side, but just as we step forward, a presence shifts in my periphery.

I glance back.

King Silas stands near the dais, his expression dark, his scowl barely concealed as his eyes follow me. There is no sympathy in his gaze, no shared grief. Only the cold, seething resentment of a man who still believes I am to blame for the loss of his son.

A chill passes over me, but I do not look away.

I will not cower.

Lifting my chin, I meet his gaze with resentment of my own before I turn and walk from the hall, never once breaking my stride.

CHAPTER TWO

As soon as I enter my chambers, I claw at the laces of my bodice. The silk clings to me as if it were painted onto my skin, heavy and stiff, the fabric pressing against my ribs. It's almost as suffocating as the hold King Silas has on my freedom. I rip at the ties, impatient, my breath shallow from the weight of it all. The black skirts pool around my feet with a sigh, but there's no relief—not really. Just the ghost of the throne room still stabbing at my thoughts, wrapping around my throat like a noose.

"Your Highness," Indira says sharply as she follows me into the room, "you must remain in your mourning clothes."

I glance over my shoulder. She's standing by the doorway, her hands folded neatly in front of her, but her brow is pinched with worry. Whether for me or for her duties, I can't say.

"Must I?"

"We've gone over this. It is the custom," she says with a shrug. "A woman who has lost her betrothed is to observe a period of mourning. During this time, you are expected to wear black in public and to refrain from being seen alone with a man."

I exhale sharply. "That's ridiculous."

 11

"Perhaps. But it is tradition. And King Silas will expect you to follow it, especially since he is keeping guardianship over you. To the people of Hedera, you are a grieving princess, and anything less than a proper display of mourning will be taken as an insult."

My fingers curl into fists at my sides. I don't want to mourn Torbin. I don't want to pretend that I'm sad he isn't here, because what I feel is quite the opposite. I'm finally free from his torment, no longer repressed by his manipulation. But Indira is right. I don't want to give the king any reason to make things harder for me—or for Delasurvia. And I don't want the people of Hedera to think I'm a cold, heartless, thankless bitch.

Indira watches me for a moment. "For now, it is important to do what is expected of you."

"I'll wear my black trousers." My voice is hoarse as I step toward the armoire. "Is that good enough?"

"Barely." Her tone is disapproving but not cruel.

I yank open the doors and tug free the dark trousers and a loose black tunic. The material is plain, less regal than that of the gowns I'm expected to wear but still acceptable. Still in line with the appearance of a grieving princess. Whatever that means.

The king's words still echo in my skull. The subtle condemnation in them. His gaze when he spoke of Torbin's fall—not letting me forget that I was the one who pushed him.

Indira watches me as she gathers my discarded dress from the floor. "You're also expected to stay in your room most of the time, so why does it look like you're planning on going somewhere?"

I shove one leg into the trousers, then the other. "I need to see my uncle, Indira," I say, my voice low but unwavering. "Surely, you can understand that."

There's a beat of silence, then the soft rustle of fabric as she steps closer.

"There hasn't been any change," she says, softer now. "Perhaps if you give it more time—"

"He needs family by his side." I fasten the front of my tunic, the motion stiff with tension. "No matter if he's conscious to realize it. And

I'm the only family he's got. We're blood." And after what the king said today, I need to see someone who might still remember who I am beneath all the mourning lace and silk.

Indira hesitates. "Then at least allow me to accompany you—"

"No." I turn to her, gentler this time. "Sir Holden will escort me."

She doesn't look pleased, but after a moment, she dips her chin in a slow nod. "Very well. But please don't linger long. It wouldn't be good if anyone saw you dressed like this."

"I won't linger," I promise. "And thank you."

As she slips quietly from the room, I sink down onto the edge of the chaise and run my hands over my face.

Nadya had gone to her own rooms after the king's announcement. She'd offered a squeeze of my hand and a faint, tired smile, but I could see how the weight of the day pressed on her too. A part of me wanted to pull her close, to ask her to stay and provide me the emotional strength I need, but I didn't. I couldn't. She deserves better than to carry my worries alongside her own.

I draw in a deep breath, tying my hair back with a ribbon from my vanity. I catch my reflection in the mirror. The dark circles beneath my eyes, the faint cut across my lip from where I bit down too hard in the throne room. The warm almond undertones of my skin seem cold and almost grey in this light. I don't look like a princess or the commander of the Delasurvian Royal Regiment, but rather the ghost of one.

I turn away from the mirror and march toward the door. When I open it, Sir Holden stands there, ever the picture of propriety—rigid in posture, jaw set tight. His eyes sweep over my attire, but he says nothing, just offers a brisk nod.

"Your Highness."

"Let's go," I murmur.

We step into the corridor together, the torches along the stone walls flickering with the movement of air. The castle feels too quiet, too aware. As if it's listening. Judging.

"Where to?" he asks, voice low.

"To see my uncle. And don't try to talk me out of it."

A dry huff escapes him. "I gave up trying to talk you out of anything a long time ago."

I glance sideways at him as we walk. "Smart man."

He smirks, just faintly, but it vanishes as quickly as it appears. "He's been through a lot," he says quietly. "But if he's as strong a general as the rumors say, he'll fight his way through this."

I don't answer. Because I'm not sure if he can. No one, myself included, understands what kind of twisted power the tsar has. I have no idea how to fix my uncle because I don't have a clue what the tsar did to him.

Biting the inside of my cheek, I flex my fingers in an attempt to alleviate the buzzing that courses through my arm. It's not unpleasant, but it's distracting. I should be exhilarated at the thought of my magic— as mysterious as it still is—awakening in my blood. The problem is that the feeling also serves as a reminder of Torbin and how he stabbed me in the hand to stop me from sending a warning to Delasurvia. To my uncle.

It was excruciatingly painful, but the attack resulted in an inexplicable buzz developing in my body, originating at my stab wound and slowly expanding through my body.

I haven't told Dante about the power stirring inside me. Not yet. It's not that I don't trust him—I do. If anything, once I understand what's happening to me, he will be the first person I want to tell. But after waiting so long, after nearly giving up hope, I need a moment to claim this for myself. Fae magic is supposed to manifest by the breaching age of twenty-one, as natural as breathing. If it doesn't, there is only one fate: madness. The mind fractures, unable to hold what should have been. It happened to my brother, the madness eventually leading to his death. I had spent years preparing for that possibility, waiting for the first signs of my own unraveling. But now, my power is waking, slow and unsteady, like embers sparking but not quite catching fire. And before I reveal it to anyone, before I am faced with the fact that I've got something inside me I cannot control, I first need to do everything I can to understand it.

The halls are eerily silent at this hour, the usual hum of castle life reduced to the occasional flicker of a torch against cold stone. Shadows stretch long and lean across the floor, reaching like skeletal fingers in the dim

glow of lantern light. My steps are soft, but every shift of my weight against the marble sends the faintest echo through the corridor, a sound I once wouldn't have noticed—because I wouldn't have been awake to hear it.

A shiver prickles down my spine. How many times had I wandered these halls, unaware, moving like a specter while my mind remained locked in sleep? My feet had guided me through these very corridors, even through the secret passageways, my body knowing the paths better than my waking self. I had no recollection of those journeys, no memory of slipping from my bed and moving through the castle like a ghost. But I had always known afterward that I'd done it, because I was never where I was supposed to be when I awoke.

Ezra's powder helped. Still helps. A few pinches in my evening tea, and the incidents have stopped. At least, I think they have. There's always the quiet fear that one night, I'll wake to find myself standing in the woods again, my feet damp with dew, the moon glaring down at me like an accusation.

Along with the wolves.

I didn't know it at the time, but the wolves had always been there, watching over me. At first, I thought they were hunting me, that their golden eyes in the dark were a warning, but now I know the truth. The wolves serve as guardians to the fae.

But I'm still unsure if they can protect me from what's to come.

I round the final corner, the heavy, wooden door to my uncle's chamber coming into view. A lantern glows dimly outside, casting a soft halo of light against the stone. My steps quicken, my pulse steadying with purpose. Whatever he has to tell me—whatever secrets his fevered mind has been holding on to—I need to hear them.

I stand at the door and cast a glance at Sir Holden, who gives me a nod before turning with his back against the wall to stand sentry.

I knock softly, only so I don't alarm Mylo, who's been sitting faithfully by my uncle's side, watching and waiting for any improvement to his condition. I suck in a deep breath and brace myself for whatever awaits on the other side. As my hand twists the doorknob, my mind is tangled in the memory of Mylo staggering through the gates, my uncle

 15

slumped against him, barely clinging to life. Mylo and Sir Holden had supported his weight, bringing him to an empty room so I could try to heal him, my heart in a panic as I desperately attempted to mend the damage the Shadow Tsar had inflicted. And just before unconsciousness took my uncle, his grip tightened weakly around my wrist, his voice rasping the words that have haunted me since.

"Your father is alive."

I swallow hard as I enter the room. I don't know if those words were the ramblings of a half-conscious man, or if they hold the weight of truth. But I have to know. And if he's awake now, if he can speak, I need answers.

The guest chamber he now occupies is warmer than the hall, but the tall windows show a darkening sky. The fire in the hearth casts golden light over polished floors and embroidered drapes. It's a beautiful room, though its grandeur has faded with time. Dust once gathered in the carved, wooden trim, and the air had been thick with disuse before I had the servants air it out, change the linens, and light fresh candles. Now, the scent of beeswax and lavender lingers, though it does nothing to ease the tightness in my chest. My uncle lies motionless beneath a heavy, woolen blanket, his face pale against the shadowed curve of the pillow. The steady rise and fall of his chest is the only reassurance that he's still breathing. Still fighting.

His body has mended in the days since he arrived—a combined effort between his healing powers and mine—but whatever the tsar did to him lingers. He hasn't used his telepathy powers to speak to me, and he hasn't woken since he uttered those damning words out loud.

"Your father is alive."

If that's true, what does that mean? Does it mean my father has been held prisoner by the tsar? When the tsar captured my uncle, were my uncle and father reunited in a dungeon cell? Did the tsar mean to deliver a message to me by dumping my uncle's broken body by the border for Mylo to find? Was he threatening to do the same to my father?

"Your father is alive."

Unless he meant...

I shake my head, unable to fathom it. Surely, if my father were the tsar, someone would have realized it was King Axel Westergaard. Surely, word would have gotten out, that not only was the ruler of Delasurvia not dead, but he had also taken on a new identity.

But if he *is* the tsar, that means he faked his death and abandoned his family. That means he ambushed the previous Tsar of Dulcamar and usurped him. For what? He already ruled a kingdom. What would he have needed with Dulcamar? The questions make my head spin, and the whole idea makes no sense, so I'm convinced it can't be true.

Mylo sits in the corner, his massive frame nearly swallowing the high-backed chair beneath him. For the first two days, he paced the chamber in restless silence, a man of action forced into stillness, but exhaustion must have settled in, and now he sits as he watches over my uncle with a sharp-eyed patience. As I step inside, the floor creaks, and his head lifts. He stands immediately, towering over me, and I have to tilt my chin up to meet his gaze.

"Has he stirred?" I whisper.

Mylo shakes his head, his broad arms crossing over his chest. "Not once." His deep voice is edged with frustration, as if he'd expected his sheer will alone to wake Kormak from his state. "I don't like it."

A quiet knock pulls my focus toward the door.

Ezra steps in, his robes dampened from what I now realize is rain. He runs a hand over his salt-and-pepper hair, sending raindrops flying. His face is pale with exhaustion, and he carries a small, leather satchel under one arm. There's something fragile in the way he moves, as if the weight of all he knows is pressing too heavily on his shoulders.

He glances at Mylo, then at me. "You're here," he says softly, his tone threaded with relief. "Good."

I nod once. "Have there been any changes?"

Ezra crosses to the bedside, setting the satchel down and studying Kormak's face with a frown that pinches the corners of his eyes. "He mumbles sometimes. Unintelligible fragments. Painful memories, maybe. His brow knots as if he's dreaming—but the dreams don't bring peace. His grunting and twitching have worsened. It tells me the pain is

 17

growing, not fading."

I step closer, the scent of dried herbs and the sharp sting of alcohol tickling my nose. Kormak lies still, his chest rising with shallow breaths, his features drawn and sunken. My stomach clenches. He's suffering, and I don't know how to make it stop.

"Is there anything else we can do?" I ask. "Anything we haven't tried?"

Ezra hesitates, and in that moment, I can see he's been holding something back. He looks to Mylo, who gives a single, silent nod, and then Ezra steps toward me.

"There is one thing," he says slowly. "An elixir—a highly concentrated compound that some alchemists consider too risky. Not only is it... *widely unconventional* because of its volatility, but there are very few magisters who have access to a key ingredient." He meets my gaze. "I must be transparent, Celeste; its effectiveness is inexact. But it's also the only thing I know of that might draw him back."

My heart thuds. "What does it do?"

"It jolts the nervous system," he says. "In some cases, it can force a body caught between consciousness and unconsciousness to snap awake. But it's not a gentle rousing, Celeste. It's like calling lightning into a house already smoldering from fire."

I flinch at the image. "Could it hurt him?"

"It could," Ezra admits. "If his mind is too fragile, or if the damage done to him was... more taxing than we realize, it might worsen his state. Confuse the memory. Even burn through the parts of him that haven't healed yet. Some texts say it's been used in cases of poison. Others say it unmoored a patient's mind so badly, they never came back at all."

My breath hitches.

Regarding me, Ezra draws a breath. "But I've studied this version of the recipe carefully. I believe I can make it stable—if we act now. Your uncle's heartbeat is weakening. If we're going to try... it has to be soon."

The silence between us thickens. Rain whispers at the windowpanes. Mylo says nothing, his jaw clenched, his gaze pinned to the man who basically raised us both.

 18

Ezra watches me patiently.

I wrap my arms around my waist, fingers digging into the fabric of my tunic. My thoughts race, clashing and loud. I see my uncle's smile in my mind. His steady voice. The way he always told me the truth, even when it hurt. He was always there for me, risked everything by seeking out the tsar because of me. I can't let him fade without doing everything in my power to stop it.

But what if I make it worse?

What if this breaks him in ways I can't fix?

Still, doing nothing would mean losing him, anyway. And I can't bear the thought of not trying.

Fuck.

I look at Ezra. "Do it."

His eyes search mine for a long beat, as if to be sure. Then he nods once. "It won't take me long to prepare, but first, I'll need some of his blood."

I stiffen. "Why?"

Ezra crouches beside the bed, unfastening the clasp of his satchel. The leather creaks as he opens it, pulling out a slender, glass vial and a roll of soft cloth. "To test the elixir properly," he says, his tone calm and deliberate, "each formulation must be attuned to the blood of the patient. I need to take a small sample and let it interact with the base, test it so there's no chance the tonic could react badly."

He produces a thin, curved blade that's about a quarter the size of a dagger, delicate and wickedly sharp. "It won't be deep," he adds. "Just enough for a few drops."

I nod, but the air feels tighter in my chest. I move beside him, gently taking my uncle's arm and rolling up the sleeve of his nightshirt. His skin is hot, flushed, slick with fever-sweat. The sight of him like this—so limp, so unlike himself—sends another wave of helplessness crawling through me.

Ezra presses the edge of the blade to the inside of Uncle Kormak's forearm, and though the motion is quick, my stomach still knots. Blood wells slowly from the shallow cut. My brow furrows when I note that it's thick and dark, not the healthy crimson I hoped for. I steady my uncle's

wrist, holding it gently as Ezra lets the blood drip into the vial.

"Almost there," he murmurs.

I clench my jaw, summoning my power into my palm. The moment Ezra seals the vial with a twist of its cork, I press my hand to the wound. Warmth pulses through my fingers, knitting the skin back together with a soft hiss of heat. The cut vanishes, but the worry inside me doesn't.

"He shouldn't have to bleed at all," I whisper.

Ezra slips the vial into a padded slot in his satchel and places the blade back into its case. "I know," he says quietly. "But sometimes healing takes a few steps backward first. I'll start preparing the elixir now. It needs to steep while the blood bonds to it."

I close my eyes for a second and swallow down the anxiety clogging my throat.

Ezra rises, giving my shoulder a light touch. "I'll send word the moment it's ready."

I nod, but I don't move. My hand remains on my uncle's arm as Ezra turns and disappears into the corridor beyond.

I rake my fingers through my hair and inhale deeply. The silence that follows is heavier now. Every breath, every second, feels like it could tip the scale in one direction or the other.

Mylo moves to the window, his hand resting on the sill, eyes on the storm beyond.

And I stay beside my uncle, reaching out to place my hand gently over his. His skin is cool and clammy, the strength beneath it buried— hidden, not gone. Not yet.

Please, I think. *Please come back to me.*

Mylo scrubs at the growing hair at his jaw, tension wound tight through his frame. "The full moon's coming. You know what that means."

I do. The carnoraxis are never quiet for long. And if the past year has taught us anything, it's that when the moon swells full, the beasts follow.

"I should be out there," Mylo continues, his voice roughened by the weight of duty. "With the squad. They'll need every sword." He shakes his head, focus fixed beyond the window. In the direction of Delasurvia.

"Sitting around while those things crawl closer, it feels wrong."

"It *is* wrong," I murmur. "We should be with them."

The words settle between us, heavy and unyielding. For all the king's speeches and black mourning veils, the kingdom won't stop bleeding while we bow our heads.

"We'll meet our squad, then." I give him a nod. "Both of us."

He glances at me then, searching my face. "And the king? The mourning period?"

I let out a soft, bitter laugh. "Let him object." My pulse thrums faster at the thought of his wrath, but I shove the fear down. "I'm the commander of the Delasurvian Royal Regiment. My duty is to the people. Not to King Silas's reputation."

"You don't think he'll punish you for defying him?"

"Let him try." I lift my chin, though my heart slams harder against my ribs. "He can't afford to lose me—not when his precious kingdom still needs an heir."

For a moment, there's only the sound of my uncle's shallow breaths and the faint crackle of the fire in the hearth. Mylo watches me closely, the tension in his stance easing. But only slightly.

"You're serious," he says at last.

"I'm serious."

His mouth curves into the barest hint of a smile, an edge of approval beneath his usual gruffness. "Good. I didn't want to sneak out without you."

I huff softly, shaking my head. "As if you could."

A beat of silence lingers between us before Mylo shifts, resting his hand lightly against the pommel of his sword. "We'll leave in three days' time," he says. "Right at the full moon."

And maybe by then, my uncle will have awoken.

I give Mylo a nod, though my thoughts twist and turn beneath the surface. There's more to this than duty, more than the need to swing a sword. Every instance in which we face the carnoraxis brings us one step closer to taking down the tsar.

And this time, I won't sit idly by while the moon rises.

 21

CHAPTER

THREE

It's been two days since Ezra administered the elixir. Two long, agonizing days of sitting at my uncle's bedside, watching his chest rise and fall in shallow rhythms, waiting for a flicker of change upon his tense features, a slowing of frantic movement behind his closed lids. Of hoping for a shift of breath, for his hand to reach out for mine, anything to suggest the tide has turned.

But there's been nothing.

Ezra warned me it might take time. *"This kind of magic,"* he said, *"is not a sword; it's a siege. It doesn't win with one swift strike. It chips away, softens the resistance, until the body begins to remember how to fight."* His words were calm, meant to steady me. But they couldn't stop the way hope frays at the edges when met with silence.

As I saddle Thora and check my provisions, I fight the gnawing at my mind, the voice that questions if I should stay. It's not as if I'm abandoning my uncle to an empty room. Ezra reassured me he would constantly monitor him, journaling his progress or lack thereof. And if I can trust anyone to take necessary measures to improve my uncle's condition, it's Hedera's skilled magister.

That reassurance, plus Nadya's promise to sit in my uncle's room as long as she's got her pile of books with her, is mollifying enough for me to join Mylo on our quest to meet our squad.

I cover my uniform with a long, hooded cape. We leave early enough that there aren't many guards looming, and we take the hidden path through the forest behind the stables so we're not easily spotted. Soon, the castle fades behind us, a jagged shadow swallowed by the mist curling through the trees. Mylo rides ahead, his frame solid and unmoving as his horse glides across the path. I keep close, the chill morning air brushing against my cheeks, but it isn't the cold that quickens my pulse. It's the freedom.

For the first time in weeks, there are no eyes watching me. No guards shadowing my every step. No suffocating weight of the mourning attire. Just the steady rhythm of my horse beneath me and the open trail stretching wide and endless.

We reach a clearing, and the wind hums through the grass, carrying the sharp scent of pine and distant rain. With every stride, the knots in my chest loosen, the pressure I've carried since Torbin's assumed death easing—if only a little. Out here, no one demands answers I can't give. No one asks me to sit still while the world teeters on the edge of ruin.

I urge my horse faster, the cool air tearing through my hair as I catch up to Mylo. He doesn't speak, but when our eyes meet, I catch the glint of shared relief. We're doing something again. Not standing idly by while the world succumbs to a madman.

A branch cracks somewhere behind us.

I pull the reins sharply, heart slamming against my ribs as Thora slows beneath me. Mylo reacts just as quickly, drawing up beside me, his hand drifting to the hilt of his sword. The air, which a breath ago felt so open and free, now presses in too tightly.

Another sound, closer this time. The snap of underbrush. The whisper of movement cutting through the stillness.

I train my eyes on the edge of the forest, expecting a guard. Maybe one of the men under the command of Farvis—the king's lackey—sent to drag me back to Ivystone before the king notices I'm missing. Or

worse, something unnatural. Something that doesn't care who I am as long as there's blood to spill.

I loosen my dagger in its sheath, scanning the shadowed treeline. Mylo shifts in his saddle, his whole body tense as his gaze sweeps back and forth.

A shape emerges from the trees.

My pulse stutters—fingers curling tighter around my weapon— until the figure moves fully into the sunlight.

Broad shoulders. The familiar set of his jaw. And those eyes— burning with something fierce and undeniable as he charges ahead and then reins in his horse a few paces behind us. I should have known Dante wouldn't let go of me so easily.

A sharp exhale slips from my lips as tension drains from my limbs, replaced by a flood of something warmer, softer, though no less dangerous.

Mylo smirks. "Looks like we didn't leave undetected, after all."

"I hardly doubt a man of your size could go anywhere undetected." Dante's gaze turns from Mylo to me. "And you truly underestimate my ability to sense when your presence leaves the castle."

I let out something close to a laugh, but there's no mistaking the thrum of my heart reacting to his words. He's not talking about magic. He means this connection we have. It's the same explanation for the way a room lights up when he enters it.

And of course he followed. Of course he knows me well enough to understand I wouldn't stay behind while others bleed for my kingdom.

Mylo shakes his head, though there's a faint smirk pulling at his mouth. "The stubborn bastard's got a way with words, I'll give him that."

Dante doesn't even look at him. His gaze stays locked on mine, steady and unyielding, as if the rest of the world could crumble and it wouldn't pull his attention away. "I'm not here to stop you. I'm coming with you."

I lift my chin, though the corner of my mouth betrays me with the hint of a smile. "I figured as much."

And I don't stop him. Not that I could.

24

We travel all day, stopping only to give the horses a rest and to fuel our weary bodies with food. There's so much I want to talk to Dante about, but the small moments we have on our journey don't feel like the right times. It's not just about wanting him to hold me, or to be reminded of what his lips feel like devouring mine. We haven't discussed the fact that I pushed Torbin from the tower, that the king plans to legitimize him, that we are to be betrothed once the mourning period ends. I don't know how he feels about any of it. For all I know, he's opposed to the king's plan. For all I know, he blames me for Torbin's absence from his life, just like his father does.

If anything, the journey gives me plenty of time to think.

Night has fallen by the time we reach the meeting point. In the stretch of the rocky hillside, tucked beneath the shadow of an abandoned, wooden watchtower, the air hums with quiet anticipation—the kind that always comes before battle. Even from a distance, I spot the flicker of a whetstone against steel, the faint glow of campfire embers pulsing like a heartbeat in the dark.

We guide our horses through the tall grass, and the sound of our approach stirs the figures huddled near the base of the tower. A blade flashes as Aila stands first—always the quickest to reach for a weapon. Isaac follows, pushing to his feet with a low grumble, his sandy hair ruffled by the night breeze. Giorgi, crouched near the fire, narrows their eyes as they straighten—until recognition settles in, and their mouth falls open.

"Commander?" Giorgi's voice carries just enough disbelief to make me smile.

Isaac lets out a low whistle. "Well, shit. Didn't expect to see you tonight."

Aila doesn't wait for permission. She closes the distance between us in three quick strides, staring up at me and shaking her head. "Commander. We thought you'd be locked up tight under the king's watch until the mourning ended."

I shrug, dismounting with an ease that belies how fast my heart still beats from the ride. Since she mentioned the mourning, word must have

already reached Delasurvia about Torbin's supposed death.

"The king doesn't decide where I go," I say, my chin held high. "Not when the full moon is upon us."

She embraces me, patting me on the back in camaraderie.

Isaac snorts, bending over his sword to resume sharpening the blade. "If you're hungry, you're out of luck. It's Giorgi's turn to cook."

"Ungrateful bastard," Giorgi mutters, though there's no real bite in their tone. They lift their chin toward Mylo. "Brought the big guy with you, too, I see."

Mylo swings down from his horse, brushing a hand over the pommel of his sword. "Someone's got to keep you and Isaac from killing each other."

Aila's focus shifts to Dante, still straddling his chestnut-brown stallion, and the warmth in her expression cools to something of bemusement.

As Dante sweeps his gaze over the squad with quiet intensity, the glow of the fire catches on his features—the sharp angles of his face that momentarily leave me breathless. He doesn't speak. Just gives them a nod, one they return with the same quiet gravity. They're not exactly friends. I don't think they can dismiss the fact that his blood ties him to a ruthless king and a prince who turned malicious. But after what we've faced together, what we survived the night the carnoraxis tore through Ivystone, they are still allies. And in battle, that means everything.

Giorgi sets down the stick they were using to stoke the fire and makes their way to the horses. Dante mutters his thanks as Giorgi gathers the reins and leads the animals toward the narrow stream trickling nearby. The sound of hooves fades into the quiet, leaving the rest of us in the faint glow of the fire.

Aila is the first to break the silence. "How's the general?"

At first, I can't answer. I don't have it in me to tell my squad that his condition is getting worse. And a part of me is afraid to bring up Ezra's elixir, for fear it was the wrong decision.

"He's holding on," I answer instead. "The magister is doing everything he can. He and Nadya are watching over him while I'm here."

Isaac drags the whetstone along the edge of his blade, the scrape loud against the hush settling over the camp. "Good. The old man's tough. I'm betting on him to pull through."

Aila grins faintly. "If anyone can survive being half-poisoned, it's your uncle."

Mylo and I exchange a glance, neither of us willing to clarify just how bad it's gotten. Maybe if we don't say it out loud, the gods will reward us by bringing my uncle's condition back to normal.

Aila jerks her chin toward the top of the tower, where a lean figure descends the ladder, an axe strapped to his back. "You remember Lorne, don't you?"

My gaze follows hers, and once the man reaches the ground, I catch the familiar gleam of amber eyes beneath a fall of silver-blond hair. His features are still young, perhaps a year or two behind my own, but there's a maturity in the quiet way he moves. His face is spattered faintly with freckles, his expression closed but alert.

He brushes ash from his trousers before giving me a half-bow with practiced ease. "Commander."

"Lorne," I say, surprised. "Of course. From the southern campaign. I remember seeing you at strategy briefings in Delasurvia. I didn't realize you've transferred to our unit."

"That was my decision," Aila says, her fists planted on her sides. "With you and Mylo preoccupied in Hedera, I asked him to transfer in to fill the gap. He's a skilled soldier, and we're lucky to have him."

Not to mention he's fae, with the magical ability to throw sound. Pretty useful.

Lorne shifts slightly but remains standing at attention. "It's an honor to serve under your leadership, Commander. And under General Moorgrin's, of course."

At the mention of my uncle, his voice softens. There's real concern there, the kind that can't be faked.

"He hasn't woken yet," I admit. "But he's still fighting."

Lorne nods once, solemnly. "He's a damned legend, if you don't mind me saying. We need him back."

"Yes, we do," I murmur.

As we settle into the camp, my eyes constantly flit to Dante. He keeps himself busy, helping Isaac sort weapons and occasionally strolling down to the stream to check on the horses. He's not comfortable enough around my squad to keep still, but I don't push him. I don't try to force him to like my squad or vice versa. It will happen naturally or not at all.

The fire crackles steadily, sparks rising like fleeting stars, vanishing into the dark velvet sky. The moon hangs high and full above us, bathing the hills in silver, while a low breeze drifts through the red valerian growing at the edge of the ridge. Its scent is sharp and faintly bitter, threading through the sweeter aroma of jasmine and distant pine.

I sit beside the flames, close enough to feel their heat on my shins. Across from me, Aila sharpens her blade with slow, practiced strokes, the whetstone whispering against the steel. Her eyes are focused, but I can tell by the way her brow pinches that her thoughts are elsewhere.

I glance around camp—Isaac slouched against a log, Giorgi biting the inside of their cheek as they poke the fire with a stick, Mylo sitting quietly at the perimeter with his gaze scanning the trees, always alert. Dante lingers near the outskirts of the woods, his silhouette a steady, silent thing in the moonlight. He leans against a large tree, and every so often I catch sight of the red glow from the end of his cigarello.

My attention returns to Aila. "Any word from the camps?"

"Still overcrowded. Feels like we're constantly running low on clean water and dry shelter. But... the food helps."

"They are arriving undetected?" My throat tightens. King Silas could only get Mersos to agree on providing goods to Delasurvia if we agreed to close down the refugee camps. As far as I know, Silas is unaware that we've kept them open, and there are officially no provisions being delivered to any of the camps. Not by Mersos merchants, anyway.

Aila nods. "As you requested, we've made sure the team rerouting a percentage of goods is keeping it under wraps. And as far as the rest of the regiment goes, they're in the dark. The fewer people who know about this, the less likely King Silas or the triarchs of Mersos will find out."

"Good." I release a long breath. "The king's been increasing his

patrols. You never know where he's got soldiers watching. Or spies listening." I give her a gentle pat on her shoulder. "Thank you, Aila."

"Of course, Commander."

"Not just for keeping abreast of the camp situation. For all of it. I wish I could be in two places at once, but if I abandon Hedera, Silas will make sure Delasurvia suffers."

Aila's gaze softens. "You're doing what you can, and I know you haven't forgotten us. It's my honor to carry on here while you have to put up with that pompous king."

A few heartbeats pass in silence, filled only by the crackling fire and the whispering wind. I tilt my head toward the stars, their light distant and unmoving over my homeland. I can't help but wonder if I'll ever return there for good, if I can protect Delasurvia from within its borders. It was never my intention to be on the throne, but since I've been forced into this position, I should use it to my advantage. For my people.

The night closes in around us. Steel glints in the firelight. Boots scuff over gravel. Lorne and Giorgi keep watch for the beacons while the others rest and regenerate. The hum of tension lingers like a held breath. But for the first time in weeks, I feel something solid beneath me again. We are together. And that means we still have a chance.

"I'll get more wood," I offer, needing an excuse to stretch my limbs and steady my thoughts.

Dante pushes off the tree before anyone else can move. "I'll come with you."

The words are casual, but they pull at something deep inside me—a familiar ache I've had to bury since the king's decree ripped us apart. For weeks, there's been no room for us. Not in the castle. Not in the aftermath of Torbin's fall. But out here, beyond the walls of Ivystone, we're just us again.

I grab an axe from the supplies on the ground and head toward the edge of the trees, the brittle grass crunching softly beneath my boots. Dante falls into step beside me, quiet and sure. Always close, but never too close—not when anyone might see.

Not until we're swallowed by the shadows.

 29

The air grows colder beneath the canopy, thick with the scent of damp earth and pine. I continue deeper into the trees, scanning for a fallen branch suitable for the fire. I feel Dante's eyes on me, and though I've longed for a moment alone with him, it takes me a second to work up the nerve to turn his way. Is it the guilt? Is it fear of rejection? I can't wrap my head around this uncertainty that's suddenly clogging my throat.

Spotting a few good-sized branches on the forest floor, I stop. With a deep sigh, I finally turn to face Dante. His eyes shine, even in the darkness, and as he steps closer, I'm transfixed by his height. How have I already forgotten how tall he is, the outline of his broad shoulders? I press my lips together, trying to get my brain working well enough to speak.

"It's been a crazy few weeks," I say.

"Feels like months. If it weren't for our balconies facing each other, I don't think we'd have seen much of each other at all."

So many nights, I'd step out onto my balcony, just as the sun was setting. It was the only time Indira would leave me alone. Dante made it a habit to go onto his balcony as well, but he was too far away to speak to. We'd spend many sunsets—when he wasn't trapped in meetings with the council— simply gazing at each other over the empty distance between us, unable to communicate, unable to comfort each other. It wasn't much, but when the timing worked in my favor, it had quickly become the favorite part of my day.

"True. Luckily no one caught on. I'm sure the king would have made me switch rooms if anyone had seen us. But it was frustrating not being able to talk to you. I almost—" I cut myself off with a laugh.

"You almost what?"

"I almost attempted to write you a note. To find a bow and attach the note to an arrow so I could shoot it at your balcony."

"I would have loved to see you attempt that." He chuckles. "You might have hit me instead."

"Maybe. I could aim better with my dagger, but I don't think it would have made it that far."

30

"We'll have to test your theory and see."

As we gaze at each other, our smiles slowly fade. All the questions I have come back to press down on my resolve.

"How... are you?" It sounds completely ridiculous when I say it out loud, but it's the most pressing question on my mind. "I mean, we haven't really spoken since..." I swallow back the lump pressing into my throat, feeling the urge to apologize. For what, exactly, I can't be sure.

For him losing his brother to the tsar.

For my part in it.

"Dante, I'm sorry." It comes out in a hoarse whisper.

He steps closer, his eyes searching my face. "Celeste, listen to me. It's not your fault."

"But I *pushed* him." Whatever Torbin became in the end—cruel, power-hungry, dangerous—there was a time when he and Dante were nearly inseparable. Brothers in blood. Best friends in everything else.

"You had no choice. I was there, don't forget." His voice is softer than I expect, cutting through the stillness like a blade sliding from its sheath. "He could have killed me. He almost killed our father. I didn't lose him when he fell from that tower; I lost him way before that. I see that now."

I release a breath as a weight lifts from my shoulders. I hadn't realized until this moment how important it was for me to hear him say those words.

"I can see that this has been troubling you."

I shake my head, not wanting to make this about me. "Dante, your whole world has been turned on its head. I'm worried about how you're handling it all."

A muscle ticks in his jaw. "This isn't the first time my life's taken a turn, Princess." The words are even, but I don't miss the edge beneath them.

I swallow hard, wishing I could ease the tension that never seems to leave his shoulders.

He comes nearer, and I lift my head just as his hand rises between us. He brushes back a strand of hair that's slipped free from my braid, his

fingers lingering when they find my cheek. "But it's good to finally know what's been going on in that pretty, little head of yours."

I shiver, helpless against the soft drag of his thumb across my skin. The air pulls tight around us, thick with everything we've left unsaid. If we were at Ivystone, if anyone were watching us, I would have to step back, put the space between us that the king demands. Instead, I reach for him. My palm presses flat against his chest, and beneath my touch, his heart beats as fiercely as my own.

His gaze softens. For all the armor he wears—on his body, on his heart—this is the piece of him no one else gets to see.

His hand covers mine, fingers warm against my chilled skin. "What about you?"

I let out a humorless laugh. "What about me?"

He drops his hand to my waist and pulls me closer until we're mere inches apart. "This whole ordeal with Torbin can't be easy for you."

"He's not dead, Dante." At least that's what I suspect. "And even if he is, I've killed before."

"In battle. Or defending lives. But I highly doubt you've pushed someone you once cared about off a castle tower."

My brows scrunch together as my gaze lowers.

He lifts my chin with a finger. "He was your childhood friend. There was a time you cared for him. And you have a good heart, so I know you aren't taking this lightly."

Neither is he, no matter how convincing he thinks he is. He puts on a good face, but I can feel it. A hidden sorrow buried beneath layers of stubbornness and a mask of indifference.

"Of course I'm not taking it lightly." I move my hand to his arm, giving it a squeeze. "My heart breaks for both of us."

He nods, leaning down to press his forehead against mine. "Then we grieve together. For the man he used to be. And we can lean on each other to get through it."

But we can't, entirely. Not physically, and not yet, anyway. We're not to be seen alone together, so it's only stolen moments like this when we can comfort each other. Until the mourning period is over and he's

legitimized for our engagement, no one must find out about us.

Us.

I'm not even entirely sure what that means, but it feels like too big of a subject to bring up right now. Or maybe it's my nerves preventing me from asking the questions I really want to ask.

The thought leads me down another path. "Torbin's absence is not the only thing changing your world." I pull my head back from his and raise my brows. "You're about to become a prince."

"That's yet to be determined."

"What do you mean? It's Silas's plan, and I doubt he's going to change his mind." I can still remember the fury in the king's face when he proclaimed that Delasurvia promised him an heir. He'd made it clear that if Torbin couldn't do it, he'd see to it himself. I can only thank the gods that he'd decided to legitimize Dante instead, and that he would be the one to continue his line with me as his bride.

"It's not entirely up to him." He must see the confusion in my features, because he continues. With a sigh, he releases me and drags a hand through his hair. "The purpose of the tour is not only to introduce me to the other realms as the king's son, but to get each realm's consent."

I blink, letting this information sink in. "So his decree means nothing if the other realms disapprove?"

"Farvis had to explain it to me since a royal legitimization claim hasn't been made in almost a century. Apparently, before anyone born outside of the king and queen's marriage can be legitimized as a royal heir, they have to get the blessing from the majority of the realms. Otherwise, there would no doubt be bastards lined up seeking their places in line for the throne."

That makes sense. "The majority. So five out of eight?"

"Six, actually. The propositioning realm is a given. So we would need five more. The realms included in the tour will consist of Podrosa, Bastos, Messanya, and Mersos. My father requested an audience with Alphemra, but they are not known to even respond to correspondence. And he won't even consider reaching out to Dulcamar."

I tilt my head. "That's only four."

 33

"Delasurvia would be the fifth." The corner of his mouth quirks up. "But there's no need to travel there."

Because the reigning monarch would make the decision.

Me.

Which means, in the end, Silas would need my consent in order for Dante to be proclaimed a legitimate prince.

Holding back a smile, I raise a brow. "You're awfully presumptuous if you think I'm so easily swayed in your favor."

"If it's convincing you need," he says as he tucks that misbehaving strand of hair behind my ear again, "I'd be happy to schedule a private appointment with you."

Before I can respond, Lorne's voice booms from the watchtower. "Beacons!"

Dante and I dart back to the camp just as Giorgi runs up the ladder to confirm Lorne's claim.

"Looks like Robinburg," Giorgi announces, their breaths coming out in short spurts as they hurry down the ladder with Lorne following.

I stretch my neck to check in that direction and can just make out a burst of flame flaring high on the ridge.

As if performing a well-choreographed dance, my squad and I move at once, gathering our supplies and heading for the horses.

My mind is still reeling from what I've learned about the upcoming tour, but all of that—and all of the unspoken questions I have—will have wait. The people always come first.

CHAPTER FOUR

We crest the ridge just before the village, the wind howling in our ears and the scent of smoke already thick in the air. But it isn't the fire that first catches my attention. It's movement—fast and low—at the edge of my vision.

I snap my head to the side.

Wolves.

Dozens of them. Their lean bodies streak through the trees like shadows come to life, silent save for the thrum of their paws against the earth. They run parallel to us, matching our pace with unnerving precision. Their coats range from pale silver to deep black, and their eyes gleam gold in the moonlight.

Not one of them looks at us. Not one breaks formation. They know where they're going.

"They're back," I whisper, breath clouding in front of me.

As if answering me, howls erupt into the air.

Aila turns in her saddle, eyes widening as she takes in the sight. "Gods," she breathes. "There are more of them than last time."

She's right. I remember the wolves at Ivystone—how they emerged

from the trees and fought at our side during the siege. A full pack of them had come at the time, but I feel as if the pack has tripled in size.

Something stirs deep in my chest, knowing that a bond exists between the wolves and fae. Ezra taught me about the connection during one of my lessons. And I can't help but feel as if I've known, somewhere deep inside of me, that that bond had always been there.

But I still don't know if that means they answer to me.

One of the larger wolves glances my way, its coat a burnished grey, eyes like molten gold. A quiet understanding passes between us. They know what's coming. They've come to fight.

We thunder into the valley, the wolves keeping pace, and the first shouts rise through the trees.

We arrive at Robinburg to a scene that has my heart thrashing in my throat. The village is already ablaze—not from the carnoraxis, but from the villagers themselves. In their attempt to thwart the beasts, the fire has spread and grown out of control. Flames curl along the edges of thatched rooftops, licking at the night. Smoke thickens the air, causing every breath to clog my lungs. Shadows move in the chaos, figures darting, weapons flashing. And then, unnatural movement. The hulking, sinewy forms of the carnoraxis tear through the village, their emaciated bodies twisting as they lunge for their prey.

The villagers are fighting back, but they are no match for the beasts. And the tsar has made it clear that anyone who stands in the way of his hunt for third-born fae will be slain for their efforts.

One of the men lunges forward with a torch while the group with him takes cover, but the carnoraxis swipes the torch out of his grasp. The man falters, and it only take a second for the carnoraxis to rip into him with his jagged teeth.

Fuck!

A gust of wind whips past, nearly knocking me off my feet as I dismount. I spot a young girl standing in the town square, hands lifted, eyes aglow as she wrestles with the air itself. Fae. With air-wielding powers. The blast slams into a carnoraxis, forcing the creature back on its haunches, but the effort clearly costs her. Her arms tremble, her power

already waning.

Nearby, a man throws out a burst of fire, searing the claws of another beast before it swipes at him. He ducks, but not fast enough. Its talons rake across his shoulder, sending him spinning to the ground.

They're trying. Fighting with everything they have. But it won't be enough.

"Move!" I snap, charging forward, my sword drawn.

My squad surges into the battle, and the wolves rush in so quickly, I can't track their movements. Aila and Giorgi have already leapt from their saddles, blades flashing as they cut through the smoke. Isaac covers them, loosing arrows with brutal precision, the shafts sinking deep into the snarling beasts. Mylo roars as he throws himself into the fray, his sword carving a path through the carnoraxis closing in on the struggling fae girl.

An echoing scream rings out to our left.

It doesn't come from the villagers.

Lorne stands near the edge of the skirmish, one hand raised, his fingers curved like he's clutching invisible threads. The scream bends midair, warping and soaring toward the far end of the square. A cluster of carnoraxis jerks their heads in that direction, drawn by the illusion of fresh prey. Snarling, they veer off-course, allowing Aila to drive her blade cleanly through the exposed side of another beast's throat.

A second sound follows—footsteps pounding across flagstones, panicked gasps—and the creatures give chase, unaware they're pursuing nothing but smoke and sound. The moment of distraction gives us just enough time.

And then the wolves descend.

They crash into the carnoraxis from the flanks, claws tearing, jaws snapping. The beasts recoil in surprise, their unnatural shrieks echoing through the village. A black-furred wolf leaps onto the back of one of them, sinking its teeth into the creature's spine. Another lunges beneath a carnoraxis, tearing its leg out from under it.

The tide begins to shift.

I stare for half a heartbeat, awestruck by the savagery and precision

of the wolves' assault. They're not just fighting. They're coordinated. Tactical.

A burst of light flashes to my left. Isaac shoots flaming bolts from his crossbow, the one my eye follows piercing into the back of a beast stalking one of the children.

"Let's finish this," I mutter, charging into the firelit chaos.

I don't stop to think. I race hard into the village square, my heart pounding, my pulse a war drum in my ears.

Dante is right behind me, sword in hand. "The fire is out of hand. We need to get the villagers clear!"

He's right. They're fighting bravely, but they're scattered, uncoordinated. And the buildings around us are falling apart from the flames. If we don't intervene, they'll be ripped apart or consumed by the fire before the night is through.

A carnoraxis wheels toward me, its sunken, black eyes gleaming. I meet its charge, twisting my body at the last second to avoid its swipe before I bury my sword deep into its ribs. A piercing shriek. A spray of blood. And then I'm turning, searching for the next enemy.

A scream pierces through the chaos. High-pitched. Desperate.

I spin toward the sound, checking to see if it's merely another of Lorne's illusions. My pulse spikes as my gaze snaps to a house already half-consumed by fire. Smoke billows from the windows, black against the night sky, but through the shifting haze, I see him. A boy, no older than eleven, clutching the ledge of an upstairs window, his face streaked with soot, his mouth open in a wordless cry for help.

He's trapped.

Dante sees him too. "Shit," he mutters, already moving, but the flames are spreading fast, licking at the timber walls, devouring the lower floor. There's no way up from the inside.

My eyes flick to the trellis climbing the side of the house, its ivy-wrapped latticework trembling in the heat. It won't hold forever, but it doesn't have to.

I sprint forward, sheathing my sword in one fluid motion before grasping the trellis and hauling myself up. The wood groans beneath my

weight, but I ignore it, my muscles burning as I climb. The heat singes my skin, smoke stinging my eyes, but I grit my teeth and keep moving.

The boy spots me, his wide eyes shimmering with terror. "Please," he chokes out. "I-I can't—"

"You can," I say firmly. "I need you to climb onto the ledge. Can you do that?"

He nods frantically, his small hands scrambling for purchase as he inches forward. I'm nearly there. Just a little higher—

A guttural snarl splits the night.

I twist just as a carnoraxis bursts into view below, its sunken eyes gleaming, its elongated limbs moving with unnatural speed. It's seen me. It knows I'm trapped.

And it's coming.

My fingers curl around the hilt of my dagger, heart hammering. No time to hesitate. I whip the blade through the air, sending it spinning straight for the beast's throat. The dagger sinks deep, its jeweled hilt catching the firelight for a split second before blood sprays from the creature's neck. It staggers back with a strangled hiss, its claws swiping at the wound as dark ichor spills down its chest.

It won't die from that. Not right away. But I've bought myself seconds.

"Now!" I bark at the boy.

He whimpers but obeys, scrambling onto the ledge just as I reach him. The trellis wobbles violently, the heat from the flames nearly unbearable now. I grab his arm and pull him against me, bracing for the descent.

And then the trellis gives way.

We drop. The world tilts—wind whipping past my face—before I twist midair, forcing us sideways. We hit the ground hard, my back slamming against the dirt, my arms tight around the boy to shield him.

I barely get a breath in before I hear the ragged breathing.

The carnoraxis is still alive. And it's furious.

I shove the boy toward Dante, who's already rushing forward. "Take him!"

Dante catches him without question, but his gaze locks on mine, tight with concern. My senses tell me he's about to charge in to help me, but another beast appears at his back. Dante's falchion slices toward the aggressor.

I don't let myself linger because the carnoraxis I've thrown my dagger at lurches, dark blood still leaking from its throat. Its eyes are locked on me, hungry and wild. I rise to meet it, drawing my sword in one smooth motion, my muscles thrumming with adrenaline.

It lunges. I sidestep. Its claws rake empty air where my ribs had been a breath ago. I pivot, blade flashing, and drive my sword deep into its chest. The beast lets out a keening wail, its talons twitching as the last of its strength ebbs away. Blood bubbles at its grey lips before it finally crumples, its weight crashing into the dirt.

I exhale sharply, the pounding in my ears slowing as I step forward, yanking my dagger from its throat before wiping both blades clean.

Dante is still holding the boy, his expression unreadable as he watches me. A fallen carnoraxis, sliced in two, lays at his feet.

When an eerie whistle pierces the air, I whip my head around. Isaac stands atop an overturned cart, his crossbow steady as he takes aim at the beast charging toward Aila. She's quick, dodging its initial swipe, but it's closing in too fast. Too close. With a sharp *twang*, Isaac's arrow flies true, burying itself deep in the carnoraxis's eye socket with a sickening crunch. The creature staggers, clawing at its ruined face before it collapses to the ground, motionless.

Aila, panting, doesn't even spare Isaac a glance as she lifts her sword and plunges it into another carnoraxis at her feet. "About damn time, Isaac."

Isaac reloads smoothly, shaking sweat from his brow. "You're welcome."

Not far from them, Mylo bellows as he lifts a dying beast off its feet, shoving it back into the smoldering wreckage of a cart. The wood creaks, splinters—then the weight of the beast sends it crashing into the blaze. The fire engulfs it instantly, a shriek tearing from its throat before it finally goes silent.

Mylo turns back to the fight, his blade already swinging, already searching for another enemy. But there aren't many left.

The larger wolves in the pack growl at the remaining carnoraxis. The monsters, sensing their dwindling numbers, begin to retreat—some limping, others scrambling into the trees, their gaunt forms swallowed by the darkness.

It's over.

Not won, not really. Too many homes are in ruins. Too many bodies lie still in the dirt, their blood turning the soil dark. All I can think is it could have been worse.

41

CHAPTER FIVE

The campfire hisses softly as I stoke the embers, pushing a half-burned log deeper into the pit with the tip of a branch. Sparks rise into the night air like startled fireflies, spiraling up toward the stars. My legs ache. My arms feel like dead weight. Every breath still tastes faintly of smoke from the burning village, and the leather of my gloves is stiff with ash.

But we made it.

Behind me, the rest of the squad moves in and out of the circle of firelight, slow and heavy-footed, exhaustion tugging at their limbs. Mylo groans as he drops onto a log beside the flames, rolling his shoulder with a wince.

"Next time, maybe let the carnoraxis know we prefer *not* to be tackled into carts of splintered wood," he mutters. He winces as he rubs at a forming bruise on his collarbone.

Aila, already seated, snorts and leans back on her palms. "Next time, maybe try ducking."

"You're hilarious," he deadpans.

"Don't encourage her," Isaac says without looking up, carefully inspecting the fraying fletching on one of his arrows. His cheeks are still smudged with soot, and there's a fresh tear in the sleeve of his tunic. Most of us have washed up using the water from the stream, but Isaac's first priority is to check on the weapons.

"Why not?" Aila grins, unbothered despite the makeshift sling around her arm. "I'm brilliant when I'm concussed."

Giorgi lets out a low, tired chuckle from where they're curled up near the fire, already half-wrapped in their cloak. "We're alive. Let's call that a win."

No one argues.

Dante stands a few paces beyond the light, his back half turned to the group, arms crossed as he surveys the woods. Always watching. Always still. I feel his presence even when he doesn't speak. There's something about the way he moves—controlled, calculated, yet wound tight, like he's holding something inside, something he never lets loose unless he has to.

I notice, too, how often his hand drifts to his shoulder. Subtle. Subconsciously. But there's tension in the movement. Pain he's trying not to show.

Once the others begin settling in, blankets pulled tight and boots unlaced, I rise and walk toward him.

"You're injured," I say softly, stopping just beside him.

"I've had worse." His voice is low, quieted by the hush of the woods.

"Hold still." I lift my hand toward his shoulder, and though he doesn't move, I feel the way his body stills completely as my fingers find the fabric of his shirt. He doesn't flinch, but he doesn't stop me, either.

I press my palm against the wounded muscle.

Warmth gathers in my chest, then flows outward, through my arm, through my fingertips. Magic, gentle and steady. I feel it rush into him, mending what I cannot see. It's subtle, like weaving golden thread through torn seams.

His gaze finds mine, heavy-lidded but clearer now that the pain has dulled. "I'm a little surprised you brought us straight back here. I thought it was routine for your squad to find a tankard or two to drain before turning in."

 43

I lift a brow. "Would you have preferred that?"

He shrugs with his good shoulder. "Wouldn't have mattered. So long as I got to spend time with you."

I huff, though a smile tugs at the corner of my mouth. "You say that now, but you've never been subjected to Mylo and Isaac's pub songs. They're always off-key, never in sync, and louder than necessary."

"Sounds charming."

"They once cleared out an entire tavern with a chorus about a charming goat."

He laughs, low and rough, the kind of sound that vibrates through me more than I expect. "And here I thought battle wounds were the worst part of these missions."

"Believe me, the looks we've gotten from pub-goers smart more than any cut I've ever suffered."

When I draw my hand away, he exhales slowly.

"Thank you," he murmurs.

That heavy-lidded look he's giving me makes me want me to put my hands back on him. And not just on his shoulder.

There isn't a moment to dwell on that thought, however, because Dante cups my cheek and swallows up the distance between our lips. Perhaps it was our time apart, the weeks of missing his touch and his kisses, but I don't think I've been so conscious of every nerve ending in my body as I am in this moment. I'm completely fixated on the caress of his lips upon mine. My skin comes alive, not wanting the contact to end. His tongue meets mine, and I let out a small whimper. Dante's hands glide over my shoulders to my back, sending a shiver down my spine. His fingers graze over the curves of my ass before pulling me closer, until we're flush against each other.

He's hard. And, gods, it's been so long. But we're not exactly alone out here. As much as I want him, this isn't the time or place.

When he breaks the kiss, I look up—and his gaze meets mine. That look again. Unspoken, unreadable, but impossibly full. As if he wants to say something, but words would only ruin it.

Before I can speak, a sharp crack breaks through the trees to our left.

My hand goes to my dagger instantly. Dante steps in front of me.

We both turn, eyes scanning the dark. Another sound—closer this time. A rustle of underbrush, the crunch of dried leaves beneath paws.

And then it emerges.

A wolf pup, no more than a few months old by the look of it, stumbles into the clearing, its legs a bit too wobbly to support its round, furry body. Its coat is the color of snow-spattered ash, and one of its ears flops to the side. There is a slightly darker marking over one of its eyes that looks like a lopsided heart. The pup blinks up at us, tongue lolling as it pants.

I freeze.

"Oh," I whisper. "I don't know if I can handle how cute you are."

The pup trots forward a few steps, then stops and tilts its head at me like it's trying to figure out what kind of creature I am.

"Don't move," I murmur to Dante as I sheathe my dagger. "If its mother is near, I don't think she'll take kindly to strangers."

Sure enough, as my eyes sweep the treeline, I catch it. A pair of golden eyes watching from the brush. Unblinking. Waiting.

"She's there," I whisper. "I think she's letting it approach me."

"Or testing you," Dante mutters.

The pup pads closer, snuffling at my boots. A gentle breeze makes its fluffy fur ruffle. My heart turns into something soft and fragile inside my chest. I want to touch it, to scoop it into my arms and nuzzle it. But I stay still, respectful. My fingers itch.

"Go on," I whisper to it. "Go back to your mama. She's watching."

The pup doesn't listen. Instead, it plants its front paws on my leg, wagging its tail wildly, and lets out a tiny, excited huff.

"Okay," I say softly. "That's adorable and not helping at all."

Dante shifts beside me. "Celeste."

"I know." I cut him off. "I know."

Slowly, slowly, I crouch, my eyes darting between the pup and its mother, back and forth.

The wolf pup climbs into my lap with an awkward flop, heavy and warm and squirming. I lift it carefully, cradling it against my chest. Its

heart flutters wildly beneath its ribs. It shifts in my arms, sniffing at my chin, its warm breath reminding me of freshly baked bread.

The mother doesn't move. But her eyes stay locked on mine.

"I'm giving them back," I whisper. "I promise."

She answers me with a soft growl. A warning that I should not betray her.

I cross the dew-slicked grass, every footstep deliberate, my breaths short. At the edge of the trees, I bend and set the pup down. It sits for a moment, wagging its tail as if confused by the separation.

"Go on," I whisper again, backing away with slow steps. "Go home."

Finally, the mother wolf emerges from the brush, silent and massive, her fur dark and speckled with leaves. She walks with the grace of something ancient. Wild. She lowers her head, picks the pup up by its scruff, and vanishes into the dark.

I don't breathe until they're gone.

A pair of arms wraps around me from behind.

"I swear..." Dante mutters against my hair. "One day, you'll be the death of me."

I lean back against his chest, feeling the thrum of his heartbeat. "Why? Because I make friends so easily?" I turn in his arms, giving him a teasing grin.

"No. Because you keep offering yourself to dangerous beasts."

"Hmm." I tilt my head and grin. "And yet *you're* the one holding me."

He huffs a laugh. "Exactly."

Our gazes feed each other's for a moment before he leans down and presses his lips against mine. Before it can deepen, he pulls back and presses an impossibly small kiss to the side of my head. "As much as I'd like to spend the rest of the night kissing you, we need to get some rest."

I play off my disappointment with a laugh. "You're bossy when you're worried."

"I'm always worried when you're near danger."

I rise up on my toes to press one more kiss, impossibly tiny, to his lips. "Then you'd better get used to it."

He smiles, brushing his knuckles down the side of my cheek. "You better keep that headstrong attitude when we return to the castle. If the king has discovered you ran off again, he won't be pleased."

I sigh and rest my forehead against his chest. "He never is."

CHAPTER SIX

The moment Ivystone's towering walls come into view, unease grips my chest like a tightening fist. It's not the usual dread that comes with returning to the castle—not the suffocating weight of politics or mourning veils or the king's ever-watchful gaze. During the last mile of our journey, the worry I carry for my uncle grew with every step. I can only offer a prayer up to the gods that Uncle Kormak has finally awoken.

I glance at Dante, but his expression is unreadable, his focus fixed ahead as we guide our horses through the outer gates. If I know him, his worry lies with how the king will punish me if he knows I've run off with my squad during the mourning period. And how he'll punish us both for being together when it is forbidden.

Mylo peels off toward the stables, but before Dante and I can follow, a line of guards steps forward, barring our path.

One of the guards takes an additional step, his posture as straight as a board. "The king demands your presence. Immediately."

The words are for both of us, but his eyes are locked on me.

I lift my chin. "The king can wait. I'm going to see my uncle first."

"I'm sorry, Your Highness," the guard says. "He insists."

My stomach knots. Not just because I knew I'd have to deal with Silas, but because I'm desperate to see how my uncle is doing and the fucking king is getting in the way.

Dante exhales sharply, barely masking his frustration, but he doesn't argue as we dismount. I pull at the hem of my jacket, steeling myself, and together, we follow the guards through the stone corridors. They do not lead us to the throne room, but rather to his private chambers.

The moment we step into the room, I know this isn't going to be a quiet reprimand.

King Silas stands at the back of his chaise, hands grasping the velvet back, his entire body thrumming with barely contained rage. His piercing eyes, devoid of any warmth, fix on me first, then flick to his son.

"You," he spits, "have disgraced yourselves."

Dante stiffens beside me, but I don't lower my gaze. I've never been one to bow before the weight of the king's anger, and I won't start now.

Silas strides toward us, his boots echoing against the marble floor. "You were meant to be in mourning," he snarls, pointing a finger at me. "Not gallivanting across the countryside like some reckless soldier."

I set my jaw. "Your Majesty, I think it would interest you to know that the carnoraxis attack was in Robinburg, which lies on the border of Hedera." My voice remains even, though my pulse hammers against my ribs. "I don't think the attacks are limited to Delasurvia anymore. This concerns Hedera, too. If you want to protect both kingdoms, then I should be allowed to carry out my duty."

The king's face darkens. "Your 'duty'?" The words are a growl, laced with fury. "Your duty is to play the part of the mourning would-be bride of my son. As is expected by both kingdoms."

"Both kingdoms expect us to thwart any threat against them," I bark back. "Have you even thought to take my warning about the tsar seriously? Even if I'm wrong, what would it cost you to send some men north to Dulcamar to check if my claims are valid? If Torbin actually survived the fall, and the carnoraxis carried him to—"

"Enough!" Silas's voice reverberates through the room like a thunderclap. He narrows his eyes and points a finger at me. "Do you take

 49

me for a fool? Just because I do not feed you reports of my actions does not mean that I am not doing my kingly duties. I've sent men up to Dulcamar. Osrem is with them, since he was Torbin's advisor and might have insight. So do not assume that I have ignored your claims."

My breath hitches. "Have any returned?"

A muscle feathers in his jaw, and he straightens. "These things take time. But no one has yet to come rushing back to tell me my son is still alive."

And they probably won't come back at all. Especially if Osrem is with them. Osrem was loyal to Torbin, which means he is probably loyal to the tsar. I'm willing to bet the king's men are already dead.

Silas turns to Dante now, the fury shifting to something sharper. "And you." His voice drops to a venomous hush. "You were not supposed to be with her."

Dante's fists clench at his sides, but when he speaks, his voice is calm. "I'm not going to sit idly by while she rides into battle alone."

Silas's eyes flash with something I can't name, his anger a roaring flame. "You can and you will. Do you think I can afford to lose you?" His voice rises, echoing through the hall. "It's a moot point now because Princess Celeste is forbidden from fighting in the attacks."

"What?" I shake my head. "No, we had an arrangement."

"Your arrangement was with Torbin, and he is dead." His words strike harder than I expect. "And if you think I'm going to let the same fate fall upon the both of you, then you're even more a fool than I believed. Not to mention that if you die in battle, Princess, Delasurvia is mine."

I open my mouth to contest, but the king raises a hand.

"It's over. Your role as commander must now be set aside, as we agreed, to keep that priceless womb of yours safe and sound until it serves its fucking purpose. You will mourn my son until the tour ends, and then you will marry Dante and provide an heir. Otherwise, Delasurvia and its future are forfeit."

For a fleeting moment, I think I see something deeper in his eyes. Not just anger, not just control, but fear. Not for me, but for the

precarious future he's built. A legacy that hinges on my survival.

The realization coils in my gut, hot and twisting.

I could push back. I could tell him that my life, my choices, are not his to dictate. But my principal would come at a cost. And King Silas knows I won't betray my people. He knows he has the power here, and he will not let me forget it.

I don't go to my room after the king's reprimand. I don't even bother changing out of the mud-streaked pants I wore during the mission. My boots leave damp prints across the stone floor as I make my way down the corridor, the weight of guilt clawing tighter with every step.

There was no way for Dante and me to properly part from each other with the king watching, but I push that thought aside as I rush into my uncle's chambers.

The scent hits me first. The heat and the sweat that chokes the air.

The fire in the hearth is banked low, but the air is stifling, heavy with damp linens and something sharp beneath it—acrid and bitter. Ezra stands at the bedside, sleeves rolled, carefully wiping a cloth over my uncle's chest. The sheet beneath him is soaked through.

"Ezra," I breathe, panic already knotting in my stomach. "What happened?"

He looks up. There's no alarm in his features, no outward panic. but the tension in his shoulders speaks enough. "The fever came on yesterday evening." He wrings out the cloth in a basin tinged pink with herbal tincture. "Quickly. Fiercely."

My gaze drops to my uncle. His skin is flushed deep red, mottled and glistening with sweat. His jaw is tight, teeth grinding in unconscious torment. One of his arms twitches, and a low groan slips from his throat. Not coherent. Not present.

I step closer, unable to keep the fear from my voice. "He's gotten

worse."

Ezra's gaze flicks to me. "But this was expected."

"'Expected'?" My voice rises. "He's burning alive."

"This is the turn," Ezra says gently. "There's a reason the elixir is controversial, Celeste. It's brutal. It stirs what little strength the body has left and forces it to fight. But it's a knife's edge. Either the fever will break, or..."

He doesn't finish the sentence. He doesn't need to.

I worry my lip as I fight off the overwhelming feeling that my knees are about to give out. My eyes well up, but I sniff back the tears.

"There's another aspect to it, I'm afraid," Ezra says.

I'm not sure how much more I can take, but I nod for him to continue.

He dips his head and inhales deeply. "I believe his healing magic might be fighting the elixir."

"'Fighting it'?" I shake my head. "But aren't the two trying to do the same thing?"

"Yes, but magic doesn't behave like science. Magic has its own rules, rules we may not even understand." Ezra folds his hands together. "I suspect the two properties, so to speak, may be at war inside his body."

"So the magic is fighting the elixir, and the elixir is trying to overcome the magic?" My knees weaken, and I find the edge of the nearby chair before I collapse onto it. I press a hand to my mouth, watching as another tremor ripples through my uncle's body. "Did I make a mistake?"

"No." Ezra's voice is firm. "You made a choice. A hard one. And now... we wait."

Uncle Kormak lets out another hoarse, strangled sound, his back arching slightly off the bed before collapsing back with a *thud*. My chest aches with helplessness.

"I can give him something to ease the worst of it," Ezra adds. "But it won't wake him. Only his body can do that."

I grip my knees, nails biting into fabric. "He's in pain."

"He is." Ezra doesn't sugarcoat it. "But pain isn't always a sign of loss.

Sometimes it means there's still fight left."

I stand and hover near the bed. I want to comfort my uncle, to use my healing power to ease his pain, but at the same time, I'm afraid anything I do might stop the elixir from working.

His eyes soften. "You're not going to help him by unraveling."

I swallow hard. "I know."

He nods. "You're still in your uniform. Maybe you should freshen up, take some time to clear your head."

I exhale shakily. "Yes. Okay. I'll clean up and get some air."

Ezra places a hand on my shoulder. "Good. Go find Nadya, perhaps. I imagine she's worried about you."

I move in a trance toward the door but pause at the threshold to glance back once more. My uncle shifts under the blankets again, teeth bared, sweat trailing along his temple.

"Send for me," I say, my voice hoarse, "the moment the fever breaks."

Ezra doesn't hesitate. "You'll be the first to know."

I force myself to walk away. But the weight of the room sticks to my skin like steam. And I don't know if I'm walking toward clarity or abandoning a man I cannot bear to lose.

 53

CHAPTER SEVEN

After I've bathed and dressed in clean clothes—a black mourning dress to appease the king as well as Indira—I search for Nadya. I find her in the library, hunched over a thick, leather-bound tome that looks like it's survived a hundred storms. Her elbow rests on the edge of the table, one finger absently twisting a coil of her hair as her eyes flick across the page. She's so engrossed in the text, she doesn't notice me enter.

The air smells like parchment and old smoke, faintly sweet with dried lavender and bay leaves tucked into the crevices of the shelves to keep the moths out. It's one of the quietest places in the citadel, but right now, I welcome the hush. My thoughts have been screaming, but here, they're not as loud.

"Nadya?" My voice sounds hollow in the stillness. "Do you have a moment, or should I come back when your skin's finished fusing with the parchment?"

She startles slightly, blinking up at me before a warm smile curves her lips. "You're back."

I nod, crossing the room to her side. My body still feels like it's in motion from being on horseback all day, but it's my thoughts that won't settle. After we greet each other with a hug, I sink into the seat beside her. "I checked on my uncle. He doesn't seem to be getting better."

Nadya closes the book and shifts my way, her gaze softening, growing serious. "I know. When his fever started, I panicked. But Ezra told me he thinks it means the elixir is working."

I nod, running a hand through my hair, the strands still damp. "He wasn't so open with me. He simply said we have to wait to see if the fever breaks. I couldn't stand to see him thrashing, so I came to find a distraction."

"He said the same thing to me." She sighs. "That's why I came here."

"Have you been here all day?"

"Don't tell Indira, but I've been here since last night. Only left once, sneaking to the kitchen to grab something to eat."

I give her a questioning smile. "Why shouldn't I tell Indira?"

"I've been hiding from her. I guess I left a mess in one of the rooms... well, one of the guards and I left the mess. He has a special way to enjoy berries." She grins and coyly averts her eyes. "Anyway, I thought I'd give her some time to calm down, and I don't think she's stepped foot in the library in years."

I can't help but laugh. It's good to know that some things haven't changed, and I lean closer to her to take her hand, grateful for her company.

She gives my hand a squeeze, her grip steady and warm. "Celeste. Ezra knows what he's doing. He's the best magister I've ever met."

I manage a faint scoff. "You don't know many magisters, though. Do you?"

Her lips quirk upward, but her voice remains soft. "With all that knowledge and cleverness, I can't imagine a better magister could exist. Which is why I put all my faith in the one I do know. Ezra's calm, but he's not careless. If he thought your uncle was beyond saving, he wouldn't still be fighting."

Her reassurance settles something in my chest—not quite relief, but a fragile thread of steadiness. "I suppose."

"Oh! Have you seen the king?" She grimaces. "I tried my best to

 55

cover for you, but when he forced Indira to admit you hadn't been to your room for a few days, he caught on."

"It's not your fault. And yes, Dante and I went to see him."

She wags her brows. "Dante, huh? I figured he was with you."

I release her hand and give her a playful nudge. "We weren't alone together, if that's what you're thinking. There was another attack, this one closer to Hedera."

"So the attack on Ivystone wasn't a solitary incident? I figured they'd only crossed the border because of Torbin."

I don't answer right away. My uncle's voice replays in my mind, and my stomach churns from his words. Is my father really alive? Is he the tsar or just one of the tsar's prisoners? Was the tsar—father or not—using the carnoraxis to get to me, and that's why they were in Hedera?

"We can't be sure," I finally answer. "But it looks like I won't be much help with the effort anymore. The king has henceforth forbidden me to ride out into battle."

"That hasn't exactly stopped you before. Besides, when he leaves for the tour, he won't be around to keep you trapped."

Except I fear it will be even worse then. He'll most likely triple the guards, and I wouldn't put it past him to keep me locked up, not just in the castle, but in my room.

"We'll see." I shake my head. "For now, I need a distraction. Something to keep me from staring at the door and willing Ezra to walk through it with good news. And something to keep me from foolishly planning a vendetta against the king."

Nadya taps the edge of her book. "Then you're in luck. I've got a distraction that comes with age-old history, sorcery, and possibly a little family drama."

I raise a brow. "All that from one book?"

She flips it open again, revealing curling script and a faded sketch of women in cloaked robes. "Someone was diligent about keeping note of who was going where and when."

I laugh. "I wasn't aware that gossip was considered history."

"Well, if I've learned anything, it's that oftentimes powerful men

who are afraid of the truth getting out suppress the voices of the authentic."

I sit up straighter. "Okay. I'm listening."

She leans in, excitement returning to her voice. "This particular section talks about a small traveling band of mysterious women from Bastos. Supposedly, they journeyed through Terre Ferique before the plague of poisonous plants began spreading."

"Doing what?"

"The opinions are mixed." She lifts a shoulder. "Some say they caused the corruption. Others say they were trying to stop it. Either way, they were rumored to be powerful, wielding magic unlike anything that's documented elsewhere. Not born magic like with fae or sirens. Learned magic. Witchcraft."

The word floats around the room like dust in beams of sunlight.

"Witches traveling through Terre Ferique? I'm surprised they weren't stopped." Through the centuries, there's been a big debate on witches. Many people believed that any magic not inherited was stolen. Twisted. That it came from somewhere dark and not from the gods.

"Eventually, they *were* stopped." She closes the book with a *thud* that resonates through the room. "They were killed by assassins once they'd reached the shores of the Batu Basah Ocean."

"If the witches got that far, then they must not have been very good assassins." I tilt my head. "Who hired the assassins?"

She lifts a brow. "No one knows."

"That's ominous."

"Anyway, I thought it was interesting, mostly because that's where my mother's side of the family came from. Bastos. Particularly Cista."

I'm guessing that's what she meant by *family drama.* "You never told me that."

She smiles crookedly. "My mother doesn't talk about it. She was born in Delasurvia. Hetchling, to be exact. But her parents moved from Bastos before she was born. The only family I know of still living there is my great-aunt. Haven't spoken to her since I was little. Haven't spoken to anyone back home in Delasurvia in a while, either."

 57

Something cold twists in my chest. "Your mother hasn't written since we moved here."

"No," she says, looking down. "Not even a message. But that's not new. She doesn't enjoy writing. She says she's bad at it, but I think it's just an excuse."

"I'm sorry, Nadya."

"It is what it is." Nadya leans back in her chair, fingers drumming lightly against the closed cover of the book as her expression changes. "Can you imagine witches so powerful, they destroyed most of the world and wiped out the existence of dragons with poisonous plants?"

"That's intense, yeah."

She tilts her head after a moment. "I've always wondered what it would be like to have magic."

I blink at her. "Magic like that?"

She shrugs one shoulder. "I would never be that sinister, but, you know, some kind of mystical power. Something I could learn to control. To use."

Though I'm struggling to figure out my own powers, I don't dismiss her curiosity. I tilt my head. "What do you think you would do?"

A mischievous gleam lights in her eyes. "I think I would start small, just to test things out. Maybe I'd enchant the furniture in any room Indira enters to shift slightly so she's always running into something. You know, just to keep her humble."

I snort, covering my mouth to hide the laugh, but it escapes, anyway—light and unexpected. "That's what you'd use ancient power for? Magical redecorating?"

"Imagine the chaos. Every court function ruined by a trail of bumps and grunts. Or if she's hunting me down to scold me, I could easily outrun her." She sighs wistfully.

I shake my head, but there's a smile tugging at my lips. "You're ridiculous."

"Ridiculously brilliant," she counters, then she runs her hand along the spine of the book. "But seriously, if there's even a sliver of truth in these old texts—if witches once protected this land—it makes me

wonder."

The thought hovers between us, daring and delicate.

Before I can respond, the door creaks open behind us.

"There you are," Indira huffs, her heels clicking briskly across the polished floor. She eyes the book in front of Nadya with the disdain of someone who has no time for musty tomes or ancient curses.

"Oh, were you looking for me?" Nadya feigns innocence.

Indira's nostrils flare, but her lips are pressed into a line, as if she's trying to control herself. "I will deal with you later. But for now, you both must come with me. Immediately."

"For what?" I ask, already dreading the answer.

"Preparations are underway for the funeral," she says. "The king has announced it will take place in two days' time, and the queen has summoned the royal seamstress. You are to be fitted for your funeral gowns." Her gaze cuts to Nadya. "You, too."

Nadya groans and pushes the book away. "Mourning and fashion. Those certainly go hand in hand, don't they?"

"If you've ever been to Podrosa," I mumble, "I'd say that's spot on."

 59

CHAPTER EIGHT

The fitting isn't as horrendous as I thought it would be, but I'm glad it's finished. The corridor leading back to my room from the fitting chamber is colder than I remember. The stone beneath my boots chills the air, and the hush that haunts Ivystone feels heavier than usual. Since Nadya rushed off as soon as the seamstress was done with her, I head down the hall alone. I want to get back before sunset to see if Dante is on his balcony. Our evening rendezvous don't always work out. Sometimes Dante is holed up in the council chambers with his father and Farvis. And sometimes Indira lurks about longer than necessary, making it impossible to step out onto the balcony at all. But I hurry toward my room with hope in my heart. Even if it's just for a glance at him.

A murmur of voices drifts from the half-closed door to the king's lounge, and though I know I shouldn't stop, I do. I press a hand to my heart as dread fills me.

The voices sharpen—King Silas's low, cutting tone and Queen Eleanor's softer one, frayed at the edges. I creep closer, pressing into the shadowed alcove beside the door. I probably shouldn't loiter, but I've learned that what people say behind closed doors is far more honest than what they say in public. And when it comes to the king, this may be the only way to hear any truth he has to share.

"You are too hasty, Silas," the queen says, her voice taut but measured. "This plan to legitimize Dante, it feels rushed."

"It's not your concern." The king cuts her off, the words like a blade unsheathed. "You lost the right to speak of heirs long ago."

A pause. Then, quieter, "I gave you a son."

"Only one. And he is now gone," he sneers. "Do not expect me to wait for your approval to secure the future of this kingdom."

Her breath hitches, a small, broken sound that scrapes at my chest. "I tried to give you more."

"And you failed me at every turn," the king says, as cold as winter steel. "I am not to blame for it. I gave you plenty of seed with which to bear another heir, and yet here we are. Emptyhanded."

The silence that follows is thick and jagged, the kind that makes my throat ache to swallow. I should go. This is none of my business.

When the queen speaks again, her voice trembles. Not with fear, but with rage barely held in check. "Do you think I *planned* to miscarry? That I wanted to feel life inside me, only to have it ripped away?" Her voice cracks on the last word, raw and unguarded. "Perhaps if you hadn't been so rough—" She breaks off, swallowing a sob. "Perhaps Torbin would have three siblings standing in line for your precious throne."

"Don't you fucking dare—" A roar rips from the king, sharp and vicious. There's a clatter, a glass shattering against the stone floor, and then the sound of movement. Fast. Threatening. A thump.

Oh, fuck!

I curl my fingers around the hilt of the dagger hidden beneath my skirts. My heart pounds, each beat screaming at me to act. To stop him.

I step forward.

A voice cuts through the air from down the hall, and I freeze.

Farvis rounds the corner at the far end of the hall, his heavy boots echoing with easy authority. There's enough rage within me not to care if he sees me, but when two guards appear behind him, I step back into

the shadows. My heart hammers against my ribs, acknowledging that I'd be outnumbered if I tried to burst into the king's private lounge, even if it's to reach the queen before—

The door to the lounge flies open.

Shit.

The king storms out, his jaw clenched, his face a thundercloud. His hand curls into a fist at his side, knuckles pale against the dark-green silk of his attire. For one breathless moment, I wonder if he's seen me, if I'll pay for standing here, listening.

But he doesn't even glance my way.

Farvis bows low as the king approaches, falling into step beside him without a word. The guards pivot and follow. Farvis speaks quietly with the king, and their voices fade as they disappear down the corridor, leaving only the distant echo of footsteps behind.

I exhale slowly, my grip on the dagger loosening. The rational part of me knows I'm no match for the king, not with his entire army at his command. But the part of me that has spent months seething beneath the weight of his decisions still aches to follow him. To make him bleed for every cruel word he hurled at the queen.

Instead, I need to make sure Queen Eleanor is all right. For all I know, he's left her unconscious on the floor. I step forward, pressing my palm against the door to the lounge. Through the thick wood, I hear nothing but the queen's soft, broken sobs. I don't know what he did, but at the very least, she's alive.

I should go to her. I should offer comfort, something, anything to lessen the hurt of knowing she's lost three children before they ever had the chance to live. To tell her it's not her fault, and that she has every right to blame Silas.

Would my presence help? Or would it be one more reminder of all the things she's lost?

I check the hall again, making sure no one is around. When I finally work up the nerve to open the door, I find the sobbing has stopped, and the queen is gone. I turn a full circle, wondering if my eyes somehow passed over her, but she's nowhere to be seen. Then I remember the secret

 62

passageways and realize she must have slipped through one.

Gritting my teeth, I leave the lounge and head back to my room. But in my head, I make a mental note. One day, the king will pay.

CHAPTER NINE

'm not looking forward to today. It's not just the suffocation of the funeral gown, but the weight of what's expected of me.

The grand prayer gallery looms ahead, its towering stone archways draped in heavy black banners embroidered with gold ivy. Gleaming candelabras line the path toward the altar, their flickering flames casting wavering shadows over the polished marble floor. A faint scent of myrrh and smoke lingers in the air, mingling with the hush of whispered prayers and the occasional muffled sob. To either side of the altar, running almost the entire length of the prayer gallery, large, floor-to-ceiling windows let in the pale morning light.

Courtiers, nobles, and prominent citizens of Hedera fill the hall, clad in black silks and somber wool, their faces veiled with sorrow—or something dangerously close to resentment. Their grief is palpable, and for the families who lost loved ones, my heart breaks for them. But some of them cry for the fallen prince, and for them, I can only feel pity that they believed he was worthy of their tears.

Nadya walks beside me, her hand looped through my arm in silent solidarity. I don't need to look at her to know she's gauging the crowd, watching the way people shift, the way their eyes follow me. I notice it, too.

The weight of their stares presses against my back as I move through the hall, their judgment like static in the charged air. Some glance away when I meet their eyes, unwilling to make their disdain fully known. Others do not. For once, I'm grateful for my veil. This one is longer than the mourning veil that's attached to my black coronet. This one covers my face, though I'm sure everyone can still see me. They hold my gaze, their expressions tight with barely concealed bitterness, as if they know I am the reason their prince is gone.

I refuse to falter. I straighten my spine, lift my chin, and step forward with measured grace, my dark veil cascading over my shoulders like armor. Let them glare. Let them whisper. I know the truth—they mourn a man I could not save, but they do not know the monster he became.

And I don't believe that he is dead.

Nadya leans in, her voice barely a breath. "They're looking for someone to blame."

I exhale slowly, steadying myself as we near the front of the hall. "I know."

And they'd be right to blame me. I did mean to kill Torbin that day if it meant saving Dante. So if they're looking for a villain, here I am. The problem is I'm going to be their queen one day, and it will be difficult to carry out the duties of protecting the people and standing up for their rights if none of them trust me.

Nadya and I make our way to the front of the gallery, where rows of darkly dressed nobles and courtiers sit in solemn silence. The seats reserved for the king and queen remain empty, their absence stretching like a void across the room. No one speaks louder than a whisper, and the quiet is thick with grief, reverence, and an uncertainty perhaps only I can sense.

At the center of the altar, where a casket should rest, there is only an ornate pedestal draped in black silk. A golden circlet—the prince's coronet—sits atop it, a symbol of what has been lost. A pattern of gold ivy leaves embellishes the crown, each leaf sparkling with emeralds. Since

 65

Torbin's body was never recovered, this is what serves as the focal point of the service in place of a casket.

Leaning against the pedestal, shining under the candlelight, is a longsword with a decorative hilt. It may have been one of Torbin's swords at some point, but it is not the sabre he had sheathed at his side since I came to Ivystone. The sabre was still attached to him when he fell, and it's most likely at his side today.

I swallow hard, forcing my expression into something unreadable. No one else questions Torbin's fate. No one else wonders if the carnoraxis merely carried him away rather than tore him apart. But I saw the way they descended on him, the way they shrieked and keened as they dragged him into the darkness. Almost as if they cried for him. It should have been his end, but something inside me burns with doubt.

Torbin is too determined, too ruthless, to be claimed by death so easily. And the potion he took time and time again made him strong, stronger than any normal human. Strong enough to match a fae. And those beasts served him—or at least were ordered to serve him by the Shadow Tsar. My gut is telling me the carnoraxis carried him off to save him.

A hand on my wrist pulls me from my thoughts. Nadya gives me a small, pointed look before guiding me into my seat. I don't argue. I settle into place, folding my hands in my lap as the room waits for the arrival of the king and queen.

Footsteps echo, and I force myself not to look over my shoulder. When I catch sight of a tall form emerging at the head of the aisle, I only slightly turn my head to find Dante standing there. He pauses between the rows of chairs, as if he's gazing upon the pedestal before him. But his eyes are on me. Subtly. Unnoticeable to everyone except me and Nadya.

His funeral suit is fitted perfectly, the high collar framing his strong neck, and gold brocade on his lapels and cuffs giving the black velvet jacket a distinguished look befitting a prince. My heart flutters at the sight of him, especially since he never made it to his balcony last night. Even though I knew he had been summoned to Silas's private quarters after dinner, I still continued to check for his appearance every few

minutes, well into the night. Indira incessantly asked me to stop pacing, but she thought I was merely unsettled because of the funeral, not because I longed to catch even a short glimpse of Dante.

He doesn't nod or move his mouth, and neither do I. We have learned to keep our silent communication undetectable. He just blinks, and I blink in return, before he turns and takes his seat across the aisle.

The great doors at the back of the prayer hall swing open, and the murmured conversations dissolve into hushed reverence. This time, I do glance over my shoulder. King Silas enters first, his broad shoulders squared, his chin lifted with the self-importance of a man who believes even his grief must be seen as grand. His funeral attire is regal, an embroidered black coat lined with gold threading. His long cloak, edged in dark fur, sweeps the marble floor as he walks, the heavy footfalls of his polished boots echoing in the vast chamber.

Queen Eleanor follows a few steps behind, draped in a flowing gown of deepest obsidian. Black lace veils the bodice, trailing down her arms in sheer, delicate patterns, and a thick band of jet beads circles her throat like a chain. A veil, also black, cascades from an intricate golden comb in her hair, framing a face as pale as moonlight. But beneath all the elegance, she is a woman hollowed by loss. Her movements are slow, deliberate, like someone navigating through an endless fog. Her hands, covered in elegant, black silk, tremble where they clutch at her skirts, and though her gaze is lowered, the sorrow is prominently etched into every strained line of her expression.

Perhaps it is more than that. I can't help but replay her argument with the king in my mind. This woman is not only grieving the loss of one son, but the many children she never got the chance to hold. And perhaps she is grieving the life she is trapped in, married to a powerful, merciless man who has no respect for her.

Several high-ranking nobles and trusted courtiers flank the king and queen—lords, council members, and the king's advisors, including Farvis, who keeps his face carefully blank as he escorts them to their seats facing the altar. They take their places with a solemn grace, across from the pedestal where Torbin's coronet gleams beneath the dim candlelight.

 67

Neither the king nor queen glance my way as they pass. There are no cold, condemning stares, no sharp glares filled with quiet accusations. But their indifference is just as unsettling.

The silence stretches, thick and expectant, until the sound of approaching footsteps shifts the air in the room. Soft singing from a small choir of girls at the back of the room causes everyone to turn their heads. The high priestess enters, her long ceremonial robes whispering against the stone floor, and all eyes remain on her as she travels up the aisle.

She ascends the altar, placing herself behind the podium, and turns to the crowd, her eyes sweeping over us while her face remains stoic. The flowing silver and white of her robes are almost identical to her pulled-back hair. When she lifts her hands in a gesture of quiet reverence, I straighten in my seat, as does the rest of the crowd.

The singing stops, and the stillness in the room is almost too loud.

"The gods thank you for your witness today. It is not only in life that we serve them, but in death as well." The high priestess's voice, smooth and unwavering, carries through the great hall. "Beneath the watchful eyes of the gods, we bow our heads to honor the life of His Royal Highness, Prince Torbin Copperhammer. Though his body was lost to the darkness of battle, his spirit lingers in the halls of memory, etched into the hearts of those who knew and cared for him. A prince of strength and ambition, a celebrated hunter, a warrior who fought for his kingdom, and his name shall not be forgotten."

She pauses, letting the words settle, letting the weight of them press into the stillness. The unease is almost unbearable. I fight the urge to cover my ears and close my eyes.

"Death is but a doorway, a passage into the eternal beyond. We mourn because we are left behind, but those who have passed walk new paths unknown to us. May the gods guide the Ivy Prince with mercy. May they grant him peace. And may those who loved him find solace in the legacy he leaves behind."

Her gaze sweeps over the gathered crowd, lingering on the king and queen before shifting toward the empty space where a casket should have

been.

"Let us not dwell in sorrow, but in remembrance. Let us not speak of what was taken, but of what remains. Prince Torbin's deeds, his victories, his joy, and his trials—all have shaped the course of this kingdom. We honor him today, and always."

She lowers her hands, signaling the moment of silent reflection, and the hall is swallowed by quiet grief. The stillness worms itself into my stomach and turns it sour.

Almost a minute into the silence, whispers reach my ears. Nadya's brow scrunches as she turns to look past me. I follow her gaze to find a young woman whispering to her friend, her cold eyes on me. She doesn't even bother to look away when I match her stare, but when Nadya clears her throat with a menacing edge, both women slink back in their seats, one of them going red in the face and averting her gaze, the other giving Nadya a onceover, as if measuring how much of a threat she might actually be.

I turn away from them, and I catch Nadya clenching her jaw as she faces forward. I let my gaze drift toward Dante, and I see the way he pulls his hands into fists when our eyes meet. Very carefully, I shake my head. His jaw goes rigid, but then he releases a breath and returns his focus to the altar.

When the high priestess speaks again, I tune her out. My thoughts go from the whispering women to my uncle to the fate of my kingdom. It isn't until King Silas rises from his seat and steps forward, his heavy, black robes trailing behind him like a shadow, that my mind returns to the present. The prayer hall falls into silence, every pair of eyes locked on to the king as he replaces the priestess behind the podium and lifts his chin, his expression a masterful display of solemnity.

"My son," he begins, his voice deep and steady, "was a man of strength, of honor. Even in his youth, Torbin proved himself worthy of the Copperhammer name. At the rife age of eleven, he downed his first stag. I remember the first time he ever bested a man with his sword—he was but thirteen years old, yet his skill with a blade already surpassed that of grown warriors. And it was not only his strength and hunting skills

 69

that made him exceptional. It was his loyalty. His devotion to his family."

His gaze flickers to Dante, and I feel the weight of it between us. "When I first learned I had another son," he continues, "Torbin was the one who insisted that Dante be brought into our home, that he be given a place among us. He would not see his brother cast aside. He believed in unity, in blood, in the duty of a prince to protect those who belonged to him."

Dante's posture is rigid, his jaw clenched as he holds the king's gaze. I don't know if it's grief, guilt, or something else entirely that flickers behind his eyes, but I know this much—Torbin may have once been kindhearted, but that version of him, the one who fought for his brother to be a part of his life, ceased to exist when he became a ruthless, uncaring creature who only used others to benefit himself.

I swallow hard as the king's voice changes, losing its practiced reverence and taking on a sharper, more cutting edge.

"But Torbin deserved more than this." His grip tightens on the arms of the podium. "He did not deserve to be lost to the wretched hands of fate. He did not deserve an end so obscene, so unworthy of his station. And if the gods are just, then they will see to it that those who ever held ill will toward my son"—his voice drops to a low growl—"will suffer their wrath."

His gaze snaps to me, cold and venomous. It's only a fraction of a second, but I feel it like a blade to my chest. My hands curl into fists at my sides, my nails biting into my palms.

Fucking lies. All of it.

Torbin was never the golden son the king paints him to be. And Silas himself—his grief is nothing but a performance. He is cruel to his wife. He was cruel to his son. And this was the example Torbin learned from. Now the king stands here, acting as if Torbin had been some beacon of righteousness. As if he didn't drive his own son into darkness. The hypocrisy and posturing are enough to make my blood boil.

A strange, heated buzz starts low in my chest. My pulse thrums harder. My breathing sharpens. The prayer gallery is too warm, too stifling.

Thunder rumbles, and the windows darken from the approaching clouds.

I shiver, startled by the sudden shift in the air. A gust of wind rushes through the chamber, rattling the heavy drapes and snuffing out several candles at once. The murmurs start almost instantly, heads turning to the ominous clouds that can be seen through the large windows, like a shadow swallowing the sky.

The king keeps speaking, but I barely hear him over the pounding in my ears. My breath comes faster, and the buzzing sensation spreads, tingling at my fingertips. The moment my fury peaks, lightning cracks.

The sky erupts. Rain—no, hail—crashes against the stone walls of the citadel, against the panes of glass, driven by merciless winds. A bolt of lightning strikes somewhere close, followed by a deafening boom that shakes the very foundation of the prayer hall. And just as the king utters his final word, one of the large windows shatters with a violent, splintering crash.

Glass explodes into the hall, and a collective gasp ripples through the gathered mourners. Instinctively, I raise a hand pulsing with power as the shards rain down, scattering across the marble floor, but none of them touch me or Nadya. Torbin's golden coronet tumbles from the pedestal, much the same way that Torbin himself fell from the tower. The wind surges inside, extinguishing more candles, sending the banners of mourning into a wild frenzy.

I inhale sharply, my heart hammering, a harsh sting behind my eyes. What... just fucking happened?

CHAPTER TEN

The prayer hall is in chaos. The king's guards move swiftly through the crowd, ushering the courtiers toward the heavy double doors, their voices sharp with urgency. Among them is Sir Holden, who pushes his way to me. Once he's certain I'm secure, he escorts me forward. I move with Nadya at my side, weaving through the dispersing crowd. My skin still tingles, the phantom sensation of that buzzing energy lingering in my fingertips.

Nadya pulls her shawl closer around her, her curls tossed by the wind. "That was spooky. Almost as if King Silas angered the gods."

I keep my face carefully neutral, though my heart is still pounding. I don't know what to believe. But the way the storm arrived, the way my own emotions had surged moments before, the sudden pain that came along with it... Was it just coincidence? Or did I somehow cause this?

The pain that blossomed behind my eyes makes me wince for a moment before it begins to fade.

Before I can dwell on it further, a familiar voice cuts through the commotion.

"Princess. Lady Nadya." Indira strides toward us, her dark brows

drawn in concern. Even in the frantic atmosphere, she carries herself with her usual poise, her hands folded neatly in front of her as though nothing could ruffle her. "Let's get you to your rooms."

But before Indira can get us to follow her, I notice the crowd parting in the hall. My heart leaps into my throat when I realize they are moving aside for Mylo. His tall and muscular form heads quickly toward me with wide eyes.

My breath catches. "Mylo?"

"Commander! Your uncle is awake."

For a moment, I don't move, hardly able to believe what he's saying. Nadya takes my arm, practically shaking me. "Celeste, go. Sir Holden can escort you."

Before I can respond, she gives me a reassuring nod and turns, following Indira and disappearing into the sea of black-clad mourners being funneled out of the hall.

Clenching my jaw, I turn on my heel and hurry toward my uncle's room with Sir Holden in tow. As Mylo leads the way, my mind is burdened with worry.

He's awake. That should be enough to calm the storm in my chest, but it doesn't. What if it's only for a moment? What if he slips under again before I get there? What if the elixir damaged him somehow? The thought knots my stomach. I should be grateful. I *am* grateful. But the underlying fear is persistent. It curls beneath my ribs, whispering of fevers and failing breath. Of too much lost time.

Mylo bursts through the chamber door, stepping aside quickly so I can enter. The scent of tinctures lingers in the air—earthy and bitter, with something metallic beneath it. I rush into the dim chamber, my skirts brushing the stone floor.

Ezra stands by my uncle's bed, blocking my view as he removes a soaked cloth from my uncle's head. When he turns to me, I notice the tight line of his shoulders has eased, though the shadows under his eyes remain. "Ah, you're here," he says, taking a step back.

Uncle Kormak's weary eyes meet mine, and I let out a sigh of relief. He's propped slightly against the pillows, blankets tucked up to his

 73

waist. His face is gaunt, paler than I've ever seen it, with deep hollows beneath his eyes and the kind of stillness that speaks of pain long endured. Now that he's awake, I can see he's grown thinner, but his chest rises and falls with steady breath, for which I'm unbelievably grateful.

"Celeste, my dear," he rasps, his voice like dry leaves scraping across stone.

For a breath, I can't move. Then I cross the room and drop to sit on the edge of the bed, clutching his hand in both of mine. It's colder than I expect, dry and frail, but the moment he squeezes back, I nearly lose what little composure I have left.

"Thank the gods," I whisper, the words catching in my throat. "You had me so worried."

A faint smile tugs weakly at his lips. "Don't you know I never give up until my duties have been fulfilled."

Behind me, Ezra steps away to give us space, retreating to the shadows by the window. Mylo drops into a chair near the hearth, releasing a long breath as if he'd been holding it for weeks.

I glance back at my uncle, brushing a strand of hair from his forehead. "Please tell me you're all right. Tell me the pain is gone."

He nods faintly, eyes half-lidded. "I feel sort of like I did during my first years training, when I was a cadet and my commander made our squad run uphill until our bodies gave out and crashed upon the rocks."

"You're safe now," I say softly.

His brow furrows, as if only now realizing that for a while he *wasn't* safe.

"I... don't remember arriving," he mutters. "I don't remember much, actually. Only fragments. Ice. Darkness. The pain."

My stomach knots. "Mylo brought you here. Found you at the border. But do you remember who took you?"

He grimaces, and something flickers across his expression, an echo of pain too sharp to conceal. "No. I'm trying to recall, but it's as if there's a missing piece of my mind I can't find. I remember Lord Stregasi coming to the Garrison and telling us about Prince Torbin and the Shadow Tsar. About the pit. I remember setting out—" He shakes his head. "The rest

is a blur."

I squeeze his hand and lower my voice. "You said some things when you got here. Some of it was incoherent, but one of them was... You said my father is alive."

His expression clouds. "What?"

"You don't remember?"

He slowly shakes his head, looking genuinely confused. "I'm sorry. It's hazy. Like a dream. Like a nightmare without details..." He trails off, eyes narrowing in thought. Then he meets my gaze, swallowing hard. "I'm sorry, Celeste. Maybe it was the fever talking."

Mylo pushes off the wall, his voice gruff. "He wasn't all there when I brought him here. Kept talking like someone was watching us. Said he saw wolves' eyes in the trees."

I glance between them, uncertainty tightening in my chest. He can't remember any of it. Is this just a temporary side effect of Ezra's elixir, or is his memory of the abduction gone forever? The thread of hope I'd been following, the hope that I'd get some answers, slips loose, replaced by something warped and unsettling. Confusion. Doubt.

Kormak's eyes open again, clearer this time, and he turns to Mylo. "If it's truly been weeks, I'll need to get back to Delasurvia soon. The people need their general."

Mylo frowns. "You just woke up. We're not even sure how stable your condition is."

"I'm awake. I'll manage." Kormak's jaw hardens. "We should leave in the morning, Mylo."

"Tomorrow?" I protest. "That's too soon. What if—?"

"Whatever Ezra gave me worked," he contests. "My strength is returning by the minute."

"Please. Give yourself a week, just to be sure."

He sighs. "Three days, then. That's my final offer." He glances over my shoulder. "I have Ezra here to help me get back my strength. And my healing magic will speed things along. I'll rest here a while longer, but we can't stay."

I glance at Mylo, whose jaw tightens further. His loyalty pulls in

 75

opposite directions. But after a beat, he nods.

"I'll gather provisions," Mylo says, then he turns to me, his gaze unreadable. "And speak to the stablehands."

When he leaves, silence settles again, thick and too heavy.

My uncle's hand twitches in mine. "Don't look at me like that," he mutters. "I'm still here. I'm a survivor."

I manage a small smile, but my thoughts are spiraling. He may be here... but part of him is still lost. "I'm glad you're awake, Uncle. Now please rest."

Ezra doesn't say a word as I head into the corridor outside my uncle's chamber. He follows, as if sensing my apprehension. He stares into nothing, arms folded, lips pressed into a line too tight to be casual.

I step closer. "Did you know he wouldn't remember?"

He exhales slowly and glances at me. "I wasn't sure, but I suspected."

We walk in silence down the hall toward the eastern gallery, the quiet echo of our boots on stone filling the space. I stop by one of the narrow windows, the glass fogged at the corners, the world outside drenched from the storm. Ezra stops beside me.

"So the potion saved his life," I say, though my voice is hollow. "But it stole his memory."

"Perhaps the elixir tried to heal his suffering by erasing it. Or his mind tucked the memory away. Sometimes the brain shields itself from trauma. But between that and the elixir, the memories could be gone. Or just buried so deep, they might never come back."

A beat passes.

"I just—" I swallow, my voice catching. "I'm pretty sure the tsar was sending a message when he let my uncle go. But if he can't remember anything, we'll never know what the message was."

"It's possible your uncle *was* the message. Not what he said. Not what he remembers. But what his condition implied." He straightens. "It seems the tsar knows you. Knows your heart. He didn't need to send words."

Unless he really is my father and he meant for my uncle to deliver the truth. For what, I can't be sure. To convince me to join him? To scare

me?

A chill races down my spine that has nothing to do with the rain outside. I get the message now. The tsar is willing to hurt the people I love if I don't comply.

CHAPTER ELEVEN

The great dining hall is already alive with quiet murmurs and the soft clink of silverware when Nadya and I enter. The vaulted ceilings stretch high above, and golden sunlight spills through the arched windows, casting long, slanted beams across the grand oak table where the king and queen sit at its head. Chandeliers glisten overhead, catching the light in tiny prisms.

Despite the lavish spread of eggs, sausages, fresh-baked breads, and an assortment of fruit laid across the table, the air is stiff with formality. Servants move soundlessly, refilling goblets and setting out steaming plates, their heads bowed.

Though the feast smells tantalizing, eating is not my priority this morning. I need to speak with the king, and I already know he's not going to like what I have to say.

Dante sits at the table, across from his father. But because we're not supposed to interact with one another, he gives me nothing more than a subtle nod, which I return. They are the same subtle nods we've exchanged for every morning and evening meal, and the only reason I can tolerate it is because of our secret, nightly plans to gaze at each other from our balconies. Plans that rarely work out.

Still, I take in his appearance, as if committing it to memory for my dreams. His dark hair is not as neatly combed as it was during the funeral, the soft waves askew, as if he'd recently raked his fingers through them. Instead of the crisp finery of court, he wears a simple black tunic, the laces on the front undone enough that the top of his chest is on display. I try not to stare as I take my seat.

King Silas does not bother masking his discontent as he dabs his mouth with a linen napkin, then tosses it onto his plate. "How nice of you to join us, Celeste."

Even though she wasn't addressed, Nadya speaks up from beside me, her voice careful but firm. "Of course. It would be a shame if Her Majesty's fine breakfast went to waste."

The queen shifts slightly at the mention, her gloved hands straightening the silverware beside her plate as if she were trying to line up everything perfectly. Though her features are as carefully composed as ever, I don't miss the tightness in her brow or the way her gaze lingers on her untouched plate.

"I'm glad I was able to catch you before you left the meal, Your Majesty," I say to the king, keeping my voice strong but cordial. "My uncle has finally recovered from his illness."

"Praise the gods," Queen Eleanor says quietly.

"Yes, praise the gods," I say, nodding. "He is urgent to return to Delasurvia, to return to his duties. He would like to go back the day after tomorrow. And I would like to ask your permission to accompany him back home to ensure his safe return."

The king's gaze sharpens on me. "You ask much, Princess." His voice is calm, but the undertone cuts like glass. "Surely, your uncle needs time to get back on his feet."

"His people need to see that he is alive. That he's recovering. It will settle them. Strengthen them. You told the courts that Delasurvia now falls under your protection. So let me do what I must to ensure the people's confidence in that unity remains intact."

Silas's mouth tightens. "You've only just returned from one unsanctioned ride. Am I to believe that you won't go chasing another

 79

fight? You have a history of succumbing to your whims."

"I believed coming to you first would show that my request is in good faith." I hold my chin up. "I thought you'd appreciate the fact that I'm asking permission rather than leaving of my own accord. And since you've forbidden me from joining my squad for any more missions, it's my duty to assign the interim ranks of my squad, hand the reins over to my lieutenant and promote my first sergeant."

"I'm certain your uncle could deliver the message for you."

"He's been absent for too long to be abreast of the current situation. And it's protocol for the commanding officer to pass the baton personally."

He sighs. "Could you not simply send a nightfeather?"

"Begging your pardon, Your Majesty, but even you wouldn't deliver classified regiment instructions by messenger birds. There's too much risk that the confidential information could be intercepted." I force myself not to smirk, but I know he can't argue with my point. "There's protocol to uphold. The regiment should witness me handing over the reins of commander to my lieutenant, and because my first sergeant has gone above and beyond in her duties, she deserves to be appointed as the new lieutenant in person."

His brow furrows. "Another woman in a lead role? Do you not have enough proper men to carry out your cause?"

I want to spit back in his face, but I simply hold my jaw rigid. "I vow to be swift with this undertaking and return before you leave for the presentation tour. That way, you can be assured that I'll be under lock and key while you are away."

I see the flicker in his expression. Annoyance, perhaps. Or something colder. The king studies me a moment longer before reclining slightly in his chair, drumming his fingers against the tabletop. "Actually, I've had a change of mind. Things are moving more quickly than I originally planned. We've received prompt responses from most of the other kingdoms, and the presentation tour can begin in two weeks' time."

I blink, looking between him and Dante. Dante's expression tells

 80

me this is news to him. Even the queen looks up, obviously unaware of this change.

"So soon?" I ask.

The king nods, as if the matter is already decided. "I will not give the nobles and common folk time to speculate or turn their loyalties elsewhere. And since you have a tendency to disobey my rules, I do not trust you to sit put if I leave you alone in my castle. You, Princess, will be coming with us."

My stomach knots. I wasn't expecting to be hauled along on the tour. Not only does the fact that the king being able to watch my every move for the next couple of months unsettle me, but this means I will need to extend my act of playing the grieving betrothed, feigning sorrow as I'm veiled in black like a spectacle for neighboring kingdoms.

I glance toward Dante, and I actually catch a slight upward tick of the corner of his mouth. That's when I realize this is good news for him.

Because it means we won't have to spend months apart.

Sure, we can't be seen together in public, and we have to hide our feelings for each other when other eyes are around. But I don't have to sit here, locked up, wondering what he's doing, how he's handling being on display while his fate is being decided, and maybe we'll even be able to find a moment or two to actually exchange more than a longing look.

The king jabs his fork into a slice of sausage and shoves it in his mouth, eyes locked on me. "So, to answer your request, Princess, yes. You have my permission to escort your uncle and take care of your duties. But you must make haste and be ready to pack for the tour when you return. And once you hand over your reins, I don't want to hear another word about your fucking regiment."

CHAPTER TWELVE

I try not to let the king's announcement frazzle me as Nadya and I make our way to Ezra's lesson room. The only thing that eased the blunt was the king's acquiesce that Nadya was permitted to accompany me. I have a feeling he doesn't trust her to not turn his castle into a party hall in his absence.

Because Ezra was helping my uncle recover, lessons were put on hold. Now that Uncle Kormak is in the clear, I find myself looking forward to spending some time learning something. Mostly, I'm still wondering about the storm that suddenly hit during Torbin's funeral and if I had anything to do with it. If anyone has a semblance of a theory that could explain what happened, it's Ezra.

Nadya and I step into the scent of parchment, ink, and dried herbs. Shelves line the stone walls, crammed with tomes bound in cracked leather, their spines worn from decades, perhaps centuries, of handling. Bundles of herbs hang from the rafters, suspended to dry, while glass bottles of various tinctures glimmer in the dim light from the room's narrow windows. A sturdy desk sits at back of the room, papers strewn across its surface in ordered chaos, and behind it stands Ezra.

The magister watches us enter, his brows raised, like he's glad to see us. The dark circles have disappeared from under his eyes, and his usual tunic looks freshly cleaned. It lightens the weight from my chest that he seems to have gotten some rest after the exhausting efforts he went through to bring my uncle back from the brink.

"Celeste, Nadya," he says, his arms stretched out at his sides. "Lovely to see you in my lesson room."

I understand the truth behind his words. He's glad we're meeting here instead of in my uncle's chamber, frustratingly throwing ideas at the wall to see what sticks.

Ezra studies me for a beat longer before gesturing toward the chairs arranged before his desk. Nadya and I settle into them as he lowers himself into his own seat, hands folding over the parchment before him. "Is there a particular subject you'd like to begin with today?"

Nadya lifts her hand before I can even open my mouth. "Actually, yes. If it's okay with Celeste. I read something in the archives. About a trio of wandering women from Bastos who traveled across Terre Ferique before the poisonous plants began spreading. Supposedly powerful, possibly witches, possibly tragic figures who died before their work was done." She leans forward, resting her hands on her knees. "You wouldn't happen to know anything about them, would you?"

Ezra arches a brow. "Witches from Bastos? Now there's a tale I haven't heard in some time." He sits back in his chair, rubbing his jaw with a hand that's ink-stained along the knuckles.

"You were around back then, weren't you?" she teases.

Ezra chuckles. "Hardly. I may feel ancient when I wake up some mornings, but I'm not quite that far gone."

Nadya grins, undeterred. "But you've heard about them? Read some things?"

"That much is true." He grows thoughtful, his fingers drumming lightly on the desk. "There have always been stories. The most credible accounts mention three women cloaked in robes who moved from Bastos through the central lands. They were said to have unnatural magic, power that wasn't innate, like the fae or sirens."

I exchange a glance with Nadya, her curiosity shining in her expression like a lit match.

Ezra continues, his tone drifting more scholarly now. "Some magisters believe they were trying to warn the kingdoms. Others say they were trying to stop something. And still others think they triggered the plague themselves—made a deal with the old gods and failed to control the consequences."

"Do any of the records say who they were?" I ask. "Names, lineage… anything?"

"Not directly," he replies. "But there are more than a few accounts of their journey, each with similar details. Those descriptions repeat, even when the language changes. I've always found that consistency the most intriguing part."

"So it's real," Nadya says softly. "Or real enough that people remembered."

Ezra's gaze sharpens. "Enough that people feared them. Bastos isn't known for its love of rules, but even they tried to bury the old stories. Magic like that was seen as chaos. Uncontrollable. And anything that couldn't be chained was considered dangerous."

I fold my arms, something twisting uneasily in my chest. "Isn't that how they see all magic they don't understand?"

"Precisely." Ezra nods. "But what's buried tends to grow roots, not vanish. That's why the land feels as if it's holding its breath these days. Too many unanswered questions. Too many old powers stirring."

A chill pricks across my skin.

Nadya runs her palms over the silk of her dress, smoothing it out. "What happened to them? The women."

Ezra's voice is quiet now. "They were ambushed on the coast. No official account names the killer. But some texts claim they saw what was coming—and went willingly into the sea."

I frown. "Why would they do that?"

"Perhaps they believed their part was done and someone else would rise after them." He gives us both a long look. "Someone stronger."

The silence that follows is thick, and I can feel Nadya holding her

breath beside me.

Then Ezra stands, stretching the tension from his back. "Come. I think we've talked enough about the past. Let's see what your magic has to say today."

"My magic?" I fidget, squeezing my fingers, as if subconsciously trying to keep the magic at bay.

"Yes, Celeste. Tell me. Are there any new developments?"

"Your powder is still working." I decide it's easier to start with truths he already knows. "No night wanderings. So that's good news."

He waits a beat. "Is this your way of telling me there's bad news?"

"Not *bad* news, really."

"But something unexpected, perhaps?" Ezra tilts his head.

I glance at Nadya. She doesn't know that I felt my body buzzing during the storm. She doesn't know about the pain that shot through my head. I didn't tell her my suspicions, mostly because I'm frightened to admit them to myself.

"The day of Torbin's funeral," I begin, already feeling my mouth go dry, "there was a storm that suddenly blew in."

"Yes, I remember." Ezra waits for more, but his expression changes when I remain quiet. "No. That can't be."

"What?" Nadya scoots to the edge of her chair. "What can't be?"

Ezra straightens his shoulders, studying me for a moment longer before facing Nadya. "Celeste suspects she may have influenced the storm."

Nadya whips her head in my direction. "That was you?"

"I don't know." For some reason, I feel ashamed. "Maybe."

Her jaw drops. "Impressive!"

Ezra paces, his hands clasped behind his back. "Tell me everything. What you were feeling, emotionally and physically. Even the small details might help us understand."

I take a minute to compose myself before I recount the details for him. How I was filled with anger because everyone was being told Torbin was dead, that he was some honorable man who should be revered. Frustrated because I felt Torbin was still out there, that the tsar was

planning something big, but the king refused to listen. I told Ezra about the buzzing in my blood, within my bones, the zing of power coursing through me, and how the sky darkened.

But I don't mention the bolt of pain.

"Interesting." Ezra watches me for a long moment, then sighs. "I've been scanning every book I have, searching for anything that might explain how the fae who hid their powers during the Age of Blood regained them. There are plenty of histories that claim it was a deal with the gods, that their magic was returned as some divine gift." He scoffs slightly, shaking his head. "But I believe there's more to the truth than that. If the fae could hide their magic, there must have been a way to retrieve it—something deliberate, something tangible."

I frown. "And you think I could find that answer?"

"I think you might *be* the answer." His gaze is sharp, unwavering. "Which means we need to keep searching for it within you. This... magic you wielded at the funeral, perhaps it was an extension of the energy force you seem to have developed."

Energy force. It sounds so powerful, but I feel so far from being able to control it.

"If not, it's an entirely different path, which adds another mystery to our puzzle."

"Just what we needed," I joke.

He gives me a smile, and I can't help but notice it's lined with pity.

"Let's first try to concentrate on the parts of the puzzle we might be able to gain insight on." His eyes go toward the windows. "I suggest we try it now."

I swallow, shifting my hands in my lap. "Here?"

Ezra's lips twitch. "I was thinking about the southern courtyard. It's private, walled in. No one will see." He tilts his head. "Unless you're afraid?"

I narrow my eyes at him, standing from my chair. "Lead the way, Magister."

The wide courtyard is littered with the scattered petals and leaves of magnolia trees. The copse of trees shades the area, their broad, waxy

leaves rustling slightly from the morning's breeze. Sunlight filters through the branches, dappling the stone pathway and the patches of grass beyond. A peaceful scene—if not for the heavy weight pressing on my chest.

Ezra, hands clasped behind his back, surveys the courtyard as if inspecting an army outpost. "Nadya, step to the center," he instructs, tilting his head toward the open space.

She lifts a brow but obeys, strolling to the middle with an air of exaggerated elegance. "Am I to be sacrificed?" she muses, shooting me a playful grin.

Ezra ignores her and turns to me instead. "I want you to summon the wind—not a storm, not a gust, just a whisper. Gather the petals around Nadya."

"Am I controlling weather? Or is it simply energy force focused on the petals?"

"Do you have weather-wielding fae in your lineage?"

I bite the inside of my cheek. The mother had telepathy magic, as does my uncle. My grandmother could create illusions, and my great-grandfather had fire-wielding magic, according to what my mother told me when I was young. "I don't think so."

"Let's play it by ear and see how it feels to you."

I inhale slowly, stretching out my fingers, feeling the energy like a hum beneath my skin. It rises with my breath, coiling inside me, and as I exhale, I release it—a soft pulse outward.

A few petals shift. Then more. Like dancers stirring from a long slumber, they rise from the ground and swirl around Nadya's boots, climbing higher until they spin at her waist.

Nadya watches them in delighted awe. "Not bad," she teases, spinning once, sending them twirling outward.

Ezra, seemingly unimpressed, crosses his arms, his eyes narrowed. "Now, have them follow her."

Nadya scoffs. "I prefer to be chased by roguish men and curvy women."

"You don't need my magic for that, my friend," I say.

 87

I breathe out again, this time with more focus, pushing the magic toward her. The petals obey, drifting in a slow, weightless dance as she takes a few steps. I adjust, keeping them in her wake. With the lift of a finger in the air, I push one up to tickle her cheek.

She gasps, then laughs outright. "You little menace."

"Run," Ezra suggests, his tone entirely too amused.

Nadya doesn't need another invitation. She takes off, laughter ringing through the courtyard, and I chase her—not with my feet, but with my power, urging the petals after her like a playful storm. They catch in her hair, skim her shoulders, flit ahead of her, as if guiding her steps.

She ducks, swerves, and twirls, but they stay with her, and I realize something. I'm not straining. I'm controlling it.

The thought makes me bold. I push a little more, sending the petals rushing at her all at once, blocking her view, and she yelps, losing her footing when she trips over an exposed root. She tumbles onto the grass in an unceremonious heap, laughing breathlessly as I send the last of the petals cascading over her like a silken blanket.

I run toward her, my laughter lifting my spirits.

Until a sharp pain slices through my head like a burning blade. I almost wince but quickly school my features, keeping a smile plastered on my face.

Nadya grins up at me, twigs tangled in her curls, her stomach bouncing up and down as she giggles. "That was fun."

"Don't ever say I never brought you flowers," I tease.

"I'd say that was a success," Ezra says as he comes closer, offering Nadya a hand and pulling her to her feet.

I would agree, if only it didn't feel like it cost me.

 88

CHAPTER THIRTEEN

$\mathcal{S}$ ir Holden walks a step behind me as we head for the stables, the path before us golden from the early morning sun. Despite the king's suggestion that we take a carriage to Delasurvia, my uncle and I both declined. The journey will be much quicker on horseback. While Mylo and Uncle Kormak gather last-minute provisions, Sir Holden and I have the task of fetching the horses.

When the stables come into view, I spot a familiar figure moving about near the doors, and a small smile ticks up the corners of my mouth. Dante's hair is windswept, his cheeks slightly flush, and the sight of his broad shoulders stirs a fluttery feeling in my stomach. He's accompanied by an unfamiliar guard, and my smile is replaced with a frown. I should have guessed that the king doesn't trust his own son. Dante appears to have just returned from a ride, and the new guard tagging along watches every move he makes.

Though I'd very much like to talk to Dante before I leave—even just to say a chaste goodbye—I'm not certain I'll be able to get near him without butting heads with this lurker.

I glance over my shoulder at Sir Holden. "Do you recognize that

 89

guard?"

Sir Holden nods once. "The king appointed him to trail Lord Stregasi as his Royal Ward. Name's Sir Donovan Greystone."

A Royal Ward. I suppose that makes sense. Silas no doubt wants to make sure his only remaining son is protected, especially during the upcoming tour.

When we're a couple of yards away, Dante spots me and does a double take. Our eyes lock, and in that moment, I can tell he wants to swallow up the distance between us. Instead, he takes in a long breath before he averts his gaze, pretending to be highly interested in removing his riding gloves.

Sir Donovan regards us, his back straightening. Broad-shouldered and built like a fortress, his strawberry-blond hair is clipped short, and his brown eyes assess me with a cold, impassive stare. He doesn't bow, doesn't offer a greeting. Just stands there, arms rigid at his sides like a sentry carved from stone.

I steel myself for his disapproval of my appearance at the stables when Dante happens to be here, but how else am I to retrieve my horse?

"Donovan," Sir Holden says, breaking the silent tension. "Allow me to introduce you to Her Royal Highness, Celeste Westergaard, heir to the Delasurvian throne."

I almost smirk. It doesn't escape me that Sir Holden has used my full title on purpose to get a rise out of Dante's guard.

Probably realizing a proper response is expected of him, Sir Donovan blanches before greeting me with a bow. "Oh, yes. Of course. Pleased to meet you, Your Highness."

I nod my greeting. "Sir Donovan."

His focus returns to Sir Holden. "I was told the princess and Lord Stregasi are to avoid being seen together."

"We need to grab our horses," Sir Holden explains, "and then we'll be on our way."

"It will just take a minute," I put in before he has a chance to argue that a princess could send someone else to the stables for her. "Paul was instructed to prepare them for us ahead of time."

Sir Donovan's eyes go between me and Sir Holden before he nods. "Have you been told about the wood paths?" Sir Holden asks him, walking closer to the guard and clapping him on the back. "Very important to keep your eyes on." He uses the position to turn Sir Donovan to face the woods—and away from me—and then points toward the trees.

I take this as Sir Holden's way of giving me a moment with Dante. The man is no fool, and it occurs to me now that under all that muscle and armor, he also has a heart.

I slip into the stables, and Dante takes my cue, following me into the dim hall that leads to the horse stalls. The stable smells of fresh hay, oiled leather, and shit, and the lanterns lining the wooden beams cast flickering shadows.

In the next moment, there's a firm but gentle hand on my elbow. The touch sends a thrilling shiver up my spine.

"How long will you be gone?" he asks.

There's no trying to talk me out of it. No telling me it's too dangerous to leave the castle. He doesn't even insist on coming with me. And though I wouldn't mind being able to spend time with him and wouldn't argue if he did want to come along, it lifts a weight off my chest knowing he respects my decision. That he knows my strength and skill and doesn't question if I'm capable of heading off without him.

It's not a squad mission; it's a mere escort and return. Though one never knows what could be waiting out there, ready to strike.

"Before the week is up," I respond, checking over his shoulder to make sure we're still alone.

"Well, I'm sure you'll keep Sir Holden safe," he teases.

"If he doesn't annoy me," I tease back. "So that's your new watchdog."

He lets out a sigh. "The king couldn't be dissuaded, but it's nothing I can't handle."

His hand drifts down to mine, and our fingers brush against each other, slow and soft, a whisper of a caress igniting something deep in my chest. For a moment, I forget where we are, forget that we're supposed

 91

to be careful. There's only the sound of our breathing, the distant chatter of stableboys, and the way his gaze locks on to mine with something longing to be said.

The sound of boots crunching on gravel causes us to take a step back from each other. I turn toward Thora's stall, where Paul emerges, leading my horse toward me. Another stablehand brings Mylo's horse along with two others, and Sir Holden appears beside me to take their reins.

"Thank you, Paul," I say while admiring by raven-black mare.

Paul gives me a nod. "Your Highness. May the gods watch over your journey."

When we exit the stables, Sir Donovan stands beside Dante. The Royal Ward steps aside to give us room, but not before allowing his gaze to linger on me, assessing my every move. It makes my skin itch, but I don't let it show.

"I wish you a safe journey," Dante says, "and a safe return."

I hate that our conversation has to be this short. I would love to ask him what's going on behind the closed doors of the council chambers, to ask him how he's handling this impossible situation he's been forced into. I want to tell him about my powers, even about the pain it causes me. But there's no fucking time.

I force the emotion out of my voice and incline my head. "Thank you, Lord Stregasi."

Though I know I should avert my gaze as I pass him, I can't break the hold he has on me. He shifts, as if he's about to turn to head in the opposite direction, and it takes every ounce of control I have not to run up to him and throw my arms around him, to capture his face in my hands and press my lips to his. But I don't. He gives me one more long look—a look laced with a plea to be careful—before he turns and strides away.

As Sir Holden and I head toward the castle gates to meet with Mylo and my uncle, I brush a hand along Thora's neck. Her coat is warm, the rise and fall of her breath steady beneath my palm. The morning air carries the scent of damp hay and old wood, and a breeze whispers a cool greeting against my cheeks.

As the soft *thud* of hooves against packed earth echo behind us, I peer up at the sky, feeling positive that we'll have good weather for our journey. The sunlight has brightened to a pale gold, gleaming against the dewy grass.

By the time we reach the gates, Mylo and my uncle are already waiting with all our gear. Uncle Kormak wears a thick riding cloak, the hood pushed back to reveal the shadowed hollows of his cheeks. His uniform was ruined, bloody and torn, and had to be disposed of, so he now wears borrowed clothes from the Hederan court. His skin is less pallid now, but there's a rawness behind his eyes that speaks of how recently he was near death. Still, he takes the horse's reins from Sir Holden with his usual authority, chin high, his gaze sharp as it flicks toward me.

"Are you ready?" he asks.

I glance up at him, then tilt my head. "Shouldn't I be asking you that? I'm not convinced your lungs won't collapse halfway to the border."

Mylo, already on his horse, smirks. "I told him that. As the interim commander," Mylo says, pausing to emphasize the title, "I take my job to look after all regiment soldiers seriously. But he just grumbled something about being harder to kill than a weed in spring."

Uncle Kormak's brows rise in a gesture that lands somewhere between amusement and warning. "That weed still outranks you."

Sir Holden checks the cinch on his saddle with quiet focus, but when I glance at him, I swear I see the corner of his mouth twitch. He meets my gaze briefly, and I catch the faintest gleam in his eye before he looks away. The man's carved from stone, but even the granite of his demeanor can crack under a well-aimed joke.

I swing up onto Thora's back with practiced ease, adjusting the fall of my cloak so the wind doesn't rip at the hem. Mylo takes the lead, urging his horse forward. The guards at the gate give Sir Holden a nod, clearing the way without ceremony, having been informed of our departure ahead of time.

The sound of hooves on stone fills the air as we ride through, a steady rhythm that thrums through my bones. The castle looms behind

us, ivy-strung and towering, its high ramparts casting long shadows over the road. I don't look back, but a part of me remains behind.

A day and a half later, the gates of the Garrison rise into view just as the sun tips behind the hills, casting long, bronze shadows across the earth. Familiar banners ripple in the breeze—a brilliant, gold phoenix, its wings spread wide against a bronze backdrop.

Home.

The stone walls, though weatherworn, still stand proud. The scent of fresh earth, saddle oil, and pine wraps around me as we approach the outpost. Beyond the gates, I catch the bustle of soldiers lining the courtyard, armor glinting in the fading light, weapons strapped but peace lingering in their stance.

The sound of hooves on gravel alerts the guards. A shout hits the air, and the portcullis begins to rise.

"You sent word?" Uncle Kormak asks.

"Yes. They've been expecting us," I respond.

He nods stiffly beside me, his cloak pulled tight around his shoulders. The ride has taken its toll, but he's masked it well. That same steady look of command hasn't left his face since we crossed into Delasurvian territory. His soldiers will see a general, not a ghost dragged back from the brink.

As we ride into the courtyard, the shift in energy is instant.

There's a heartbeat of stunned silence, and then the cheers rise.

"General Kormak!"

"Commander!"

The shouts echo through the Garrison like a bell. Helmets are lifted, fists slapped against chests in salute. The noise surges like a tide, and I glance at my uncle just in time to see the flicker of emotion cross his face—something between pride and disbelief.

Aila pushes through the crowd first, her dark, chin-length hair swaying behind her. Isaac isn't far behind, nearly tripping over a coil of rope someone abandoned in their excitement. Giorgi appears at the edge of the group, nodding, and Lorne trails after them all, quieter but smiling.

"General, you old beast," Isaac calls, his grin stretching wide. "We knew you'd pull through."

Mylo dismounts first, boots thudding against the dirt. "Of course he did. He's got the strength of a lion."

"Looks like he's got the hair of one too, now," Giorgi says, chuckling. "Let me know if I should have Matilda fetch her shears."

"All in good time." Kormak swings down from his horse with a grunt, his landing just a pinch less solid than it used to be. But the soldiers don't see it. They're too busy cheering, clapping each other on the backs, some even stepping forward for a handshake or a bowed head of welcome. He accepts it all without fanfare, giving nods and brief murmurs in return, but I can tell it's wearing on him already.

I maneuver to the ground but stay near Thora a moment longer, watching the scene unfold, watching the light in my people's eyes. They needed this. Needed to know he was still standing. That Delasurvia hasn't lost everything.

Soldiers and servants alike approach me to welcome me back home, and although I extend my thanks to them, my gaze keeps darting back to my uncle. A weight has lifted from my shoulders seeing him here, in his element.

As if feeling my relief, Uncle Kormak turns my way with the hint of a smile. *"Thank you."*

His voice in my mind causes grateful tears to well in my eyes. I give him a nod and turn to hand Thora's reins to one of the stablehands who appears at my side.

Sir Holden dismounts beside me and says nothing, but as always, I feel the weight of his gaze as he does a quick sweep of the yard, ever vigilant.

Aila reaches me next, clapping me on the back. "Commander," she

says with mock sternness. "Sticking around?"

"For a while, at least," I reply.

"It's good to see you back home."

"Yeah, it's good to be back." The words come with a strange ache. She must see it. "What's going on?"

I gesture toward the keep. "Walk with me?"

She nods. "Lead the way."

As we cross the yard, I catch Lorne speaking with my uncle, and Giorgi muttering something to Mylo that makes them both laugh. The sky above is streaked with the softest pinks and dusky violets, the first star flickering just above the tower spires. The breeze carries the air from the sea; it smells like seaweed and forthcoming rain. I hadn't realized how much I missed the scent.

Aila and I step into the Garrison, the stone corridors of the army barracks cool and familiar. Boots echo against the flagstones as we make our way to the war room, the iron handle strong and cold beneath my palm as I open the door.

Inside, the long table remains exactly how I remember it: maps stacked neatly, the large one of Terre Ferique spread across the center like a battlefield waiting to be fought.

I close the door behind us and turn to face her. "I wanted to speak to you alone."

Aila straightens a little. "You've got that look."

"What look?"

"The one that says you're about to throw something heavy in my lap and expect me not to blink."

I exhale, almost smiling. "Is there any other way?"

She leans on the table with both hands, bracing. "All right. Hit me."

I take a deep breath. I find it hard to say the words because I know, once it's official, I will feel like a part of me is missing. So I decide to broach another subject first. "Any word from the scouts sent up to Dulcamar?"

"They've returned with no intel," she tells me. "The fortress is almost impossible to approach. Giorgi says there may be a way in

 96

through the underground river that comes in from the Batu Basah Ocean, but that tunnel is ridden with deadly nightshade, so we're unsure it's our best course."

"Giorgi knows best about these things."

"We still have one troop out," she adds. "I can send word as soon as they return."

I nod, steeling myself for what I need to tell her.

"And regarding the carnoraxis attacks," she adds, "they've already crossed the borders. One attack has gone as far as the border between Hedera and Podrosa."

"Thanks, but you can pass on all this information directly to Mylo."

Her brows dip down. "Commander?"

I tap the table, releasing a long exhale before I continue. "I'm not stepping down. But King Silas is insisting I take a... hiatus. He wants me focused on court appearances. The legitimization tour."

Aila frowns. "He's pulling you out of field work?"

"He already has," I say, quieter. "I'm not permitted to meet up with the squad anymore. Not unless it's a royal-approved engagement. He made an exception for my uncle's return, and to do this handover in person."

Her expression darkens. "You're the commander. You're our best."

"And you'll still have me. Just not right now. You have to understand, I'm doing this for the good of Delasurvia." I walk to the map, fingers brushing the edge of the parchment. "I didn't want to leave without ensuring the regiment is still in good hands. That the work continues. The camps are still operating, even if quietly. The villages still need protection. I'm naming Mylo interim commander. I've already spoken with him, so he knows what to expect. But he needs someone by his side to pick up the pieces he might miss. A good second."

Aila blinks. "Me?"

"Don't act so surprised," I say with a laugh. "You'll make an excellent lieutenant. You know the squads, the terrain, the rhythm of the field. Hell, you're more updated on the current status of things than I am at the moment. You're ready. You've *been* ready."

For a long moment, she doesn't speak. Then she softly says, "You trust me with this?"

"With everything."

She nods once, the corners of her eyes shining just slightly in the torchlight. "Then I won't let you down."

"I know." I give her a wink. "That's why I chose you."

The ever-present tension in my chest eases a bit.

Because even if I can't be here... I know my people are still being protected.

By two of our own. Two of my very best.

"Isaac and Giorgi are going to be pissed you chose me above them," she jokes.

"No, they won't. They know how good you are."

As Aila and I step out of the war room together, the sounds of soldiers engaged in discussions fill my ears. Exhaustion is pulling me down, but if I can get this announcement out in the open, it will one less thing I need to deal with before I'm ready to pass out in my old room.

Aila moves ahead of me without hesitation, climbing up on a table and placing her thumb and finger in her mouth to create a loud whistle. As the din of the crowd fades, she holds a hand out to me. I take it and jump onto the table beside her.

"Listen up," I call out, my voice ringing across the courtyard with a clarity that silences every clang of metal and murmur of conversation. "It's truly great to be back in your presence and to see that you're all holding up the integrity of Delasurvia. I'm sure you're all curious as to how things will be moving forward, given the circumstances." There's no need for me to get into the theories of Torbin's survival; Aila's been keeping the regiment informed in my stead. "In order to keep Delasurvia safe, especially under King Silas's watchful eye, I must take a temporary hiatus of my duties as commander."

Boots shuffle, and heads turn as murmurs fill the room.

"I would never abandon you without knowing you're in proper, skilled hands, so I am grateful to be able to inform you that Mylo Yaroslav has been appointed as your interim commander during my

absence, and Aila Chen will serve as the new lieutenant. I know you will be well led under their care."

Mylo jumps up on the table, making the entire thing shake. "That means if I give an order, you follow it. If I say jump, you ask how high."

"And if anyone has an issue with this arrangement," Aila adds, "then I suggest you take it up with the sharp end of my dagger. I'm sure it'll be happy to hear your complaints."

Laughter breaks through the air like a snapped arrow string. Isaac raises his mug in a mock toast while Giorgi gives a dramatic, sweeping bow. Even Lorne cracks a crooked grin, clapping his hands in congratulations.

I fight the knot forming in my throat. It feels like the last time I'll stand on this side of the command, but I remind myself it isn't permanent.

Aila turns to me. "Come on, get washed up. The kitchens have been working on a welcome meal. It's not comparable to the royal feasts you must be used to, but the ale's strong and the bread's soft, and I figure that's enough to count as a celebration."

I nod, letting out a small laugh. "Sounds perfect."

I make my way to the small room I called home when I lived here. It's unchanged—plain walls, a narrow bed, a low chest for storing gear. But when I glance out the window, I catch sight of the distant castle beyond the stretch of fields. Its towers are just visible in the fading light, draped in violet dusk like a wound hidden under fine silk.

Taking in the shadowed windows, I remember Bennett, and my chest tightens. He never lived to see what became of me. Never learned of my betrothal. Never met Dante. Was gone long before Torbin fell.

I close the curtains gently and sniff back the threat of tears.

After washing and changing into dark trousers and a cream blouse, I re-braid my hair and roll up my sleeves. My dagger rests at my hip, familiar and steady. It's the first time in weeks I've felt like myself. No silk gown, no veil stitched in mourning lace. No heavy-handed king telling me what I can and cannot do.

The regiment's dining hall is already buzzing by the time I enter. The

sprawl of tables is simple—rough-hewn benches, mismatched cutlery—but the scent of stew and baked bread fills the air. Roasted root vegetables, salted meats, buttered rolls. More than I've ever seen on the Garrison tables. Not as decadent as Hedera's feasts, but a far cry from what we had when Delasurvia was starving.

I slide onto the bench beside Aila, across from Giorgi and Isaac. Mylo and Lorne sit farther down with Uncle Kormak, who only nibbles at a roll and drinks sparingly from a tin cup. His eyes seem far off, as if still watching a battle play out behind his eyelids. He's here, but only just.

Isaac lifts his mug, his eyes on me. "It's great to have you back, Commander."

I give him a nod. "How about just 'Celeste'?"

"Nah. You'll always be 'Commander' to me." He chuckles before tossing back his mug, his throat bobbing as he finishes the entire contents in one go. When he's done, he slams the mug on the table and lets out a long, loud belch.

"Nice one," Aila says, deadpanning. "Real proud."

"Shut up," Isaac says. "You're the one who can belch the entire Delasurvian motto."

Giorgi laughs so hard, they almost choke on their ale.

Beside me, Sir Holden approaches, his hair still damp from washing up. He takes the spot to my left and lets out a groan.

"Everything all right, Sir Holden?" I ask, pouring him some ale.

"It's been a long day, Your Highness." He takes the ale and gives me a nod.

"You think *your* days are long," Isaac begins. "Try being attached at the hip to this guy for most of it." He juts a thumb at Lorne.

Hearing him, Lorne shakes his head, but there's a hint of a smile playing on his lips. "Why are you so mean to me?"

"Have you met you?" Isaac bursts into laughter before Lorne can respond, but then he shoves Lorne's shoulder playfully.

Mylo leans closer to Lorne. "Just say the word and I'll make sure his eyes are so black, they match his boots."

I shake my head, leaning my elbows on the table and facing Lorne.

"I take it you're finding your place all right with my squad?"

He shrugs, amber eyes glinting in the firelight. "Yeah. Isaac only pulls a prank on me every *other* day, so things are improving."

"Don't pretend you don't love it," Isaac says. "You know you're not really part of the squad if you're not putting up with our shit."

"I'm honored, then," Lorne replies, lifting his drink.

Before anyone tosses out another jab, a shadow appears at my side. A young courier, dust still on his boots, holds out a sealed parchment.

"Message for Commander Westergaard," he says. "Came in not long ago."

"By nightfeather?" I ask, taking it from him. It's heavier than a usual scroll—weighted. "It must have been strong to carry something like this."

"No, Commander," he says, brow furrowed. "Not by nightfeather. Came by griffon vulture."

The words still the entire table. Even Mylo looks up. Aila mutters something under her breath, and Giorgi stops chewing.

Griffon vultures are bigger, faster, stronger—and native to Dulcamar. The winged beast is the main symbol on their banners.

I meet my uncle's eyes across the table. His expression sharpens as I untie the seal.

Inside is a black, leather cord. At its center hangs a narrow strip of metal—long, forked at one end, the surface etched with subtle, curling lines. It looks simple at first, but something about the weight of it in my hand feels... off. As if it hums with purpose I don't understand.

Beneath the cord is a small scrap of parchment. *For the future prince.*

I stare at the message, then the pendant, then back again.

"Do you recognize this?" I ask, holding it up for my uncle to see.

His face pales.

"Come, Celeste," he says, pushing up from the bench with deliberate care. "We should talk. Alone."

With that, the warmth of home is gone.

Uncle Kormak's office is dim, dustier than I remember. A low fire flickers in the hearth, recently stoked, and the scent of old parchment

and beeswax polish permeates every corner. The thick, stone walls muffle the clamor of the Garrison beyond, and here, in this quiet place, the weight of what I'm holding sinks deeper into my palms.

He moves slowly behind the desk, brushing off a few scattered papers, righting a tipped-over inkwell, settling back into the shape of the man he used to be before the fever stole the color from his cheeks and the sharpness from his eyes.

He doesn't sit. Instead, he turns to face me fully, his jaw tight, his expression unreadable. "Do you remember how your father felt about sirens?"

The question drops like a stone in my chest. I nod once. "Yes."

But the word scrapes my throat raw.

What I don't say is that it was something I hated about him. That I'd overheard his slurs and cold commands. That I'd seen the way he'd bristle when any mention of Messanya reached the court. That he'd called their songs deceitful, their bloodline tainted, as if power that took the shape of beauty could never be trusted.

That he'd imprisoned Dante's mother.

That he most likely had her killed.

Uncle Kormak nods slightly, eyes narrowing on the object in my hand. "That pendant, that collar... it's a restraint. A kind of shackle, though not in the way you'd expect."

I study the metal again. I'd thought the shape strange, like the head of a fork. Elegant, almost. Now it feels sinister.

"It was crafted by black market artisans," he continues. "Years ago. Axel started using them when he imprisoned the sirens here, in Delasurvia. He couldn't risk their magic influencing his soldiers, so he had these made. The metal's tuned to react to vocal frequency. When a siren tries to hum or sing to access their glamour, the metal sends a vibrational shock into the throat of the siren and stops their magic."

"A vibrational shock?"

"Like a tuning fork against bone. The frequency reverberates through the throat. Violently. It silences them and causes just enough pain to make them think twice before trying again."

I clench the leather cord tighter between my fingers. "So it's torture."

"Yes," he says without hesitation. "But masked as precaution. It's only ever used on prisoners. Because outside of chains and cells, it's... control. Abuse."

My skin prickles with heat, a fury rising in my chest that I don't know where to aim. "I've never seen one before."

He leans on the desk, his voice low. "You wouldn't have. They're meant to shame, not warn."

The weight of the message begins to settle into place.

"It's a threat," I say, the words barely above a whisper. "To Dante."

Uncle Kormak nods once. "Knowing that a griffon vulture delivered it, I can only assume it came from the tsar."

My stomach twists. "Or Torbin. What if he sent it? What if he's alive and... this is his way of saying Dante won't have power over him? That even if Dante becomes a prince, he'll never win?"

I look down at the pendant. The etched lines shimmer faintly in the firelight—like veins. Like scars.

"He's toying with us," I say. Whoever sent this is trying to make me believe that Dante is vulnerable. That his voice—his birthright—can be taken from him.

CHAPTER FOURTEEN

'
ve been back at Ivystone for two days, and I haven't seen Dante once. Not because I haven't tried. But because the palace walls have grown thicker in my absence, its halls more crowded with courtiers and guards and attendants eager to keep Dante and me on opposite ends of every corridor.

Things have apparently moved forward quickly while I was away. The first thing I was told—by Indira, as I'd been stripping out of my gear upon my return—was that the king would be throwing a banquet, and everyone was required to attend. But it was Nadya who filled me in on how word regarding Dante's legitimization had traveled quickly throughout Ivystone. Apparently, courtiers love to gossip.

The servants finish styling our hair for the banquet and leave the room. The black mourning dress I'm stuffed into is stifling, but at least I don't have to wear the half-veil, as it isn't required at meals.

"Do you think the king is trying to save face by jumping in front of the rumor?" I ask Nadya once we're alone. "Making it official before the whispers take over?"

I'm relying on Nadya for information, since Indira will only tell me

so much, and, I couldn't even find Ezra to ask him. Evidently, he's been sequestered to join the tour to continue my lessons because the king wants my schooling to be finished before the wedding. So Ezra's been busy preparing for the new task.

"I heard that most of the other realms sent their nightfeathers rushing back with their responses to King Silas's request to hold an audience with them. Apparently, they're all desperate to make peace with Torbin's passing by welcoming a new heir."

"Something about that doesn't sit right with me. Don't get me wrong, this is good news for Dante, but I feel as if the other realms aren't blinking twice at sweeping Torbin's... *demise...* under the rug."

"It's a mad world, I suppose."

"With even madder kings and queens."

"We'll soon see," Nadya says, checking the back of her dress in the mirror. "We leave for the legitimization tour tomorrow morning."

Barely enough time to catch my fucking breath.

Half an hour later, we stand at the edge of the banquet hall beneath a vaulted ceiling. The murmur of the crowd presses in on me, causing the same annoyance I feel when an insect flies too close to my ear. Servants approach us and lead us to our table near the back of the hall.

I'm seated nowhere near Dante. The king made sure of that. I sit with Nadya, flanked by ladies of the court who barely look at me save for brief condolences offered in hollow tones. I nod in return, grateful I have an excuse not to be lively. Mourning, after all, doesn't pair well with wine and conversation.

The king has hidden me in the back because he doesn't want me seen tonight. Not as anything more than the grieving princess. Not as Dante's future. That is one rumor we need to keep quiet. Not just for Dante's sake, but for the legacy of Hedera.

But tonight, I don't mind being hidden. There will be enough eyes on me in the coming months to make my skin itch. So for once, I'm grateful for his plotting.

I try to catch a glimpse of Dante, but there are so many people in the room, and I'm seated so far away. I shift slightly, craning my neck to

see around the flurry of velvet sleeves and embroidered silk that crowds the high table. And then a courtier with a tower of hair piled upon her head finally moves out of the way, and I see him. Dante sits beside the king like a trophy finally brought out for display. His tunic is black, finely cut and embroidered at the cuffs in gleaming silver thread, with a narrow collar that fastens just beneath his throat. His dark hair is combed back but remains unruly at the ends. I can tell he's putting on a show—most likely as he's been instructed—with his shoulders broad, spine straight, and polite smile. But the flicker in his eyes betrays his discomfort. The king claps him on the back now and then between gulps of wine, loud and proud, as if every gesture is meant to hammer in the claim—*mine, mine, mine.*

My heart tightens. It's been more than a week since I last saw him. He hasn't returned to the balcony, not since I came back from Delasurvia. I told myself he's been busy, kept occupied by the king's plans, by endless meetings behind closed doors. But still... I miss him. And when his eyes lift, skimming the room, they find mine in an instant—like a match struck in the dark. Something pulls taut inside me, sharp and electric. I want to continue holding the look, but once again, the king pats Dante's back, and his focus is pulled away.

The banquet hall is filled to capacity. Musicians play a gentle melody in the corner, while servants pass between the rows of long tables with platters of roasted meats, braided breads, and dried fruits soaked in brandy. Gold light flickers from the hundreds of candles set in polished sconces, and I can't help but notice how sharply the green and gold banners gleam above the hall tonight—brighter somehow, more triumphant. The court is dressed for celebration, not grief.

The king stands at his table, and the room goes quiet, the crowd listening with rapt attention.

"As I'm sure you've all heard," King Silas begins, his voice echoing easily through the hall, "the rumors are true. I plan to legitimize my son Dante."

The room hushes all at once, save for a few gasps and the sound of a goblet being set too hard against wood.

106

"I am pleased to announce that we have already received word back from four great realms of Terre Ferique. Podrosa, Bastos, Messanya, and Mersos have all accepted the invitation. The legitimization tour will begin tomorrow, with our first stop in Podrosa. From there, we travel to Bastos, then onward to Messanya and Mersos."

There's no mention of Alphemra. The land of the fae rarely deigns to host visiting kings. I doubt they'll make an exception now, even for a legitimization.

King Silas spreads his arms as if bestowing a blessing. "Tonight, let us take joy. Let us raise our cups to strength, unity, and legacy. We feast as we ask the gods for to bless our journey. Tomorrow, we ride."

But then he pauses, letting the murmurs quiet again.

"This legitimization is more than formality. It is necessity. With my son Dante, the future of Hedera is secured. The Copperhammer name will continue. The bloodline will endure. And through him, our kingdom will not only survive—it will thrive."

He lifts his goblet. "To Hedera. To legacy. And to the future king."

A round of polite applause follows. I catch some smiling faces in the court, murmurs of approval and toasts raised. But there are others— silent, still, unreadable. I wonder which camp they fall into. Loyalists of the late prince, perhaps. Or skeptics, unsure if a bastard belongs on the throne at all.

The musicians strike up a more festive tune. Plates are replenished. More wine is poured. Nadya leans over to murmur something, but I miss it because I'm watching the dais, where Queen Eleanor sits beside her husband.

She doesn't raise her glass. She doesn't even lift her eyes.

Normally, she comes to life in moments like this—when the court is full, when music swells through the halls and the torches burn high, when there are people to distract her from the isolation of her chambers and the man beside her. But tonight, there is no brightness in her expression. No attempt to feign joy. She remains still, her hands folded in her lap, her head tilted ever so slightly toward her goblet, though she hasn't touched it. Her hair is pulled back elegantly from her face, but it

does nothing to lift the shadows beneath her eyes.

I wonder if this moment feels, to her, like the final blow. Not just the legitimization of Silas's bastard, but the quiet erasure of the child she lost. As if the court has decided to move on without him—to drink, to feast, to toast a future prince while the memory of the first fades into silence.

My throat tightens. Despite what he became, Torbin had always been kind to his mother. At least from what I witnessed. Maybe Torbin was the queen's only joy, her last true tether in a marriage that never offered warmth. If so, what must it be like to sit here now, surrounded by revelry and flattery, while her grief still pulses like a wound too deep to close?

She doesn't look toward the guests. She doesn't look at Dante. She simply stares ahead, as if the flickering candlelight might burn away the ache in her chest.

A part of me aches to rise, to walk to her side, to press a hand to hers and promise that she isn't forgotten. That I will protect her in whatever small ways I can. That she still matters.

But I don't move.

I can't risk what it might mean for either of us to show even that much softness in front of this court.

So I remain seated, watching her as the music begins and the laughter returns to the hall—louder now, gilded with false delight.

And Queen Eleanor remains still. A porcelain figure in a kingdom already rewriting its history.

My goblet is half-full, my food untouched. I toy with a slice of duck, stabbing it halfheartedly with my fork. The conversations around me are a soft murmur, none of them directed at me. I don't mind.

Not until I hear Torbin's name. My ears perk up, expecting to hear my name next, but instead of mine, I hear Dante's.

"—heard he was in the tower that night."

My head turns slightly.

"Dante?" a young woman whispers, her voice cautious. "Do you think he had anything to do with it?"

"Don't be absurd," another says quickly, voice hushed but firm. "He's to be a prince now. That kind of talk is treason."

The third woman doesn't respond. She just lifts her goblet and takes a long drink.

"I used to think he was handsome," the first woman says. "But he's a siren, so I think it was just his magic tricking me."

I stiffen, suddenly remembering the collar sent to me in Delasurvia. A part of me doesn't want to tell Dante about it, not wanting to add another thing to the list of worries he must already have, but if it was sent as a threat, then he has the right to know.

"Just because he looks fuckable doesn't mean he's worthy of being a prince," one of the women says.

My grip tightens around my fork. I want to turn, to glare, to say something that will make them choke on their honeyed fruit.

But I don't.

Not tonight.

Not with every move I make watched. Every whisper weighed. Every glance between me and Dante carrying the potential to be catalogued like evidence.

I chew a piece of bread and stare at the tapestry on the far wall. Ivy climbing up a tower of gold, threaded in silver and green. The king jumped to make this announcement so the whispers would stop. If he thinks this court is done whispering, he's wrong. They've only just begun.

When I glance back toward the high table, Dante is no longer seated. He's at the king's side now, moving through the crowd like a dog on a leash. King Silas wears the expression of a man thoroughly pleased with himself, pausing before lords and counts as if expecting them to fall to their knees as he shows off his shiny, new toy. And most of them do—bowing their heads, clasping their chests, murmuring greetings with the kind of reverence I've never once seen them offer to Dante before.

It startles me, the way they've turned so easily. Some of these same men used to scowl at him from the shadows of council chambers, barely concealing their distaste. Now, they lean forward to shake his hand, to

mutter some respectful phrase or another. I suppose loyalty bends where power flows. It all feels like pageantry—scripted, shallow, a show meant for the king's pleasure more than Dante's acceptance.

Then come the ladies. A wave of velvet and perfume. They drift toward him in practiced formation, each one angling to catch his eye, offering the curve of their hands as if awaiting his kiss—which he cleverly avoids by taking their hands and bowing instead. They laugh at things he hasn't said, smile too sweetly, tilt their heads just so. I recognize a few of them. Two of them, at least, once stood at the edge of the royal gardens murmuring that Dante shouldn't have been allowed to remain in Hedera. That a true queen would have turned him away. That the court was growing soft.

Now their eyes gleam when he so much as glances in their direction.

I set my fork down. The taste of rosemary and roasted fig has vanished from my tongue. All that's left is bitterness.

Nadya turns to me, her brows pulled together. "Are you okay?"

"I think I need some air," I say quietly. "Or maybe just sleep. My stomach's turned."

Nadya starts to rise. "I'll come with you."

I shake my head gently. "No. Stay. You actually enjoy these kinds of things." I try to smile, though it feels thin. "Besides, we'll be stuck together in a carriage for the next few months. I'm sure you'll get plenty of me soon enough."

She huffs a soft laugh. "Fair point. Get some rest, then. I'll tell you all about it tomorrow."

She pats my hand, and I rise, smoothing my skirt, careful not to draw too much attention. Most eyes are on Dante, anyway.

At the edge of the room, just before I slip into the corridor, I glance back one last time. He must sense it, because his gaze lifts across the crowd and lands on mine. A pause. Then the faintest of nods, subtle and sure.

It's not a kiss. Not a word.

But it's enough.

For now, anyway.

CHAPTER FIFTEEN

A note lies on my pillow when I get back to my room.

The parchment is folded once, tucked neatly against the hem of my turned-down blanket. No seal. No crest. Just the faintest scent of cloves and spice. My pulse stutters.

I scan the corners of my chamber, but the shadows reveal nothing. No creaking door, no fading footsteps. No Indira lurking around. Only silence.

I unfold the note.

After midnight. Use the secret passage. I made sure it's safe. Please come.
—D.

I read it three times, as if my eyes can't quite trust what they're seeing. A thousand thoughts crowd into the space behind my ribs, but one rises above the rest.

We haven't been alone together. Not really. Not since before Torbin's fall.

Even on the mission to Robinburg, we were surrounded by Sir Holden and my squad, forced to keep our distance by duty, watchful eyes, and too many ghosts. There's always been someone watching. Someone listening.

Tonight... could be different.

Except for Indira.

Assigned to watch over me by order of King Silas himself, she's taken her post as my nighttime chaperone with maddening devotion. Every evening, she settles into the armchair by the hearth, her boots kicked off, a book in her lap and a steaming cup of tea in her hand. She doesn't sleep. Not until I do.

Until tonight, if I can carry out my plan.

I glance toward my vanity, where the drawer holds a small container.

Usually, before I go to bed, I take a pinch of Ezra's sleeping powder, mixed in my water or tea. It hasn't failed to keep me from wandering in my sleep like I used to when the nightmares rip me away. It normally works quickly to relax my muscles, lulling me into a deep sleep and making it almost impossible to get out of bed.

It also worked on Torbin, that evening in the tower. It weakened him enough so that I could overpower him and force him off the balustrade.

So a little pinch in Indira's tea should be sufficient to incapacitate her long enough for me to sneak out for a few hours.

I sit at the vanity and slide open the drawer, fingers trembling slightly as I open the container and spill a small amount into a silk handkerchief. The powder is pale and fine, almost weightless. I quickly fold the handkerchief to close it securely around the powder.

When the door to my room opens, I slip the pouch of silk into the pocket of my robe and smooth my expression, grabbing a brush and glancing at Indira in the mirror.

She enters, yawning dramatically. "You know, if the king intends on making this a permanent thing, I'm going to ask for a cot instead of this chair." She carries her usual mug in one hand, a book tucked beneath the other arm.

I smile faintly, taking my place at the vanity. "You should be happy. We leave for the legitimization tour tomorrow. Maybe you'll get your

own room."

She snorts and plops into the armchair. "I suppose you wouldn't imagine it, being a princess, but servants usually have to share rooms when we travel. There will probably be six of us stuffed into a room the size of your armoire."

I feign a laugh, brushing my hair slowly, watching her in the mirror. "Have you ever been to any of the other realms?"

"Podrosa, once. But I was young. It rained the whole time, and my boots fell apart. That's all I remember." She sets her book in her lap, fingers curling around the mug.

My palm tightens around the pinch of powder. "That's about as far as I've traveled as well. From what I remember, anyway. Even when my parents attended the symposiums the realms used to hold, Bennett and I would stay in Delasurvia with my uncle."

I step away from the vanity and walk toward her, the powder clutched between my fingers.

"I'm not looking forward to Bastos," she says. "The temperature there doesn't agree with me."

"It's a shame we're not going to Alphemra. I would love to see where my mother's side of the family lives. I don't even know if they would know who I am."

She lifts her brows, clearly about to respond, but I tip my hand toward her book instead.

"You always read the same story?" I ask.

She huffs. "Not always. But I'm a creature of habit and always drift back to my favorites."

With a flick of magic, subtle and controlled, I nudge the book off her lap.

It falls with a soft thump and skids beneath the chair.

Indira groans. "For the love of figs—" She sets the mug on the side table, then leans forward, stretching, fingers swiping at the leather spine.

I use my magic to nudge it just out of her reach, and as she bends lower, I tip the powder into her tea.

It dissolves in a whisper.

By the time she straightens, book in hand, I'm smiling faintly and heading back toward my bed. I let my silk robe slip from my shoulders, draping it over the footboard. Beneath, my nightgown clings softly to my frame, featherlight and cool against my skin.

Indira blows on her tea and takes a sip. "Try to sleep, Your Highness. We leave early."

"Goodnight, Indira," I say, sliding beneath the covers. "I hope you get some rest as well."

She nods, already settling deeper into the chair. I keep my eyes on the ceiling, but my senses are taut—listening for every breath, every shift of weight. My fingers curl around the dagger strapped to my thigh beneath the sheets.

Dante said the passage was safe. Still, I'm not foolish enough to go unarmed.

Minutes pass. The fire pops. And my thoughts wander.

I hope my uncle is okay.

Will my squad be all right without me?

Are the Delasurvian people still being fed?

I hope the refugee camps are thriving.

How does Dante feel about being betrothed to me?

The fire pops again, and Indira's breathing has noticeably slowed.

And then a snore resounds. Soft. Steady. Genuine.

I exhale slowly, heart hammering, and sit up to glance over. Her mug rests empty on the side table. The open book slips from her hands into her lap.

Though I can't help the twinge of guilt that flickers beneath my ribs, it worked.

I'm sorry, Indira.

I throw back the covers and rise, grabbing my robe, and move in silence toward the wall behind the wardrobe where the secret passage's door is hidden.

The panel opens with a whisper, and the cool hush of the passage greets me like a sigh. It's been weeks since I've crept these halls, weeks since the air felt so still and secret around me. I slip inside, pressing the panel closed behind me, the soft click of the latch sounding far louder in the quiet than it should. The torchlight from my room vanishes, swallowed by the dark.

I wait a moment to adjust. I'm barefoot, and though the chill of stone seeps into my skin, the thought of Dante waiting for me keeps my body warmed. My silk robe glides against my legs as I move, trailing softly along the narrow corridor, and I keep one hand on the wall, fingers brushing across uneven stone. My other hand rests lightly against the hilt of the dagger strapped to my thigh.

I worry my lip. My heart is loud in my chest—not from fear, not tonight. Anticipation rises, hot and quiet, curling low in my stomach. It's been too long. I've suffered behind too many stolen glances, agonized from longing for too many nights of merely gazing at each other over the distance of our balconies.

I round the bend where the corridor forks and follow the narrow path that leads to the hidden entrance near Dante's chamber. My fingers find the familiar notch in the wall, the pressure point where the panel gives way. I press it open just a sliver—

Voices make me freeze.

Low and firm. One of them unmistakably the king's.

"Just remember that they are expecting a prince," King Silas says, his tone a murmur of steel and strategy. "Each realm has already concocted their own idea of what you are, and it's your job to shatter their presumptions. You are to present yourself as confident—but not arrogant. Cordial. Respectful. But still every bit of man your father is."

There's a pause, and then the familiar rustle of fabric. The king pacing, perhaps.

"I want them to see what I see," he continues. "A man worthy of the Copperhammer name. One who commands attention without demanding it. You are my son, and that will mean something—if you carry that honor properly."

Silence follows, and I hold a hand to my chest, wondering if they are done speaking.

After a moment, the king's voice comes again, this time softer.

"Because that's what you will be when this is all over, son. A Copperhammer, by all rights."

My breath catches.

I can't see Dante, but I can feel the stillness in the room shift. The silence stretches a moment too long.

When he finally speaks, his voice is quiet, almost a whisper. "Understood."

It's just one word. But I can hear the weight in it. The conflict.

All his life, he's lived in the shadow of a crown not meant for him. All his life, he believed he didn't belong. Now, with a few words, the king has offered him what he's always been denied: acknowledgment. Belonging. A name.

Even if it comes at a cost.

"Get some rest," the king says. "Your entire world is about to change."

CHAPTER SIXTEEN

ootfalls sound, followed by the scrape of a chair, and then the tread of heavy boots across stone. A door opens. Closes.

I don't dare move.

I wait until the footfalls fade completely before I press my hand to the panel again, my pulse now louder than ever in my ears.

As the secret door slides open, the glow of candlelight fills my vision. I squint against it for a moment, adjusting to the change in illumination.

His back is to me, but then he straightens. He glances over his shoulder before turning completely in my direction and stepping closer. Dante's gaze slowly strokes over the length of my body before he takes my hand and tugs me into the room.

My breath catches, and I feel the urge to say something, just to give myself enough time to adjust to the intensity of his eyes. "Pretty late for the king to pay a visit."

He runs a thumb over the back of my hand. "He's in a dark place and wants to ensure this tour goes his way."

"Why would he think it wouldn't? It's what you want, isn't it?"

 117

"I'm not doing this for him." He tips my chin up with a finger. "And if you don't know what I want by now, Highness, you haven't been paying attention."

His eyes darken as he traces my jaw with his thumb. The connection of our skin sparks an eruption of energy so intense, I can feel his pulse in my blood.

"I have to tell you something." The words come out so fast, I have to catch my breath. "A message was delivered to me when I was in Delasurvia. Meant for you."

"For me?" His brows lower. "What kind of message?"

"It said, 'For the future prince,' and there was an item included."

He waits a moment, but when I don't continue, he prompts me. "What was it?"

"It was a black, leather cord, like a band or collar. And there was a pendant shaped like the head of a fork."

He blinks, taking that in. "Like a tuning fork?"

"Yes. Do you know what that is?" I'm hoping he does so I don't have to explain the horrible thing.

"I've heard of it, yes." He doesn't elaborate, and the look he's giving me tells me he's heard of it because of my father. He must have known that my father used the collar to keep the sirens he imprisoned from using their powers. To keep Dante's mother from glamouring my father's guards when she was locked in Delasurvia's dungeons. "Do you think it was from the tsar?"

"It was one of the thoughts I had, yes." I swallow. "The other was... your brother."

He drops his gaze, most likely absorbing that possibility. After a moment, he nods. "Not even a prince yet and I've already got enemies."

"It's an empty threat, Dante. They can't touch you." I say it more to convince myself.

The corner of his mouth ticks upward. "Not with you watching my back."

I can't help but smile. "I'll gladly be your sworn protector."

"It could call for some extremely close contact." He trails his hands

around my waist. "You think you can handle it?"

"I'll give it a try." I fist his shirt, pulling him closer until his lips crash upon mine. I soak in his kiss, making it my mission to memorize the feel of his mouth, the taste of his tongue. There's no telling when we'll get the chance to be alone again, so I intend to commit every bit of him to memory.

He nips at my bottom lip before trailing his teeth down my throat, causing heat to blossom between my legs. I gasp as his mouth finds my collarbone, his fingers tugging my hair at the nape of my neck. It's just painful enough to heighten my senses. I arch into him until our bodies are flush, and when I feel his hard length press into me, the heat between us elevates to an inferno.

"Gods, I want you." My voice is a hoarse whisper.

"Is that so, Highness?" he asks between kisses peppered at the top of my breasts. His hands snake around and cup my ass. "Where?"

"On top of me, inside me. Everywhere."

"And I want you. I need your sweet pussy pulsing around my cock. And I want your eyes on mine while I make you cum."

His words make me melt against him. His mouth returns to my neck as his finger drag my robe from my shoulders. Before it drops to the floor, he snatches it with his hand and slips the silk belt from its loops.

"What are you—?"

"Shh." The corner of his mouth rises as he holds my upper arms and steers me backward. "Just making sure I've got you where I want you for as long as necessary."

When we reach his bed, he takes me by my waist and effortlessly lifts me onto his mattress. The movement causes my thin nightdress to raise above my navel, exposing my underwear to him.

And the dagger sheathed to my thigh.

He smirks, his gaze slowly coming up my body until our eyes meet. "Expecting trouble, Highness?"

"One can never be too careful." I reach for the strap. "Should I—?"

He wraps his hand around my arm to stop me. "No. Let me. I'm in control now."

I'm too turned on to respond. His hungry gaze roams over me for a moment before he gathers my wrists together and wraps the silk belt around them.

I bite my lip, my excitement for what he has planned intensifying. He nudges my legs apart with his knee and hovers over me while he fastens the belt to one of the cast-iron bars of his headboard.

"Lord Stregasi," I tease. "You're so naughty."

He raises a brow. "You show up in my room wearing this," he starts, indicating the gauzy material barely concealing my breasts, "something so thin, it makes my cock twitch, and you think *I'm* the naughty one?"

The smile that begins on my mouth gets stolen away by his lips, his kiss deep and passionate. I try to hold on to the kiss, but his lips trail down my jaw, my throat, and when he reaches my breasts, he deftly grabs the material of my nightgown and rips it in half as if it were nothing. My nipples harden as they are exposed to the air, and Dante doesn't hesitate to descend on one, and then the other, nipping and sucking each into his hot mouth as I emit tiny gasps and writhe beneath him. I'm soaking wet watching him trail his tongue down the curves of my breasts, down my quivering stomach, until he reaches the waist of my underwear.

He lifts his head, his eyes locked on mine as he scoots back, and his fingers trail down to the strap of my dagger's sheath. He gently unbuckles it and pulls it away from my body, then he lets his feather-light touch traverse up my thigh before tugging at the material of my underwear. He takes his time, slowly pulling the material down my legs, his gaze taking in every inch of me. I squirm, desperate to reach out and pull him back on top of me but unable to move because my hands are restrained.

"Something wrong, little pirate?"

I smirk at the nickname—something he derived from his taunts about Delasurvians having pirate backgrounds. It used to annoy me, but now it gives me a thrill when he says it.

He slides off the bed, and once he's on his feet, he yanks his shirt off with one swift move. Candlelight flickers on the sculpted muscle of his chest and arms.

"Just... impatient," I say, my chest heaving from the thrill of

anticipation.

"I can see that." He steps out of his shoes and undoes the button of his pants, then pulls them down along with his underpants. His hard cock, now free, indeed twitches. He shakes his head and clucks his tongue. "You're soaking my sheets, Princess. I think I might need to punish you."

I can only hum in response, my body quaking, desperate for his touch. But instead of stepping toward me, he turns around and traipses to a small table by his chaise. I'm so confused about what he's doing, but the mystery is exhilarating. When he turns around to face me again, he's holding a flower he plucked from the vase. He twirls the stem between his fingers as he saunters back to the bed. I realize then that it's a peony.

"Tell me again what you want," he demands, climbing onto the mattress one leg at a time until he's kneeling beside me.

"I want you."

He uses the soft petals of the peony to caress my cheek. "Be more specific. What do you want me to do to you?"

"Dante, please."

He trails the flower down to my chest, outlining my breasts with feather-light strokes. My pulse races, my senses in a frenzy.

"Tell me," he says, his voice low and sultry.

"I want you to touch me. I want you to fuck me." I pant, my blood rushing in my ears. With him, there's no need to hold back, no need to worry about accidentally becoming with child. Preventing pregnancies is one of the many powers sirens possess.

He smirks, running the peony down my abdomen. "Hmm, I'll make a deal with you."

Is he fucking serious?

"You stay perfectly still," he continues, "while I play with your gorgeous body. And if you remain quiet, I'll give that wet pussy exactly what it's craving."

He challenges me with his gaze. I want to protest, to make him stop this game so I can have him, but I also want to play along, to enjoy this time with him. Because after tonight, we're going to have to pretend we

121

don't have feelings for each other. We're going to have to keep our distance and we won't be able to touch each other. We'll be watched closely and might not be able to find a stolen moment to be together for a long while.

"Can you do that, Highness?" He slides the flower down between my legs, lightly twirling it.

"Yes," I whisper.

He lets out a low chuckle. "That's my good girl."

It takes every ounce of control not to squirm, not to moan as he traces the contours of my body, teasing and stroking, caressing my skin, bringing the flower to skim my inner thighs and dance over my throbbing pussy. He glides the petals up over my pebbled nipples, and I almost arch into the feel of it. I open my mouth but don't release the gasp of pleasure.

I beg him with my eyes, but he only smirks.

"Don't move, little pirate," he repeats, running the peony over my breasts again, but this time, he follows the touch with his lips.

I fight the urge to moan when he laps at one nipple and then gently grazes his teeth over it. It's too much, the yearning, the desperation, the fucking anticipation. This is torture. Sweet, sweet torture. I close my eyes and throw my head back, the fire inside me making me dizzy.

The flower trails back down to between my legs, and he teases me with it, stroking up and down. Once, twice. On the third caress, I almost buck forward, so desperate for more. The light touch of the petals over my clit has me grinding my teeth with need. His teeth trail over my nipple as he glides the flower over my center. My whole body is burning with need.

He teases me again, stroking my clit with the silky flower, the pressure too light. I push my hips up to meet the touch, but he pulls away with a chuckle. I almost growl in frustration, but then he strokes over my center once more, and then the flower falls away, only to be replaced by his fingers a second later. He slides two fingers along my opening, and this time, I can't hold back the intake of breath.

"So fucking wet," he breathes into my breast.

Oh, gods. I don't know how much more of this I can take.

He strokes his fingers through my wetness again and then circles my clit. I rock my hips forward, seeking out more of his touch. He told me not to move, but I can't stop myself. Thankfully, he seems to have given in to his desires and slips his fingers into the velvet heat of my core. He growls low in his throat, kissing his way back up to my mouth as his thumb applies the perfect amount of pressure on my swollen nub. When he slides his fingers deeper inside me, I cry out. The belt cinches tighter around my wrists as I writhe.

My head thrashes, my back arching to get closer to him. "Don't stop. Please."

He kisses me hard, slipping his fingers out of me.

I actually whine this time, which causes him to chuckle. But before I can protest, he reaches up and unties the belt. With my hands finally free, I reach for him, my palms on his shoulders and my fingers digging into his skin.

"More. Dante, please."

He positions himself between my knees, his gaze locked with mine as he wraps a hand around his erection and strokes himself once. Twice. Three times. I can't help but stare at the drop of precum that beads at the tip.

"Don't fret, Princess. I'm not stopping yet. I intend to fuck you so thoroughly, so diligently, until you're so soaked in my cum that the scent of me cleaves to you for months."

My hands go to his hips, the need in me driving me to the brink.

He places the head of his cock against my entrance, covering it with my wet arousal. His mouth parts, and his lids grow heavy with lust. His eyes are on mine as he pushes into me, and the room echoes with my cry of pleasure. He slides in further, stretching me as he glides every inch of his hard length into the hot center of my core, until he's fully seated. My pussy clenches around him, as if it's fighting to keep him there.

"So good and wet," he says, his voice gruff. "You take my cock so well."

His mouth comes down to devour mine as he pulls almost all the

way out of me and then thrusts back in. I tighten my hold on him as he pumps in and out of me, my small gasps growing louder. I'm burning up. I'm on fire, and the heat is delicious. He reaches down and wraps one arm under my knee, lifting my leg until it's propped on his upper arm. His strokes reach deeper at this angle, hitting that sweet spot that makes the world blur, and the sound of our wet bodies slapping together fill the room.

"Fuck," he growls, low and slow.

He undulates, and I run my fingers over his sweaty skin, grasping and pulling him closer. This fire is consuming me, and I need him to stoke the flames higher, higher. He shifts, wrapping his arm around me and lifting me until I'm sitting in his lap, his cock still deep inside me. I gasp at the feel of it, the completeness of it. As if I wouldn't be whole without it. He leans forward, leaving sloppy kisses all over my breasts as I lift my hips, sliding up his length and pushing back down, soaking his cock in my hot desire.

"Oh. Dante!"

"Yes, love, keep going," he urges. "I want to remember every moment of this. I need the image of you riding my cock to last the entirety of this tour."

He reaches between us and rubs my clit as I rise and fall, grinding and stroking his hard, thick length with the quivering walls of my pussy. Our moans and whimpers call out and answer each other, our slick skin growing hotter with every thrust, every plunge. He grabs a handful of hair at the nape of my neck, twisting the strands in his fingers, and tugs, exposing my neck to him. He devours my throat as we fuck, and my heart is thrashing in my chest. His thumb on my clit moves faster, and my breathing picks up. I'm so close.

"Cum for me, Celeste."

"Oh, gods." I'm at the edge of a cliff, ready to soar.

The desire crescendos, and Dante grabs my hips and slams me down onto him, shuddering. My pussy pulses, my orgasm flaring inside me like an explosion. Dante practically roars as he shoots his hot release into me, flooding us both in cum.

His hold on me is tight, unrelenting, our foreheads pressed together. I can feel both our hearts pounding as if in unison. Our skin is covered in sweat, making us slide against each other as our breathing slows to normal.

He holds my gaze as he tucks my damp hair behind my ears. "Beautiful."

"Amazing," I reply, stroking his cheek with my thumb.

There's something in his gaze as his eyes travel over my features, and though it remains unspoken, I understand. I tilt my head and press my lips into his. I soak him in, relishing in the feeling of being in his arms, being covered in his sweat, his scent. This isn't just sex. This man isn't just holding my body. He's holding my heart.

"What do you say, Lord Stregasi?" I give him a coy smile. "Good enough to last the entirety of the tour?"

He lets out a short laugh and shakes his head. "I don't know if I'm strong enough to restrain myself. Keeping my hands off you for the next few months, it's going to be hard."

I raise a brow and look down between our bodies. "Feels like it already is."

CHAPTER SEVENTEEN

've barely slept. Dante and I took advantage of almost every minute we had alone together, only drifting off for a couple of hours, our naked bodies tangled in his sheets. The dawn's light announced that our time was up. It took every ounce of willpower within me to finally leave his room and find my way back through the secret passageways.

I know I'm getting back too late. Ezra's powder would have certainly worn off by now, and I can only imagine what Indira must be thinking. When I reach the panel that accesses my room, I push it open slowly, peering around to see if she's around.

Instead of Indira, I find Nadya. Her eyes are wide as I slip into my room, and she looks over her shoulder at the closed door.

"Where have you been?" she whispers.

"I... got tied up." I can't help but smirk to myself. "Where's Indira?"

Nadya lets out a sigh. "I asked her to fetch us some tea. She burst into my room about twenty minutes ago asking where you were. I convinced her that you woke up early to get some books from Ezra you wanted to take on the tour."

"She bought that?"

"I doubt it, but if you hurry up and get ready, maybe we can get down to the carriage before she can badger you." Nadya is already dressed in a light-yellow dress, her hair pinned up in an elegant bun. "What's this?" she asks, reaching for my hair.

My eyes widen for a minute when she pulls a peony petal out from my strands.

I instantly snatch it away from her. "Nothing."

She studies me for a moment and then slowly nods. "Yeah, okay. I'm sure you'll tell me later." She gives me a smile and a wink. "Good for you. Now get ready."

Despite the fact that I love Dante's scent on me, I know I can't travel for the next couple of days brewing in my own sweat-stained skin, so I wash up and get dressed in a traveling dress suitable for the mourning period. I grab the black tiara with the veil, but I decide to wait before putting it on. Servants arrive to bring my traveling chests down to the carriage, and before I know it, we're loading up the entourage to head out on our way.

Before I climb into my carriage, I catch sight of Dante, and I immediately want to rush back into his arms. But I can't. It's time for us to play our parts, to pretend there is nothing between us. I school my features as I place the mourning tiara upon my head. We only have to endure the duration of the tour, and soon after that, we won't have to hide anymore.

The carriage rocks gently beneath us, its wheels bumping over the uneven dirt road as the royal caravan snakes its way across the golden plains of eastern Hedera. Outside the window, wildflowers sway in the breeze, painted in soft hues of violet and amber. In the far distance, the mountains rise like sleeping giants beneath a pale-blue sky, their snowy caps catching the late morning sun.

Inside, the carriage is warm and polished, with smooth, dark paneling that gleams faintly in the shifting light. Velvet cushions, deep green and gold-threaded, soften each jostling movement. Across from me, Nadya is curled into the corner, her boots tucked beneath her as she reads, one gloved finger tapping lightly against the page. Her book makes me think of Ezra, who rides in a separate carriage, probably with his nose in a few books of his own.

At the front of the caravan, the king is in his royal carriage with Farvis and a couple of his advisors, but separate from the queen. I noticed, when we were leaving Hedera, that she entered her own carriage with her ladies-in-waiting, while Dante boarded a carriage that used to belong to Torbin. I can't help but wonder if that makes him uncomfortable or not.

I lean against the frame of the window, cheek resting in my palm, and let the rhythm of the ride lull me into a kind of haze. The wind slipping through the small, cracked window cools the back of my neck, and my mind wanders to the night before, and how Dante and I spent every moment we could exploring each other's bodies. When I close my eyes, I can still feel his hands on me, the taste of his lips, the feel of him filling me.

My eyes snap open, worried that Nadya might be watching me, but her nose is still buried in a book.

I smooth the folds of my dress over my lap, absently tracing the embroidery along the hem. The gown is a dark grey, cinched at the waist with a twisted black ribbon. A constant reminder of the role I'm being forced to play.

My thoughts drift, unbidden, to my uncle. Is he eating? Sleeping? Does he even remember what happened to him? The last time I saw him, his skin was still too pale and his eyes too dim, like the light inside him hadn't quite returned. I don't know if he'll ever be the same.

Nadya sighs. "Are you going to tell me about your night, or are you going to keep it a secret forever?"

The corner of my mouth slides upward. "You don't always tell me about your little night meetings."

"You don't really want to hear about them, do you?"

I laugh. "Not really, no."

She drops her voice to a whisper. "Were you with Dante the entire night?"

I can't hide my smile. "Yes. I don't know if the gods would approve of half the things we did, let alone the king."

She lets out a giggle and swats me playfully. "Oh, Your Highness," she teases, "so very scandalous."

"There's only one thing I regret."

"Honestly, Celeste, it only hurts for a minute. You just need to—"

"No! Not that." My cheeks heat, and I have to laugh. It takes me a second to recover. "I had meant to tell Dante about my powers, but it... slipped my mind, given the circumstances."

"Oh, that." She giggles a little before continuing. "Well, it's not like you won't get a chance to speak to him again. The king can't be watching you the entire time. Besides, you said you wanted to find out more about controlling the magic first. And it's not like you're keeping a secret from him."

I worry my lip and nod. "That's true."

There's a brief silence, the kind that hums with quiet comfort.

"Are you reading another one of your torrid love stories? The kind with knights in shining armor and fair maidens sighing in meadows?"

She laughs. "No meadows. No sighing. Did your parents ever read you the story about the sun dragon and the moon dragon?"

That gets my attention. I shift to face her more fully, curiosity tugging at the edge of my tired thoughts. "I seem to remember a bit of that, yes."

"This is an account by an historian who translated accounts from a seer, making a case that the story has some true origins."

"Really? Remind me how the story goes."

"There were once two mighty dragon species," she recites, her voice dipping slightly into a storytelling cadence. "The sun dragons—creatures of flame and light—and the moon dragons, born of darkness and shadow. They ruled the skies in ancient Terre Ferique, powerful and

proud, but never allies. Always adversaries."

I listen, intrigued despite myself.

"The tale says that whenever a great shift came upon the world—a changing of thrones, the rise of a powerful force—these two species would stir. Wake from their slumber as if called to take sides and champion a leader. But they were too destructive. Every time they fought, they left the world around them in ruins. So a curse was cast. It bound them to dormancy, locked them away."

"Sleeping dragons," I say. "That sounds familiar."

Nadya's voice lowers, the tone laced with eerie reverence. "And the curse said this: when the sun is blocked by the moon, the dragons would awake, and their final battle would begin. And then only one would survive. The other would perish forever. One cannot survive so long as the other lives."

I tilt my head. "I vaguely remember it, but it was just a tale told to children. Unfortunately, dragons are extinct. Died out centuries ago."

She shrugs, the corner of her mouth twitching. "Or maybe they're just sleeping, like the story says, waiting to be awoken when the world shifts. When the moon blocks the sun. I don't know. Stories have to start somewhere."

"I guess we can't count anything out." I glance out the window again, watching the distant clouds unravel across the blue horizon. The tale sits in the back of my mind, strange and oddly persistent.

Sun and moon. Fire and shadow. Locked in a battle that could end the world.

The caravan comes to a slow halt on the outskirts of a quiet village nestled between rolling, green hills. The next leg of our journey will be over mountains too treacherous to conquer at night, so we need to stop and rest at an inn until morning. The evening air is cool, scented with

damp earth and the faintest hint of honeysuckle from the distant forest. Lanterns flicker to life along the cobbled main road, casting a warm, golden glow upon the inn's timbered façade. The establishment is modest compared to the grandeur of Ivystone Citadel, but there is an undeniable charm to it—its walls washed in soft cream, the windows framed by dark wooden beams, and flower boxes spilling with violets and ivy.

The sound of carriage doors unlatching and booted feet striking the road fills the quiet, and I step down with care, smoothing the skirts of my black traveling dress. The fabric is wrinkled from the day's wear, traces of sweat marking the seams, but I keep my chin lifted, remembering to play my part—not as a soldier, but as a princess. Sir Holden is immediately at my side.

The rest of the caravan begins to disembark in a slow, practiced rhythm. Guards move into place, alert but not tense, and attendants begin unloading satchels and cases from the backs of the wagons. The creak of leather, the clink of bridles, and the low voices of nobles fill the air with a kind of buzzing quiet.

Two carriages ahead, King Silas descends, his posture as rigid as the blade at his side. His expression is unreadable, but the tension in his jaw is unmistakable. A moment later, a second carriage door opens, and Queen Eleanor steps out, a soft, onyx-colored shawl wrapped around her slender frame. Her eyes do not find the king.

Though they stand a couple of feet apart, the distance between them feels colder than the dusk air.

The words from the fight they had play in my mind.

"I gave you plenty of seed with which to bear another heir, and yet here we are. Emptyhanded."

"Perhaps if you hadn't been so rough—"

"Don't you fucking dare!"

My throat tightens, the ache of it sudden and sharp. Eleanor wears grace like a mask, but I've seen what's beneath. The quiet grief, the way she carries it in her eyes. And I've heard the king's voice—clipped, cruel, never softened for her sake. I know what he's capable of.

 131

A flicker of movement draws my attention to the next carriage as Dante steps down, his silhouette backlit by the lanterns. He rakes a hand through his wind-tossed hair, and my heart stumbles over itself.

Gods, he's beautiful.

His tunic is travel-worn, the laces at his collar loosened, but still, he looks every bit the prince he's being presented as. When his eyes lift and find mine, the world dulls around the edges. Just for a moment.

His expression softens, just slightly, and I feel it—low in my chest, in the pit of my stomach—the thing that draws me to him like a tide sweeping me into the shore.

I force myself to look away. There are too many eyes. Too many rules. And I'm afraid there would be no disguising the heat behind our gazes.

A shuffling of feet and mumbled voices break the silence, and the innkeeper and his family step out in a practiced line, their heads bowed, hands folded respectfully. A chorus of greetings rises, warm and full of pride at hosting the crown.

Stablehands hurry forward to tend to the weary horses, bowing their heads respectfully as they take the reins. The innkeeper, a round-bellied man with a kindly face, stands at the entrance, wringing his hands in nervous excitement. His wife, a tall, sharp-eyed woman with flame-red hair, swiftly directs their staff to prepare for our arrival. The weight of our presence is not lost on them.

As we step closer, the innkeeper steps forward, bowing so low, his forehead nearly brushes his knee. "Your Majesty," he says, voice trembling slightly. "It is our greatest honor to host you and your royal delegation of Hedera. Everything is prepared to your liking."

King Silas merely nods, stepping past him with a slow and deliberate stride. A pair of swinging iron lanterns creak in the breeze above the entry as the door is pushed open and our party begins to file in. Queen Eleanor follows, moving with quiet grace, her black mourning attire a stark contrast to the inn's cozy glow.

Dante lingers behind them, his gaze sweeping the area as if assessing every shadow, every movement. Our eyes meet briefly before I turn away,

taking in the inn's surroundings.

The honor of housing a royal entourage is apparent in the meticulous care given to the surroundings. The hearth crackles invitingly within, a contrast to the crisp, night air settling over the village. The scent of roasted meat mingles with pipe smoke and the faint tang of vinegar from the mop water still drying in the corners. The floorboards gleam from recent scrubbing, and though the ceiling beams are low and thick with age, they carry the place's history like strong shoulders bearing familiar burdens. Not a single cobweb to be found. It is a pleasant enough place to rest, but even here, miles away from Ivystone, there is no true reprieve from the weight of duty that has us all in its clutches.

The innkeeper leads the king and his courtiers toward the wide, winding staircase. As the king and his men pass, the innkeeper gestures with both pride and humility. "Our suites on the uppermost floor overlook the town square. They're the quietest in the house, if not the most spacious."

Dante moves with them, shoulders squared in his black coat, the silver fastenings catching the light of the chandeliers. His expression is unreadable, but just before he follows the rest of them up the steps, he glances back at me.

It's a fleeting look, but his eyes find mine like a touch in the dark, and something in my chest shifts. When Sir Donovan steps in and blocks the view, a muscle feathers in Dante's jaw.

Nadya nudges me as we linger in the foyer, waiting our turn. "I don't think I've ever seen Dante look so uncomfortable. You think he's going to survive the trip?"

I murmur, "I think he doesn't have a choice."

"Mm. It's tragic the way he's jumping through loops for the king. I liked him better when he was mysterious and half-brooding."

"You like anything with a jawline."

"Speaking of," she whispers, tilting her chin toward the tavern's bar as the innkeeper's wife emerges from the back hallway. Behind her, a tall man with rolled shirtsleeves and sun-warmed skin lifts a crate of bottles and sets it on the counter like it weighs nothing at all. His muscles ripple

with the movement, and when his eyes catch Nadya's, he grins—slow and deliberate.

Nadya bats her lashes, her hips swaying a touch. "That's a dangerously pretty man."

I let out a small laugh, hiding my mouth immediately when I remember I'm supposed to me in mourning and not giggling like I have no care in the world. "You're going to get me in trouble," I whisper to Nadya.

"Sorry. I can't help that I'm observant."

The innkeeper's wife gives me a slight curtsey as she approaches. "Your rooms are just up this way, Your Highness. I'm sure it's not what you're used to, but the beds are warm and the linens are clean."

"Thank you," I reply, inclining my head.

We head up the narrower stairwell tucked between the tavern and the back hallway, Sir Holden trailing behind us with the quiet steadiness of a shadow. He doesn't comment, just positions himself at the landing outside our door like a sentry cast in stone.

Inside, the room is modest but comfortable. Two beds, each with thick quilts and downy pillows, flank a small, carved dresser with a mirror cracked at one corner. A basin sits on the washstand near the shuttered window, where warm evening light filters in, catching on the floating dust motes like fireflies drifting through amber.

The air smells of lavender sachets, most likely tucked beneath the mattresses, and old wood warmed by sun.

"There we are," says the innkeeper's wife, placing a key on the table beside the door. "If you need anything, don't hesitate. Dinner will be served downstairs at seven sharp. You'll hear the bell." She dips a curtsy and disappears back down the hall with the whisper of her skirts.

As she departs, Indira shuffles into the room, inspecting it with curiosity.

Nadya immediately flops back onto the nearest bed, arms spread wide, a satisfied groan escaping her lips. "After all those hours in the carriage, this feels like heaven."

Indira makes a noise of disapproval and folds her arms. "Don't get

134

too comfortable. You both need to get ready for dinner."

Nadya smirks, not moving an inch. "Come on, Indira. You've been trapped in an even more cramped carriage than we have. Don't tell me your rear isn't screaming for mercy."

There's a pause.

Then Indira exhales with exaggerated patience and settles into the overstuffed armchair beside the dresser. "Fine. But only because the bench cushions are about as soft as a knight's breastplate. And only for a minute."

I smile faintly, letting the door click shut behind me as I step farther into the room.

The quiet of the inn wraps around me like a blanket not quite warm enough. It feels like a pause in the middle of a battle, one of those rare breaths where the dust hasn't yet settled and no one is shouting orders. Just space.

I cross the room and sit on the bed meant for me, letting out a long breath. My body seems to thank me for the momentary rest. It's a small reprieve, but I'll take it.

CHAPTER EIGHTEEN

The common room of the inn has been transformed—at least, as much as a common room can be. The wooden tables have been pushed aside to make way for a single long one, polished until the waxed surface glows in the flickering lamplight. The innkeeper cleared the space himself, having barked orders to his staff with military precision, and now oversees the evening like a general watching over his prized battalion. His shirt is freshly laundered, his apron crisp, and he moves between bar and table with the focus of a man determined to impress. He doesn't sit—wouldn't dare. But every time a platter is brought out or a cup refilled, he is nearby, murmuring to his staff with a hand at his hip and a hawk-like eye on every detail.

The air smells of roasted pheasant and rosemary potatoes, warm bread and sweet apple glaze. The fire in the hearth crackles steadily, throwing gold and amber light across the beams overhead. Outside the inn's mullioned windows, the sky has turned a deep indigo, the first stars already visible between the branches of the tall trees that surround this edge-of-nowhere village.

Guards sit at the far end of the room, near the windows, eating from heavy, wooden plates and keeping their voices low. I catch sight of Sir Holden among them, speaking quietly to Sir Donovan as he saws into his meat. None of the servants dine with us, though I don't know if they eat somewhere else or not at all.

I've changed out of my traveling clothes into something simpler—still dark enough to befit mourning, but less suffocating than the gown from the road. A high-collared tunic in black velvet with long, flowing sleeves, and a long skirt that flows to my boots. No veil. No fanfare. But the mask of sorrow is still present.

Ezra sits beside Farvis, the two of them already deep in conversation when I arrive with Nadya. The king is at the head of the table, relaxed, confident, like he's already conquered this village just by arriving.

I slide into the seat across from Dante.

He's dressed in black again, though his tunic is looser now, the collar open enough to show the edge of his collarbone. His hair is damp and curls slightly at the ends, where it brushes the backs of his ears. I try not to look too long, but I catch him holding his gaze as well.

The chatter rises slowly around us. The king compliments the inn's cider. Farvis offers some veiled opinion about the road being better maintained than he expected.

One of the waitresses—a curvy young woman with honey-blonde hair and a flush that suggests she's had a few sips of that cider herself—leans over Dante, her hand resting on his shoulder as she sets a bowl in front of him.

"I hear you're the future prince," she says, her voice too sweet to be accidental.

Dante's mouth curves slightly, but he keeps his tone polite. "Only if the king has his way."

"Oh, I'm sure he will," she says, her eyes darting to Silas and back. "If there's anything you need tonight, my lord, anything at all..." She leans a bit closer, and her bodice shifts just enough to reveal her intent.

On the outside, I keep my expression neutral. On the inside, I'm already calculating the exact angle I'd need to throw my dagger into the back of her hand without nicking Dante's skin. It wouldn't take more

than a flick of my wrist, and it would be embedded in her flesh before anyone realized what had happened.

But I don't move. I reach calmly for my cup and sip the watered wine.

The king chuckles. "You'll have to grow accustomed to such attention, my son. Royal blood draws many eager eyes."

Farvis doesn't laugh. He wipes his mouth with the edge of his napkin and turns toward Silas. "Your Majesty, if I may—there's word spreading through the merchant routes. Whispers of the tsar's beasts crossing more borders than we realized. If the carnoraxis reach Podrosa, or gods forbid, Bastos, the alliance will fracture. The nobility there already mistrusts Hederan steel."

Silas waves his hand lazily. "Then we remind them that Hederan gold speaks louder than fear."

Farvis frowns but says nothing more.

Beside me at the table, Nadya's already locked eyes with the barkeep. He's behind the counter, pretending to wipe mugs with a cloth that's clearly just for show. His gaze is fixed on her, and when he nods once, slow and deliberate, I know something's coming.

Sure enough, one of the waitresses delivers a drink with a sprig of mint tucked in and a tiny, blue flower balanced on the rim. "Compliments of the bar," she says, then she glances quickly at Nadya and scurries off.

Nadya grins. "Well. It's not quite a royal ball, but I do love local charm."

I shake my head at her, but it's hard to hide my amusement.

I lift my fork and eat, but the warmth in my chest has little to do with the food and everything to do with the pair of storm-grey eyes that meet mine when no one else is looking.

Another waitress arrives with a tray of glazed duck. She lingers a little too long when she sets Dante's plate down, her fingers grazing his bicep. "Do let me know if you require anything else," she murmurs, looking at him through her lashes. "Our cook goes easy on the salt, but don't hesitate to ask if you need something with more spice."

If she doesn't get her hands off him, I'm going to find the nearest salt dispenser and shove it up her—

"Thank you," he answers flatly.

I keep my gaze fixed on my cup. Pretending not to notice. Pretending it doesn't matter. But my fingers tighten around the stem of the goblet just the same.

Across from me, Dante catches my eye. And his lip fucking twitches. Like he's amused. Like he can sense my jealousy and it's fucking pleasing him.

But there's something else. A look in his eyes that reminds me of the night we spent together. My body warms.

That's right.

He doesn't need some desperate waitress to get his fill of spice. He's got me.

I hide my smirk in my cup and avert my eyes.

Farvis speaks again, turning his attention now to Ezra. "Would it be possible to predict the tsar's next move? Through maps or magic? Anything?"

Ezra lifts a brow, sipping from his cup before answering. "Magic rarely lends itself to straightforward strategy. But pattern, movement—those are things we can observe. If the beasts behave with any consistency, we may be able to anticipate the next strike."

"Then this tour must accomplish more than handshakes and gift-giving," Farvis mutters.

"Oh, we'll offer more than that," King Silas says, lifting his own goblet in a mock toast. "We'll remind them of Hedera's wealth, as well as its strength. After all, we've got Delasurvia's regiment, the most skilled in Terre Ferique. Knowing that, no ruler will wish to stand on the wrong side of a war."

Of course he would use his guardianship over me to claim an army that isn't his. But it's all part of his plan to strengthen Hedera. Aside from needing me to secure an heir, the king needs my regiment. And those are the only reasons he hasn't sent me away. He could easily find another noblewoman to procreate with his son, but my soldiers are unmatched

in skill, and he knows it.

Another platter of steamed greens and herb-roasted duck is set down, and I glance toward the fire. Its light plays against the flagstone floor, throwing dancing shapes along the walls like ghosts circling the room. As the conversation continues, the waitresses circle time and time again to refill our cups—especially Dante's. The voices blend in my head, and I find myself wishing I could shut them out.

After dinner, Nadya and I go back to our room and spend over an hour holding our stomachs and not moving. It's good to fill our bellies with warm food, but we may have overdone it.

After another hour, I'm feeling back to normal, and Nadya must be too because she's changing into one of the dresses she usually wears when she she's planning to see a lover.

"Don't tell me you're meeting up with that barkeep."

Nadya grins. "Okay. I won't tell you."

"He won you over with that drink, didn't he?"

"He had me the minute his eyes sparkled. No dressed-up drink necessary. Though the little cornflower was a sweet touch, don't you think?"

My heart flutters. "I prefer peonies."

Her brows draw together. "Okay. Anyway, I've got to go. He may or may not have hinted that that busty waitress would be joining us."

Hmm, well I guess the busty waitress took the hint that Dante wasn't interested.

"Cover for me," Nadya adds, "in case Indira comes looking."

I follow her to the door. "Absolutely."

She leaves, and after hooking the latch, I wander over to the window. The night sky is clear, and as I gaze at the sky, I get the feeling the stars twinkle brighter here than they do at Ivystone.

A gentle knock sounds at the door. I steel myself, thinking up a lie to tell Indira. Unless it's Nadya, having forgotten to douse herself with perfume. With a sigh, I stride across the room, unhooking the latch and pulling open the door.

But it's not Indira or Nadya.

Dante stands in the dimly lit hallway, his expression unreadable in the flickering glow of the lanterns.

I almost gasp, instinctively darting a glance past his shoulder to ensure no one sees him. "What are you doing?" I whisper, reaching for his sleeve and yanking him inside before anyone can take notice. The door clicks shut behind him as I turn, breath unsteady. "How did you get past Sir Greystone, Sir Holden, *and* Indira?"

He smirks, stepping closer. "I have my ways."

I narrow my eyes. "You used your glamour on them, didn't you?"

He doesn't answer—at least not with words. Instead, his hands come up to cradle the sides of my face, his palms warm against my skin. His gaze searches mine, dark and intent.

"I'm surprised you got this far," I say, yet I can't stop myself from arching into him. "I thought for sure at least one of those waitresses would have cornered you by now."

"Don't you know better by now?" His thumbs move in lazy circles on my jawline.

"What do you mean?"

"There isn't a person in the world who could keep me away from you."

And then his mouth is on mine.

His lips are warm, insistent, stealing the breath from my lungs before I even think to resist. My fingers tighten around the front of his tunic, torn between pulling him closer and pushing him away before Indira walks in on us.

But my resolve, my clear thinking, my cautiousness—it all shatters beneath the weight of this kiss. His hands slide back, threading into my hair where it's loosened from its pins, tilting my head as he deepens the kiss with aching reverence.

I let myself fall into it, into him, for just a moment. A moment where there are no titles, no mourning period, no prying eyes. Just Dante and me.

Then reality crashes back in.

With a sharp inhale, I press my palms against his chest and break

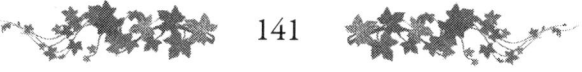

the kiss, stumbling back a step. This isn't his private room back at the castle. We're on the presentation tour now. There are too many factors that could ruin this for both of us. "Dante, we can't—"

"I know," he murmurs, his voice husky. But he doesn't move away. He gently brushes my hair from my shoulders, taking slow and steady breaths, like he's struggling to restrain himself. "I'll go."

He should, but those two words are like daggers to my gut.

His breath is uneven as he studies me, and my heart pounds against my ribs, my body still burning where his hands were. His gaze is locked on mine, as if waiting for me to agree with him, that it's best if he goes. If I tell him to leave, he will. But I can't seem to form the words.

Instead, I step forward, closing the distance between us, tilting my chin up just enough to meet his lips again. Just one more kiss. One small taste to get me through the night. A groan rumbles low in his throat, and then his arms are around me, strong and sure, one hand cupping the back of my head while the other splays across the small of my back, drawing me flush against him. His hard length presses against me through our clothes.

Heat flares through me like wildfire. I should stop this—I should pull away before it becomes impossible—but gods help me, I don't want to. His mouth moves against mine, slow at first, almost tentative, like he's savoring each stolen second before it's ripped away. But then his grip tightens, fingers tangling in my hair, and I melt into him, my hands wandering up his chest, over the firm muscle beneath his shirt.

He sucks in air through his teeth as my fingers trace the scar just above his ribs. His own hands move, skimming down my waist, gripping my hips like he's anchoring himself to me. His name is a whisper against my lips, reverent, like a plea.

His hands roam back to cup my ass. "Gods, Celeste. I don't know how I'm going to survive this tour without being able to touch you."

"If it's your sense of touch that's neglected, those waitresses were more than willing." My words are teasing, but I'm not sure they belie my lurking jealousy.

"You think I *wanted* their hands on me? It took every ounce of

control to not tell them to fuck off. To stand up and shout to the world that I belong to you. To say that, not only can they not have me, but no one else can have *you*."

The corner of my mouth ticks upward. "Lord Stregasi, we're not betrothed to each other quite yet."

"You think I give a fuck about semantics? You are mine." His hand glides between my legs, cupping me there and making me whimper. "This. Is mine."

I'm so hot and wet, and when his thumb strokes the bundle of sensitive nerves at my center, I gasp and push into him. "Fuck it." I throw my arms around his neck and grind into his fingers.

He lets out a deep moan as he devours me with kisses, and my head spins as he guides me backward, his hand still stroking my pussy.

A loud series of hammering thumps makes us freeze in place.

We jolt apart as the books Nadya had piled up on the nightstand tumble, hitting the wooden floor loudly and landing in a chaotic heap.

My pulse is still thrashing when, from the other side of the door, Indira's sharp voice calls out. "Your Highness? Are you all right?"

Dante's breath is ragged, his eyes dark with lingering heat as he looks at me. I press a hand to my chest, trying to will my heartbeat back to something resembling normal before answering. He slowly slides his fingers away from my core. My body is screaming with disappointment, but my brain slowly gains clarity.

"I'm fine." I force the words out evenly, still watching him. "Just— some books fell."

A pause. "Why is your door locked?"

Dante lifts a brow, amusement flickering across his face despite the tension still crackling between us.

"You know, um, safety? I didn't want any strangers walking in," I say smoothly, though my voice is a touch too breathless.

Indira doesn't sound convinced. "You should be sleeping, Your Highness. Shall I fetch you a tea?"

"Yes," I say quickly. "That would be—thank you, Indira."

I listen as her footsteps retreat down the hall, and the moment she's

gone, Dante exhales a quiet laugh, shaking his head.

"You're going to get us both killed," I jest.

"Worth it."

I swat at his arm playfully, then steel myself to release him. It's so hard to let him go, so hard to not get swept up in that storm brewing in those grey eyes. I swallow hard, still caught in the gravity of his gaze. He lifts a hand, brushing his knuckles across my cheek, and my breath hitches.

Then, before I can think better of it, I grab the front of his shirt, pulling him down into one last kiss.

It's slow, lingering, as if he's memorizing the feel of me before he forces himself to leave. When he pulls back, his forehead presses against mine for the span of a single breath, and then he's gone, slipping through the door before anyone is the wiser. I press my fingers to my lips, steadying myself, knowing these next couple of months are going to push me to my limits. *Gods help me.*

CHAPTER NINETEEN

I squint out the carriage window, holding a hand over my brow. The sun glares unforgivingly off the pristine white stone of Ironshield Keep in Podrosa, its towering walls smooth and unblemished, as if no enemy has ever dared lay siege to them. The fortress is impressive, a true testament to Podrosa's unwavering order—nothing out of place, nothing left to chance. Even the banners, deep crimson with the insignia of a silver sword pointing down, encircled with black thorns, ripple in the breeze at perfectly even intervals, as if the wind itself has been trained to obey the land's strict customs.

The moment my foot touches the ground outside the carriage, I feel the weight of expectation pressing down on me. I immediately school my expression into one of a sad princess.

A formation of Podrosan guards—Ironshields, as the guards are called—stands at rigid attention, their polished breastplates gleaming, their expressions carved from stone. Behind them, nobles line the courtyard in perfect rows, dressed in the deep reds and dark greys of their homeland. Not a single hem is out of place, not a single head tilts too far in curiosity. Even their bows and curtsies are uniform, executed with seamless precision. Almost as if they were machines.

This is a land that does not tolerate missteps.

At my side, Nadya exhales a low breath, barely audible over the rhythmic clang of the castle bells announcing our arrival. "They look like they'd march straight off a cliff if someone ordered them to."

I suppress a smirk, keeping my expression solemn as I sweep my gaze over the assembled court. She's not wrong. Podrosa has always been rigid, its people raised to follow rules above all else. Still, there is power in their discipline. They thrive on order, on absolute control, and I have no doubt their castle operates with the same ruthless efficiency.

The sound of boots crunching against the pale gravel draws my attention as the royal carriages in front of ours are tended to. A footman is at the king's carriage in an instant, opening the heavy door with the reverence one might use for a holy relic. King Silas steps down, draped in his customary black, the sun glinting off the golden threads woven through his tunic. Though his expression is neutral, his mere presence seems to draw every pair of Podrosan eyes, a ripple of tension threading through the crowd as if his reputation alone precedes him.

Queen Eleanor then disembarks her carriage, her veil short but dark, matching the folds of her somber gown. The breeze catches the edge of her sleeve, fluttering it like a warning flag, but she remains composed, chin slightly lifted. Her steps are light, but her face is harder than I remember—drawn tight, hollowed beneath the cheekbones.

Then Dante emerges. He moves like a shadow, stepping into place beside them, silent and composed, but even so, he is watched. Judged. The Podrosan court does not hide their curiosity the way the Hederan court pretends to. Their gaze follows his every move with an intensity that borders on calculation. He does not shrink from it. He meets it, eyes like storm light behind a curtain of dark lashes. Still, he spares a glance for me—fleeting, careful. But I catch it. And I carry it.

As the royals take their places a few paces in front of Nadya and me, the entire delegation begins to form a neat line of representatives. Hederan courtiers adjust their posture and fix their expressions into masks of civility. I fall into step with the rhythm of it—because I must.

A glance over my shoulder reveals the rest of the courtiers following us in a haphazard formation. Among them are Indira and the queen's maidservants as well as Ezra, who walks beside Farvis.

We ascend the stone steps, and mere seconds later, the great doors of the castle groan open on iron hinges. At the center of the entrance stands a beautiful woman around my age. Princess Orida Trevose, the only daughter of the Podrosan king and queen, holds her posture perfectly, the sleek fall of her golden hair catching the sunlight like polished silk. Her chin lifts imperceptibly as she surveys our party, cool elegance covering her like a second skin. Her gaze remains on Dante for a second longer, and I feel as if the judgment has already begun.

Beside her stands her cousin, Lord Marcos Trevose. His once-clean-shaven jaw is now framed by a neatly trimmed beard, just enough to lend a sculpted gravity to his otherwise-boyish features. I can't help but notice that it suits him. Gone is the awkward heir who once tripped over his own feet while presenting me a bundle of withering lilies. In his place is a man who stands with quiet confidence, shoulders squared beneath his finely tailored coat of burgundy.

Our eyes meet, and there's a pause, a flicker, like the moment before a page turns.

Something unreadable passes across his face—curiosity, perhaps. Hope. His gaze lingers just long enough for it not to be accidental. And when the corner of his mouth lifts in a slow, measured smile, I feel a ripple of unease stir at the base of my spine.

Not because he is unkind. But because I know that look.

A man testing the waters. Wondering if time and tragedy might have changed my mind. This was the man whom I rejected for Torbin. If I had decided differently, I would be standing at his side now, as his bride.

Though I didn't choose him, the look on Marcos's face tells me his offer is still on the table. Only, he wouldn't be able to broach the subject while I'm in mourning. Not that it would do any good, anyway. King Silas has already nipped that idea in the bud.

I remind myself that Marcos doesn't know about Dante or the king's plan. No one outside of a select circle does.

147

They have no idea about the engagement the king has yet to announce.

They have no idea about the kiss that still lingers in my thoughts like the echo of a song I can't quite shake.

Still, there is something in Marcos's expression that softens the edges of what I remember. He doesn't leer. He doesn't posture. He only watches—measured, polite. Disciplined.

As our ensemble lines up, Dante realigns himself until he's at my side. The firm line of his jaw tightens ever so slightly, and I realize he's noticed Marcos staring at me. I feel the simmer of Dante's attention, the subtle shift in the air between us.

You are mine.

I bite back the smile that emerges with the memory of his words.

"King Silas, Queen Eleanor," Princess Orida says, her voice smooth and formal as she dips into a curtsey. She wears the same severity as her courtiers, her gown a deep garnet with no embellishments. "Welcome to Podrosa. My father and mother await your presence in the great hall." Her gaze flickers briefly to Dante and me before returning to the king. "If you will follow me."

Without waiting for a response, she turns sharply on her heel, leading us through the towering corridor.

The moment I step inside Ironshield Keep, I feel it in the air, woven into the very stone beneath my feet. The courtiers standing in two perfect rows along the great corridor hold their spines ramrod straight, their hands clasped neatly behind their backs. Not a single strand of hair is out of place, not a single garment wrinkled or out of alignment.

Their fashion mirrors the rigid order of their kingdom—long, high-collared coats for the men, not a lapel or cuff out of place. The women wear modestly-fitted bodices with structured skirts that fall to their ankles, the fabric stiff and unyielding. Dark colors dominate, navy and charcoal and deep crimson, with not a single hint of excess ornamentation. I see no jewelry on anyone. Nothing unnecessary. Nothing indulgent.

Even their hair is styled with meticulous precision, the men's

cropped close, the women's either bound in tightly coiled braids or twisted into severe buns, nonetheless covered with a coif. No loose strands. No softness.

And none of them makes a sound.

If not for the methodical clicks of their polished boots against the pristine marble floor, I might believe them to be statues rather than people. Their expressions remain carefully neutral, not a single whisper exchanged between them. Even their bows, as we pass them in the corridor, are identical, dipping their heads at the same precise angle before straightening in unison.

Podrosa's castle reflects the strictness of its people. The walls, made of pale limestone, are unadorned, save for banners of the royal crest. No paintings. No unnecessary embellishments. The floors are pristine marble, so polished, they gleam under the chandelier's glow, and every door we pass is of thick, dark wood reinforced with iron. Even the guards standing at their posts appear sculpted from stone, eyes forward, hands firm on the hilts of their swords.

The grandeur is undeniable, but it is an imposing kind of beauty, meant to inspire obedience rather than awe.

And it makes me want to fucking squirm.

As we approach the great hall, the enormous doors are pushed open in perfect synchrony, revealing the thrones at the far end of the chamber. King Harold and Queen Agatha sit with absolute authority, their attire mirroring their subjects—structured, impeccable, and utterly devoid of warmth.

"Your Majesties," Princess Orida announces, her arm sweeping wide. "King Silas Copperhammer, Queen Eleanor, and the Hederan court."

King Harold's gaze sweeps over us, assessing. Calculating. Then he gestures for us to step forward, and the weight of the room settles heavily on my shoulders.

The king and queen sit on matching ebony thrones raised upon a dais. King Harold is as severe as his surroundings—a broad-shouldered man with black hair cut close to his scalp. His square jaw is clean-shaven,

lips pressed into a firm line that does little to soften the chill in his pale-grey eyes. At his side, Queen Agatha is a study in perfect composure. Her dark-brown hair is pulled into a flawless knot at the nape of her neck. Both king and queen sit with their backs rigid, their expressions unreadable.

King Silas strides forward, every step echoing through the hall. His black robes brush the floor behind him, the gold embroidery glinting under the light as he bows his head with measured respect. "Your Majesties," he says, his voice deep and authoritative, carrying effortlessly in the vast chamber. "It is an honor to stand once more before the esteemed rulers of Podrosa. Though many years have passed since our last meeting, I hold the memory of your hospitality with the highest regard."

A long, heavy silence follows his words. Podrosans value ceremony above all else—it would be an insult to interrupt their king's measured consideration. When King Harold finally inclines his head, the movement is slow and deliberate, as if weighed by the weight of duty. "Hedera's presence honors our court, King Silas," he replies. His voice is low and even, each syllable clipped with precision.

I notice that Queen Agatha doesn't speak up, only giving a solitary nod in agreement with her husband.

Silas stretches out his arms to free them from his cloak. "Today, I come before you not only to formally present my son Dante, but to reaffirm the alliance and cooperation between our lands."

"We receive you in the spirit of peace and would first like to extend our condolences on the death of your son Torbin."

"You are very kind, Your Majesty. Thank you."

I almost shudder. It seems so cold, so devoid of emotion. It's hard to believe either of them is actually sincere. I glance at Queen Eleanor, whose gaze is trained on the floor.

King Silas's lips curl faintly at the corners and with a wave of his hand, his attendants step forward, carrying heavy coffers they set in front of the dais. "As a sign of appreciation for allowing us to have an audience with you, we have brought you tokens of our gratitude."

150

The first is a chest of polished blackwood, its surface inlaid with veins of silver. Silas steps toward it, opening the lid himself as if only he has the power to do so. I stretch my neck a bit, but not enough to be noticed.

"Finely crafted steel," King Silas announces. "Ceremonial blades forged by the finest Hederan smiths, each one engraved with the insignia of both kingdoms entwined—a gesture of unity."

King Harold's brow lifts by the smallest fraction, and when one of his guards steps forward to examine the craftsmanship, I catch a flicker of approval behind his stern mask.

"For your archives," Silas continues, gesturing to a second offering. "A bound collection of maps—each painstakingly detailed—outlining the trade routes between our realms and beyond." The parchment gleams with fresh ink.

Ezra is called to the front, and it is his duty to bring the item to Queen Agatha. She accepts it with a graceful nod, her long fingers tracing the elegant leather binding before passing it to an attendant.

Two of Silas's men step forward, carrying a velvet-lined trunk carved with Hedera's crest. When they unlatch it and ease the lid open, the torches around the room seem to dim in comparison to what rests inside.

I blink in surprise.

Dragon scales.

I step forward instinctively, drawn by the shimmering contrast within. One is pale gold—no, not gold, something more radiant. A yellowish white like the heart of the sun, with a sheen that dances as the light shifts. The other is darker—blue-black, like midnight ink spilled across glass, with an iridescent halo at the edges that makes it look like the stars have taken root in its surface. Each scale is about the size of a soldier's breastplate.

A sun dragon and a moon dragon. It was only a few days ago when Nadya regaled me with the tale.

I can't be sure that the dragons these came from were actually sun and moon dragons, but still, my throat tightens. I've never seen anything like them before. Delasurvia doesn't deal in dragon scales. We trade in

 151

coin and gold and well-earned respect.

It's hard for me to grasp the idea that Silas would part with such treasures. I wonder if he truly values the alliance, or if this is merely the smallest edge of the hoard he holds. Somehow, I suspect it's the latter.

"For the throne of Podrosa," Silas says smoothly, his tone practiced, regal. "A token of trust from Hedera. Scales retrieved and preserved from the great age before the dragons fell. May they serve as a reminder of strength and dependability."

King Harold's eyes narrow slightly as he regards the scales, the way one might study a weapon instead of a gift. I might be imagining it, but I swear he shifts forward, almost as if he wants to stand but is holding himself back. He nods once. Queen Agatha says nothing, but she visibly swallows as her gaze lingers on the scales.

And I... I can't stop looking at them. The way one glows like fire. The way the other drinks in the light like shadow.

The king and queen exchange a glance—brief but filled with unspoken meaning—before King Harold speaks again. "Hedera's gifts are generous, King Silas. We accept them in good faith." His words are as rigid as his posture, but the slight dip of his chin signals the closest thing to gratitude one can expect from the ruler of Podrosa. "And we will extend our hospitality, as is proper. Our chamberlain will show you to the rooms we've readied for the duration of your visit."

Before the chamberlain can step forward, Queen Agatha inclines her head with the elegance of someone born to diplomacy. "Princess Celeste," she begins, her voice soft but clear, like still water over glass.

I curtsey to her in greeting. "Your Majesty."

"I would like to express my sorrow to you on the loss of your brother," she says. "King Bennett was always an honorable man when we met with him, and you have our sympathy."

It takes me a second to find my voice. "I'm much appreciative, Your Majesty."

Her smile is perfectly measured, touched with warmth, but not too much. "Should any of you require anything—fresh linens, tailored garments, a bath drawn to your liking—our staff is at your disposal.

Dinner will begin promptly at seven. We hope that will give you ample time to rest and prepare."

"Then we can begin the main event tomorrow," King Harold adds. "Bright and early."

The main event'? I suddenly fear the Podrosan royals plan to parade Dante through the streets of their land for everyone to judge.

King Silas offers a gracious nod. "Your hospitality is appreciated."

Queen Eleanor inclines her head to her, the softest of smiles gracing her lips.

As the courtiers begin to shift and the room starts to loosen its rigid spine, I turn just enough to glance behind me. Lord Marcos, still standing off to the side, meets my eyes. He gives me a polite, wordless nod—just enough to be noticed, not enough to be scolded for presumption.

The chamberlain steps forward with a bow. "If you'll follow me."

Beside me, Nadya leans closer, her voice barely above a whisper. "This place is like one long rulebook come to life."

Dante shifts into motion, but before he takes his place beside his father, he casts me a silent look. *Mine.*

It's so hard to not smile as I fall into step with the rest of the royal party. The sound of our boots echoes faintly through the cold halls of Ironshield Keep. A fortress that doesn't bend. A castle built to demand control—and crush anyone foolish enough to test its rules.

As I cast one last look at the coffers in front of the dais, a thought occurs to me. The fine gifts King Silas brought to the Podrosan royals might not be symbols of gratitude for their hospitality. Knowing the lengths Silas would go to in order to get his way, I don't think it would be wrong to call those gifts a bribe.

CHAPTER TWENTY

here's nothing special about the room I'm given at Ironshield Keep. The walls are plain concrete, there are no curtains framing the windows, and the bedsheets are a boring white. Aside from one side table next to the bed and one cushionless, wooden chair, the room is devoid of furniture. There isn't even a mirror for me to check my reflection, and I don't have Nadya to let me know if I have bags under my eyes because they've separated us.

At least there's a fireplace to keep the room warm, though this one looks as if it hasn't been used in ages.

I probably should rest, but the room is too dull and so compact that I feel the walls closing in around me. After I've paced the room ten times, I know I have to break out of its confines. My body has been in a state of rest for too long, trapped in a carriage not spacious enough to stand in, and this place isn't much bigger than that. My muscles need attention, and I need to hone my skills.

When I open the door, Sir Holden glances at me from his post.

"Your Highness?"

"Sir Holden, I need to train." I keep my eyes on him, steeling myself

for an argument, but none comes.

"Let me see what I can do." With a curt nod, he turns and marches down the corridor.

Thankful that the servants already delivered my trunks to my room—and surprised that they fit—I search for some trousers and a tunic I know I can move in. I'm expected to be wearing my mourning dress, so I pull my long cloak over my clothes and fasten it in case I come across anyone in the castle.

But I can't take another minute in this room, so I head for the hall. When I open the door, I'm met with a familiar face. My eyes widen, first from surprise that she's standing at my door, and second because of the significant swell of her belly.

"Marette?" I step out to greet the woman who used to be engaged to my brother.

Before he died.

Before he succumbed to a madness that she didn't know how to handle.

She dips into a partial curtsey, her hand on her abdomen. "Your Highness."

"No, please. It's just 'Celeste.'"

We were never so formal when she lived at the castle in Delasurvia. It's why I didn't call her *Lady* Marette. She was meant to be my sister-in-law. And up until she called off her engagement to my brother, we'd become close.

I don't blame her for leaving. The madness that claimed Bennett was a frightening thing to watch. There's still a chance it could claim me. I can only hope that this buzzing feeling that runs through me when it chooses to means I've escaped the madness. But I guess that's yet to be seen.

"I apologize for not being present for your arrival," she begins. "I wasn't feeling well and was bedridden."

"Don't apologize." I glance at her belly. "When will the baby be born?"

"One month yet." There's a soft smile on her face that tells me she's

happy. Whatever life she has now, whichever man she's with, she seems to have found her happiness. After a moment, her smile falters. "Celeste, I'm sorry about Bennett."

She means more than his passing, I think. I can see it in the way her head dips and her gaze goes to the floor. She might not regret leaving my brother, but she still carries the guilt.

"Thank you," I respond, reaching out to squeeze her hand.

Her voice lowers. "I did love him, you know."

"I know." I could tell. It wasn't just about the crown. She would have made a fine queen, a devoted wife, and any child she would have carried by him would have been in line for the crown instead of me.

"You haven't had an easy year, have you?" She gives a slight shake of her head. "The attacks, Bennett, and now Prince Torbin. I'm not sure how you're holding it together."

"Honestly, neither am I."

I know she assumes I'm sad about Torbin being dead. If only she knew the reality. That he betrayed his kingdom and is a pawn in the Shadow Tsar's twisted plan.

Could I tell her? Would she believe me? Or would she think I've gone mad like her brother? Or worse, would she report what I tell her to her king? Or mine. Silas would never forgive me for that, and he would most likely punish Delasurvia for it.

"It was kind of King Silas to claim guardianship over you," she says. "And I'm glad he brought you along on his son's presentation tour so I could get this chance to see you."

I pull my cloak tighter around myself. "I'm glad I got the chance to see you, too."

We hear footfalls and turn to see Sir Holden approaching.

"That's my Royal Ward," I tell her.

She nods. "I'll let you go, then. But we'll meet again tonight at dinner."

"Seven sharp," I say, but I doubt she hears the mockery in my voice.

She flashes me a small smile before walking away.

"Who was that?" Sir Holden asks once she's out of earshot.

"Lady Marette. An old friend." I let out a breath. "Ready?"

"Follow me."

After leading me through what feels like endless corridors, Sir Holden pushes open a heavy, wooden door. His expression is unreadable as dust motes swirl in the golden shafts of afternoon light spilling through the tall windows of a large room. The air inside is thick with disuse, the scent of aged wood and forgotten history hovering like a ghost.

"This is the best I could do," he mutters, stepping aside so I can enter. "No one's used this wing of the castle in years. You should be undisturbed."

I take a slow breath, relief settling into my bones. "Thank the gods. I was going to die of boredom otherwise."

The room is cavernous, lined with old wooden chairs stacked against the far wall, their upholstery long faded. A few broken weapons hang on rusted mounts above an empty hearth, relics of battles long past. But the floors are sturdy, the space wide enough for movement, and the windows flood the room with warmth despite the thick stone walls.

It will do.

Sir Holden stays near the door, arms folded, his gaze sweeping the hall like a sentry on post. "Just try not to break anything. Or yourself."

"No promises." I shrug off my cloak, already feeling the itch in my muscles.

I stretch first, arms overhead, twisting my torso until my spine pops satisfyingly. Then I drop to the floor, boots scuffing wood, and knock out a series of push-ups. The first dozen come easy, but by the twentieth, my shoulders burn in a way I've missed. I push harder, switching to knuckle push-ups, then clapping between them, the slap of my palms echoing in the hollow space. Sweat beads at my brow, but it feels good to shake off the stiffness of days trapped in that carriage.

When I rise, Sir Holden lifts an eyebrow, as if quietly impressed, but he doesn't comment. He just steps farther into the room, beginning to unwrap the cloth bundle of practice blades he brought.

The door creaks, and a slow clap punctuates the air.

I glance over my shoulder, pulse hitching even before I see him.

Dante leans against the doorway, arms crossed over his chest, dark hair tousled, his black tunic fitting snugly over broad shoulders. There's a familiar glint in his eye, but something sharper beneath it, and when his gaze drops briefly to my chest, then back up, I realize he's noticed more than my warm-up.

"You're slipping," he says, pushing off the frame, his voice smooth but edged. "Endurance like that will only get you halfway through a fight."

I smirk. "I'll keep that in mind next time I'm climbing castle stairs in full armor."

"I know ways to strengthen your muscles," he adds, circling me now. "If you'd let me show you."

Sir Holden, no doubt sensing what's coming, places the collection of weapons in my hands before letting out a grumble and heading for the door. "I'll be outside, trying not to roll my eyes."

He shuts the door behind him, leaving me alone with Dante's lingering stare.

"You're suddenly the expert when it comes to my training?" I challenge, picking out a dulled dagger to practice with, one that isn't sharp enough to pierce skin.

"You could say that I've been studying your moves." He takes a matching dagger from the collection and places the rest of the weapons on a nearby stool.

"I haven't had any complaint about my moves before," I say, taking a defensive stance as he nears.

"No complaints, Highness. Merely... suggestions."

Without warning, he lunges. I pivot, but he's already grabbing for my waist, spinning me before I can find my footing. His grip is sure but not bruising, his hands dragging heat along my sides. I twist free, elbowing his ribs, and dart a couple of steps away.

"You're distracted," he taunts.

"You're smug," I snap, pouncing forward to sweep his leg.

He jumps it, damn him, and catches my arm mid-spin, yanking me

 158

close.

For a heartbeat, our bodies are flush—his chest rising and falling against mine, our breath shared between barely an inch of space.

"You're slow to react," he murmurs, his gaze flicking to my mouth.

"Maybe I just don't want to bruise that pretty face of yours," I retort.

He chuckles as I shove off his chest, and we circle again. My body is awake now, alive in every tendon and nerve. I fake left, then duck, and jab the hilt of the dagger into his side. He stumbles back, catching himself with an arm, but he pivots quickly in a move that places him behind me, his dagger at my neck.

I decide to play dirty and push my ass into him. The distraction pays off, and when he hesitates, I grab his wrist and twist, twirling my body away as I disarm him.

He smirks and shakes his head, but it only takes a second before he ducks and rushes me, dodging my swiping blade, wrapping his arms around my waist and using the momentum to knock me off my feet.

I instinctively use a countermove, pinning my knees to hips and pushing one of his shoulders back until I've flipped him onto his back. Now my dagger is at his neck as I look down at him, my hair falling loose from my braid like a curtain over his face.

For a heartbeat, we just stare at each other, chests rising and falling, breath mingling.

"Looks like I win," I say.

His smirk returns, and he runs hot palms up my hips before caressing the curves of my ass. "I beg to differ."

He's right—I'm distracted when he slides his hand around my waist and spins us until he's on top of me. His face is so close, his storm-grey eyes darker now, his mouth parted just slightly. My heart thunders, demanding things I don't dare give into here.

He leans down, just enough that his nose brushes the side of mine, and my breath stutters. I think he's going to kiss me, but instead, he lets out a sigh.

"We need to get ready for the dinner," he says lowly, his voice rough.

I almost groan. I'm hungry now, but not for dinner.

He pushes himself to standing, then offers me his hand. Reluctantly, I take it, and he pulls me up, steady and close.

Trying to clear my head from the glorious feel of Dante's body pressed into me, I take a breath and a much-needed step back. "So, what do you think of Podrosa?"

"It's as stiff and unforgiving as I remember."

"You've been here before?" I know he must have traveled through Podrosa when he moved from Messanya to Hedera, but that didn't mean he'd spent any time here.

"On a couple of occasions," he says "But never for long."

I almost ask him if he's ever bedded any women here, but I decide I don't want to know. Instead, I sway the conversation elsewhere. "The king and queen seemed open to welcoming you. I wonder what this 'main event' they spoke of entails."

His chin dips a bit, his eyes far away for a moment, and I wonder if he's worried about making the right impression on the tour. "I'm sure it's nothing extraordinary. Podrosa doesn't care for veering from the norm."

"I've noticed." I offer him a supportive smile. "In any case, I'm sure you'll win them over with your charm—magical or otherwise."

The corner of his mouth inches upward, but before he can reply, Sir Holden enters the room. "Sorry to interrupt, but Sir Donovan is headed this way."

I give Sir Holden a thankful nod.

Dante takes my hand, surprising me when he lifts it to his lips and gently kisses my knuckles. "I'll see you at dinner, Highness." He releases me and quickly turns, leaving me in the sun-warmed silence.

CHAPTER TWENTY-ONE

The grand dining room of Podrosa is as severe and disciplined as the rest of the castle. The vaulted ceiling arches high above, its heavy beams polished to a near-black sheen. No elaborate chandeliers hang here. Instead, wrought-iron sconces line the walls at even intervals, casting a clean, bright light without a hint of warmth. The walls themselves are slate grey, unadorned but for a singular crest of Podrosa displayed above the far wall—a silver sword and black thorns on a field of crimson. Precision defines everything in this space. The long dining tables, crafted from solid oak, are arranged in rigid lines, their polished surfaces free of any embellishment beyond the crisp, white linens. Servants move about the room with quiet efficiency, their faces expressionless as they place silverware with near-mathematical exactness. Not a movement is wasted. Each step they take is practiced, as if choreographed.

A subtle tension tightens across my shoulders the moment I notice the arrangement of the tables. Men occupy one side of the room, while women sit separately on the other, divided by a narrow aisle. It strikes me as strange—outdated, even—but here in Podrosa, the adherence to tradition is as unyielding as the stone walls around us.

We step farther into the dining hall, the air heavy with the scent of roasted meats and boiled potatoes. Men and women already file into their assigned places.

Nadya leans toward me, her brows raised in disbelief as we approach the table reserved for women. "I take it back," she murmurs under her breath. "This place isn't a rulebook. It's a prison sentence."

I stifle a laugh, biting the inside of my cheek, until a familiar voice halts me mid-step.

"Princess Celeste."

I turn.

Lord Marcos Trevose stands just to my left, his crisp attire immaculate, the dark blue of his coat lined with silver embroidery that matches the signet ring on his finger. He looks every inch the polished nobleman, yet there's a flicker of warmth in his eyes that softens the sharpness of his features.

"My condolences," he says, bowing his head slightly. "I cannot imagine the weight of your losses."

I incline my chin, keeping my expression appropriately solemn. "Thank you," I say gently, the words stiff in my throat. "It's been… difficult."

His eyes study me for a beat too long, as if searching for the truth beneath my carefully composed exterior. "If you ever find yourself in need of someone to speak with, I hope you'll consider me." He pauses, then adds, "My best friend died in the southern campaign last year. It changes you—grief. Leaves a mark no one else can see."

The honesty in his voice catches me off guard.

"I'm sorry," I murmur, meaning it. "I hadn't heard."

He gives a faint smile. Tired, not bitter. "Few did. He wasn't a prince or a commander. Just someone who mattered to me." He straightens slightly. "Loss can be… easier when it's shared."

Something in my chest tightens. I realize he'd been grieving when his family proposed our engagement, and I probably didn't make things better by rejecting him. I don't know how to respond to him, so I simply

nod.

Behind him, movement catches my eye. Dante sits at the king's table, facing me. His gaze is fixed on Marcus for a moment, but his expression is unreadable. The flicker of a raised brow is the only indication he's watching. No rigidity in his shoulders, no twitch in his jaw. But I know him well enough by now to recognize the restraint in his silence.

I force my expression to remain neutral. I am mourning. And I'm not supposed to be gazing at the future prince.

Marcos follows my gaze, and when he sees where it's landed, his brow lifts slightly—not in amusement, but in curiosity. Luckily, Dante has already turned his head, answering some question Ezra has asked.

"It's been a long time since someone's gone through legitimization," he says, his voice low and thoughtful. "I wonder if Lord Stregasi is truly up to the challenge."

I blink, caught off guard. "'Challenge'?" I echo, careful to keep my tone neutral. "I imagine he's as prepared as anyone could be."

There's a wrinkle of his brow, but Marcos doesn't press. The corner of his mouth tilts again in something almost contemplative. "I suppose we'll find out soon enough."

"Excuse us, cousin," Princess Orida says as she approaches along with his sister, Lady Marette.

When he bows and steps aside, they glide toward their seats like a gentle breeze wrapped in silk.

Marcos steps back farther, his hand resting briefly over his heart in a silent farewell. "Enjoy your evening, Princesses," he says, then he turns, nods to his sister, and makes his way to the men's table, his steps even and composed.

I take my seat beside Nadya, spine straight, lips tight, and allow the mask to fall back into place. Nadya shoots me a quick look, her brows raised, having obviously listened in on my conversation with Marcos.

Taking one more glance around the dining hall, it stuns me that no one objects to the women being separated from the men. Even the king and queen do not sit together. I turn to Orida, wondering how she feels

 163

about the custom. "Is it always like this?" I ask, keeping my voice light. "The separate tables, I mean."

Her pale brows lift slightly, as though the question surprises her. "Of course," she replies, her tone as even and measured as everything else in Podrosa. "Men and women have distinct roles in our society. Each knows their place, and we do not blur those lines. It is the way it has always been."

"And no one ever questions that?" Nadya presses, her dark eyes sparkling with barely concealed curiosity.

Princess Orida offers a serene smile that does not reach her eyes. "What is there to question? Tradition keeps our kingdom strong. In Podrosa, we do not mistake novelty for progress."

I don't miss the faint edge in her voice, the subtle correction lurking beneath her words. This is how things are. This is how they will remain. I bite back the urge to challenge her, reminding myself that we are here to strengthen alliances, not debate the merits of gender roles.

I glance at Marette, who runs a smoothing hand over her belly. She simply smiles at me, as if to say she accepts the tradition. I return the gesture and give her a nod. After all, she seems happy, and who am I to argue that she shouldn't be?

As the first course arrives, my focus shifts to the food placed in front of us. The presentation is orderly and plain. Nothing decadent or excessive. No exotic spices or elaborate garnishes. Just practical, functional sustenance. A platter of roasted chicken, neatly carved and portioned. Steamed root vegetables arranged in rows of perfect symmetry. A simple barley stew, the aroma hearty but unremarkable. Even the bread is cut into identical slices—thick and sturdy rather than soft or sweet.

I glance at Nadya, who eyes her plate with the same bewilderment I feel. "At least we won't starve," she whispers, spearing a carrot with a deliberate jab of her fork. "Though I can't promise I won't die of boredom."

A flicker of amusement warms my chest, but it fades as I lift my gaze across the aisle again. Dante is speaking with one of the Podrosan lords,

his face calm, though I sense the restraint beneath it. The men surrounding him seem intent on scrutinizing every word, as if measuring his worth against some invisible standard. Another leans in, asking a question I cannot hear, and Dante answers with the smooth charm that comes so naturally to him. Yet something about the way the Podrosan nobles observe him unsettles me. It is not mere curiosity. It feels like an evaluation—an interrogation disguised as polite conversation.

I only catch snippets, especially when King Harold addresses King Silas, but I don't dare let on that I'm listening.

"I do want to commend you on your decision to terminate refugee intake at the Delasurvian border," King Harold says. "Uncontrolled migration leads to instability, which no realm can afford to endure. Especially when our enemies strategize against us."

I grip the handle of my fork, my knuckles turning white from squeezing it, all while keeping the irritation out of my expression.

"Yes, these measures are necessary," King Silas replies. "I've doubled our forces at the borders of both Hedera and Delasurvia."

"Was that decision made before the recent carnoraxis attack at your castle, or the result of it?"

I sneak a glance at the king, whose jaw stiffens at King Harold's question. "It's an ongoing campaign," Silas says. "We are constantly correcting any miscalculations our scouts have reported. The progression to perfection takes practice, as they say."

I almost let out a groan, knowing the king is taking no such measures.

For a fleeting moment, my gaze lands on Dante. Our eyes lock, and he licks his lips after sipping his wine. The noise of the dining hall recedes, leaving only the heat coiling low in my stomach. I grip the edge of the table to steady myself, longing to cross the distance between us. But here, under the weight of so many watching eyes, that is impossible.

A movement beside me draws my attention back to Princess Orida, who observes my lingering gaze with an expression of cool detachment. "The future prince appears to make quite the impression," she comments, though her tone is unreadable.

"He has a talent for that," I reply, forcing a polite smile.

"Once he's legitimized, he could make a good match," Marette interjects.

My breath gets stuck in my throat. Did she see the look Dante and I shared? Will she say something to the king that might shatter the ruse we're being forced to engage in?

But then I see that she hasn't said it to me, but to Princess Orida. The princess gives her a hint of a smile but quickly schools her features. "It's too soon to speculate," Orida says. "He must first endure the tour, and for that, I wish him success."

Nadya and I exchange a glance, and she bites her cheek before lifting her glass to hide her face. I should have guessed that the realms would see a new prince as an opportunity to unite the kingdoms through marriage. The thought pricks at my skin in an intolerable way, even though I know King Silas would never let that happen.

Would he?

CHAPTER TWENTY-TWO

It is early morning when we are invited to the Podrosan tournament grounds, as they call it. It looks more like a huge outdoor arena to me, with a semi-circle of tiered viewing benches that look out over the expansive space. To the left and right of the seating area, high stone walls are draped in banners of deep crimson and black. The scent of warm earth and polished steel lingers in the air, mingling with the distant clamor of the city beyond.

I sit between Nadya and Queen Eleanor in the shaded viewing box, the heavy folds of my mourning gown pooling at my feet, suffocating in the midday heat. The sun beats down from a cloudless sky, glaring against the pale stone walls of the arena and forcing me to squint through the brightness. Sweat trickles between my shoulder blades beneath the velvet, and I can already feel a dull ache building behind my eyes.

The Podrosan court is gathered around us—nobles draped in plain, red attire, guards stiff and alert along the stone perimeter, courtiers whispering into gloved hands. Just below our viewing box, Lord Marcos Trevose stands among the other lords. His outer robe is a shade deeper than the Podrosan crimson, belted in polished onyx that glints when he

167

turns toward the sun. Silver embroidery coils at his cuffs and collar, etched in symbols of his house—a mark of old nobility.

He notices me watching and offers a shallow nod, the corner of his mouth lifting in that familiar, measured smile. Respectful. Thoughtful. Perhaps still hopeful.

I look away quickly, my gaze shifting to the arena—but his words return to me in a murmur, low and uncertain: *I wonder if Lord Stregasi is up to the challenge.*

At the time, I'd assumed he meant the diplomacy. The scrutiny. The maneuvering through a foreign court built on brittle, ancient pride. But now, as my eyes adjust to the brightness and take in the mountainous course beyond the arena sand, my stomach twists.

This isn't politics; this is a trial.

The arena sprawls wide and open, a vast expanse of packed earth enclosed by towering stone walls. But beyond that lies the true test—the mountainside itself, carved into a brutal gauntlet of obstacles meant to break even the most seasoned warriors.

Wooden beams stretch at precarious angles, forming narrow platforms that jut like broken teeth from the rock face. Thick ropes hang from overhanging ledges, some coiled taut, others swaying lazily in the breeze. Jagged outcroppings form handholds—but I could swear their surfaces are rough, perhaps even sharp. This place feels like a trap disguised as a challenge.

I blink and glance to the left, where the Podrosan king stands speaking with a man in uniform—a soldier, but not like the others. His skin glows faintly golden under the sun, and when he raises a hand, the very rock beneath the lowest section of the course shudders. The stone settles, reshapes. Earth magic.

My throat tightens. He's fae. And loyal to the Podrosan court.

They built this course with more than muscle in mind.

I turn my attention to the center of the arena, where Dante stands, his dark tunic clinging to him like it's painted on. He rolls his shoulders back and stretches his fingers, the tendons in his forearms catching the light. I follow the movement of his throat as he swallows. Steady.

 168

Focused.

Did he know this trial awaited him? Whether he did or didn't, there's no turning back now. Everything is riding on this. Not just his title. His worth. His name. His future.

And mine.

I glance over my shoulder and catch sight of Ezra, whose hand rubs at his chin, his brow wrinkled as he studies the rock face. He spots me and tries to give me a reassuring nod, but I know there's no confidence behind it.

For a brief moment, my focus lands on Princess Orida. She leans forward, a faint smile on her face as she stares at Dante. She shifts in her seat, her hand coming up to wave in an effort to get his attention, but he doesn't notice her. But she doesn't let it bother her. She whispers something to the lady beside her, and they both modestly hide their mouths behind their hands.

A hush falls as King Harold steps forward, his voice ringing out over the crowd.

"In Podrosa, we do not crown a man untested." He inclines his head to King Silas, who returns the nod. Then he gestures toward the mountainside. "This is the path that forges warriors. Every soldier in my army has proven himself upon these stones. And any man fit enough to call himself *prince* must prove the same."

There is a beat of silence that seems to stretch on.

"The Ironshields of Podrosa are famous for their accurate aim with an arrow. The objective of this trial is to hit a bullseye on the target at the top of the ridge. But first, Lord Stregasi, you must climb."

My eyes shift back to the mountainside. One of the overhanging ledges shifts, making the ropes sway. I glance back at the fae, who waves his hand in a swiping motion, guiding the rock formation. This isn't fair. The fae has no doubt been instructed to make the structure impossible to ascend.

"If you reach the summit," King Harold continues, "you will have to best one of my finest warriors in order to retrieve the bow and arrow, which await you." A faint grin pulls at the corners of his mouth. "If you

get that far, you merely need to hit the target dead center to finish the trial."

Tension tightens like a drawstring around the entire arena.

Dante gives a small nod. "Simple enough, Your Majesty."

He says it in jest, but I can feel the aggravation in his tone. The bell tolls and he launches forward.

A gust of dust lifts behind him as his boots hit the earth, racing for the base of the course. The first incline is a cruel mess of wooden slats unevenly jammed into the mountain's surface—meant to mimic steps but spaced like a snare. He climbs fast, barely slowing as he leaps from one to the next. A slat cracks beneath him, but he's already moving, catching a higher ledge.

He reaches for the next grip—his fingers land, hold, swing. The crowd murmurs. A sharp breath leaves me as he narrowly avoids another collapsing beam. But when he grabs hold of the stone grip above him, the mountain shakes and the grip disappears into the cliff face.

I gasp as Dante's body swings down, almost slipping from the first grip, but he holds fast and manages to grasp the edge of a plank to his right. Using his upper body strength, Dante pulls himself up onto the platform.

The first split in the course looms ahead. There are only two options: left or right. From our vantage, I see the flaw—the central beam of the right platform is cracked at the root. The moment he steps on it, it will break away.

My heart slams against my ribs. I lean forward, fingers clawing into the edge of my seat. He stretches out his right arm.

No. No, not that one.

"Go left," I whisper.

But my mind isn't whispering. It's screaming.

"Go left. Go left, Dante—"

A flash of pain lances behind my eyes, hot and piercing. I wince, clutching my temples. The world wavers slightly around me, my breath catching.

Dante pauses mid-motion. His head turns—just a fraction—

toward me.

A strange sensation zips across my skin, like static, or a hum, or... awareness. As though something in him absorbed my words.

Then he moves.

He jumps left.

The right platform collapses a breath later, exploding in a rain of splintered wood and stone.

Nadya's hand tightens on mine.

My stomach twists. Did I... help him?

I shake my head, but the pressure behind my eyes grows sharper, blooming into something deeper, heavier. My vision swims for a second, but I blink it away.

He keeps climbing.

The next section demands a leap toward a dangling rope. He doesn't hesitate—just leaps, catches, swings. His boots skim the air as he ascends, each pull of his arms drawing him higher, the rope swinging violently from his momentum.

Then comes the wall. A slick stretch of rock, sheer and cruel. The final ascent. Dante grabs the lowest crevice, hauls himself upward. His muscles strain, neck corded, sweat glistening along his jaw.

The fae by the king waves his hand through the air, and the mountainside shudders.

Dante slips.

"No," I gasp, rising slightly in my seat.

I don't think. I just feel.

Raw energy rises inside me, clawing for release. I shove it forward.

A pulse bursts out—vibrating through my bones and through my skin. And Dante's body shifts, swinging upward so that his hand catches hold of the crevice. I let out a breath, knowing the pulse I sent was enough. Just enough.

He strains to pull himself up. As I focus on his efforts, a sharp, wet sting blooms in my nostrils. I swipe at my upper lip—and come away with blood. I stare at it, stunned.

"Celeste," Nadya whispers beside me, her eyes widening. "Your

nose—"

"I'm fine," I mutter. But I'm not.

The air around me crackles faintly, and as I glance down toward the Podrosan fae. He's watching me. Not openly. Not accusingly. But watching. His gaze lingers too long, brows furrowed, as if trying to solve a riddle written in starlight.

I sit back slowly, heart hammering. I wipe the rest of the blood away with the edge of my sleeve and force my face to stillness.

Dante claws his way upward, hand over hand, muscles flexing. At last he reaches the summit, and the crowd erupts in applause.

All at once, the world seems to shake. The semicircle of tiered benches shifts, rumbling as the entire structure seems to ascend, intact. The fae has elevated the seating area so that we get a better view of the summit. I shudder at the fae's power. It's nothing like I've ever seen before, and I can understand now why King Harold has made him part of his retinue.

The Ironshield soldier at the top of the cliff side steps forward with his blade drawn. Dante's shoulders heave from his climb, but after a moment, he unsheathes his falchion.

His opponent—a broad-shouldered soldier bearing the crest of Podrosa—adjusts his grip on his longsword, rolling his neck, as if this were merely another day of training.

King Harold rises from his seat, lifting a hand for silence. "This challenge is a test, not a duel to the death," he announces, his deep voice carrying across the space. "One must simply disarm the other."

The Ironshield lunges first.

Dante sidesteps easily, pivoting on the ball of his foot as the blade sweeps past him. He parries the next strike with a sharp clang of steel, his grip firm but relaxed. The soldier presses forward, launching a series of rapid slashes—textbook maneuvers meant to overpower an opponent early.

Dante weaves between them like water slipping through fingers.

He doesn't just block—he redirects, each deflection calculated to unbalance his opponent rather than merely stop the blow.

The soldier grits his teeth, frustration creeping into his movements as he adjusts his footing. He tries to press Dante toward the edge of the cliff, but Dante shifts, twisting his sword in a tight circle to disengage before stepping back to reset.

They circle each other, the sunlight casting their shadows long against the sand.

With a sharp feint to the left, Dante forces the soldier to adjust his defense—only to pivot sharply and strike from the right. The soldier barely blocks in time, the force of the impact sending him stumbling back a step.

The court murmurs, their intrigue growing.

The soldier recovers quickly, setting his jaw as he goes on the offensive again. He aims high—a downward slash meant to drive Dante to his knees—but Dante meets it with a high guard, then twists, rolling his blade along the Podrosan's before flicking it away. The disarm is near-seamless, the opponent's sword flying from the summit through the air.

The arena erupts into applause.

Dante steps back, lowering his blade as the Podrosan soldier exhales sharply, shaking his head with something that might be reluctant respect.

King Silas nods in approval, and beside me, Queen Eleanor clasps her hands in her lap, unreadable as always.

All that's left now is the target.

Dante's heavy breaths make his body unsteady as he nocks the arrow and takes aim.

"Steady, Dante. Concentrate."

I realize then that my fingers are aching from gripping the chair so tightly, but in the next moment, that sharp pain shoots across my eyes, quickly replaced by that strange, calming static.

The arrow is loosed, and everyone jumps to their feet with shouts of triumph.

I release a slow breath, the tension easing from my body at last.

He won.

CHAPTER TWENTY-THREE

The courtyard empties in a swirl of restrained excitement and murmured praise, the Podrosan nobles moving toward the long feast tables set beneath carved archways, where plain pastries and mead await. The scent of baked bread rides the wind, but it does nothing for the churning in my stomach.

I search for Dante, but the crowd makes even catching a glimpse of him impossible.

My legs still feel unsteady, my breathing uneven. A headache pulses behind my eyes, like something clawing from the inside.

"Come on," Nadya whispers, her hand already closing around mine.

She pulls me gently through the dispersing crowd. I'm dimly aware of familiar faces—the Ironshields, the courtiers in dark red and black—but none of them see me, not really. They see the princess who stayed perfectly still while the king's son proved his worth.

Not the woman who bled from her nose and nearly passed out trying to keep him alive.

We slip through a narrow passage flanked with faded tapestries, until Nadya pushes open a door and leads us into a dim, unused lounge—

its walls lined with empty display shelves and tall windows veiled in dust-smeared glass. The light is soft in here, scattered. Quiet.

As soon as the door closes behind us, Nadya rounds on me.

"Celeste," she says, her voice low but urgent, "what happened out there?"

I lean against the nearest column and slide slowly to the floor. "I... I don't know."

She kneels beside me, her hands fluttering, clearly unsure whether to hold my arm or just give me space. "Was it your magic?"

I shake my head, but not in denial. In disbelief. "It was beyond my control. I needed to help him. I just... thought it. Willed it. I called out his name in my head, and he turned. Then again, later—when he slipped—I pushed... something. I felt it leave me."

"Like when you chased me with the flower petals?"

I start to tremble. "Yes, but much... wilder. Like I had no control over it."

She straightens and goes to one of the windows, as if making sure no one is looking for us. "Do you think you're developing your uncle's power? The telepathy?" Nadya's voice is kept a whisper. "It would make sense, since it's in your family."

"Fae aren't supposed to have more than one special power." The strength, speed, and healing nature of fae is part of our race, but each fae usually develops a singular power that rises above all that. "How could I have telepathy too?"

Nadya's brows pull tight. "And the nosebleed? That's never happened before."

Before I can answer, Ezra steps into the room, his robes gathered in his fists, his brows furrowed as he studies me. "There you are. I've been looking for you," he says, shutting the door behind him. "Are you all right?"

"No," Nadya says quickly, standing near me and folding her arms. "She is not all right. She's bleeding from the nose and barely able to stand."

"I'm fine," I say. My physical turmoil has nothing on the mental

anguish troubling me. "Ezra, what the hell was that? A fucking trial? Did you know they were going to make Dante go through that?"

"Not exactly, no." Ezra steps closer to me. "As I mentioned, there hasn't been a legitimization tour in over a century. The trails are a very old custom, a way for a bastard making a claim for his place in line for the throne to prove his worth. The realms took these claims seriously centuries ago, knowing anyone worthy of a royal title could simply *ask* to be legitimized; they had to earn it. The trials were created as a way to measure one's worth, as well as to deter those who were not up to the challenge."

It makes sense, in a cruel sort of way. "Did Dante know he was going to have to go through all this?" He hadn't mentioned anything about it to me, but maybe he didn't want me to worry. Or maybe he believed the realms wouldn't carry out this old tradition.

"I don't believe he did. Not until they brought him out into the arena, that is. But luckily, it seems he passed the test."

"Yes." I swallow hard. "About that..."

Ezra narrows his eyes. "Tell me exactly what happened."

I take a deep breath before I push myself up to stand before him. "At first, I just saw the danger. The platform Dante was about to jump to— it was loose, ready to fall. I was thinking *go left* so hard, it felt like I was screaming it in my own head." My voice thins with the memory. "Then he looked toward me. He turned, just for a second, as if hearing me. And then he jumped the other way."

Ezra exhales slowly, blinking at me. "So... you didn't speak the words aloud?"

I shake my head.

"And he responded? As if he'd heard you?"

"I don't know," I say again, weaker now. "It could've been coincidence. But then when he slipped, I felt panic rise like a tide, and I just shoved the energy out. Like I did when we practiced with the magnolia petals. Except I don't think I even meant to. It was just a reaction. The energy burst forward before I could question it."

Nadya looks at me for a long, still moment, her expression

unreadable.

Ezra paces back and forth for a bit, tapping his bearded chin with his finger. "Telepathy runs in your family. Your uncle."

"Yes," I whisper. "But until today, the only magic that caused a buzzing in my body was from the energy-force magic—if that's what we've decided to call it. I've never... *spoken* to anyone before. Anytime my uncle spoke to me that way, I've heard him, but I could never answer."

"Her nose bled," Nadya said. "When she used the magic."

Worry sharpens in Ezra's features like a blade being honed. "Is this the first time this has happened, Celeste?"

"The nosebleed, yes. But there have been other... consequences when I've used my magic before."

He doesn't ask me. He simply waits for me to continue.

"Headaches. A pain behind my eyes that makes everything go black. Twangs in my gut, sometimes."

Nadya puts a hand on my arm. "Oh, Celeste."

"It doesn't last long." Even to my own ears, it sounds like I'm making excuses, dismissing something serious as if it were nothing.

It takes a moment before Ezra breaks the silence. "Your power hasn't fully manifested. Not truly. What's happening now... I believe your body is trying to decide what to do with the magic that's been hidden away. The pressure of it is building behind a locked door, and some of it is bursting through."

I blink at him. "And the pain?"

"Cracks." His expression is grim. "The door is sealed, but the magic is leaking through, uncontrolled. It's not meant to trickle out this way. It's meant to be unlocked. If it continues to claw through the cracks..." His voice trails off, and his eyes flick away.

"Say it," I demand.

Ezra meets my gaze again. "It could break you."

The room goes eerily still to the point my ears ring. The air tastes like old dust. My hands feel clammy despite the chill in the castle.

"I don't feel broken," I say softly. "I just feel... tired. Like I'm being tugged in too many directions."

"You are," Ezra replies. "You're holding in something that wants out, and it's trying to escape by any means. Your body, your mind—they're paying the price."

I lower my head into my hands. "What do I do?"

"For now?" He exhales slowly. "Nothing. No more magic. No more desperate pushes. Not until we know more."

"How?" Nadya asks. "How do we find answers?"

Ezra straightens, his voice cautious. "I've been conversing with the Podrosan magister. He may be able to point us in the right direction. Ironshield Keep has one of the oldest libraries in Terre Ferique, if not *the* oldest. If the king permits me access, I might be able to find something. Maybe even a record of a similar case. A fae whose magic was locked from within."

"And if he says *no*?" I ask.

Ezra's jaw tightens. "Then I'll find another way in."

A flicker of hope stirs in my chest, but it's paper thin. Fragile.

And still, at the edge of it all, my thoughts drift to Dante.

I wonder if he felt it too. The push. The call. The thread between us. I wonder if he suspects. Or if he simply thinks he survived the trial on his own. And what will his reaction be, knowing I helped him? I'm sure if it had been Torbin, he would have reacted with anger. But surely Dante would understand. Wouldn't he?

Part of me wants to tell him everything. But I don't have all the answers yet.

CHAPTER TWENTY-FOUR

The fire crackles low in the hearth, casting slow-turning shadows on the stone walls as I perch on the edge of the bed, tugging loose the pins from my hair. My head throbs—sharp behind my eyes, dull at the base of my skull, like something's been pressing outward all day, trying to escape. I wince as the last pin comes free.

"You should rest, my lady," Indira says, standing near the window. "I would offer to draw the curtains, but there aren't any. I could light the balm candle if you like."

"I'll manage," I mutter, massaging my temple with two fingers. "I just need a moment to breathe without everything spinning."

She turns from the window with a frown, a neatly folded nightgown in her hands. "You're still pale. Are you sure you don't want tea? I could fetch something mild for the pain—though, I admit, their teas taste like boiled parchment here."

I groan softly. "Gods, I can still taste the flavorless pudding from last night's dinner. If that's what they do to desserts, I don't want to know what they do to tea leaves."

Indira snorts, placing the gown on the bed beside me. "Suit yourself.

But if you faint, I can't promise I'll catch you."

She's halfway to the door when the faint sound of a knock on the open frame draws both our eyes.

I've been in my room since after the trial, but Nadya told me Dante hadn't been at lunch. Nor were the kings or Farvis, so I assumed he'd been pulled into some post-trial meeting. Now he's dressed in simple dark linen, damp curls pushed back from his face, his eyes searching.

"I heard you weren't feeling well," he says, studying my face. "Thought I'd check on you."

Indira arches a brow, her arms crossing. "She needs rest."

"And tea," I add suddenly, rising just enough to smooth the skirt of my gown. "That actually sounds... like the perfect remedy."

Indira levels me with a knowing look. "Mm-hmm." Her gaze flicks back to Dante. "Leave the door open, my lord."

"Of course," Dante says with a gentle nod. "Sir Holden and Sir Donovan are right down the hall as well." He steps aside as she brushes past him. He waits until her footsteps fade, then steps inside.

He doesn't talk right away—he just looks at me. A long, quiet look that slides beneath my skin.

"You didn't come to the feast," he says.

"I think you're being generous with the word 'feast,'" I joke. "But I couldn't. The headache... and everything else."

He nods once, his hands curling into the back of the chair near the hearth. "I understand."

I pat the space beside me on the bed. "Would you like to sit?"

He hesitates only a heartbeat, then moves, the mattress dipping slightly beneath his weight. We're close, not quite touching, but the heat between us is immediate, unmistakable.

"I didn't know they were going to put you through that," I say quietly. "When I saw the arena, I thought it would be a sparring match, maybe a duel. But that course—Dante, they were trying to break you."

"They were doing what they've done to every soldier and every would-be heir in over a century," he replies. "No bastard has ever been legitimized without proving he can survive the same trials their kings

once did. It's an ancient tradition, which Podrosa obviously hasn't forgotten."

I lift my hand to his jaw without thinking, brushing my thumb along the faint bruise forming beneath his cheekbone. "You look like you held your own."

His eyes shutter slightly before meeting mine. "I was fueled by the thought of you watching."

A smile tries to tug at my lips, but it fades too fast. "I did watch. Every second. And I felt so... helpless." My fingers fall back to my lap. "Dante... something happened."

His brow lifts.

I exhale slowly, sorting the threads of thought into something that might resemble an explanation. "I don't know if it was me, not entirely, but when you reached the point where you had to choose left or right, I saw the trap. And I—I thought it. I screamed it in my head. *Go left.* And you did."

He blinks, his brows plunging. "I... thought I was imagining it. You called out to me?"

"In my head, yes." I shake my head.

His eyes widen. "Celeste, have your powers manifested?"

I take a long, deep breath before I begin. "It's a long story, and I'm not even clear on all the facts. It started after Torbin stabbed me," I murmur.

I tell him about the buzzing in my body, about how I was able to push and pull things after that, about the magnolia petals in the courtyard. And then about calling his name at the trial.

He waits, listening patiently.

I shift, fingers knotting together. "And when you slipped from the cliff side—I pushed. I didn't even know I was doing it. But I shoved the energy forward, and it helped you catch the ledge."

His thumb moves in slow circles over my knuckles. "And does Ezra know?"

"He's been trying to help me understand it. I don't have control over it. Not yet. Ezra says the magic hasn't truly been released. That it's seeping

181

through. Breaking me from the inside. Because sometimes..."

Dante's eyes narrow. "Sometimes what?"

"Sometimes, when I use the magic, it... hurts me. My head gets this pressure, a sharp pain behind my eyes. And today, after I pushed out the energy, I had a nosebleed. It felt like my mind was unraveling." I meet his gaze.

Dante goes still.

His gaze sweeps over my face as if trying to see the damage, to catch every ripple of fear beneath the surface. His hand tightens around mine.

"You shouldn't use it again," he says softly, but there's steel beneath the words. "Not until Ezra understands more. Not until we know it won't harm you."

"Dante—"

"Not even for me." His voice drops even lower, his brow furrowed in a way that makes my chest ache. "I can't stand the thought of you hurting, especially because you're trying to protect me. I'd rather fall from every cliff in Podrosa than make you bleed again."

My breath catches, and I try to ease the tension with a half-smile. "You know you can't tell me what to do."

He doesn't smile back. He leans in, his voice a quiet command. "Celeste, I'm serious. You bleed for no one."

I blink.

The room feels too still, like even the fire is frozen in place.

I don't answer, but inside, my answer is already clear.

There is no universe in which I'll sit idly by if he's in danger. I'll bleed. I'll burn. He just doesn't get to know that yet.

The floorboard creaks, and we both start slightly as Indira steps back in with a tray balanced in her hands, steam curling from the teacup perched neatly at the center.

She sets it down with a soft *clink*, her eyes flicking between us, taking in the closeness, the weight of the silence. "King Silas is looking for you," she says to Dante, her voice clipped. "He didn't sound particularly patient."

Dante sighs, then rises, but not before he gives my hand a gentle

182

squeeze.

"Get some rest," he says, his thumb brushing against my knuckles. "And don't forget what I said."

He turns and disappears through the doorway, the corridor swallowing him up.

Indira watches him go, then lifts the teacup from the tray and hands it to me.

I blow on the brown liquid before taking a sip. Immediately, my face twists. "It's worse than I imagined."

She doesn't laugh, but her lips twitch. "Drink up, Your Highness. It was a rough day, but our time in Podrosa has only just begun."

 183

CHAPTER TWENTY-FIVE

A sharp, blaring horn shatters the stillness of the night. I jolt upright in bed, heart pounding, the distant sound cutting through the stone walls like a blade. For a breath, I wonder if I imagined it, until it comes again, long and urgent, followed by the rapid clang of bells. Not just an alert. An alarm.

Something is wrong.

I throw the covers aside and scramble to my feet, my pulse quickening. Across the room, the moonlight spills in thin, silver streaks through the tall windows. The walls, so still and austere during the day, seem to hum with unseen tension now. The steady rhythm of boots hitting stone grows louder as I snatch my dagger from the belt I left on the chair. My fingers curl tightly around the hilt as another horn blast shudders through the air.

The full moon casts a cold, silver glow over the palace grounds, where torchlight flickers wildly against the stone walls. Beyond the towering gates, dark figures race through the fields, their movements swift and unnatural.

Carnoraxis.

I yank on my trousers and boots, my hands trembling as the horn wails again. Outside my door, the sounds of footsteps echo in the corridor—Ironshield soldiers, judging by their brisk, measured cadence.

By the time I step into the hallway, Nadya bursts out of her room, her dark curls spilling over her shoulders. "What is that sound?" she hisses, wide-eyed.

"Trouble." I grab her arm, pulling her along. "We need to find out what's happening."

The marble floors are cold beneath my boots as we hurry toward the grand staircase. More guards flood the halls, stern-faced men in their crimson uniforms, their hands on the hilts of their swords. Each of them moves with practiced precision, their formation perfectly aligned, even in the chaos. It would almost be impressive if the air weren't thick with tension.

As we reach the grand foyer, the towering double doors stand open. The Podrosan king and queen emerge from a side chamber. King Harold's broad frame is stiff with authority, his dark hair gleaming beneath the light of the chandeliers. Queen Agatha glides beside him, her expression composed but her knuckles white where they clutch the folds of her ivory robe.

A guard bows low before them, his voice taut. "Your Majesties, the western perimeter has been breached. Creatures—dozens—advancing toward the city." He swallows hard, his composure cracking. "They are unlike anything our forces have faced."

Behind them, Hederan soldiers pour in from their quarters, swords drawn, their heavy boots clattering over the polished stone.

My pulse quickens as I search the crowd. Where is Dante?

I push closer, my robe slipping off my shoulders as I strain to hear the guard's next words.

"They move fast," he continues, his voice faltering. "Too fast. And the way they tear through flesh—" His words cut off with a shudder.

The king's jaw tightens. "Sound the second alarm. Mobilize the outer guard and reinforce the gates. Nothing gets through."

"Yes, Your Majesty." The guard spins on his heel, but I step forward

before I can think better of it.

"Let me fight," I say, my voice steady despite the icy dread curling through my chest.

Every head turns toward me. The king's mouth pulls into a frown, his disapproval palpable. "You are a guest of this kingdom. And a mourning one, at that."

Before I can reply, another voice cuts in.

"Celeste, no." Marcos steps into my path, his brow furrowed beneath tousled, dark hair, his red cloak hanging open at his shoulders. He looks equal parts horrified and perplexed. "You can't mean to go out there. It's not your place. Not now."

I lift my chin. "My place is at the front of the line, defending the people."

He shakes his head, glancing toward the king and queen as if to appeal to their reason. "You'll be breaking every rule of this court. You're in mourning. It's forbidden. The consequences—"

"Rules don't save lives," I snap. "I've seen what those things can do. If I stand by and watch more innocents die, then what good are any of your precious rules?"

The king's face darkens, but I don't wait for his retort. Because for all his rigid adherence to protocol, even he can't deny the truth: neither he nor his soldiers have seen what's coming.

I turn back to Marcos, whose jaw hangs open. "You've always been kind to me," I say quietly, too quietly for anyone else to hear. "Please. Don't stop now."

He swallows, clearly torn, but he steps aside.

I don't waste another second. I let my robe drop, draw my dagger from its sheath, the weight of it familiar in my grip, and bolt into the night.

As I force my way past the soldiers at the gate, a shadow falls over me. I turn my head to find Dante charging beside me. We don't break our stride as we hold our weapons in our grasps.

"You didn't think you were going to face this horde without me, did you?" he asks.

 186

"What took you so long?" I tease.

He moves with easy confidence, but I see the flicker of worry in his storm-grey eyes when they meet mine. He's already dressed for battle—black leather fitted to his frame, the hilt of his falchion gleaming at his side.

The cool, night air brushes against my skin, thick with the scent of rain on distant earth. The smell of smoke drifts faintly on the breeze, but there's something else beneath it: an acrid, coppery scent that makes my stomach twist. I know that smell. *Blood.*

In the field between the castle and the oncoming carnoraxis, orderly rows of Podrosan soldiers flood into formation. Every movement is precise, mechanical. Nothing like the easy, fluid readiness of my own regiment. Dante and I push our way through, rushing out in front of the troops.

A deep, thunderous bellow rolls over the plains—a sound I know too well. The open fields stretch toward the dark treeline, but even from here, I see the shadowed figures moving—too fast, too many.

The guard captain—an older man with greying hair beneath his helmet—calls out orders. His voice is clear, cutting through the din. "Archers, take position!"

Dante curses under his breath. "Let's move."

The horde descends, and the battlefield is chaos. Shadows twist through the moonlit fields, monstrous and fast. The shriek of a carnoraxis splits the night, sending a chill through my blood as I sprint toward the thick of the fight, my dagger already slick with blackened gore. The Ironshields are holding their line—rigid and precise, as expected—but the sheer number of beasts is threatening to break through.

I cut down one lunging for a wounded soldier, the blade slicing clean through its neck. My heart hammers in my chest as I scan the field. I've fought these creatures before—too many times—but this is different. I am not with my squad. With them at my side, our defense would be well coordinated, a dance so well-rehearsed, there would be no question of the steps we needed to take.

 187

But these soldiers, to their credit, are disciplined, moving with impressive coordination. One to my left reloads his crossbow faster than I've ever seen—his aim nearly as sharp as Isaac's—as he releases a bolt that takes down a beast mid-leap.

A shout pulls my attention across the battlefield. A Podrosan soldier, his leg pinned under the weight of a fallen carnoraxis, struggles against the creature's last death throes. His sword lies inches beyond his reach, his face pale as the beast's claws twitch closer to his throat. None of the other soldiers are close enough to help.

I don't think. I move.

I dart across the blood-soaked ground, knees bending low as I drive my blade into the beast's side. The creature howls in agony, but I twist the blade deeper, feeling the sickening give of its ribs before it collapses, still.

The soldier gasps, pulling his leg free with a wince. Blood streaks his cheek, but his eyes widen when he sees me. "Your Highness!" His breath stutters. "You... You saved me."

"Get back to the line," I order, keeping my tone firm as I offer him a hand. He grips it tightly, hauling himself upright with a hiss of pain. "And next time, don't let them get that close."

He nods quickly, still looking at me like I've sprouted wings. "Thank you," he says, his voice raw.

"Go!" I bark, pushing him toward his comrades.

I pivot back to the battle, but his words linger in my mind. He'll report what happened, I know it. And I almost wish I could see the look on the Podrosan king's face when he learns that an outsider—a woman—was the one to save one of his men.

Another beast lurches toward me. I raise my dagger again, the blood pounding in my ears as I meet it head-on.

A final carnoraxis lunges from the treeline, its jagged teeth bared as it charges the remaining guards. One soldier is too slow to raise his sword. I sprint forward, and with a sharp twist, I drive my blade into the beast's exposed throat. It collapses, twitching as black blood pools beneath its heavy frame. The guard stares at me in wide-eyed disbelief,

his mouth opening and closing as if words have abandoned him.

"You're welcome," I say breathlessly, yanking my dagger free.

The air is thick with the acrid stench of blood and burnt flesh, but the sounds of snarls and screams have faded. All that remains are the distant crackles of dying fires and the sharp orders of Podrosan captains calling their soldiers to regroup.

I wipe my blade against my thigh, scanning the battlefield for any remaining threats. The ground is littered with carnoraxis corpses, their twisted forms steaming in the cool, night air. Bodies of soldiers—Podrosan and Hederan alike—are scattered between them. My pulse thunders in my ears, but the adrenaline coursing through my veins begins to ebb, leaving behind a sharp ache in my limbs.

I turn, searching, until finally I see him.

Dante's hair falls messily across his brow, damp with sweat, but it's his eyes—stormy and fierce—that hold me captive. His falchion hangs loosely at his side, the silver blade slick with carnoraxis blood.

For a heartbeat, neither of us moves. The world narrows to the space between us—every breath we take and every bruise we'll feel tomorrow.

CHAPTER TWENTY-SIX

The audience chamber in Podrosa is as austere as the king himself—tall, grey columns carved with geometric precision, not a curve or flourish in sight. The ceiling looms high above, vaulted like a cathedral, but the windows are narrow, and the light that filters through them is cold. The scent of oil lamps and soap imbues the air, sharp and faintly metallic.

Ezra and I stand before the king, who scowls at us from his throne on a raised dais. He refused to hold an audience with anyone after the attacks, and it wasn't until this afternoon that he agreed to a closed-door discussion with King Silas. I'm fully expecting Silas to reprimand me for stepping out of my mourning role and charging into battle, but even he can't deny that my efforts helped save the people in the Ironshield Keep.

But I'm sure King Harold doesn't want to acknowledge that fact. Especially because I'm a woman.

Ezra bows low beside me, his expression composed, as always, but I keep my spine straight. I won't fucking grovel.

King Harold's dark-grey robes pool around him, perfectly pleated, and his eyes—narrow, pale, and heavy-lidded—flick between us with evident disdain.

Beside him, Queen Agatha perches like a breath of silk in a room full of granite. She is still and quiet, her expression unreadable, though I feel her gaze settle on me now and then, thoughtful and lingering. Unlike her husband, she does not seem displeased by my presence.

"Thank you for agreeing to see us, Your Majesty," Ezra says, his voice smooth and diplomatic. "We come only to request access to your library. There are texts here that do not exist elsewhere in Terre Ferique—especially regarding historical magic and the wars of the second era. Her Highness and I are conducting research that may prove vital to understanding the recent attacks."

He pauses, then adds with quiet conviction, "As the princess's appointed magister, it is my duty to educate and advise her in every way I can. To deny her the knowledge she needs would be a disservice, not only to her future, but to the realm she will one day help lead. Your library holds centuries of wisdom—lessons written in blood and ash and survival. To let those lessons gather dust while threats rise around us is folly."

Ezra's gaze remains steady, respectful, but firm. "The opportunity to study those texts while we are within reach is not one I take lightly. And I would not have brought it to your attention if I did not believe it mattered."

The king's lip curls, a slow, deliberate gesture. "And you expect me to open my archives to you freely? After the spectacle your princess made of herself in my kingdom?"

I tense beside Ezra, my hands clasped before me to hide the way my fingers dig into my palms. For now, I remain silent.

"She helped stop the carnoraxis from slaughtering your people," Ezra replies calmly. "Your own soldiers were overwhelmed. Without her aid, the toll might have been far higher."

"She's a woman," King Harold spits, rising from his throne like a stone giant uncoiling. "And what she did was unnatural."

My jaw clenches, but I force myself to breathe slowly through my nose.

 191

King Harold stalks a few paces forward, robes swishing against the smooth floor. "Our people value tradition. Honor. Order. Not this foreign spectacle of disrespectful women wielding blades in battles the gods never meant for them to take part in." His voice rises now, echoing across the chamber. "If word spreads that Podrosa was defended by a mourning princess, what message does that send to my enemies? That our warriors cannot protect their own gates? That we needed a *girl* to save us?"

He doesn't say it outright—but I hear it in every syllable: shame. He is ashamed that I was needed. Ashamed that my skills eclipsed his soldiers'. That I embarrassed him.

I lift my chin. "I did what I was trained to do. What I swore to do." I take a slow breath. "I will not apologize for saving lives."

His eyes narrow like slits in old stone. "No. I expect you won't." He turns, sweeping back toward his throne with finality. "Your request is denied."

"But the library—" Ezra begins.

"Is closed," King Harold snaps, without so much as a glance back. "To foreigners. To women. To those who forget their place."

He drops into his throne as if the conversation were over. The guards at the sides of the chamber shift subtly, hands falling to their blades. A warning.

At his side, Queen Agatha stirs. Her gaze lands on me for a moment before she lowers her chin.

I stand frozen, fury pounding like war drums beneath my ribs. For a moment, I wonder what would happen if I reached for my magic—if I let it swirl just enough to make the flames in the sconces tremble, or the wind outside howl against the stained-glass windows. Just enough to remind him that his arrogance is not power.

But Ezra's quiet voice stops me. "Come, Princess."

I follow Ezra from the room, the king's silence a weight between my shoulder blades.

The hall outside the throne room feels colder than it did when we entered. Ezra walks beside me, arms folded, his brow drawn into the

thoughtful crease it wears when he's fighting the urge to argue further.

"I should've known," I murmur. "Podrosa would rather pretend the world only works if it's resting on the shoulders of obedience and order."

Ezra exhales through his nose. "He fears perception more than consequence. If word spreads that a foreign princess had to protect his people—"

"Then his ego shrivels," I say dryly. "And gods forbid his manhood follow."

That draws the faintest curl of Ezra's mouth. But it's fleeting. He glances at the tall, stained-glass window lining the corridor, its light casting fractured blues and golds across the floor. "There may be another way. The king is inaccessible—but his court is not. Perhaps I could speak again with the palace magister. If I convince him to lend me access to the texts, I could study them in private. Quietly."

I glance at him. "You think he'll help?"

Ezra arches a brow. "I think he might be more open-minded than the man who employs him. And I doubt he enjoys seeing his library padlocked by fear."

We round a corner, our footsteps hushed by a faded runner rug. But before we reach the next alcove, a boy steps into our path.

A page. No older than thirteen. His eyes are downcast, his voice polite as he bows. "Your Highness. Magister. The queen requests your presence."

My brows lift. "Queen Agatha?"

He nods once, not quite meeting my gaze. "If you'll follow me."

Ezra and I exchange a look. There's caution in his eyes, but also curiosity.

We follow the boy through a discreet side corridor, winding past a tall alcove lined with stone urns and a pair of disapproving statues. The route is narrow and quiet—meant for servants, not royalty—and when we finally reach the door to which he gestures, it is unremarkable. Unadorned. The page raps once, then opens it and bows, gesturing for us to head inside.

Queen Agatha of Podrosa stands at the center of a modest solarium,

framed by pale-blue drapes and a table set for tea that looks untouched. Her posture is impeccable, hands clasped before her, not a hair out of place. But her eyes are not cold like her husband's. There's a quiet steel behind them. A spark of something not yet dulled by years under his thumb.

"Your Majesty," I say, dipping into a graceful curtsy.

"Please," she says softly, "there's no need for ceremony here."

Ezra and I straighten. I study her carefully, unsure what this is. Pity? Gratitude? A test?

"I wanted to thank you," she says, her voice even. "For your bravery during the attack."

I blink. "You saw?"

"I saw enough. Word travels quickly within these walls. You saved lives. Including my cousin's boy." Her lips twitch faintly. "I fear my husband's pride is louder than his gratitude. But I see clearly where he refuses to look."

I glance at Ezra. His expression is neutral, unreadable. But his hands are loosely clasped behind his back in the way he always stands when he's waiting to see whether a blade will be drawn or a gift offered.

The queen steps forward. "You wish to study our library. I see no harm in that."

I blink. Hope flares in my chest. But before I get carried away, I hesitate. "Will it cause trouble for you?"

Queen Agatha's mouth flattens. "I've learned there is no need to tell my husband every detail of what I decide." A pause. "There is a servant door near the east corridor, beside the shrine of the Weeping Saint. It opens into the library's east wing. My steward will ensure the main entrance is locked and the staff cleared for the next two hours. The kings and the men are taking a tour of the barracks, so you should proceed undisturbed. No one will see you."

My heart lifts, but I temper it with caution. "Thank you. Truly. We'll be quick."

"You have two hours," she says. "After that, the men will return from the barracks, and questions may be asked." Her gaze sharpens. "Find

what you need."

I swallow thickly and nod.

Queen Agatha turns, gliding to the curtained door on the far wall before pausing to look back at me. "Terre Ferique needs women like you, Princess. Even if most men would rather deny the truth."

Then she vanishes through the curtain.

As soon as I fetched Nadya, we headed for the east corridor. She's the probably the fastest reader out of the three of us, so having her along is a big advantage.

Our steps are muffled by the worn, velvet runner, and the sconces are devoid of candlelight, so we move through shadow. The hush in the air isn't natural; it feels pressed down, like even the palace itself knows we shouldn't be here.

The door is exactly where the queen said it would be: tucked into a narrow alcove beside the shrine of the Weeping Saint, barely visible beneath an arch of stone.

Ezra tests the handle. It opens with a soft groan.

He pushes it open just wide enough for us to slip through.

Inside, the scent of old parchment and wood polish hovers around me like a cloak. The Ironshield Keep's library is nothing like the one at Ivystone. It's cavernous, its ceilings vaulted and laced with slender buttresses, its walls lined floor-to-ceiling with arched bookcases. Gold filigree gleams along the spines of thick tomes. In the center of the room, narrow tables are arranged in perfectly straight lines, each one stacked with neatly arranged scrolls and catalogs. The windows are shuttered to protect the books from damaging light.

It feels like we've stepped into a sanctum. Something secret and sacred.

"When can I move in?" Nadya asks, gaping at the walls of

bookshelves.

"I'm sure they'd let you, if you marry Lord Marcos," I tease.

"I prefer the princess," Nadya retorts, "but I think she's got her eye on someone else."

My gut sours at her words, though I know deep down, Dante wouldn't choose her over me. At least, I don't think he would. Unless King Silas suddenly has a change of heart and wants to unify Hedera with Podrosa instead of Delasurvia.

Once we're sure no one will disturb us, we waste no time. I pry open a pair of shutters so we don't have to work in the dark. Nadya takes the far end of the room, rifling through indexes while Ezra and I split off toward the tomes labeled by era and subject. The sunlight bathes rows upon rows of gilded script and brittle scroll cases. It's overwhelming— so much history, so many voices pressed between dusty pages—but I try to trust the pull in my gut, hoping it leads me to what we need.

We search for books that might mention fae, witches, or rituals that hide magic. Even if the subject comes close, we flip through as if searching for buried treasure. I read a dozen passages. A dozen more. Each promising something, each ending in a dead end.

I glance at the clock. We've been here an hour and haven't gotten any further to understanding anything. Even a small clue would make this stealth mission worth it.

On a sigh, I move on to the next bookcase in the row, gliding my fingertips along the spines as I read them. When I come across a tome titled *The Turn of the Fae*, I slip it out and bring it to the nearest table. The pages don't reveal text as much as illustrations in a variety of styles, telling me there wasn't just one person who contributed to the book.

The first section is about ancient fae, and the word *ancient* is fully befitting, because the illustration depicts the fae walking along with and interacting with the gods. And the fae drawings resemble the ones I used to see in children's books, with wings and pointed ears, the air shimmering around them. According to this book, this is what the ancient fae people looked like.

"Ezra," I call, since he's supposed to be the smartest one in the room.

"Do you believe the fae used to look like this?"

He comes over, bending a bit to see the illustration better. "Ah, yes. They were believed to have been molded from the image of angels, according to what I've read"

"But this isn't what fae look like now." My ears, and the ears of all the fae I know, do have a slight angle to them, but nothing close to the pointed ears depicted in the book.

"The legend is that the angelic-looking fae were feared by the people of Terre Ferique. This caused the fae to become lonely, and the feeling of not being accepted caused a deep sadness. So the fae made a deal with the gods." Ezra shifts to sit in the chair beside me. "You see, apparently fae didn't used to be only limited to one power when their magic manifested itself. But the fae were willing to sacrifice in order to be one with the people, to be seen as the same community. So they asked the gods to take their wings, to make them look more human, and as a payment, they would reduce their arsenal of powers to just one."

"That's wild," Nadya says. "I don't know if I could do that."

"Really?" I tilt my head. "I mean, I guess if it were for something like love, I could understand."

Nadya gasps. "Oh, yes. I can just imagine it. A lovely fae, willing to sacrifice her wings and her ear tips and her... glitter, I guess... so she would be accepted by the man she loves."

I let out a small giggle. "There's no doubting what kind of books you've been reading."

She gives me a smile and a shrug before continuing her search. Ezra lets out a small groan as he stands, returning to the bookcase he'd abandoned before I called him over.

I flip through the pages, hoping the book might mention fae hiding their magic and getting it back, but there's naught to be found.

Ezra finds a book mentioning a great execution of witches, but nothing helpful comes out of those pages, either.

Moving on to a new section, I trail my fingers across the spine of a thick volume bound in faded, green velvet. Something about the texture draws me to it. I slide it free and take in the illustrated cover of a man in

 197

armor, standing in the foreground with a sword pointed in the air, with a sail-finned dragon roaring in the background.

I read the title out loud. "*The Slayer of Hedera and the Final Age of Flame.*" I glance over my shoulder.

Ezra nods. "It's on our curriculum to go over, yes. The tale of a warrior from centuries ago who became obsessed with conquering dragons. What had started as a mission to track down and conquer one rogue dragon turned into a compulsion to slay dragons for their scales when he learned their worth. Strong as steel and resistant to flame, dragon scales quickly became more valuable than gold. Some said they held ancient magic. They were discovered to have medicinal qualities, used in potions to stave off incurable fevers. Some believed they could strengthen the blood, prolong vitality. Dull pain. And then, of course, were the rumors that they had the power to make one immortal."

A shiver runs through me, and I rub my arms.

Ezra continues, his voice lower now. "Once word of the worth of dragon scales began to spread, the king at the time—King Haldric—saw a different future for Hedera. Prosperity became his obsession. And he took the dragon slayer under his wing to build his fortune."

I swallow. "Torbin once brought me to a cave entrance in Hedera," I murmur, my fingers drifting along the edge of the page. "We were just children. He said it was an old slayer's den—where a dragon slayer used to sleep between hunts." The memory rises slowly, like mist from a forgotten glade. "I remember how excited he was. He wanted to go inside, kept saying we might find old bones or buried treasure. But the moment I saw that dark mouth yawning open in the rocks, I froze. I was convinced there were monsters inside. I told him I wasn't going any farther."

Nadya shivers. "I would have said the same."

My smile is faint but sharp at the edges. "He teased me. Called me 'a coward.' Said he thought I was brave—stronger than the other girls. That I disappointed him." I shake my head. "It stung more than it should have. So I took his horse and rode back to the castle without him. Left him standing there alone."

 198

Ezra's eyebrows lift slightly, but he doesn't interrupt. Nadya looks like she's holding back a smile.

"He walked all the way back," I continue softly. "Found me sulking in the castle later, pretending not to care. But he had flowers. Wild ones, barely tied together. And a small box of sugared dates he must've stolen from the kitchen." I glance between them, a strange ache spreading beneath my ribs. "He said I was his best friend. That he was sorry for making me feel small. And I believed him."

For a long moment, no one speaks. The memory hangs between us, whole and bittersweet.

"It's strange," I add, barely above a whisper. "Even back then, he could be cruel. But he never wanted to lose me. Not really. If he thought he had, he'd do anything to win me back."

Nadya reaches out, her fingers brushing mine. "That doesn't mean you owe him anything."

"I know," I say. And I do. "I knew it even then. That's why I took the horse."

Ezra lets out a thoughtful hum beside me. "That cave... Was it tucked into the cliffs south of Hedera's southern pass?"

I glance at him. "I think so. Why?"

His brow furrows. "There's a vault hidden in the rock face there. It's said to house a portion of Hedera's dragon scale reserves. It would've been sealed—heavily warded—but Torbin always did know all the secret passageways. Perhaps he meant to show you the wealth. Not bones or treasure. Gold and scales."

Instead, he inadvertently showed me a side of himself he probably hadn't meant to.

I close the book. "Well, I guess we can check that lesson off our list."

"Do not fret," Ezra replies, inspecting a scroll from the middle of the table. "There's no shortage of lessons."

"Yay," Nadya says, devoid of enthusiasm as she strolls away from the table.

I take the dragon slayer book back to its respective shelf before perusing more titles.

Nadya meanders by a far shelf, humming as she glances at the spines. Suddenly, a large tome falls from a shelf she just passed, landing with a *thunk* on the floor behind her.

"Oh!" She remarks, twirling to gape at the book. She holds a hand to her heart and looks at me. "Did you do that?"

I shake my head. "No."

She bends and picks up the fallen book. "It practically *jumped* off the shelf."

When Ezra and I come over to her, I study the cover bound in deep-navy leather with an inlaid sigil gleaming on the front: a silver circle atop a four-pointed star.

"There's no title," I say. "What is it?"

"No idea." She flips the book open. "The text is... strange. I don't recognize the language."

"May I?" Ezra asks, approaching her side.

She hands him the book, but he shakes his head after a few moments. "It's not in any lexicon I know. And I've studied thirty-seven."

Nadya exhales, clearly disappointed. "Maybe it's nothing. Look at these swirls. There's no way that's a language."

Ezra blinks, eyes darting between her and the book. "'Swirls'?"

She lowers her brows. "Yeah. Look. Right there." She points to something on the page.

"I see shapes," he says. "Like squares and triangles."

I stand, abandoning the dragon slayer book. "Let me see."

When I approach them, Ezra holds the book out so I can study the page. Except I don't see swirls or shapes. "This book must be enchanted. I see a series of straight lines and crosses."

Nadya's eyes widen.

Ezra flips a page. "Peculiar."

"I suppose this book isn't meant to be read by just anyone." Nadya runs a hand over the print, shaking her head. "Which means there are secrets in here somebody worked hard to hide."

Then the clock above the library door chimes the hour, and we all stiffen.

200

"Time's up," Ezra says. "Quickly, put everything back where we found it."

Nadya takes the book from Ezra, her hand smoothing over the sigil on the cover once more before returning the book to its shelf.

I draw the shutters closed, and we hurry back down the secret hall. The door clicks shut behind us, sealing off the passageway to the library with a quiet finality. We step into the corridor, shadows curling along the stone floor, the sconces casting a dull, golden light. Nadya exhales, rubbing her arms against the chill.

"Well," she mutters, tucking a curl behind her ear, "we didn't get what we came for, but at least no one's chased us down."

"Princess Celeste?" The voice cuts through the silence like a blade. I freeze.

We all turn at once to see Lord Marcos Trevose standing a few paces down the corridor, gawking at us with wide eyes. His hand, gloved in soft, brown leather, hovers near the hilt of the ornamental dagger belted at his waist—not a soldier's gesture, but one of uncertainty.

He strides forward studying the three of us. "You were—" He looks past us, to the faint seam in the wall that betrays the secret passage. "Were you in the library without permission?"

Ezra's mouth tightens. Nadya's eyes flick to mine. I can feel the tension between the three of us, can feel it in my chest, tightening with each beat.

Podrosa does not forgive rule-breakers. Not easily.

"Marcos." I keep my voice barely above a whisper. "Please."

His eyes narrow slightly.

I reach out to take his hands. They're cool and slightly stiff with tension. He glances down at the connection, blinking slowly.

"I've always valued your friendship," I tell him.

His lips press into a line, unreadable. Behind me, Nadya shifts her weight. I can sense Ezra readying himself to speak, but I squeeze Marcos's hands and lean in just a little closer.

"We meant no harm. We only wished to read for an hour or two." I hold my empty hands up for him to see. "Nothing was taken. Nothing

damaged."

He glances toward the sealed passage again, clearly torn. There's a flicker of hesitance in his eyes, but it conflicts with what I can only assume is a sense of duty. Podrosan loyalty. But if he reports this, it could bring punishment for us.

He holds my gaze for a second longer, and then he gives me the faintest nod. "You should steer clear of this corridor." He turns and walks away without another word.

When he rounds the corner, disappearing from view, Nadya lets out a slow breath. "Gods, I thought he was going to haul us straight to the stocks."

Ezra's voice is dry. "We're fortunate he values your friendship."

"Come on." I glance over my shoulder. "Before someone else catches us."

"You could have told him the queen gave us permission," Nadya says, quickening her steps to keep up with me.

"No. I wouldn't do that. She took a risk giving us access, and I wouldn't betray her trust just to clear our names."

I press a hand to my chest, feeling my pulse still racing beneath my ribs. We're leaving tomorrow. We spent two hours in the most tightly guarded library in Terre Ferique, and still, we walk away emptyhanded.

CHAPTER TWENTY-SEVEN

can't remember if it's been three days or four. I've become so bored in this tiny carriage that I've even succumbed to Nadya's recommendation of reading one of her sordid romance books. It turned out to be very entertaining, but at the end, it only made me want to escape our carriage and climb into Dante's all the more.

Aside from spotting Dante at his carriage as Princess Orida took it upon herself to personally wish him a pleasant journey, I've only caught glimpses of him when the caravan has made its stops. King Silas hovers over him like he's protecting the most valuable treasure in his inventory. Dante must hate it. Even though he spent years seeking out his father's approval, Dante no doubt feels suffocated by Silas's constant presence.

I've yet to find out if the visit to Podrosa was an actual success. I would guess it was, since he passed their physical trial, but Ezra told me there's more to it than that. Political views, terms of alliances—all things I wasn't allowed to be present for when the *men* discussed them. Even after I outperformed King Harold's Ironshields.

I just hope King Harold didn't take my heroism as an insult that might sway his decision in a negative light.

Knowing Podrosa's affinity for protocol, they're probably going to follow some ancient rule, writing up a hundred-page document approving Dante's claim to the throne. Just to keep things done by the books.

Whether Dante's trial in Podrosa was a success or not, we're now approaching Baharat Palace in the capitol of Bastos, and I can't help but wonder what tests await Dante here.

Our caravan stops, and the heat is the first thing that hits me.

The moment I step out of the carriage to join the royal procession, a wave of thick, sweltering air presses against my skin, heavy with the scent of spiced fruits and something floral—heady and intoxicating. My mourning attire is instantly unbearable, the dark fabric trapping the heat and sweat against my body, and I resist the urge to pull at the stiff collar.

The people of Bastos have no such burdens.

They line the wide stone street leading up to the palace, watching our arrival with unabashed interest. Sheer silks and lightweight linen hang off their bronzed skin, the thin fabrics flowing with the occasional warm breeze. Still, most of their skin remains uncovered. Gold glints from their ears, wrists, noses. Chains drape from collars; beads and bangles clink softly with every lazy movement. Intricate tattoos of vines, animals, and symbols wind up their arms and across their backs, some swirling along their ribcages, half-visible beneath gauzy wraps.

But it's their eyes that make my breath hitch.

Unlike the rigid stares in Podrosa, the people of Bastos drink us in with slow, smoldering glances, their dark eyes gleaming with curiosity— and maybe something more lascivious. Women and men alike gaze at Dante with open appreciation, their lips curling at the corners, as if already picturing how they might lure him away. But they do not only look at him.

I feel it too, the slow drag of their gazes down my form, lingering where my dress clings to me. I stand taller, my chin high, pretending not to notice the way some of them whisper behind their hands, their expressions playful, amused.

Nadya, walking close beside me, exhales a long breath. "So," she murmurs, just loud enough for me to hear. "This is Bastos."

The great palace sprawls before us, a breathtaking sight of domed rooftops and white stone towers, the architecture intricate and elegant. Arched entryways are draped in silks of every jewel tone, the banners depicting Bastos's royal sigil—a copper viper coiled beneath a silver crescent moon—fluttering in the warm breeze. Guards stand lazily at the entrance, but there's nothing indifferent about their posture. Their tunics are open to their waists, exposing corded muscle and bronzed skin, their scimitars and axes strapped loosely at their hips, as though daring someone to test their speed.

A dainty woman in a copper top that exposes her stomach and a semitransparent, long skirt saunters toward us from the palace gates. Her pastel-pink hair is chopped at chin level, and there's a thin, gold chain loosely connecting her right nostril and her right earlobe.

"Welcome, Your Majesties, Your Highness, and Lord Stregasi. I am Jalelle, the palace chamberlain. I hope your journey was pleasant." She places her palms together and bows, not waiting for a response. "Please follow me. The queens are eager to see you."

We are led through the palace gates, and the air turns even thicker, scented with incense and jasmine. Musicians lounge on cushions, their fingers dancing over the strings of golden lutes, the music sultry, hypnotic. Servants glide past carrying trays of exotic fruits and goblets of deep-red wine, their bodies adorned with chains of pearls and delicate, golden veils.

The heat inside is a different kind altogether. It carries the scent of passion, embraces one's skin like a lover's kiss. I stretch out my neck and splay my fingers, fighting the urge to rip my heavy clothes off my sweat-dampened body.

"Right this way," Jalelle says, her arm flowing forward as if sifting through water.

We are brought into a grand chamber, its walls lined with draped silks that shimmer under the sunlight shining in through glass panels in the ceiling. Plush mattresses in rich burgundies and sapphires are arranged in circular formations, oversized pillows scattered between them. Ferns and palm plants sit in colorful pots, scattered throughout

the space. A feast of glistening, roasted meats, fresh figs, and sweet pastries are laid out.

And at the center of it all, lounging on an enormous, plump, round mattress, are two of the most striking women I've ever seen. Smoky, black kohl and shimmering powder accentuates their piercing eyes. Their stunning, sun-bronzed arms and legs drape over each other, completely at ease, completely unbothered by the formality King Silas brings with him.

"Your Majesties," Jalelle announces to the two queens. "May I present King Silas and Queen Eleanor of Hedera, Princess Celeste of Delasurvia, and of course, our guest of honor, Lord Dante Stregasi." She turns to us, her arm extended toward the queens. "Queens Ambra," she says, indicating the one with long, raven-colored hair dressed in sheer purple, "and Eosla," she continues, gesturing to the curvier one with turquois waves and a coy grin.

Their bodies are adorned with golden cuffs and delicate chains, their sheer gowns flowing over the curves of their figures, leaving their shoulders bare. They don't seem the least bit disturbed that their nipples are somewhat visible through the material. They have no shoes on, and they are not alone. Several lovers—men and women—lounge at their sides, some draped lazily across the cushions, others curled against them, their hands idly tracing along bare skin.

Queen Ambra props herself up on one elbow, her catlike green eyes raking over our party as a slow, sultry smile spreads across her lips.

"King Silas," she purrs, her voice like silk and wine. "You have finally arrived. Let us first extend our condolences for the loss of Prince Torbin. He was a fine man, and Bastos weeps with you."

King Silas steps forward, his black robes a severe contrast to the cascade of brightly colored silks and gauze spilling from every corner of the hall. He inclines his head with rigid formality. "Thank you, Your Majesties. Your kind words mean a lot to our wounded hearts."

"Queen Eleanor, we can't begin to imagine your loss," Queen Eosla adds.

"You have my thanks," Queen Eleanor says, her voice small in the

huge hall.

"It has been too long since our last meeting," King Silas says, steering the conversation away from his wife. "I trust Bastos continues to thrive."

Queen Ambra's smile deepens, her voice as smooth as honey. "Thrive, we do. And yet Bastos is always... *livelier* when there are guests to entertain."

A ripple of laughter moves through the courtiers sprawled on cushions and divans across the hall. The women are draped in gossamer fabrics that leave little to the imagination, while the men wear open vests or nothing at all over thin, loose breeches. The air hums with a lazy sensuality that makes my skin prickle.

King Silas's face barely shifts. "We thank you for your warm welcome. As you know, I have come to present my son Lord Dante Stregasi for consideration in the matter of legitimization, and to strengthen the bond between Hedera and Bastos."

At the mention of Dante's name, Queen Eosla straightens, her eyes bright with curiosity as her gaze sweeps over him. "Ah, yes. The future prince. Your arrival has stirred much excitement, my lord."

Dante, to his credit, bows smoothly and answers with charm I know is only halfhearted. "I'm honored to be here, Your Majesties."

The queens exchange a look I can't quite decipher, but something in the way Ambra's fingers trail down her arm suggests more than polite interest.

Queen Eosla's gaze lands on me. "Princess Celeste, we were both deeply sorry to hear about your brother's passing. He was a well-versed man and always respectful."

I offer a small smile and a curtsey in response but say nothing.

King Silas gestures to his servants, who step forward carrying a carved, wooden chest. "In honor of your hospitality, we bring gifts from Hedera. Treasures to please the senses, as we know such delights are cherished here."

I take a step back, giving the servants room to place the chest before the queens' velvet mattress. Ambra and Eosla scoot closer, their brows raised in anticipation.

 207

The chest is opened, revealing bolts of silk in rich jewel tones—sapphire, ruby, and emerald—each fabric embroidered with ivy patterns that shimmer under the light like liquid luxury.

"Our skilled seamstresses have worked their fingers to the bone," Silas explains, "to create the most exquisite and unique silks especially for you. There are also vials of perfumes crafted from rare flowers found only in the wild meadows of Hedera."

One of the servants removes a polished, wooden box from the trunk, handing it to Queen Ambra with a bow. She opens it to find a collection of hand-carved hair ornaments inlaid with mother-of-pearl and gold.

Queen Eosla rises gracefully, padding barefoot upon the marble floor to inspect the offerings. She lifts a strand of emerald silk and runs it through her fingers. "Exquisite," she murmurs, turning toward Ambra. "Don't you think, my love?"

Ambra's smile sharpens as she traces the wooden box with one finger. "Hedera always did have impeccable taste."

The king nods to another servant, who unveils the dragon scales. Just like in Podrosa, the king has chosen to gift the royals with one gold and one onyx scale. The queens' smiles widen as they gaze upon the rare items.

"King Silas," Eosla purrs. "You have outdone yourself. We are humbled by your lovely gifts."

"We look forward to hearing your proposal for your son," Ambra adds. "But you must be exhausted from your travels. Please, follow Jalelle to your rooms. We know you are not accustomed to our climate, so we have provided clothing more suited for the heat, which you'll find in your chambers."

"Tonight we feast in our celebration tent," Eosla says as she eases back onto the cushion. As soon as she's seated, fingers and lips from the queens' ensemble of lovers find her skin.

The king gives a crisp nod, but I catch the way his mouth tightens. These women unsettle him, as if he finds their boldness a challenge. And for some reason, I do, too.

CHAPTER TWENTY-EIGHT

The evening air is thick with the scent of rich, heady spices mingling with a sweet undertone of jasmine. Nadya and I follow Jalelle to the tent where the evening feast is taking place, Sir Holden trailing behind us. Except this isn't any tent I'm used to. The structure is enormous. It towers above us—vast, sprawling, and shimmering under the light of the moon.

Inside, rich fabrics in shades of crimson and gold cascade down the sides, their edges embroidered with delicate patterns that twist like curling smoke. The air is thick with the scent of spiced meat, honeyed fruits, and the sweet tang of wine, mingling with the faint trace of incense that drifts lazily through the warm air. Soft music hums from one side of the tent—a melody of flutes and stringed instruments, sensual and slow, as if every note is meant to coax the body into motion.

Beside me, Nadya adjusts the gauzy scarf draped low over her shoulders, her dark curls spilling from a loose bun at the top of her head. Her brown skin, shining with glittered oil, contrasts beautifully against the golden silk dress the Bastosi queens gifted her. The gown is molded to her figure, just as mine is—too thin, too revealing for the mourning period, but a welcome respite in the Bastosi heat. Bastos observes different mourning traditions than we do in the east, but at least my dress is black, so the eastern tradition isn't completely ignored.

"Well," Nadya murmurs under her breath, eyeing the clusters of people lounging on the floor, half-reclined against silk cushions. "No one can ever accuse them of not knowing how to enjoy themselves."

I can't argue with that. Everywhere I look, Bastosi courtiers move with a kind of effortless sensuality. Lovers—if they are even exclusive—share whispered secrets, bodies pressed close as they sip from jeweled goblets. Bare shoulders brush without hesitation, hands linger too long or disappear beneath clothing, and laughter swells as if nothing exists beyond the pleasures of this very moment.

Sir Holden stops near the entrance and takes his position to keep watch over me. He is immediately approached by a curious Bastosi lord holding a goblet. The handsome man begins asking Sir Holden questions, too low for me to hear.

A servant welcomes me and Nadya, ushering us forward toward a lavish spread of pillows and ground-level tables. I feel the others watching me as I approach. Though I'm glad to be out of the high-collared, long-sleeved, floor-length gown, I do find it unsettling that my shoulders and arms are bare and that the skirt of my thin, gauzy dress barely flows down to my knees. When we finally reach the section reserved for us, my heart stumbles in my chest.

Dante is already seated—broad-shouldered and impossibly composed in the middle of this decadent chaos. His black attire stands in striking contrast to the gilded fabrics around him, and the sharp angles of his jawline seem even more severe under the flickering candlelight. Instead of a tunic, he wears a silky, black vest that lies open to expose his muscular chest and abdomen. It's so hard not to stare and admire his body.

I can feel the pull of him like gravity, and when his storm-grey eyes meet mine, the air between us seems to hum.

With no subtlety whatsoever, a servant gestures to the cushions beside him.

Of course.

Nadya quickly moves from my left to my right, forcing me to take the cushion directly next to Dante. When I flash her a look, she pretends she didn't do it on purpose, batting her lashes at me in feigned innocence.

With a controlled breath, I lower myself beside Dante. As I settle, my thigh brushes his in the confined space, and every nerve in my body sharpens. He's close—too close for me to be able to convincingly ignore his presence. I almost sigh at the feel of his warmth seeping through the thin fabric of my dress. I try to steady my breathing, but the air is thick, heavy with scents and sounds and the undercurrent of temptation that touches everything in Bastos.

"A fortunate coincidence," he murmurs low enough that only I can hear.

I arch a brow, refusing to let my voice betray how much I feel his nearness. "Or a risky one."

The corner of his mouth curves into a wicked smile, and my stomach flutters traitorously. His gaze travels down my body, and he tilts his head slightly.

"What are you doing?" I whisper.

"Trying to figure out where you're hiding your dagger under that tight dress."

It's my turn to give him a wicked smile. "Wouldn't you like to know."

"Make no mistake. I would take absolute delight in figuring it out."

My skin heats, the hot sensation trickling down my back. I release a breath that's dangerously close to a sigh, and Dante's gaze darkens.

I make a point to look away, swallowing down my urge to move closer to him. And it's a good thing I do, because the king's glare stays on me for a moment. It's a warning he won't let me forget.

A rustle of movement draws my gaze to the left, where Queen Ambra lounges with a goblet in hand, one of her lovers feeding her slivers of sugared dates. She catches me looking and winks.

Beside me, Nadya clasps her hands together, her smile wide as servants begin laying out the feast. Platters piled high with honey-glazed meats, jewel-bright fruits, and spiced pastries fill the tables. Wine flows

 211

like water, the deep-red liquid shimmering in cut-glass decanters. A golden bowl holds figs dripping with syrup, while delicate flower-shaped sweets are dusted with crushed petals. As one lovely servant fills Nadya's glass, she rests her hand on Nadya's shoulder, letting it linger there a moment as their eyes meet.

I reach for a goblet, taking a sip to steady myself. The wine is rich and sweet on my tongue, with a hint of something floral that lingers as I swallow.

"Is everything in Bastos this... indulgent?" I ask, half to myself.

Dante leans closer, his breath warm against my ear. "You have no idea."

The brush of his voice sends a shiver down my spine, and I curse the heat rushing to my core. My hand trembles slightly as I place my goblet back on the table.

How am I going to get through this dinner?

A group of courtiers drifts closer, their conversation laced with laughter and teasing words. They look like they've had too much wine. One of them stumbles, falling halfway to the floor, pressing against me before catching herself, and causing me to lose my balance. I fall into Dante's side, and the dampness of our sweat-glistened bodies makes our skin glide against each other's.

His hand comes to my waist—steadying, possessive. For a heartbeat, neither of us moves.

"Careful," he says softly, though there's nothing careful about the way his thumb brushes against my hip.

I bite the inside of my cheek, desperate to keep my composure. Across the room, King Silas watches us with his usual air of disapproval, his sharp gaze lingering a moment too long. I shift slightly away from Dante, though every fiber of me protests the loss of his touch.

I take that moment to glance around at the others around the table. When my eyes land on Queen Eleanor, my stomach sours. She is not dressed in the sheer fabrics the rest of us wear. Instead, she wears the usual high-collared, long-sleeved dress and her ever-present elbow-high gloves. It pains my heart, knowing she is covering her bruises. I guess they

haven't healed enough during the journey to fade from view.

Unless she has new bruises she acquired since leaving Podrosa. I can't help but wonder when King Silas might have had the opportunity to mishandle her, especially since they are not traveling in the same carriage. I fight the urge to go to her, to ask her if she's all right and comfort her. And I fight the even bigger urge to confront the king and make him see the error of his ways.

Ezra gives me a small nod from across the tent. He lifts a goblet, sniffing the liquid before sipping it. I almost laugh when he wrinkles his nose, which eases my anger for the king a bit.

The laughter grows louder as more wine is poured, the Bastosi clearly unbothered by decorum or restraint. Nearby, a musician plucks a sensual melody on a lute while a trio of dancers twists and sways to the rhythm, their jewel-toned skirts brushing the floor. I settle back onto the pillows, feeling the silk slide cool against my legs, and resist the urge to glance at Dante again. But the warmth of his presence is impossible to ignore.

"So," Queen Ambra purrs, her voice dripping with intrigue. "Lord Dante, future Prince of Hedera. What is it like, to be a man who was hidden in the shadows, only to now stand at the center of every kingdom's gaze?" She lifts her jeweled goblet and tilts her head, her striking, green eyes gleaming with intrigue.

Dante, to his credit, does not flinch under her gaze. He offers her a slow, polite smile. "I wouldn't say I'm at the center of anything, Your Majesty. I'm only doing my part to ensure Hedera's proper succession."

"My son is truly humble," King Silas puts in. "But there should be no doubt that he will make a fine prince."

Dante simply nods and takes a swig of his drink.

I notice the dip of Queen Eleanor's gaze, the way her eyes lower with sadness.

Queen Eosla hums thoughtfully, leaning back against her wife with an easy elegance. "A dutiful son," she muses, brushing a lock of turquois hair behind her ear.

"But not all dutiful sons bring honor to their realms," Queen Ambra

puts in, tracing a fingertip languidly over her wife's collarbone. "It was only decades ago when my father broke ties with Tsar Pisarus, which most certainly had my grandfather rolling in his grave." She shifts her gaze to me, clearly seeing my confusion. "When my grandfather was King of Bastos, he had sworn allegiance to Dulcamar. But that was before the Age of War."

I can understand the shift in alliances. My own father made an enemy of the sirens of Messanya, but when my brother inherited the throne, he took great strides to mend their ties.

"And so it goes in times not embraced by peace," Queen Eosla says, tracing lazy circles on her wife's hand. "If the tides shift, we must shift with them."

Queen Ambra tilts her head as she studies Dante. "We do so appreciate a man who knows his duty. But surely, you must have desires of your own." Her smile deepens, the invitation in her tone unmistakable.

Dante chuckles low in his throat, a sound that sends a spark of heat through me despite the sweltering air. "I find a prince's desire should be to serve his kingdom," he says, his voice like velvet, smooth and controlled. His fingers twitch slightly where his hand rests on his knee—a movement so small, I nearly miss it.

"Yes, of course," Queen Ambra says as she flashes him a smile. "But you are also a man, and there must certainly be a passion that drives you."

I fight to control the heat that climbs up my neck.

Dante gives her a nod. "Naturally, but I'm also a man of decorum, and I know it's wise to keep my private affairs... private."

A silver-haired courtier lounging nearby gives an exaggerated sigh. "What a shame," he says, his mouth curling in amusement. "We are always eager to know what a handsome prince desires. Perhaps a bit more Bastosi wine will loosen your tongue?" He gestures to a servant, who swiftly refills Dante's cup with a golden liquid that gleams in the lantern light.

I feel Dante's gaze brush against me as he lifts the cup to his lips. My throat tightens, and I force my attention to the fruit platter in front of me. I reach for a fig, hoping to distract myself from the warmth spreading low in my belly. Nadya, ever the observant one, nudges me with her elbow, her lips curving into a teasing smirk. I pick up my goblet, shifting closer to her as I drink.

"They're practically undressing him with their eyes," she murmurs, leaning in close and keeping her voice just loud enough for me to hear. "Not that I blame them."

I shoot her a glare, but it lacks any real bite. The truth is, I can barely stand it myself. The way he looks tonight—relaxed, confident, yet utterly untouchable—only makes me want him more. But I cannot afford to let my thoughts wander, not here, not when the king is watching us so closely.

"Lord Dante," Queen Ambra calls again, her smile wicked. "I hear you are quite skilled with a blade. Is it true that your falchion never misses its mark?"

"I do my best," Dante replies smoothly, but there's a tautness in his jaw. There's bound to be a trial the queens have arranged, and I'm sure Dante is wondering if this is a clue to what they have planned.

One of the queens' lovers, a lean, dark-eyed man wearing little more than a sheer robe, leans toward Dante with a playful glint in his eye. "If you ever tire of swords, we could find other ways to test your skills."

I press my lips together tightly to stop myself from reacting, but the heat prickling along my skin betrays me. Dante shifts slightly closer to me, his thigh brushing mine on the cushions. The contact is fleeting—just enough to steady me, but not enough to satisfy the ache curling in my chest.

Queen Eosla watches the exchange with amusement but soon waves her hand dismissively. "You must forgive my court, Lord Dante. They seem to have no sense of restraint tonight."

I almost laugh at the understatement.

The evening hums with heat and decadence. Low laughter ripples through the tent, accompanied by the soft chime of bells on the ankles of the servants who drift between cushions and low tables, refilling goblets with sweet, spiced wine.

Queen Ambra tilts her head as the music shifts. The steady beat of drums grows softer, more sensual, and she claps her hands lightly. "Ah," she purrs. "A gift for our guest of honor."

Dante straightens slightly as the three women who had been dancing on the edges of the feast step into the center of the tent.

My breath hitches.

I'd noticed them before, but taking the time to study them in more detail, I have to admit that these women are stunning. From the melodic sound Nadya makes beside me, I can tell she agrees.

Scarves of sheer crimson and gold flutter around their hips, the thin silks offering only the barest cover to their soft, curving figures. The skin at their exposed shoulders, cleavages, and stomachs shimmers and sparkles in the candlelight. Glittery, beaded belts sway below their waists with each measured step, drawing the eye lower. Hair as dark as midnight cascades down their backs, threaded with delicate gold chains and ribbons. Their faces are painted—sultry, red lips and kohl-lined eyes that gleam like polished obsidian as they approach.

"Stand for us, future prince," Queen Ambra invites, her voice a husky tease.

One of the stunning women draws closer to Dante, tossing a handful of flower petals in the air over us before bending down to pull at his arm with two delicate hands. Her gold bangles clink together as she stretches between us. She has a smile that could charm anyone into letting her get away with anything she wishes.

"Yes, stand, my son." King Silas lifts his drink, laughter bubbling from his throat.

Dante hesitates just long enough to make my pulse quicken before he sets his goblet down and rises to his feet.

I force myself to hold still, to keep my expression smooth.

But inside, a different kind of heat prickles through me. A heat borne from jealousy, I painfully admit to myself.

The dancers move with liquid grace, encircling him. A slow roll of their hips, the slide of their hands skimming the air just shy of his skin. One twirls a length of silk across his shoulders, letting it slip down his chest in a teasing caress. Another traces the edge of his jaw with her fingertips, bold as anything. I curl my fingers into my lap.

I could stop her. A flick of my wrist, and the dagger hidden beneath my skirts could pin her hand to the floor.

Instead, I do nothing.

The dancers twirl swiftly around him, their breasts practically spilling from their tops, and Dante's balance sways.

I hadn't noticed before, but his eyes are a bit bloodshot. The wine they've given him must be strong. He's keeping his balance, but I can tell it's a struggle.

A chuckle ripples from the queens' mattress, low and indulgent. "The future prince seems tense," Queen Eosla murmurs, exchanging a knowing look with her wife.

"Perhaps he's merely deciding which of them to bed first," Queen Amber suggests.

"If it's too much to handle, Dante, I'll relieve you of one," King Silas quips, the amusement in his tone laced with something coarser. "Or keep all three, if you dare. I'm sure they wouldn't mind sharing."

My nails dig deeper into my palm.

Dante's lips curl faintly, but it doesn't touch his eyes. "Your generosity humbles me, Your Majesty," he says smoothly, though I notice the way his shoulders stiffen beneath the press of the dancers' hands.

One of the women—tall, with skin like gleaming bronze—slides her fingers along the open edges of his vest, pushing it farther apart. A muscle feathers in his jaw, but he doesn't pull away.

I clench my teeth as my heart pounds, the flush rising higher along my neck.

He's only playing the part, I remind myself. But that doesn't stop the ache low in my belly, the sharp twist of something I'm embarrassed I let consume me.

The women laugh softly as the music winds down. They twirl their scarves around him once more, drawing out the moment, their bodies brushing close enough to make my blood boil. But Dante only offers them a polite smile, dipping his head. "Your talents are exceptional," he

says, his voice as smooth as velvet. "Truly a welcome I won't soon forget."

The queens exchange a glance as they applaud, clearly pleased.

The three women pull on Dante's arm, forcing him to hunch forward a bit. When they each place a kiss on his cheeks and jaw, my breath leaves me, my stomach roiling. In my head, my dagger has already decapitated them all. But in reality, I keep still.

The dancers giggle, running their hands over his biceps as they sway their hips. The music fades as the dancers twirl away, leaving behind the scent of honeyed sweat and the low hum of anticipation. Heat coils around me like a second skin, thick with spice and incense, seeping into my lungs until every breath feels heavy. My hair sticks to the back of my neck. The thin silk of my dress clings to my spine.

Beside me, Dante sways as he reclaims his seat, his expression guarded beneath a veneer of amusement. But I can see the flush high on his cheeks, the way his hand tightens around the stem of his goblet. He's trying not to show that the wine is affecting him.

But the queens know it.

The queens recline on their velvet cushions like cats basking in sunlight. Queen Eosla's mouth curves into a smile as she lifts her hand, fingers glittering with rings.

"You've been a most gracious guest, prospective future Prince of Hedera," she purrs, her voice like molten gold. "But your trial has yet to begin."

I freeze. His trial? Now?

Dante lowers his goblet slowly. "Oh?"

Part of me wants to reach out and push the goblet down. More wine will only make any trial they have planned more difficult.

Queen Ambra leans forward, her silky, raven strands coiled over one shoulder like a serpent. "It's simple. All we ask is that you walk." Her eyes gleam as she gestures toward the center of the hall.

All heads turn.

At first, I don't see it. But then the crowd parts. Nobles shift aside with the eager rustle of silk and laughter until a path is exposed.

Oh, shit.

Everyone stands to get a better view.

The tiled, twenty-foot path, narrow and straight, has been cleared across the length of the hall. Its edges are flanked by two rows of golden vases interspersed with lit torches, the flickering flames casting sharp shadows onto the tile. And scattered across the tiles, coiled and shimmering like water in the firelight, are at least a dozen snakes.

My breath catches.

The snakes barely move, their movements deliberate as they hiss. Like they're waiting.

What the fuck is this?

Dante glances at me for a split second before inhaling deeply. He sways slightly as he sets down his goblet. My eyes go to the king, and even he seems rigid, the grasp on his goblet turning his knuckles white.

The queens exchange a glance of private amusement, Ambra hooking her arm through Eosla's.

"Make it from one side to the other," Queen Ambra says, her voice like velvet drawn across a blade. "But step carefully. The serpents of Bastos do not take kindly to drunken feet."

Queen Eleanor holds a gloved hand to her chest. King Silas swallows hard before schooling his features, giving Dante an encouraging nod.

"Ah-ah-ah," Queen Ambra lets out, shaking a finger at Dante. "No sword. Those are royal serpents, protected by the realm."

Dante exchanges a glance with Silas as Sir Donovan steps forward and waits by Dante's side. Dante's jaw stiffens as he unsheathes his falchion and hands it to Sir Donovan to hold on to.

Murmurs ripple through the audience. Some are watching with fear, others with glee. I shift, palms damp, and I have to stop myself from reaching for Dante's hand. Luckily, Nadya mollifies me by linking her hand with mine, giving me the support I need. Dante's bloodshot eyes catch mine for a moment as he moves around me toward the path.

Nadya tenses beside me. "They're venomous," she whispers.

A man in a violet sash moves to stand near the path—young, sharp-eyed, with a cobra tattoo winding down his arm. I swear his eyes are pitch

black. He raises a hand in a slow, practiced motion, and when he does, a few of the snakes slither to life, their heads raised and their scaled bodies gleaming beneath the firelight.

He's fae. An animal-wielder, or at least a snake-wielder. But I'm not sure if he's there to keep Dante safe... or to make this trial more challenging.

Everyone is quiet as Dante steps onto the first tile. From the musicians' corner, someone hits a drum in an unnerving tempo. Dante's shoulders rise and fall as he steadies himself, as if shaking off the haze of wine and heat. The sweat on his brow is visible from where Nadya and I stand, and the tight set of his jaw makes me nervous he's going to crack a tooth. The music starts again, the flutes and string instruments joining the pulsing drumbeat, and the air feels like it thickens in my throat.

He takes another step. Then another. The fae flicks his wrist, and the first snake shifts toward Dante with a hiss.

I nearly step forward, but Nadya's hold is strong. I glance at her with wide eyes, and she shakes her head. She's right. I have to let him complete his trial.

But my magic pulses, anyway, an anxious hum beneath my skin. I clench my teeth, trying to keep it quiet, trying not to let it leak out, but already, I feel the ache pressing behind my eyes, the dull, rhythmic throb that always precedes something I can't control.

Dante gapes at the snake, his body swaying.

"Steady, Dante. Please."

Dante straightens a bit, then he moves again, slower now. The snake is now joined by a second, both of them curling across the tile before him, rearing their heads back slightly. The fae twitches his fingers, directing them. They wave their bodies, taunting Dante.

Dante shifts sideways, his weight careful, his focus absolute. But the wine is dulling his edges. He lifts his foot and slides it forward, his eyes trained on the two reptiles. I watch the rise and fall of his chest as he takes a step forward and clears past the first two threats.

I release a breath. I hear a giggle and glance over to see the queens tittering, Ambra's arms now wrapped around Eosla from behind, her chin resting on Eosla's shoulder.

I turn my focus back to Dante, who stumbles for a breath—just enough to draw a collective gasp from the room. Laughter bubbles up from a few courtiers.

He recovers. Steadies.

King Silas stretches as if working out a kink in his neck, his hands clenched into fists.

The path ahead of Dante narrows, twisting through a dense cluster of serpents. They slither lazily, but their intent is unmistakable. With the snake-wielder's signal, one of the reptiles slinks directly into Dante's path, blocking his progress.

He has to step over it.

My heart is a frantic drum. My hands clench in front of me. I can feel the wild heat of the room, the prickle of sweat against the back of my neck.

The snake juts its head forward with a loud hiss. Dante instinctively reaches for the hilt of his falchion, the wine apparently making him forget it's not there. The realization throws him off-kilter, and he almost tips forward into the serpent.

My magic surges again.

No!

I push—barely a whisper of will, just enough to nudge the snake away from him. It works, the snake sliding a foot to the right, but the force backlashes through me like a crack of thunder behind my eyes.

Pain splinters across my skull. I flinch, head ducking, and Nadya reaches for me in evident alarm. Her gaze drops to my nose, and her eyes widen. Before I can question her, she grabs a silk handkerchief from the table and shoves it into my palm.

I wipe my face quickly, almost shuddering at the sight of the blood on the silk.

Nadya nods, letting me know I'm in the clear, but my body is still buzzing. If my magic cuts loose again, I'm going to need more than just this handkerchief.

"It's fine," I whisper to her.

But it's *not* fine. My vision blurs at the edges.

Dante has made it past the snake, but he's not at the end of the path yet. He's not walking straight, but he keeps going.

The music swells—faster, louder. The snakes are restless now, weaving through the tiles like living shadows. The fae lifts both hands and two serpents writhe into Dante's path.

Fuck!

He's swaying. Sweat glistens on his skin. His focus is slipping.

Come on. Just a few more steps.

I press my palm flat against my stomach, grounding myself as best I can. One final push—I don't even know what I'm aiming for. Just *something* to keep him upright, to clear the tile. I shove the energy outward, but it bursts sideways—wild and chaotic. As soon as I release it, I get a sharp pain in my chest.

The fire from one of the nearby torches flares too wide, causing the nobles closest to it to cry out and scatter back. Dante's arm shields his face, and I suck in a breath when I notice the instant, red blistering of his skin.

Without thinking, I send another wave of energy surging. In my mind, I sense the urgent need to heal him. The next two seconds play out in slow motion in my eyes—an icy film appearing on his scorched skin, Dante pulling his arm against his chest and covering it with his other arm, his brow scrunching over narrowed eyes, and then the straightening of his back.

Luckily, I see that the distraction has also caused the animal-wielder to falter. The snakes shift off-course. And when Dante finally steps forward again, he strides cleanly over the last tile and into the open.

The hall goes silent.

Then... applause. It's slow at first, then grows louder. The faces of the people in the crowd are filled with amazement. They're clearly impressed.

I feel like I'm going to faint, and the sharp pain behind my eyes has blossomed to the point that I see black spots dance before me. My arms are wrapped around myself, and Nadya is supporting me to keep me upright. I wince, then straighten, flashing her a look of gratitude as I breathe through the pain.

The queens lean toward each other, exchanging another knowing look before Queen Ambra claps her hands once. "Very well done," she says, stepping forward. "You've completed the path, Lord Dante."

Dante inclines his head, his movements stiff, as if he's barely holding himself upright.

I glance around, wondering if anyone noticed what I had done. No one remarks on the fire burst; no one mentions seeing any ice form on Dante's arm. Even the snake charmer seems oblivious to my magic interfering. Maybe it was the wine, dulling everyone's attention.

"But your night is not over," Queen Eosla adds, her voice dripping with amusement. "Come. The final mark awaits you."

Final mark? What the fuck does that mean?

They gesture to the flaps at the rear of the tent. Two attendants appear, draped in gauzy crimson, beckoning Dante forward.

His jaw tightens. His eyes find me, and his brows come together.

I force myself to stand up straight, hoping there's no trace of my nosebleed for him to see. I give him a nod, but he can only blink.

The attendants clap him on the shoulders, and he has no choice but to follow.

As he disappears into the night, I'm left with my pulse pounding in my ears, the taste of blood at the back of my throat, and the certainty that whatever they plan next could be worse.

Much worse.

CHAPTER TWENTY-NINE

After Dante left the tent, Nadya and I excused ourselves and headed to our rooms, though Nadya didn't quite make it halfway down our hall before being approached by someone who wanted her full attention. I couldn't be bothered to keep an eye on her, though. I didn't have as much wine as Dante did, but the alcohol did make me drowsy. On the bright side, it helped me get a restful sleep, which I otherwise might not have gotten, since I was encumbered with worry.

A soft breeze stirs the silk canopy above my bed, carrying the faint scent of spices and lavender. Morning light filters through the open window, golden and warm against my bare shoulders. The luxurious bed in Bastos is far softer than the one at Ivystone—too soft, maybe. I could stay here all day, wrapped in silk sheets and the caress of the breeze, if the world would allow it.

Well, perhaps not all day. The Bastosi heat is bound to come in not far behind the rising sun.

The door bursts open without a knock, causing me to spring into a sitting position, clutching the sheets to my chest.

"You're still abed?" Nadya's voice rings through the chamber, bright and full of energy.

I groan softly, sinking deeper beneath the covers again. "What time is it?"

"Late enough. And you'll want to hear this," she says, practically skipping across the room to throw the curtains aside.

I rub at my eyes and find her already rifling through my vanity for some rouge, her dark curls bouncing with every movement. She's dressed in a pale-turquoise gown—far more modest than what the Bastosi women wear, but the gauzy fabric still hugs her frame. Her face is flushed, and her deep-brown eyes sparkle with excitement.

"What did you do?" I stretch, feeling the pull in my limbs. The aftereffects of using my magic have left me sore.

"I asked around," she says, running a finger over one of her eyebrows. "And I found someone who knows where my great-aunt lives."

That gets my attention. I sit up fully, pushing the sheets aside. "Here? In the capital?"

"Just outside it. A little village to the south." She spins to face me, hands clasped in front of her. "And I want to go see her."

I arch a brow, still too hazy with sleep to match her enthusiasm. "Doesn't that sound... impulsive? What if she doesn't want visitors?"

"Oh, come now, what elderly recluse wouldn't want to see a charming, long-lost relative?" She plops onto the edge of my bed with a grin. "Besides, aren't you desperate to escape all of this for a little while? I know I am."

She's not wrong. While I would like to seek out Dante and find out what kind of trial the queens put him through, I'm aware that it's also likely he's already locked in endless meetings with the Bastosi lords and ladies or discussing alliance terms with the queens. All the while, I'm expected to sit in mourning, looking demure and tragic. "I suppose I could use a change of scenery," I admit, though my mind already ticks over the details. "We'll likely have to bring Sir Holden. I doubt the king would approve of us wandering off on our own."

Nadya waves a dismissive hand. "I can tolerate the walking slab of muscle if it means sating my curiosity."

"And what, exactly, are you hoping to find?" I ask, watching her closely. There's an edge of something deeper beneath her playfulness—curiosity, yes, but something else too.

"I don't know," she admits, her smile faltering for the briefest moment. "But I remember my mother's stories. There was always something... *odd* about my great-aunt. And if there's even the smallest thread to follow, I want to pull it."

"'Thread'? You mean about possibly being in the same bloodline as the Bastosi sorceresses?"

She lifts one shoulder, shooting me a shy smile. "Maybe."

I swing my legs over the side of the bed, the cool marble floor sending a shiver up my calves. "Fine. But you're waking Sir Holden and taking the blame if he growls about it."

"Deal." Nadya bounces to her feet and grabs my hand, tugging me toward the wardrobe. "Now, come on. Let's find Indira before you change your mind."

I let her pull me to my feet, laughter bubbling in my chest despite myself. "I can dress myself. And you're far too eager for a woman who snuck off with one of those Bastosi dancers last night."

"You saw that?"

"You give me too little credit, my friend."

"Much like the company I kept last night, I'm a woman of many talents," she says breezily, throwing the door open. "And today, those talents involve dragging you on an adventure."

Twenty minutes later, Indira's sharp tugs at the laces of my gown speak louder than any complaint she might voice aloud. This mourning gown is thankfully thinner than the thick gown I wore in Podrosa, but I'm already starting to feel the sweating begin.

"I'm not sure what the sudden urgency is about," she mutters, securing the last loop with a little more force than necessary. "Where, exactly, are you two off to in such a rush?"

Nadya leans against the vanity, plumping her curls with a palm. "Just a quick outing. A little air, a little exploration. Nothing too scandalous."

Indira sniffs, smoothing down a crease on her apron. "Well, I'll alert the coach master, but I'm not responsible for chasing after your guard dog. If you're looking for Sir Holden, he isn't at his post." Without waiting for a reply, she spins on her heel and strides toward the door. "And if you get yourselves into trouble, I won't be the one dragging you out of it."

"I think that's the closest thing to concern we'll ever get from her," Nadya says dryly as the door clicks shut behind her.

"She has a point," I reply, already moving toward the corridor. "Where *is* Sir Holden?"

"He's probably brooding in some shadowy corner, polishing his sword," Nadya quips, falling in step beside me. "Or sharpening his scowl. That man needs to learn how to let loose once in a while."

I think about the times Sir Holden has given me space or looked the other way when I needed him to, and I feel the need to defend him. "He's not always so serious."

"I'll believe that when I see it."

We weave through the quiet palace halls, passing open archways that let in the warming Bastosi breeze. Most of the court is still abed, nursing their indulgences from the night before. When we reach the west wing, I pause outside the door we're told is his and give a sharp knock.

Nothing.

I exchange a glance with Nadya, then knock again, louder this time.

The door creaks open, and Sir Holden fills the frame, his bare chest catching the early sunlight. His hair, usually perfectly combed, is rumpled, and a faint flush warms his chiseled features. For once, the man looks less like a sentinel forged from stone and more like, well, a man.

I can't help but smirk. Over his shoulder, I catch a glimpse of tousled sheets and the very same Bastosi lord who had been speaking far too closely to him at last night's feast is now stretched languidly across the bed.

"I—" Nadya's jaw hangs open, but I cut her a knowing glance, willing her to hold back the quip already forming on her tongue.

Sir Holden, to his credit, doesn't flinch. Instead, he squares his shoulders and crosses his arms over his chest. His expression is as impassive as ever, but there's a flicker of something behind his eyes—an unspoken request for discretion.

Tit for tat, I guess.

"Sir Holden, we would like to go out," Nadya announces, her voice dripping with false innocence. "And we need you to join us. After all, we wouldn't want to be unprotected while we explore this strange and mysterious realm."

His lips press into a thin line. "Is this an official errand?"

"Of course," I say. "Call it a... familial obligation."

He exhales quietly, the faintest hint of a sigh. Then, casting a glance over his shoulder at the half-draped man still lounging in his bed, he mutters, "Give me half an hour."

The door clicks shut.

I blink, struggling to contain the grin tugging at my mouth. Beside me, Nadya raises her brows and lets out a low whistle.

"Well," she says, laughter bright in her voice. "I take it back, Celeste. Guess he knows how to let loose, after all."

I shake my head, letting out a laugh as we head back down the corridor. "There's hope for him yet."

"And a very satisfied Bastosi in his bed," Nadya murmurs, sending us both into a fit of laughter as we traipse toward the main wing of the palace.

The morning air is thick with the familiar scent of jasmine and warm, spiced incense curling through the archways. Shimmering sunlight filters through the sheer, silken drapes, casting golden patterns on the polished marble floors. The palace hums with a lazy, decadent energy—servants in gossamer fabrics drift by, carrying trays of citrus fruits and honeyed pastries. Everything here is designed for pleasure, from the velvet-cushioned benches to the sweeping murals depicting Bastosi gods tangled in their endless indulgences.

Near the entrance, the coach master, a wiry man with sun-bronzed skin, bows low when he sees us. "Your carriage will be ready shortly, Your

Highness," he says, his voice as smooth as the wine they serve here.

I nod in acknowledgment, and I allow my mind to wander to where Dante might be. Is he still sleeping? Is he even still alive? Yes, of course, he must be. I would have heard something if whatever challenge they'd put him through had proven fatal. Did the queens make him do something sordid as his part of his test?

Gods, I hope not.

A throat clears behind me, and I whirl around just in time to see Sir Holden descending the grand staircase.

He's back to his usual, imposing self—broad shoulders squared, uniform pressed and pristine. There's no trace of the disheveled man we found at his chamber door earlier, though the faint pink at the edge of his jawline suggests he shaved in haste. If he's annoyed at being pulled from his... *extracurricular activities*, he gives no sign.

"I assume we're ready?" His voice is clipped, as professional as ever, though his gaze lingers on Nadya just a fraction longer than necessary.

"Whenever you are." I make a point to give him a polite smile.

Sir Holden's jaw tightens slightly, but then he gestures toward the front gate. "Your carriage awaits, Princess."

The carriage rocks to a halt at the edge of a small, sun-drenched clearing. Beyond it, nestled beneath the canopy of a copse of olive trees, stands a modest cottage. The walls are whitewashed, the roof thatched and slightly weathered, but the place is alive with color. Pots of herbs crowd the windowsills—lavender, rosemary, and something that looks like wolfsbane. Wreaths of dried sage and bundles of wildflowers hang from the eaves, swaying gently in the warm breeze. A stone path, half-covered in creeping thyme, leads to the front door, which is painted a faded, cheerful red.

It's quaint. Some might even say picturesque. And yet something

about it puts me on edge.

Nadya shifts beside me, twisting her fingers in the folds of her skirt. "I don't even know if she'll remember me," she murmurs. "I was only a girl the last time we met."

"Well, I guess we'll find out."

It's a little cooler here than it is at the capitol. There's a weight in the air—something that feels like it's been lingering since long before we arrived. I think of the stories of Bastosi witches and wonder if that strange thing I'm feeling in the air is a spell.

Sir Holden opens the carriage door, scanning the surroundings with his usual caution. After we disembark, he waits silently by the carriage as Nadya and I step onto the path.

Nadya hesitates, brushing her curls behind her ear. I can tell she's nervous, and I don't blame her. This matters to her. I've dragged her along to live in Hedera with me, essentially making her give up her life in Delasurvia, upending her daily life of being surrounded by friends and romantic interests and family. All of it for me. So I can give her this. I can be the supportive friend she's been to me through all of this.

I reach out and squeeze her hand to let her know I'm here for her.

She gives me an understanding smile. When we reach the cottage door, she lets out a long breath before rapping on the faded, red wood.

For a long moment, nothing happens. Out of the corner of my eye, I think the curtains move.

The latch clicks.

The door opens just a crack. An older woman peers out, her eyes sharp and wary beneath the hood of a sheer linen shawl. Her skin is rich and warm like Nadya's, though hers is marked with faint lines at the corners of her mouth and eyes. Silver streaks wind through the mass of ebony curls piled atop her head, but there's a liveliness to her expression, an alertness that suggests she misses nothing.

When her gaze lands on Sir Holden—looming and armored—her lips thin. "I don't take visitors," she says, her voice low and cool.

Nadya steps forward hastily. "Auntie Tia," she says softly. "It's me. Nadya."

The woman freezes. Her dark eyes narrow as she studies Nadya's face, as if peeling back the years. After a moment, her mouth softens. "Gods above..." She pushes the door open wider, her gaze sweeping over Nadya's curls, her warm, brown eyes, the brown skin that matches her own. "I should've known. You've got your grandmother's face. Come closer, child. Let me see you properly."

Nadya moves toward her, and Tia cups her face with both hands, studying her intently before sighing.

"You're all grown up, child," Tia says. Her voice gentles as she releases her hold.

Nadya blinks rapidly, her usual quick wit faltering. "I wasn't sure if you'd want to see me."

Tia's mouth twists faintly. "Family is family. You'll always be welcome here." Her gaze shifts to me, and she tilts her head slightly. "And if I'm not mistaken, the Princess of Delasurvia is gracing my doorstep as well." She doesn't fall into a full curtsey, but her frame bends a bit as she inclines her head.

I straighten, offering a polite nod. "It's an honor to meet you, madam."

Something flickers behind her eyes—something unreadable—but her voice remains smooth. "I met you once, when you were only knee high to me. And my condolences to you, Your Highness. I was fond of your mother, what little I knew of her. She had a kindness about her that was rare among royalty."

I swallow the ache that rises at the mention of my mother and nod. "Thank you," I say quietly.

Tia's gaze lingers on me for a breath longer than is comfortable before flicking to Sir Holden. Her mouth hardens again. "I don't like armed men near my door," she says flatly.

"He's only here to ensure our safety," I explain, already bracing for his response. "And rest assured, he will stand sentry at the carriage."

Sir Holden's jaw tenses, but after a moment's pause, he gives a curt nod.

Tia sniffs but steps aside. "Come in, then," she says, waving us

through. "If you've come all this way, I suppose you didn't do it just to stand on my doorstep."

The air inside the cottage holds a cozy warmth, fragrant with dried herbs and something faintly sweet, like honeyed pears. The space is small but well-kept, everything in its proper place. Sunlight streams through the open windows, illuminating shelves lined with glass jars, each labeled in a precise, looping hand. Bundles of herbs hang from exposed beams, their earthy scent blending with the faint tang of dried citrus. A wooden worktable dominates the far wall, its surface scattered with parchment, half-ground powders, and a delicate mortar and pestle.

A small hearth flickers beneath a wooden mantel, worn but tidy. A quaint sitting area is arranged around a low table. There's no extravagance here, but the simple beauty of the place is undeniable.

Tia gestures toward the cushioned chairs. "Sit. You're making me tired just standing there. Tell me what brings you to Bastos."

Nadya and I settle into the chairs, but Tia remains standing.

"King Silas is presenting his son Dante to the Bastosi queens," Nadya explains. "It's for his legitimization tour."

"Ah, yes. I heard rumors of a bastard son. And of Prince Torbin's untimely death." Tia crosses to the kitchenette in the corner, plucking a polished, copper kettle from a hook. "I suppose I ought to make tea—gods know you've probably been fed nothing but watered-down wine at that palace."

I smile faintly at the comment but stay quiet as I glance at Nadya, trying to assess how she's doing emotionally.

Nadya's smile is small, possibly forced, but she gives me a nod.

I switch my attention back to Tia. She moves about the small kitchen, her fingers deftly selecting herbs from hanging bundles. I feel it again—that subtle weight. That sense that there's something in the air. Watching us, maybe. Waiting for something to react to.

Tia moves with brisk efficiency, clattering down a tin of dried hibiscus and another filled with clove buds. The kettle sings not long after, and Tia pours the steaming water into mismatched ceramic mugs. Her hands are steady, her movements practiced—but there's a tension in her shoulders, like a coil wound too tightly.

She places the cups on the small table before us. "It's best drunk while hot."

Tia remains beside the table, staring at us. Nadya and I glance at each other, blinking in confusion.

"Drink!" Tia presses her lips together and runs a hand over her neck as if she'd hurt her throat. "It's just that its flavor is best before it grows cold."

My brow furrows. The cups are clearly still steaming, so Tia's worry is unwarranted. Still, I don't want to upset Nadya's great-aunt, so I pick up my cup.

Nadya follows my lead, and we both carefully press our lips to the cup rims to take a sip. The liquid burns my mouth, so I'm only able to manage a few drops, but my healing magic eases away the pain.

The scent of the tea is floral with a hint of something cloyingly sweet—honeysuckle, maybe, or dried fruit steeped in herbs. Tia is still waiting, so after blowing on the tea for a bit, I take another careful sip. There's a strange aftertaste I can't quite place, syrupy and faintly metallic, but not unpleasant.

I hum my approval, and Tia smiles, finally taking a seat in a worn, tweed chair.

I drink again.

"You're like her, you know," Tia says suddenly, her eyes on me.

I blink. "Who?"

"Your mother." Her voice softens, but just a shade. "The same dark eyes. Same warm coloring. Same quiet strength. Except her stillness was worn like a veil, whereas yours is more like armor."

The words confuse me, and I can't help but wonder if there's a hidden meaning behind them.

Nadya clears her throat, her fingers curling lightly around her mug. "Aunt Tia, I have some questions."

"I thought you might." Tia's eyes go from Nadya to me and back again. "I knew there was more that brought you here than sentimental reasons."

 233

Nadya takes another sip of tea, letting out a long breath again before continuing. "I've been reading about Bastos and its... connection to those who practice magic. And I was wondering if you know anything about that."

"Ah, yes. The infamous Bastosi sorceresses." Tia nods. "You must be reading about the dark past. Not dark because of the existence of sorceresses, but because of the bad reputation forced upon them."

"'Forced'?" I ask, leaning forward a bit.

Tia tilts her head, her gaze lowering to my cup. Instinctively, I take another drink.

"The fae and sirens claim that sorcerers and sorceresses were not born with magic, that it was stolen from the gods." Tia taps her fingers upon the arms of her chair. "But those claims were false, borne of jealousy, because a single sorceress's magic can be expanded and affect more than a single fae or a single siren. It's why they can develop seer skills, if learned enough."

"But that seems... dangerous." I'm a bit surprised that I let that slip out. If this were a stranger, I wouldn't be so restrained, but I was trying to be respectful because Tia is Nadya's family.

"Yes, it can be," Tia answers. "I won't deny that there are sorcerers and sorceresses who abuse the gift."

Nadya blinks at her great-aunt over the rim of her cup as she sips more tea and then suddenly she blurts out, "Are you a witch, Aunt Tia?" Nadya's eyes widen as soon as she says it, and she slaps a hand over her mouth. "I'm sorry. I don't know why I—"

The corner of Tia's mouth turns upward. "It's quite all right, my child. Your curiosity is obviously unsettling you." She studies us a minute before continuing. "But your instincts are right. I have it in my blood."

"I'm sorry I said 'witch,'" Nadya says.

"By all means, I welcome the name." Tia lifts a brow and shakes her head. "You see, those same people who were afraid of our powers used the word to try to scare people into hating us. At first, they called us 'heretics,' but then the name 'witch' caught on. I suppose they deemed it crueler. They thought the word was slanderous, that it would make us outcasts. And in a way, they were right. But we, who have this ability to call magic to us, embrace the word because we know it simply means our craft is strong."

Nadya has awe in her eyes. "If it's in your blood... does that mean... that it's in mine?"

I'm pretty sure the expression on Nadya's face is hope, and I'm not sure how I feel about it.

Tia rubs her chin. "There's a high chance, though bloodlines can be diluted over time. There is a way or two to check, though. Here, take my hand."

Nadya swallows hard before setting her cup down. Her gaze darts to me, and then she scoots forward in her chair, reaching out for her aunt's hand.

At first, nothing happens. But after a moment, the room warms, and the candles flicker. In the next moment, the flames blaze brighter. Nadya's eyes widen, reflecting the glow.

Tia smiles. "There. You feel that?"

Nadya nods, breathless. "What is that?"

"Our magic feeding each other. Happens when two connected bloodlines meet." Tia squeezes Nadya's hands. "Yours is quiet, but it's there."

Nadya looks as if she's going to jump out of her skin. "'Quiet'? How do I... Can you teach me to make it louder?"

Tia grunts. "My dear, I don't think I have it in me anymore to be your mentor. Not at my age. But I can help you out with the basics." She stands, and Nadya stares as she moves to an old, cluttered bookshelf. "Where in the gods' rotting teeth did I put it..."

Nadya quickly looks to me, clasping her hands in her lap. I can tell she's nervous, not just because of the way one of her feet keeps tapping, but because I can feel it pulsing out of her.

Tia whistles, then slides a tome off the shelf. For a quick moment, I'm reminded of the book that jumped off the shelf near Nadya in Podrosa. Tia comes back to stand in front of her great-niece.

Nadya reaches for the book slowly, reverently. The leather is cracked

and worn, the edges of the pages curled with age. Strange symbols curl over the cover like vines.

"Is this the *grimoire*?" Nadya's voice comes out in a whisper.

Tia chuckles. "No, child. That was lost in the Age of Blood—torn from our hands and burned by cowards who feared what they couldn't control. This here's a pale cousin. Notes written down by some of the first witches. It's got a few basic spells. Simple things like starting a flame, pushing life into a dying plant, some illusion spells. Special brews and potions to fit certain situations. There are some advanced spells near the end, like a temporary cloaking spell. Nothing grand, but it'll teach you focus. Precision."

Nadya gapes, her eyes focused on the book. "That all sounds incredible."

Her excitement scares me for some reason, and my thoughts bubble straight to the surface, unfiltered. "I don't know if Nadya could handle the consequences that come with using magic," I blurt out. "She's clever, curious, compassionate. But she hasn't seen the things I've seen or had to make the choices I've made. Not only am I fae, but I'm a soldier. Trained to fight. When situations get out of hand, I know what to do."

I bite my tongue too late, the words already out. Nadya furrows her brows at me. I've clearly struck a nerve.

Tia snorts softly. "Good," she mutters. "Soldiers break things. Witches mend them."

"I meant she's not ready," I say again, blinking at my unfiltered outbursts. "Magic can be dangerous. Unstable." I grip my mug, eyeing the tea suspiciously. *Special brews and potions to fit certain situations.* "What... What was in this?"

Tia raises a brow. "Just a little something to make sure my guests aren't trying to manipulate me."

Nadya and I stare at her.

Tia sighs but doesn't look sorry. "It's a brew that lowers your defenses, eases the truth out of you."

"Gods," I mutter, setting the mug down. "That feels like a violation."

"Lying would be a violation," Tia retorts. "Wouldn't you agree?"

I whip my head toward Nadya. "I didn't mean anything bad by what I said, and you know I'm telling the truth because—" I lift my mug to drive my point.

It takes a moment before Nadya gives me a nod, and I feel as if I've caused a small rift between us.

"I tell you what," Tia begins, gesturing toward the book. "Practice a little. Start small. And if you think it's too overwhelming or gives you a bad feeling, then simply stop."

Nadya gapes at her. "Are you letting me borrow this?"

Tia leans back in her chair, looking proud. "It's yours."

Nadya's eyes shine. "What?"

Tia shrugs. "I've had it so long, the damn thing talks back to me. Might as well go to someone who can learn something from it. Plus, you're family."

I look between them, that old ache building in my chest. I want to be happy for Nadya. I am. But there's a part of me that still curls inward at the possibility it could go terribly wrong.

"You sure about this?" I ask softly.

Nadya looks at me. "I don't know. But I want to try."

Tia snorts again, heading for the kettle to pour herself a second cup. "Good. About damn time someone in this family stopped making excuses."

I set my cup down. "In a book Nadya was reading, there were sorceresses traveling the land before the dragons died out from the poisoned plants. Do you know anything about that?"

One of Tia's eyes narrow. "Are you asking if witches started the poison?"

"Yes," I say, unable to not speak the truth.

Tia shakes her head. "This happened a century before my time. There are many mixed opinions from the modern witch community, people taking sides, especially descendants of those witches. But the dispute continues. Many say they did, but others say they were lifting magic that had already been spelled."

"So there's no way to know?" I ask.

"Not unless someone can magically revive the torched grimoire from the ashes."

Nadya's face twists in confusion, and I'm sure I mirror her expression.

"What do you mean?" I don't understand what the grimoire has to do with it.

"The grimoire contains a powerful spell that can reveal truths." Tia waves a dismissive hand. "It's the kind of magic that trickled down into reading palms and cards, even staring into crystals, trying to find answers. But the grimoire had the original spell, one that could not be replicated in any other book or retained in anyone's memory because the magic wouldn't allow it."

"Like the ultimate divination spell," Nadya says.

"Exactly." Tia gives a half-shrug. "Probably for the best. Can you imagine being able to see into the past and future and know the fate of the world?"

That could lead to dire circumstances. In the hands of someone with ill intent, it could mean utter destruction.

Tia looks between us both, eyes darker now. Heavier.

"Now it's my turn to be truthful," she says, slowly sinking into her chair. "You're right, dear." She looks to me. "In the wrong hands, this magic can be dangerous." She turns her gaze back to Nadya. "So use it wisely, child."

CHAPTER

THIRTY

zra only spent twenty minutes in my room before he gave up on fighting the heat. We were supposed to practice controlling small amounts of my magic, but neither of us could concentrate, so we called it quits for the day. I feel a little guilty that I didn't mention using my magic the previous day to keep Dante safe during his snake walk.

I also didn't mention the book Nadya's great-aunt gifted her.

Sweat beads along my spine as I pace the length of the room, fanning myself with little relief. The air in my chamber is thick, sticking to my skin in damp waves. Even at night, the heat presses against me from all sides, suffocating.

Outside, the city is still alive. Music thrums through the warm air, blending with laughter, moans, the clatter of feasting. I move to the pane-less window and peer out to the courtyard and beyond.

The courtiers are indulging in their endless revelry. Bodies tangled on silk-draped lounges, mouths seeking, hands roaming. A woman arches beneath a man's touch, gasping into the night, while another pair dances in a slow, sultry rhythm, their bodies moving as if they've long forgotten the presence of anyone else.

I wonder if every night is a party in Bastos.

I swallow hard, my throat dry despite the glasses upon glasses of water I've been drinking. Dante was taken away with the queens and their lovers an entire day ago, and I haven't seen him since. I can't exactly go around asking where he might be or what trial he was forced to face, so I have to live with this hollowness in my chest, at least for a little while.

I clench my fists, willing intrusive thoughts away, thoughts that convince me that he's been thrust into an all-day orgy, or worse, into an entire pit of vipers, without me to help him step safely through them. But the thoughts and fears fester beneath my skin. Those dancers who circled him, their hands grazing, their movements deliberately seductive... they could very well have been the least of my problems. And gods, the way the queens looked at him, as if he were something they might devour whole. But the danger he might be in worries me more. Because I don't know what I'd do if he—

Fuck. I need to stop thinking this way. Surely, he's fine. The palace would have been alerted if the future prince of Hedera had succumbed to death. Silas would be in an uproar.

I turn from the window, shaking the images from my mind, when a sharp knock startles me. I whirl, heart lurching, and cross the room in four quick strides. My pulse pounds as I unbolt the door and pull it open.

Dante stands before me.

Sweat hugs his skin, his tunic loose at the collar, his hair damp as if he's just stepped out of a fire. His breaths come heavy, lips parted slightly, and the scent of liquor lingers on him, warm and heady. His eyes— hooded, unreadable—flick over me, then past me, as if checking to see if I'm alone.

"Can I... Can I come in?" His voice is rough.

I nod and step aside, barely thinking, thankful that Indira is busy running errands for Queen Eleanor.

He enters without another word, moving straight to the nearest chair and sinking into it with a weary exhale. He leans forward, elbows on his knees, fingers laced together as he stares at the floor.

I watch him, my pulse thudding. Gods, he looks ruined.

"What happened? What did they make you do?" I ask, bracing myself.

His shoulders rise and fall with a slow breath. "Something unexpected," he says finally. "Something stupid."

I swallow hard. My heart is in my throat, hammering against my ribs. "Dante."

He drags a hand through his hair, frustration shadowing his expression. He winces when his arm comes back down. "It's done," he mutters. "I endured it."

That's not an answer.

Irritation flares sharp and hot in my chest, a desperate need for clarity. "What was it, then?" I snap, the words escaping before I can stop them. It's been hours since Nadya and I returned from her great-aunt's cottage, and I momentarily wonder if Tia's tea is still affecting me.

Dante exhales, then lifts his hands to the buttons of his tunic.

I freeze, my frustration twisting into something sharper, something more uncertain.

He undoes the first button. Then the second.

My brow furrows, unease pooling in my stomach. "What are you—"

The tunic slips from his shoulders.

My breath catches.

His arm—his entire shoulder—is covered in ink.

A sprawling design, intricate and dark, the curving lines sharp and precise, curls over the muscle. Gorgeous, detailed peonies surrounded by leaves and artistic swirls. The skin beneath it is still red and swollen, the ink gleaming, fresh.

My lips part, a gasp slipping free.

Dante leans back in the chair, letting his tunic fall the rest of the way, watching me as if waiting for my reaction.

But I can't speak.

Because for all my worrying, all my misplaced jealousy, all the tension I'd built up in my mind—this was never what I expected. And I still don't know what it means. I don't understand *how* this happened.

I exhale slowly, dragging my thoughts back into focus. Dante's chest

still rises and falls with uneven breaths, his skin gleaming with sweat, his muscles tight with lingering pain. Whatever liquor they forced on him is only dulling the edges. It won't last.

I step toward him, my bare feet nearly silent against the stone floor.

His lids are heavy, the grey of his eyes a bold contrast to his lashes as he gazes at me. He shifts in the chair and then winces, freezing in place.

"You're still in pain."

"I can't even focus on it completely." He struggles through the words. "The alcohol in Bastos really fucks with your mind."

"Well, you shouldn't have to suffer anymore." I step closer, holding my hands out, palms facing him. "Let me heal you."

He watches me a bit longer, then exhales and leans back in the chair, giving me access. When he nods, I inch closer, standing between his spread legs. I unbutton his tunic completely and carefully remove it. My fingers hover over the ink stretched across his skin. His arm is still swollen, the lines red and raised, the fresh ink gleaming in the dim candlelight.

Gently, I press my hands against his shoulder, feeling the heat of his skin, the way his body tenses beneath my touch. I close my eyes and let my magic pulse outward, coaxing the pain away, easing the sting of the needle's work.

For a moment, I'm afraid that my magic will force the ink out of his body, so I adjust, aiming my healing powers toward the inflammation without drawing out the artwork.

Dante lets out a slow breath, muscles relaxing as the worst of the pain fades.

"Talk to me," I say softly. "What happened?"

He huffs a tired laugh, shaking his head. "I thought they were going to make me sword fight. Like in Podrosa."

I smirk. "That, at least, you would've been prepared for."

He grunts. "Instead, they dragged me into town. Into some loud, crowded pub. There were people everywhere—drinking, shouting, hands on me every time I turned around." His jaw tightens slightly. "The queens kept making me drink. More and more. Concoctions I've never tasted before. I was starting to lose focus."

I keep my hands moving, my magic sinking deeper, soothing the raw edges of his flesh. "And then?"

"They led me to a back room," he says, voice rough. "I thought—" He hesitates, dragging his free hand down his face. "There was a raised cot. I didn't know what it was for. I thought maybe they were going to make me... participate in their kind of partying."

I swallow because I had the same fear.

His eyes flick to mine. "The queens wouldn't tell me what was happening. I didn't know what to expect. I was checking the room for the quickest exit. Looking for something I could use as a weapon because Sir Donovan still had my falchion. And then, a man came out of the back room."

I bite the inside of my cheek. "Oh, no."

"He was a big guy. Wide, I mean. About a half a head shorter than me, but arms like Mylo's. And for a minute, all I could think was... *fuck*."

A laugh bursts free from my lips. My mind can't help but conjure the image of Dante—drunk, brooding, and entirely out of his element—coming face to face with a man like that and not knowing what was expected.

"He told me to lie down—"

My laughter gets louder, and I have to hold my stomach.

Dante tries to glare at me, but I see the flicker of reluctant amusement in his eyes. "Then he took the needles out, and I spotted the ink. That's when it started to make sense."

I shake my head, finally composing myself as I examine the tattoo more closely. "So you chose this."

His expression shifts, something raw and unguarded slipping through the exhaustion in his eyes. "Because of you," he murmurs.

The words settle deep in my chest, making my heart stutter.

"What do you mean?" I think I know, but for some reason, I need to hear him say it.

"They're peonies." His eyes are locked with mine. "They remind me of you."

I let out a shuddered breath.

"Not just because of our last night in Hedera, but that night at my manor. The first time we... made love." He drags his teeth over his bottom lip. "After you left, the next morning, I went outside to watch you ride off. All the peony bushes around the manor were in full bloom, the scent completely surrounding me." He glances at his tattoo. "Now I have you with me wherever I go."

My heart thrums. I find it hard to breathe. "It's... I can't even begin to describe how this makes me feel."

He raises his free hand and softly caresses my cheek. Desire threads through my blood.

"Does it still hurt?" My voice is breathy.

His fingers find my waist, his thumb tracing small circles on my skin. "Not when I'm distracted."

He pulls me closer, his gaze trapped in mine, and I lean down until our lips meet. He lets out a small moan, his eyes still closed. The sound stirs something deep inside me, and I can't stop myself from moving my hands lower, down his chest, to the firm muscles of his abdomen.

When my fingertips brush the waistband of his trousers, his eyes flutter open. Grey pupils flare as he focuses on me. The intensity of his gaze drives me wild. I slip my fingers into his waistband.

"What are you doing?" His voice is slow and low.

"I'm distracting you."

He keeps his gaze locked on mine as I unbutton his pants. His erection strains against the material, as if seeking me out. My palm brushes against it, and it twitches, making me lick my lips.

"Fuck, Celeste. Do you know what you do to me?"

"I'm pretty sure I do."

I undo the remaining buttons and lower to my knees. He cups my cheek, and the heat of the night seems to intensify. I part my lips as I pull the material open and slide my hand in to cradle his hard cock and guide it free.

"Eyes on me, Highness." His voice is gruff, and his chest rises and falls with heavy breaths. Beads of sweat travel languidly down the slick

planes of his stomach.

I obey, keeping my gaze on the heated storm in his eyes as I wrap my hand around the base of his cock and give it a stroke. Two.

His teeth sink into his bottom lip as he watches me.

I lean forward, catching a glimpse of the precum on the tip of his thick length. My tongue darts out to lap at the moisture, and Dante sucks in a breath.

"Does that feel better?" I ask, my voice low and sultry. But before he can answer, I lower my mouth over the head of his cock and swirl my tongue around it.

His hips move forward, and his fingers lower his trousers a bit before they move into my hair, tangling them in the strands and tugging me closer. I press my thighs together as heat pools low in my belly. My mouth glides down his shaft, my tongue tracing every vein as he becomes even harder.

I keep my pace slow at first as I bob up and down, his cock covered in my saliva, my eyes trained on his parted lips as his breaths get heavier. His hands embrace each side of my head, guiding me to the rhythm he desires. I squeeze his base with my hand and stroke him along with my mouth. With every quirk of his jaw, every grunt that escapes his lips, I feel my power over him. And it makes me wetter.

"Like that?" I say between strokes.

"Fuck, yes. I love watching my cock fuck your beautiful mouth."

I let out a whimper at his words, the vibration of my sound causing him to moan and thrust his hips forward, leaving me no choice but to take him deeper. The head of his cock hits the back of my throat, which I relax to give him more access, and I hallow my cheeks as I continue to move up and down. I cup his balls and caress them, making him stiffen even more.

When I pull back enough to circle the crown of his shaft with my tongue, Dante throws his head back, his mouth falling open. I hum against his flesh as I continue to stroke him with my lips, my tongue, my cheeks, my hand, my pace increasing. The room is filled with his grunts and raspy groans, the sounds so arousing, I can't help but suck harder.

His hold on my head tightens, and his eyes flash with desire as he watches me.

"Fuck! Fuck, Celeste, I'm going to cum. Are you going to swallow me, little pirate?"

I moan in response as I continue the rhythm.

He makes a sound that starts with the beginning of my name but explodes into a growling groan as his hips convulse. Hot, salty ropes of cum shoot into my throat, coating it as I swallow. His fingers curl into my hair as his breath hitches, and I bob twice more, slowly, thoroughly lapping up every drop of his spilled arousal.

His breaths are still heavy as I lean back on my feet and drag the back of my hand across my mouth. As I move to stand, he grabs my arms and pulls me against his chest.

I wipe the sweat from his temples before pressing my forehead against his. When his hands caress down my arms onto my hips, slipping closer to my core, I stop him. I want him so badly, but he needs to rest and heal.

"Dante," I whisper. "I don't want you to overexert yourself."

"Too late for that."

I let out a small laugh. "No, really. You should rest. And you probably should get out of my room before someone catches us. Indira should be back any minute now."

It would be so easy for me to give in, but I know it's too risky for us to be caught like this. Or in a more compromised position. And I don't even know if my door is locked.

We could easily let our hunger take control, especially in a place like Bastos, where everyone lets go of their inhibitions and arousal seems contagious.

No. One of us has to be strong enough to stop, and it looks like it has to be me.

He cups my face and pulls me into a soft kiss that almost makes me change my mind. "All right, my queen," he says, his voice deep and soothing. "Anything you say."

CHAPTER THIRTY-ONE

The sea wind carries the scent of salt and rain as I lean over the rail of the ship, my fingers curled tightly around the polished wood. The coastline of Messanya grows clearer in the distance, a haze of sun-drenched cliffs and pearl-colored rooftops that glint like shell fragments beneath the sky. But my thoughts are still tangled in the hot-blooded memory of Bastos.

We left the capital three days ago, our carriages rattling over the cracked ochre roads that led us north through valleys of red rock and olive trees. The heat clung to everything—our skin, our clothes, our tempers. And yet nothing there burned quite like the memory of Dante walking the thin path lined with serpents.

Even now, I shudder.

But not all the memories of the Baharat Palace are bad. I smile at the thought of Dante's tattoo and the meaning behind it. That ink represents us, our coming together, and the intimate moments we shared, hidden in the artwork of a special flower I now hold as my favorite.

A seagull squawks above the ship, drawing me from my thoughts.

The farther we travel from the Bastosi capitol, the more clarity I feel. It's almost as if the air around the palace had been laced with a drug that erased inhibitions. It would certainly explain the behavior of the courtiers.

I haven't heard what the Bastosi queens decided about Dante's fate, but I can only assume that because he passed their tests, he received their approval. This whole tour is a huge mystery to me. I need to sit down with Ezra and have him explain it to me. In any case, we've made it halfway through the realms.

Two down, two to go.

Another thought occurs to me as I note our halfway point: I haven't heard from my uncle at all. Not that he uses his telepathic powers to contact me often, but after what the tsar did to him, I could find some comfort in an update from him. Even if it's just to tell me he's all right. I considered trying to "speak" to him, since Dante apparently heard my voice in Podrosa and Bastos. But whenever I accidentally used that power, it ended up hurting me, so I'm too cautious to try. Not to mention, I wouldn't even know if it would work or not.

Behind me, gulls careen and shriek over the mast, and the ship creaks as it rocks through the surf. At the stern of the ship, Nadya is curled up with the book her great-aunt gave her. She's hardly put it down since we left Bastos, and I'm not sure if I should be worried or not. Her eyes gleam with something fierce whenever she reads it, like the words are carving themselves into her bones. Maybe they are. Maybe that's how sorceress magic works.

I'm trying to be supportive. I am. But there's a shadow in her now, a hunger for answers that might lead her somewhere I can't follow. Not because I don't love her, but because I'm struggling with magic myself. I'm not sure I can help keep Nadya safe from traveling down the wrong path when I can't even figure out how to keep my body from betraying me when I use my mysterious powers.

Still, when she looks up from those curling pages and grins like she's holding the key to everything, I don't say a word.

Instead, I stay where I am, the wind tugging at the strands of hair that have come loose from my braid. Messanya unfolds in the distance—an island of music and myth—and I wonder if it will welcome us or swallow us whole.

My half-veil whips around my head in the cool breeze as we glide toward the nearest port. The waters, clear and crystalline, shimmer beneath the afternoon sun, casting waves of light against the jagged, black rocks that form the island's base. The shoreline is a mix of stark beauty, smooth, marble cliffs crowned with lush greenery and wildflowers in hues of gold, violet, and blush. Vines creep over the edges, draping themselves like delicate lace over the sharp crags below. The shore is littered with sharp, jagged rocks.

Footfalls approach, slow and deliberate. I glance over my shoulder to find Ezra joining me at the rail, the sea breeze tugging at the edges of his robes. His hands are clasped behind his back, as if he's been lost in thought—though with Ezra, it's just as likely he's been cataloging every shape of cloud and calculating their nautical implications.

"You've been quiet," he says gently, eyes scanning the horizon. "Are you well?"

"As well as one can be on a boat headed toward the homeland of the people my father used to imprison and execute," I mutter.

Ezra's lips twist. "That well, then." He leans closer to the railing, his gaze narrowing on the shore. "Do you see them? The bones?"

I follow his gesture. I thought they were jagged rocks, but I was wrong. Bones, bleached white by time and the sun, jut out from the sand and stones in scattered clusters—a grim reminder of the pirates who were lured to their deaths long ago.

"They say sirens leave them as a warning." Ezra's voice lowers. "The Messanyans never remove them. To remind anyone who comes near exactly what they are capable of."

A shiver crawls down my spine. This place feels different from the other kingdoms—older, wiser, and far more dangerous.

"Ah." Ezra straightens, shielding his eyes from the sun. "The Diapason."

My eyes lift to the enormous structure looming high above the cliffs.

The Diapason gleams in the sun like a polished blade. Its sweeping, iron beams arc like a ribcage to form a dome. The curved spires are long and slender, shaped like the tines of tuning forks. Their sleek, silvery surfaces hum faintly as the wind passes through them, sending an almost-imperceptible tremor into the air. At the top of the structure waves the Messanyan flag, the top half pearl white, the bottom half seafoam green, the two halves divided by a wavy, silver line, symbolizing the sea. At the center, the sigil of a silver harp is depicted.

"Magnificent," Ezra says, the awe apparent on his face. "The Diapason was built over a hundred years ago, when the sirens' influence grew too powerful. To prevent war, the siren nation agreed at the symposium to have it erected upon their shore. It's forged from elinvar iron—an alloy enchanted to vibrate in resonance with siren magic."

My brows knit. "Like the pendant that was sent to me in Delasurvia."

He nods. "Exactly like it. Though far larger, and much more powerful. Those tuning-fork spires? When a siren inside the structure or within fifty feet of it sings or hums, the spires react. Not just noise—they send feedback. Vibrational magic. Enough to disrupt a glamour, silence a song, even render a siren unconscious if the tone is strong enough."

My skin prickles. "So even the queen..."

"She is not immune," Ezra says. "The entire palace is attuned to the Diapason's frequency. If she were to attempt anything... *persuasive*... she'd be incapacitated before finishing her first note. That is why they used to hold the symposiums here, to assure an equity of power."

I swallow, turning back to the shore. "Seems like a cage with a pretty view."

Ezra says nothing, but his silence speaks volumes.

Another sound reaches my ears. It's faint, but the breeze catches it now and then.

"Is that... singing?" I tilt my head, trying to hear the sound more clearly.

"Yes. That sound would be the *Eirenes*, the siren peacekeepers. They dwell high in the mountains, their sole purpose being to maintain the

tranquility of the island, lulling it, so to speak, into a peaceful nation."

"So, there are no fights or disagreements in Messanya?"

Ezra chuckles. "I wouldn't go that far. But there are no disputes with the queen or her reign, as far as I know. The Eirenes don't replace the queen's soldiers, but they do a pretty good job of making her soldiers' duties easier. Think of it this way: in the same way the air in Bastos gave people the tendency to be more, um, lax with their inhibitions, the Eirenes create an atmosphere that dilutes feelings of aggression and hostility."

"'Dilutes,'" I repeat, "but doesn't totally eradicate."

"Correct."

The ship rocks gently as the wind shifts course, the white sails above us billowing with renewed force. Most of the crew is occupied adjusting the rigging, their voices blending with the call of gulls overhead. I remain at the rail, watching the shoreline inch closer, when a flicker of movement draws my eye to the quarterdeck.

Silas stands there with his hands linked behind his back as he surveys the approaching land. He emanates that smug, self-satisfied air he wears like a second skin. Queen Eleanor is beside him, her veil pinned in place beneath her coronet, the folds of her dark sea-cloak rippling against her slender frame.

She reaches up, so slowly, it almost looks like a breeze caught her hand, and attempts to adjust his crown—just slightly, a tilt here, a smoothing there. A gesture most would interpret as a dutiful wife tending to appearances.

But Silas jerks his head just enough to dislodge her fingers.

"Don't you have anyone else to bother, woman?" He swats her hand away, and I don't miss it when she flinches. "I should have listened to Farvis and left you at Ivystone."

Eleanor's hand lingers midair before retreating, folding with practiced grace beneath the other on her waist. She says nothing.

"Besides," he spits out, "you've outgrown your usefulness since your womb has withered up and dried."

The words aren't loud, and there are no guards close enough to hear

them. But I feel the crack of them in my ribs like a punch.

The queen does not respond. She simply stares forward at the water, face unreadable.

I grip the rail harder, wishing I had the freedom to step between them. To tell him he doesn't deserve to wear that crown at all. That it doesn't sit crooked, it sits bloodstained. That Eleanor shouldn't have to deal with such a monster.

But I keep my place, knowing that I can only do what's expected. For now, anyway.

I'm still watching Eleanor when a quiet rustle draws my attention from the quarterdeck. Nadya approaches, blinking against the sun as the wind plays with her curls. She adjusts the edge of her shawl, her eyes sweeping across the deck and catching immediately on Sir Holden, who walks the stretch of deck between us.

One of the crew, lean and freckled, hovers near a stack of tarred barrels, a coil of rope slung over his shoulder. As he shifts his grip, something slips from his pocket—a small, metal tool that clatters across the planks. Before he can retrieve it, Sir Holden steps forward and picks it up. Instead of handing it over to the young man, Sir Holden slips it into the crew member's pocket.

They exchange a look, but the crewman lingers, a half-smile playing on his lips as his gaze drifts appreciatively over Sir Holden's broad frame. The smile isn't brazen, but it's bold enough to spark curiosity.

Sir Holden says nothing, yet when he turns to move on, his eyes catch mine. The look is fleeting, but there's something sly in it, like he knows I've seen everything and he's daring me to say a word.

I bite my cheek and turn my attention to Nadya, pretending there was nothing to see.

When Nadya reaches my side, she exhales dramatically. "I can't blame Holden. The sailors on this ship might make me forget all about the barkeep in Podrosa."

"And the dancer in Bastos?"

She leans on the rail beside me, brushing wind-tossed curls from her cheek. "Mmm, I'll never forget her. Or her girlfriend."

 252

My eyes widen and my jaw drops, but Nadya simply laughs, leaning on the rain beside me.

"Still reading that book?" I ask, trying to keep the judgment out of my tone.

A flicker of guilt crosses her face. "I'm sorry. I just..." She hesitates, then lowers her voice. "I've been learning things. Big things. Stuff I want to show you when we're not surrounded by people who might tattle to the wrong king."

I study her face for a beat, noting the excitement thrumming beneath her words—the barely-concealed thrill that comes when she's close to uncovering something. A part of me worries what that something might be. But I nod.

"Tonight," she promises. "If the sirens haven't wiped our minds by then."

I nod, nudging her with my elbow.

Our ship docks, and a procession appears on the shore, awaiting us.

The king marches toward the bow, joined by his guards, and the queen tags along like a forgotten pet.

Dante emerges from below deck, his movements slow and steady. He advances to where his father stands, the sea breeze tugging at his dark hair. There's stiffness in his posture, and it makes me wonder if it has to do with returning to his birthplace. It occurs to me that this may be the first time he's been to Messanya since his mother died.

We disembark in careful order, the Hederan court flanked by guards in polished breastplates. Ahead, two Messanyan courtiers await us. Their beauty is so otherworldly, it borders on unnatural. The man's gleaming skin is practically gold, his dark hair curled neatly at his ears. The woman beside him moves with a dancer's grace, her pristine, white gown flowing in the wind with a slit that shows off her long, elegant legs.

The sweet song of the Eirenes tickles the hair on my ears. A strange vibration rolls through me. Nothing uncomfortable, though. In fact, I feel the muscles loosen and my mind relax. I glance at Nadya, whose posture becomes less stiff. She slowly sways her head back and forth.

"What is that?" she asks.

253

"The peacekeepers of Messanya. Their magical song has this effect. Feels like... euphoria."

Nadya's smile widens. "It's incredible. Why would anyone want to leave this place?"

Our procession stops, and I look past the king and queen at the courtiers greeting us. The woman curtseys, and the man bows.

"Welcome to Messanya," the woman says, her voice rich and elegant. It somehow feels like a warm embrace. "Queen Verina awaits you in the Diapason." She gestures to a set of carriages.

"Oh, great," Nadya whispers, taking in the steep road that leads up the mountain. "Just what I need after all that teetering on the ship. More wobbling."

I manage to nod off during the journey up the mountain, and Nadya has to shake my arm to wake me. I adjust my half-veil and smooth out the skirt of my mourning gown as the coach master opens the carriage door for us.

As soon as my feet touch the ground, I glance around, immediately finding Dante as he disembarks from the king's carriage. When his gaze meets mine, it lingers, soft and unspoken, as if his eyes alone could trace the curve of my cheek.

We assemble on a tiled walkway, Eleanor taking her place beside the king. He tolerates her nearness, but I know it's because there are so many eyes on him, watching his every move.

I end up next to Dante, our hands mere inches apart. All I'd have to do is stretch my fingers outward and I'd be able to feel his skin. When I take a chance and glance his way, his eyes find mine, as if he's thinking the same thing. His gaze softens, and the smallest of smiles pulls at my lips.

The couple who met us at the dock appear before us. They lead us

into the Diapason's grand entrance, where the air cools my skin and helps to pull me from my sleepy state. The interior is a marvel—a sweep of polished marble tiles at our feet reflecting glimmers of sunlight from between the metal spires. Silk banners float from the ceiling, the material waving in the sea-scented breeze.

The Messanyan courtiers are a vision, as if they stepped from the pages of a legend. Men and women alike wear flowing garments of smooth silks and delicate gossamer in soft, pearlescent shades. Golden cuffs and anklets gleam against golden-tan skin, and their hair flows loose in waves of midnight black, platinum, and sunlit copper. Each movement is languid, deliberate, as if they expect the world to bend for them.

I catch more than a few curious glances cast toward Dante. He doesn't react, but I notice the slight tightening of his jaw.

At the center of the space, flanked by servants, stands a woman who can only be Queen Verina.

She is breathtaking. Taller than most of her courtiers, she moves with the grace of water slipping over stone. Her long, flowy gown of seafoam green embraces her hips, cut daringly low in the front, the gossamer fabric shimmering as if woven from moonlight. Long, platinum hair falls in soft waves down her back, and her flawless skin is golden. It's as if sunlight melts when it touches her. But it is her eyes that ensnare me—a shade of violet so vivid, they seem almost unreal.

"King Silas, Queen Eleanor." Her voice is low and honey-sweet, and though I know the Diapason restrains her magic, I feel the lure of it all the same. She dips her head in the most elegant way I've ever seen. "It has been too long."

Silas inclines his head before stepping forward, his chin then lifted in that regal manner he always carries. "Queen Verina, your hospitality honors us. It is a privilege to stand within the Diapason once again."

I notice the slight stiffness in his voice, the faintest trace of wariness beneath his polished tone. For all the Diapason's protections, even King Silas is not immune to caution when standing before a siren queen.

Queen Verina's lips curve in a knowing smile as she sweeps her gaze

over the assembled Hederan court. When her eyes land on Dante, that smile deepens. "It is my pleasure to meet your siren heir. I had wondered if the rumors were true."

Dante inclines his head. "Your Majesty, I'm humbled by your reception."

"This is your home, Lord Stregasi. Of course you are welcome here."

I can't help but gaze upward at the structure we stand beneath, taking in the details as Queen Verina extends her condolences to the king and queen for the loss of Torbin. This place is intimidating, and the thrum that comes with each gust of wind is almost hypnotic.

King Silas, ever one to redirect the conversation to his advantage, gestures to the coffers his attendants carry forward. "As a token of our gratitude for granting us audience, we bring gifts that reflect the beauty and grace of Messanya."

The attendants open the chests, revealing an array of luxuries: strands of iridescent pearls, golden jewelry engraved with ivy symbols, and delicately crafted crystal chalices. When King Silas presents the dragon scales, Queen Verina's expression shows that the gift was unexpected but appreciated.

"Exquisite," she murmurs, running delicate fingers along the golden scale. "Your thoughtfulness does you credit, King Silas. I hope you find our hospitality equally pleasing."

As her voice lingers in the air, my gaze drifts to where Queen Eleanor stands, her black gown a stark contrast to the shimmering brightness around her. Her posture is regal, her face carefully composed, but I know it can't be easy for her to stand here. It's no secret that Dante was born from the affair between Silas and a Messanyan siren. Whatever the truth of that past relationship, having to be present in this place must feel like a cruel reminder of that betrayal.

"And I see you have also brought Princess Celeste." Queen Verina straightens her shoulders as she studies me.

I swallow hard and curtsey, unable to read her face. "Your Majesty."

"Lift your chin, dear," she says. "You *are* welcome here. Your father and I were not allies, but your brother did what he could to right your

father's wrongs. King Bennett was a good man, and I mourn his loss. May the gods gather you in their embrace so that your heart can heal."

"Thank you, Your Majesty." I swallow hard and fix my focus on the queen. Her words seem genuine, but I can't help the guilty feeling that lingers in my chest, simply from being the daughter of a man who hated her people.

"I look forward to seeing what kind of queen you become." She tilts her head, and for a second, her eyes dart to Dante. It's almost as if she knows.

I know the king has forced everyone to keep the engagement secret, but maybe Queen Verina isn't guessing his plan. She looks between Dante and me as if she feels our connection. But I'm in a mourning gown, so she dares not mention it.

The queen finally tears her gaze from mine and straightens her shoulders. "My esteemed guests, please allow my chamberlain to bring you to your rooms to freshen up. We have a busy schedule ahead of us."

CHAPTER THIRTY-TWO

The Messanyan and Hederan courts gather along a marble terrace suspended over a glistening bay. Above, gulls cry into the open sky, wheeling through bands of golden light as the sun rises over the horizon. A velvet wind sweeps in from the sea, rich with salt and the hum of magic, pulling in the roaring waves.

There are rows upon rows of velvet-cushioned seats filling the terrace. The center front seats are occupied by King Silas and Queen Eleanor. I sit to Eleanor's right, hands clasped tightly in my lap. The carved, coral balustrade before us at the edge of the terrace glows faintly in the low sun, and below, the sea rolls and shifts in restless motion. Nadya sits close on my other side, her fingers twisting and turning in nervousness. She knows as well as I do that another trial is about to begin.

Below us, on one side of the bay, is a wooden platform that hangs over the water.

Dante, barefoot and bare-chested, casually paces the wooden planks, his dark tattoo contrasting against his skin already bronzed under the Messanyan sun. He wears only dark breeches that stop at his knees and are damp against his muscular thighs. His hair is wet from sea spray, and he rakes it back to keep the strands out of his face. His muscles are taut, poised with tension, his expression unreadable as he waits for Queen Verina to speak.

She stands at the edge of the platform, facing the terrace, her stance and expression so confident, I believe even the sea answers to her. When she lifts a gleaming, silver trident, the crowd goes silent. I lean forward to inspect the weapon, taking in its blades that gleam wickedly in the light. It shimmers as though it's encrusted with diamonds.

"In Messanya, the sea decides who is worthy." Queen Verina's voice is thunderous, though her tone is cool. She turns slightly, her gaze narrowing on Dante. "You seek to prove your integrity and earn the respect of our court. Then you must face the wrath of our tides and earn that respect from the sea."

Dante stands tall, shoulders squared, and gives the queen a reverent nod.

If he's apprehensive, he's not showing it. In fact, he looks as if he simply wants to get this task over with. I clasp my hands tighter, feeling the unease for him.

"This is the trident of my ancestors." The queen holds the weapon high again as her robes flutter behind her. "It will be taken to the secret caverns far beneath the sea. Retrieve it, and bring it back to its rightful place. Of course," she adds, her lips curving with amusement, "our siren soldiers will ensure the trial is... thorough."

From beneath the terrace, a wisp of a woman with a shaved head approaches them. Her deep-blue robe falls from her shoulders, revealing tight bands of cloth covering her body from her chest to her thighs. She wastes no time, taking the trident from the queen and running to the edge of the platform. She dives into the bay with breathtaking grace, barely making a splash as she disappears beneath the surface.

A low murmur ripples through the crowd. I spot nobles leaning forward on their cushions, their sea-green robes catching the sunlight.

Queen Verina extends her arm toward the bay and faces Dante. "You may begin."

Dante nods once, and without hesitation, he dives. The sea swallows him whole, its surface barely rippling.

Queen Verina turns to a small group of people at the edge of the platform. Her soldiers, I'm guessing. They march toward her on her command. Three of them drop their robes, just like the bald woman did, and I catch a glimpse of daggers strapped to their chests right before they dive into the sea.

My stomach knots, and my hand finds Nadya's for comfort.

From our vantage point, the figures appear as dark shadows cutting through the crystal-clear water. The queen hasn't explained their purpose, but I know they serve as obstacles to deter Dante from reaching his goal. But to what extent they plan to use those daggers, I can't be sure.

My breath catches. The sea goes still. A drumbeat thunders once— deep and slow.

The queen nods to the other person who approached her. His ocean-blue, silk robe covers his tall form, and he has waves shaved into the sides of his head of sandy-brown hair. He faces the sea and lifts his hand—just slightly—and the waves begin to churn harder than before.

Shit. He's fae.

And he's controlling the water. As he glides his arms through the air in a fluid motion, the tide reacts by coiling, rising, and retreating. The Messanyan courtiers smile and inch forward. This is clearly entertainment for them.

My attention goes back to the sea. I can just make out the dark figures of the queen's soldiers cutting through the water. They're fast. I've seen Dante swim before, back when we rescued Dulcamaran refugees whose boat capsized. He'd been fast, but these full-blooded sirens might be faster. And they carry weapons.

I bite my cheek in frustration; it's too hard to make out what's happening below the surface. Though the water at the bay is clear enough to see the sandy bottom, the water farther out is less transparent. I watch the shifting shadows darting undersea, uncertain of what's happening. I have to hold down my knee to keep my leg from bouncing in worry.

My attention is drawn back to the fae, who lifts his arm and flicks

his fingers. The sea surges. The rumbling grows louder.

"What's happening?" I whisper under my breath.

In my peripheral vision, Nadya shakes her head.

A tremor runs through the air as the first swell rises. It crashes down with a deafening roar, the white spray reaching even the edges of the terrace. The spectators gasp. Somewhere in the depths, Dante is still swimming, still fighting. And the push and pull of the water can't be helping with his struggles.

Still, the silence stretches, and the ache in my chest tightens with every heartbeat.

Then... movement catches my eye, impossibly swift.

A siren warrior breaches the surface, a gash blooming crimson across her shoulder. "He evades us," she spits, reporting to the queen. "Even wounded, he fights like a creature born of the tides."

I clutch the balustrade harder, my pulse thudding painfully in my ears.

Wounded.

Gods, what did they do to him?

I glance to my left and catch the lowered brow of King Silas. His jaw is tight as he releases a long breath from his flaring nostrils. Queen Eleanor reaches for his hand, but he yanks it out of her reach.

On the platform, Queen Verina nods to someone on a boat near the bay, her fingers moving and shifting in a way that tells me she's speaking with her hands. The soldier she communicates with nods in return, lifting one hand to signal back something to her. With fierce concentration, he proceeds to turn a large crank connected to some kind of metal contraption attached to the boat.

A resonant *click* echoes deep within the water. The churning of my stomach tells me a cage door has been opened.

Something stirs. Movement ripples beneath the surface. At first, just a dark shadow. Then larger. Faster. And in the next instant, a shark's fin breaches the surface.

My pulse hammers.

Fuck.

 261

Dante.

They've released a *shark* into the bay.

My hands clench into fists. My vision sharpens with panic. He doesn't know. He doesn't know. My mind races, the fear turning sharp, electric.

"Dante, there's a shark!"

I don't speak it aloud, but my mind screams it. I don't know if he'll hear me, if that magic even still exists within me, but I have to try.

"Dante, a shark!"

A sharp burst of pain erupts behind my eyes, blinding me for a second. I grip the edge of the chair as my vision blurs, spots dancing across my gaze. But then I feel a tingle at the back of my head. The same sensation I felt in Podrosa when Dante reacted to me mentally calling out to him. I can only hope it means he heard me.

I lean forward, tracking the shark's movement as it heads toward a dark figure beneath the surface. In the water, the figure veers. Hard right.

The shark surges up with razor-sharp teeth, gnashing at nothing but water and air, missing him by seconds.

My breath *whooshes* out in a silent gasp. I blink rapidly, tears springing from the pain now slicing down the center of my skull.

By the time my vision clears, I can no longer see any figures in the water, and I've lost sight of the shark.

The sea begins to rise again.

Faster.

Higher.

No.

The fae on the platform lifts both hands now, and the ocean obeys. Not a wave. A wall. A monstrous, roiling tsunami, taller than the balcony itself, threatening to bear down upon the bay.

Dante's head whips up from the small waves near the edge of the bay. Behind him, the wall of water rushes forward, rising higher.

It's going to hit him. It's going to hit all of us.

The queen stands behind her fae, her features relaxed. She's not afraid because he will keep the water from touching her. But the rest of

us?

My fury makes my body react, like a string pulling taut within my ribcage. That humming thread takes over. My power stirs rampantly beneath my skin, reacting to the danger.

"Get down!" someone shouts, but I stay rooted to the edge.

People in the crowd rise from their seats, retreating to the back of the balcony.

Nadya pulls on my arm, but I don't budge.

My hands rise of their own accord. The magic surges before I can stop it, tearing through me like fire laced with glass.

I force one wave of energy toward the water surrounding Dante, pushing him far off to the side until he's out of the path of danger.

Pain lances through my skull, sharp and blinding.

But the tsunami wave rolls closer to us.

I ignore my pain and push another surge of energy out to meet the approaching water. It leaves me in a burst—raw, unrefined. It burns as if my veins were being torn from my body.

The power slices through the air, and the wave shudders.

Come on!

I push again, despite my agony. The strong pressure, hot and relentless, forms behind my eyes. It feels as if my skull could burst.

The swell of water starts to fall apart, dropping into the depths of the sea.

What's left of it breaks early, as if it's hit a giant, invisible shield. It shatters apart in a fury of foam and spray, crashing down onto the platform instead of over Dante's head. Most of the wooden planks split and splinter under its force. But the queen is safe behind the magic bubble of the water fae's magic.

As the tide settles and the waves dissipate, my gaze darts over to Dante. He watches the water for a moment before his eyes find me. He's too far for me to see his expression. In the next second, he dives under again.

I sag against the balustrade, my ears ringing. My breath comes in ragged gasps. Something warm drips from my nose.

 263

Fuck.

Another pulse of pain. A sharp jab behind my eyes.

I duck my head and wipe at my nose, and blood smears across the back of my hand. My vision swims. My ears are filled with a high-pitched whine. My fingers come away from my temple—wet.

Not just my nose.

My ear.

"Celeste!" Nadya's voice reaches me, sounding as if it were from somewhere far away, muffled. She pushes something into my hand. "Here."

I nod. Or I think I do. The world won't stay still long enough for me to be sure. I try to look at what she handed me, but everything is blurry and shifting. I tighten my hold and discover it's cloth, so I use it to wipe my nose and ear.

The high-pitched whine in my ear fades, and my vision clears. Thank the gods my healing magic is working. The crowd slowly returns to the edge of the balcony. I glance around me, but everyone is too focused on the trial to pay attention to me. Everyone except Nadya.

And the queen's fae.

He blinks at me, but I can't read his expression.

I straighten my shoulders and stare him down. It's a risky move. If he tells the queen I'm helping Dante, the trial would be forfeited, and Dante wouldn't get Messanya's approval for legitimization.

Besides, I can't be sure it was entirely my power that stopped the giant wave. I can't imagine the queen would let her audience suffer from a hit like that. And I suspect the audience believes he was in control the entire time.

I take slow, steady breaths, waiting.

Ever so slightly, the fae dips his head and turns back toward the water.

The breath I release is rasped and laced with ache. I glance down at my hands, still trembling. My pulse is a wild, frantic thing.

Below, the tide rolls out again. And Dante rises.

He bursts from the water with a roar, the queen's trident gripped in

 264

his hand, soaked and victorious. His chest heaves, hair plastered to his face, a bleeding gash where his chest meets his shoulder, but he is whole.

The Messanyan court erupts into stunned applause. Even the queen lifts her chin in approval.

But I can barely hear it.

Dante makes his way out of the water and marches toward Queen Verina. He hands her the trident with a bow. She dips her head, and it is only then that his shoulders slump with relief.

I slide back into my seat, trembling. My vision dims at the edges.

 265

CHAPTER THIRTY-THREE

'm starving. After Dante's trial, Nadya helped me return to my room to rest and heal, and I drifted off to sleep for a good two hours. Now that I'm awake and feeling myself again, I can acknowledge the loud grumble of my stomach, urging me to find sustenance.

The first thing I asked Nadya when I awoke was if Dante was all right. He'd been bleeding from the trial, and I had the desperate urge to heal him. But Nadya informed me that the queen's healers had already tended to him. I wonder if one of them was the water-wielding fae.

Nadya and I make our way downstairs to the dining hall with hopes that we'll find something to eat. The palace on the Messanyan coast is unlike anything I've ever known. It lacks the towering grandeur of Ivystone or the rigid austerity of Podrosa, yet its elegance is undeniable. Everything here feels soft—from the plush, velvet cushions on the chaise to the gauzy, white curtains that ripple with the evening breeze. The windows, flung wide open, invite the salt-laced air and the distant crash of waves against jagged rocks. Silver lanterns hang from delicate chains overhead, casting a warm glow across the pale, marble floors. Even in the quiet, the place hums with an energy I can't quite name, as if the very walls have absorbed centuries of enchantment.

The wind is quieter now. Softer. But maybe it's simply because I'm comparing it to the roaring tsunami that threatened to wipe us out.

We slip into the kitchens, where a few servants bustle about, scraping the remnants of the grand lunch from platters and decanting sauces into small jars. The air is warm, heavy with the scent of fresh bread and roasted meat, and my stomach growls loud enough that one of the cooks glances up with a chuckle.

"Apologies," I say. "We missed the lunch earlier. Is there any chance we could have something small?"

The woman, plump and red-cheeked, waves a dismissive hand. "Of course, Your Highness. We'll have something prepared in the dining hall."

Nadya bumps her shoulder lightly against mine, grinning. "Small, she says."

While the staff gathers dishes, Nadya grabs an apple from a wooden crate on the counter. She flashes it at me, her eyes gleaming with mischief. "Hey, I didn't get a chance to show you last night. Watch this."

I raise a brow. "Nadya?"

Before I can stop her, she mutters something under her breath, fingers curling loosely around the apple. A shimmer washes over it, like a ripple through glass. The apple vanishes from sight.

I stare into Nadya's seemingly empty hand. "Nadya—"

"Shhh," she hushes, casting a furtive glance toward the servants. No one seems to notice.

I gawk, my heart kicking up in my chest. "What did you—how long can you hold it?"

She bites her lip, concentrating, but then the shimmer falters, and the apple snaps back into view. She tosses it up and catches it with a proud, little smile. "Not long. But I'm getting better."

A flicker of pride wars with my worry. "You need to be careful with that," I murmur. "If anyone sees—"

"I know. I will. I just wanted to show you."

Before I can press further, one of the servants waves us along. "If

267

you'll sit in the dining chamber, Your Highness, we'll bring your meal shortly."

We thank them and head into the adjoining hall, where the long, oak table is already being laid with plates.

I glance at the spread: sliced salmon peppered with herbs, a plate of olives and soft, warm bread, figs stuffed with nuts, and a pitcher of chilled citrus water. It smells divine.

We each take a seat, and the moment I pop a fig into my mouth, I realize just how hollow I've felt all day.

Nadya watches me with a small grin. "Feeling better?"

I nod, though the ache in my muscles is a stubborn thing. I take a bite of the salmon, almost moaning at the deliciousness. "I'll live."

"You gave me a scare, you know."

I offer her a faint smile. "It wasn't exactly pleasant on my end, either."

Nadya tears off a piece of bread, her expression turning thoughtful. "You should talk to Ezra. See if he can help you regain some of your strength."

"Where is he, anyway?"

"With the Messanyan magister," she says. "Apparently, the man has an entire library of sea-based potions and remedies. Ezra couldn't resist."

I'm about to ask more when Nadya suddenly stills, her gaze fixed over my shoulder. I turn to see Dante leaning against the doorframe, arms folded loosely across his chest.

But then I catch the tightness in his jaw. The way his shoulders are squared just a little too stiffly. There's something simmering behind his gaze.

He steps forward, closing part of the distance between us. "We need to talk."

The words land differently than expected—no teasing, no easy charm.

I narrow my eyes. "About the trial?"

His silence answers me.

I push back my chair and rise. "Let me guess. Somewhere private?"

Nadya waves me off with a grin. "More for me!" she says, already reaching for the olives.

Once we're alone in the hall, Dante keeps his voice low. "I want to take you somewhere."

I arch a brow. "Is that allowed?"

"Technically? Probably not." The corner of his mouth tugs upward. "But Silas is busy talking politics with Verina, and I may have faked a headache to escape."

I shake my head, suppressing a smile. "You're a terrible influence."

"Lucky for you, then." His eyes flick toward the corridor ahead. "Besides, Sir Holden and Sir Donovan are both down in the barracks. They're being shown the Messanyan defenses, so we have some time."

It's very hard for me to resist him, but a part of me hesitates. I already risked his legitimacy by interfering with the trial. I don't want to give Silas, Verina, or anyone else cause to rip his potential title from his hold.

But then Dante's grin turns sly as he offers his hand. "Come on. Trust me."

I'm a skilled strategist and soldier, but I've already lost this battle.

We slip down the corridors like a pair of thieves, dodging the occasional guard and servant. I spot Indira outside one of the side parlors, and we have to duck into a linen alcove until she moves on, muttering about lazy nobles.

Eventually, we reach the castle's outer grounds, where a single horse waits tethered to a post beneath a jacaranda tree. Its violet blooms flutter like confetti in the breeze.

"One horse?" I ask.

Dante smirks. "Suddenly scared of sitting too close to me, Highness?"

I return his smirk and pull up my skirts to mount the horse.

He hops up behind me, the reins in his hand, as he guides us away from the castle. The proximity of our bodies is intoxicating, with his thighs straddling me, his hand resting low on my hips. We ride toward some hills, the heat and the friction coaxing me to lean back into him.

When our trail winds upward, weaving through stretches of pale-green hills dusted with wildflowers, Dante's hands glide downward to my upper thighs. I find myself arching my back so that my ass is closer to his groin, delighting in the constant rubbing of our bodies. I dare to let out a whisper of a sigh when he starts tracing slow circles on my thighs, his finger inching closer to the heat igniting at my core.

But even though I can feel him grow hard against my ass, he doesn't move his hands to where I really want them. A part of me feels like he's punishing me like this on purpose.

So I punish him back, shifting my ass back so there's no space between us.

The higher we climb, the more the islands of Messanya reveal themselves, scattered like emeralds across the turquoise sea. With the lush colors of the land against the pink and orange of the setting sun, the scene spreads before us like a painting. Surreal. Beautiful.

When we round a mossy rock formation at one of the higher levels of the mountain, Dante slows the horse, guiding us toward a veil of ivy and flowering shrubs, the sound of trickling water growing louder as we dismount. We push through the greenery, and suddenly, the world opens—an enclave of smooth rock cradling a pool of water fed by a slender waterfall that glitters in the fading light. The lagoon's water is as clear as glass, its surface shimmering with every gentle ripple. The far edge of the pool falls away into a jagged overlook, where the sea glints beyond, dotted with scattered isles.

"This is where you take your conquests?" I tease, but softly, because the place feels too sacred for sharpness. "I'm sure there were a flurry of Messanyan ladies hoping you'd invite them for a ride." I almost laugh at my own pun.

He chuckles. "There were a few, yes. But I paid them no mind."

"They didn't use their powers to convince you?"

"Response to siren powers differs with each person. The stronger someone's mind, the harder it is for a siren to glamour them."

"So, you're saying you have a strong mind."

"I'm saying there isn't a siren strong enough to sway me from the

person I truly want."

A shiver travels up my spine. "I see." My voice barely rises above a whisper.

He smirks. "But to answer your question: no. I haven't brought anyone else here. Just me. When I was younger, I'd come here when the world got too loud. When I didn't know where I belonged." He tugs off his boots, then starts to strip down to his underclothes. "But the world feels quieter with you in it."

"It's beautiful here."

Instead of responding, he lets his eyes roam over me. "Undress."

Biting the inside of my cheek, I shed my shoes and outer layers, leaving on my shift before wading in. The water bites at first, cool and crisp, but then it embraces me, up to my chest. Dante joins me, the surface rippling around his broad frame, his hair curling damply at his temples.

Above us, from somewhere higher in the cliffs, a melody carries—a chorus of voices, pure and haunting, threading through the air like silk. The Eirenes' song lulls me into feeling calm.

I tilt my head back, letting my body relax. "I think I could get used to this."

Dante splashes me, catching me mid-reverie. I yelp, water dripping from my chin.

"You're lucky my dagger's on the rocks," I warn.

"I'll take my chances."

We swim for a while, splashing and exchanging a laugh, but we're mostly quiet, simply enjoying being together in this peaceful reprieve.

I feel the energy shift as he floats closer, his storm-grey eyes fixed on mine, water sheeting down his shoulders.

"Do you ever wish you'd stayed here?" I ask quietly.

He stops just shy of touching me, his voice low. "If I had, I'd have never met you."

Then he closes the distance, his hands gliding to my waist under the water. He pulls me closer, the heat of him cutting through the chill.

For a moment, his smile falters. His eyes, still pinned to mine,

darken with something heavier, something he's been holding back.

I smooth my hands down his forearms, feeling the strength beneath his skin. "I guess it's time to talk about the trial now."

His jaw flexes. "You used your magic again."

"Dante—"

"You promised you wouldn't," he says, voice quiet but taut, threaded with frustration. "You said you'd wait. You said you'd let Ezra figure it out."

"I never promised," I snap back, chin lifting. "You asked me not to, but I never agreed."

"You bled, Celeste." He leans closer, his voice low, heated. "I could tell something was wrong, even from the water. And what I couldn't see, Nadya filled me in on."

Of course she did.

"I had to help you." The words come out louder than I intend, sharp with the emotion I've been burying all day. "They sent armed soldiers after you. And a shark! You were bleeding underwater. You could have been pummeled by a fucking tsunami. You don't get to ask me to sit and watch you die."

His hands flex, fists clenching just beneath the surface. "And what if helping me had killed *you* instead?"

I stare at him, my breath shallow. I don't have an answer—not one that would make him feel better.

He paces a few steps through the water, raking a hand through his hair until it curls wild and damp around his temples. "Gods, you're so damn stubborn."

"And you're so damn arrogant if you think you can tell me when and how I'm allowed to use a power that's mine."

He turns sharply, water sluicing off his chest, his gaze fierce enough to stop me in place. He crosses the space between us with quick, sure strides—and suddenly, he's there, his hands finding me beneath the water, one arm locking around my waist, the other curling so that his hand is tugging the hair at the nape of my neck.

The heat of him burns through the chill. My breath stutters.

"Of course you'd fight me," he mutters, his voice hoarse against my cheek. "Even when I'm trying to protect you."

"And of course you'd push me," I breathe back, "even when I'm trying to save you."

The air thrums between us, thick with something neither of us is willing to yield. My pulse hammers as his thumb grazes the side of my throat, slow and reverent, like he's trying to memorize the beat of my heart.

"I told you," he says, his forehead almost brushing mine, "you bleed for no one."

"And I told you," I whisper, "you don't get to decide that."

His jaw tightens—and then, in one breath, his lips are on mine.

It's fierce and heated, like he's trying to fuse every argument, every fear, every unspoken word into this one, soul-deep touch. It's not soft or careful. It's the collision of two storms, and I surrender to it, arms winding around his neck as the world falls away.

My heart pounds against my ribs, my body already burning where his touch lingers.

His hand wraps around my neck as he guides me backward through the water to a shallower part of the lagoon. When the backs of my thighs press against the edge of smooth rock, he pauses, breaking the kiss just long enough to meet my gaze. His storm-grey eyes are dark, half-lidded with desire as he lifts me by my waist and sets me on the flat stone, which is large enough for me to recline on. Mist from the waterfall covers us in a moist, lingering cloud.

He hovers over me, his gaze roaming over my wet chemise. Soaking wet and thin, it reveals my pebbled nipples and the curves of my breasts. He runs his fingers down my chest, his thumb grazing my nipples as he continues down to the waistband of my underwear. I lift my ass slightly as he slips them off and places them on the rock surface beside me. When he takes a step back, I whimper. The water ripples, coming up to his thighs, and I can clearly see the outline of his hard cock through the material of his underwear.

"Come back," I say, resting on my elbows on the stone.

There's a smirk on his face that tells me he has plans. "First, touch yourself."

My pulse races even faster.

His eyes are still on me as he removes the rest of his clothes and tosses them to land beside my discarded dress. The mist causes droplets of water to trickle down the sculptured muscles of his chest and abdomen. I almost forgot about his tattoo, and when I take in the beauty of the inked design, remembering he picked that design for me, I melt for him. Heat quickly gathers at my core.

"Did you hear me, little pirate? Start with your breasts." He wraps a hand around the shaft of his cock and gives it a stroke. "Show me how much you like those nipples pinched."

My chest is heaving as I glide my hands over the swell of my breasts and finger my nipples through the wet material of my chemise. I arch my back and part my lips as my thumbs and forefingers close around the hardened peaks and give them a pinch and a roll.

He strokes himself as he watches, his teeth dragging over his bottom lip. "Yeah, just like that. Are you getting wet for me, Highness?"

"Yes." My voice is a rasp.

"Open your legs," he demands. "I want to see."

I do as he says, feeling a tingle in my stomach as he instructs me. I'm on full display for him, and I shudder at the way his lids get heavy.

He takes one step closer, his gaze drawn between my legs as he continues to stroke himself. It's wicked torture. "You're more than just wet, Princess. Your pussy is soaked for my cock."

I writhe. "Then come give it want it wants."

"Only good girls get what they want, little pirate. Are you a good girl?"

"Yes." I lick my lips, following the rhythm of his fist moving up and down his shaft. "Please."

"Tell me what you want."

"I want to feel you. I want you inside me." My arousal is flooding me. "My pussy needs you."

"Touch it for me. Show me how much your pussy wants to be

rubbed." I let out an impatient moan as I move my hands over the bottom curves of my breasts and splay my hands down my stomach. When my fingers slip through my wetness, my hips buck forward.

"Nice and slow," he says. "Tease your clit, and imagine my mouth on you."

I rub at the bundle of nerves, wishing it was him. "I'm imagining it's you," I say in a whispered voice. "I want it to be your tongue."

"You want me to taste you, Highness? You want me to devour that dripping, wet pussy of yours?"

"Gods, yes." The pressure is building, hot and frantic, and I don't know how much more I can stand. "I want you to feast on me like you're starving."

"I *am* starving, Highness. I'm starving for the taste of your arousal. I want it all over my lips and my tongue. I want it to fill my mouth as you scream my name." His hand moves a little faster, and I can see the precum glistening at his tip. "Now put a finger inside. Imagine it's my aching cock."

I bite my lip, sliding my finger down to my entrance and then slowly pushing it inside. He lets out a growl as he watches me, his breathing speeding up. I pump it in and out, and then, without him instructing me to, I slip another finger in.

"Fuck." He comes closer, resting his free hand on my thigh. "Taste it. Tell me how you taste, little pirate."

I slip my fingers out and bring my hand up to my lips, keeping my eyes on him as I open my mouth and wrap my lips around my fingers. I slide them out slowly with a moan.

"Yeah?" he asks with a deep voice. "That good?"

"Mm-hmm. But don't just take my word for it." I spread my legs wider, my knees falling to the sides. "Try it for yourself."

He doesn't hesitate. He drops down until his face is inches away from my throbbing pussy. First, he kisses my thigh, gently nipping at the skin. I let out a small sigh at the feel of his lips and teeth. His tongue laps upward, directly to my center. A fire ignites inside of me. My breath leaves me as his mouth moves, his lips caressing my labia and his tongue

 275

thrusting into my center. My body jerks when his tongue darts out and circles my clit.

"Fuck," I cry out, unable to stop myself from grabbing his head and pushing into him. His wet hair tangles between my fingers.

He flattens his tongue and laps over my hot pussy, his saliva mixing with my arousal, and then I feel his fingers push into my slick heat. He sucks at my clit as he pumps his fingers in and out, making my eyes roll back in my head.

"Dante! Oh, Gods!"

"Cum for me, Celeste. I want to feel your pussy clenching around my fingers."

He swirls his scorching-hot tongue over my clit, and I swear I see stars exploding as I'm pushed over the edge. He continues to push his fingers in and out of me, riding out my orgasm.

I barely have time to catch my breath before he's making his way up my body, peppering my skin with sensual kisses. When he reaches my mouth, his lips are pink and swollen, and I moan into his kiss as he positions his body over mine.

"We're not done yet, Highness," he says, his eyes filled with hunger. "I need to feel you."

"Yes, please." I practically hiss from need. "Take me."

He drags his hard length through my soaked center, covering his cock in my arousal. "Fuck, you feel good."

I can only moan in response, needing to feel him filling me. I'm too needy, so I reach down and wrap my hand around his shaft and position his head at my entrance, my legs lifting so my thighs are pinned at his hips.

His hand joins mine, and together, we slide his cock into me. It sinks to the base, and my jaw hangs open at the feel of him. He shudders for a moment before pulling most of the way out and then slamming back into me. The burn of him stretching me is delicious, and I claw at his muscles, unable to get enough.

He grips my hips and undulates, thrusting in and out in a perfect rhythm, the friction building and sounds of our bodies slapping together combined with the whooshing whisper of the waterfall filling my ears.

"Gods, your pussy is squeezing me so good." He fuses his lips to mine, his tongue moving with a passionate caress, breathing me into a frenzied kiss.

Our pace increases, and I cry out as he drives his cock into me again and again and again—*fuck!*

He grabs one of my legs, propping it over his forearm, and rolls his hips, pushing deeper into me. He grunts with each stroke, his jaw taut as he looks down between our thrusting bodies. I look, too, reveling in the sight of us moving together, my full breasts bouncing as he grinds into me, and I whimper with every thrust. He wraps a large, hot hand over one of my breasts, his thumb circling my nipple before lowering his mouth over it, sucking and lapping at it. With his mouth still on me, he moves his hand down to stroke my clit.

It's too much, too hot, and I'm going to combust. I can feel my pussy clenching him, and I know I'm close.

"Dante!"

"Cum for me, Celeste," he moans breathlessly. "I want to feel your pussy pulsing while I fill you with my cum."

He thrusts, harder, faster, bringing me to the brink. I let out a desperate noise as my release bursts from me, my body straining, my pussy clamping around him as if it never wants to let him go. His body jerks and spasms as he lets out a guttural, "Fuuuck!"

His hot cum fills me, his ass clenched and his mouth crashing into my neck. Our breaths are erratic, hot and raspy. I feel as if I'm melting as my heartbeat gradually slows back to normal. My head is spinning with euphoria, and my body tingles with the afterglow of pleasure. Dante's lips move on my neck, pressing kisses into my skin as he moves his mouth higher, up my jaw. I turn my head so I can capture his mouth with mine, pushing his hair back from his temple and tracing his jaw with my thumb.

"So fucking perfect," he whispers, kissing me again.

We lie like this, with his cock still inside of me, as the sun disappears and the sky darkens. It isn't until the breeze cools our bodies that he

finally pulls out of me and shifts, wrapping me in his arms with my head resting on his chest. He lazily strokes my hair as we gaze up at the emerging stars.

"Do you think things will be different once you're a prince?" I ask quietly, my voice barely above a whisper.

Dante doesn't answer right away. His hand moves in slow, soothing circles against the small of my back, but I can feel the tension creeping back into his shoulders.

"Maybe," he finally says, though there's no conviction in the word. "My father, he's always measured a man's worth by the power he holds. Being his bastard made me nothing to him for years. But now..." He huffs a bitter laugh under his breath. "Now, I'm useful."

I lift my head, frowning. "You're not just useful. You're—"

"I know what I am to you, Celeste," he murmurs, his gaze locked on mine. "But to him? This title—this legitimacy—it's not about me. It's about control. As long as I do what he wants, I have value. If I step out of line..." He trails off, his jaw clenching tight.

I catch his hand, lacing our fingers together. "You don't have to play his game. Not if it costs you who you are."

His expression softens, and something unreadable flickers behind those storm-grey eyes. "I'm not doing it for him," he admits. "I'm doing it for you. For us."

My heart stumbles. "Dante—"

"This title... it's a leash. I know that." His thumb brushes across my knuckles, warm and steady. "But it's also a weapon. And if holding it means I can protect you—if it means keeping Delasurvia safe—then I'll wear the crown. And I'll do whatever it takes to make sure no one can ever touch you."

His words are heavy as they settle in my chest, a mix of fierce devotion and quiet dread curling through me. "You shouldn't have to carry that weight alone."

His lips curl into a faint smile. "I'm not. I have you."

I shift and press a lingering kiss to his lips, letting the steady rhythm of his heartbeat anchor me. "Always."

CHAPTER THIRTY-FOUR

y room in Messanya is the nicest I've had so far on this tour. It's impeccably clean, the bed is extremely comfortable, and the sea breeze sneaking in through the windows means the air always smells incredible. My room in the castle in Delasurvia—the one I had as a child, anyway—was close enough to the sea that I could view the water from my windows. Maybe that's why I like this room. And why it stings a bit to say goodbye to it.

Or maybe it's the song of the Eirenes convincing me that this place makes me feel at home. Safe. Content.

Indira has just finished packing my things when a knock comes at my open door.

"Ezra," I greet him. "Was your room as nice as this?"

"I found it quite pleasant, yes."

"Is it really necessary for us to rush off to Mersos?" I raise my brows, as if that could sway the answer.

"I believe the king deems it necessary, since the triarchs are expecting us."

"And is it entirely prudent that I come along?"

His smile is small. "I'm sure he's set on that, I'm afraid."

I hum my displeasure and give him a sideways smile. I know he's right. I also wouldn't abandon Dante. I want to support him, be with him, cheering him on during the last stop on his tour.

Not to mention, he might need me. Again.

We're almost done.

It's almost over.

A couple of servants brush past Ezra, inclining their heads to me before continuing to my traveling chest and lifting it up by its carrying handles. I step aside to give them room to haul it outside.

"Well, then," Indira says, "let me go check what's taking Nadya so long."

Once Indira is gone, Ezra steps into the room, his hands clasped behind his back.

"How are you feeling?"

My mind goes immediately to Dante and the lagoon. "I actually feel great."

Ezra narrows his eyes. "You used your power at the trial."

"Oh." *Yes, that.* "I know I shouldn't have. But I was afraid he was going to die."

"It's not only Dante's well-being that concerns me, Celeste. Nadya said it was worse this time."

I press my lips together and exhale through my nose. "I'm going to have to have a talk with my *best friend* about boundaries."

"She's worried about you. That's what best friends do."

I sigh, and when I realize there's reason to dwell in my empty room, I head into the hall with Ezra in tow.

"It's not really about control," I say to him when I'm sure no one is near enough to hear. "The magic is listening to me. But every time I use it, it feels like I'm tearing something open inside me. And the more I tear, the less I can stitch it back up."

Ezra nods. "Obviously, neither of us expected that circumstances would arise in which you would have to use your powers to such a degree. And it is a shame that we didn't take the opportunity earlier in the tour. But at this point, it's essential to increase the frequency of your magic

practice. But not too much at once."

"So, start with little ripples before taking on a tsunami."

He smiles. "Precisely." He extends his arm as we reach the ground floor, guiding me to the main doors. "I know you want to help Dante. But you need to remember that if you burn yourself out, you won't be able to help him anymore."

I nod slowly. "You're right. Speaking of lessons, Nadya showed me some magic yesterday. She cloaked an apple."

Ezra lifts his brows. "Did she?"

"She made it vanish for a few seconds. It was completely invisible. For a few seconds, anyway."

His gaze seems far off. "I'll speak with her. I don't know much about sorcery of that kind, but I can't imagine the training involved would be much different than what we've been doing. It's all about discipline, after all. Mind over matter. Practiced control with boundaries in place."

"You'll help her?"

"If she's willing." His gaze softens.

I manage a smile. "She'll like that. Especially if it means showing off."

As we step outside into the front of the castle, where the carriages are waiting, I spot most of the Hederan court gathered before Queen Verina. She's speaking openly with King Silas and Queen Eleanor, and Dante is standing silently beside his father.

"I've been meaning to ask..." I say to Ezra before we approach the crowd. "What happens after all of this? How do we know what the realms have decided about Dante?"

Ezra straightens, a hand on his chin. "There hasn't been a case like this in more than a century. Back then, the realms would discuss among themselves, weigh the intent, the worth, the risk. They'd decide and send word by nightfeather. So the king would be the first to know."

My stomach knots. "So there's no way of knowing Dante's fate until we get back to Hedera."

"I'd say the odds are in Lord Stregasi's favor, since he's been passing their tests." He pauses, glancing at me. "So far, that is. We've still got

Mersos to visit."

I take a deep breath, glancing at Dante while I slowly exhale. There's one more realm to conquer, and I'm already nervous about what trial they have planned for him.

And what it means for me.

A flutter of soft rose skirts appears at the edge of my vision, and I turn to see Nadya approaching, her spell book tucked beneath one arm and a determined glint in her eye.

"There you are," she says, a little breathless. "Everyone ready to get back on the ship?"

Ezra groans. "I'm not particularly fond of sea voyages, to be honest."

"Really?" I ask, not having noticed his aversion. "I find them enjoyable."

"That's because you're part pirate," Nadya jokes, then she bites her lip. I've told her about Dante's little nickname for me, but it isn't something Ezra would be aware of.

Luckily, Ezra doesn't seem to pay much attention to the comment.

We go forward and join the crowd in front of the carriages. Queen Verina nods to King Silas and Queen Eleanor, apparently finished speaking with them. Her eyes fall on me, and she tilts her head.

"Princess Celeste," she says, "may the tides favor your onward journey."

"Thank you, Your Majesty." I dip into a small curtsy.

She turns to Dante, giving him an elegant nod. "Lord Stregasi, it's been a privilege." Her tone softens. "You're an honorable man, and I look forward to witnessing your legacy. You are always welcome here, should you ever wish to return home."

He inclines his head respectfully. "You've been beyond kind, Your Majesty. Truly."

She gives one final smile to everyone before graciously turning on her heel and heading into the castle with her entourage.

Dante gives me one long look before entering his carriage, and I can't help but wonder what fate has in store for him next.

CHAPTER THIRTY-FIVE

We have to travel through the sweltering heat of Bastos to get to the southern realm of Mersos. The air changes as soon as we cross the border, and I swear I can breathe easier. The breeze carries the scent of fertile soil, fresh fruit, and sweet grain. Rolling fields stretch as far as the eye can see—golden wheat swaying like waves beneath the sun, ripe vineyards and abundant orchards dominating neatly divided plots across the horizon. Everything about Mersos is carefully maintained, and it seems as if everyone who lives here contributes to cultivating a sustainable environment. Diligent workers bend low, tending to the crops. Horse-driven carts are piled high with produce, trundling along dirt paths toward the sprawling city that rises beyond the farmland.

As we move through the city, there are artisans working under open stalls—cobblers repairing boots, weavers threading looms, gloved perfumers delicately blending scents in glass vials. Yet despite the bustle, nothing seems rushed. Every motion is deliberate. Controlled. Quality is important here.

The capital of Kernhart is full of a practical luxuriance, a symbol of durability, cohesion, and productivity. The streets are made of pale stone,

flat and seemingly perfect. I take in the pristine structure of Sagehold Castle, which is more wide than tall, surrounded by boundless lavender and rosemary fields on either side. The structure sits on a cliff, and the back of the castle drops off into an enormous valley, which would make it difficult for enemies to infiltrate them.

Despite its beauty, there is a sharpness to Mersos. A guardedness. I feel it in the way the workers watch us from the fields—polite, but wary. As if our presence is both welcome and an intrusion. Probably because they know how important this realm is. Mersos holds the survival and wealth of the realms in its hands. They provide more than crops. The fine silk worn by the courtiers of Hedera, the delicate perfumes that scent their chambers, the linen sheets that grace their beds—it all comes from here. If something is made or grown, it comes from Mersos. And they know their worth.

"I usually don't mind when I'm being stared at," Nadya murmurs beside me, "but this makes even me uncomfortable."

I nod slightly, keeping my expression neutral as our caravan slows at the front entrance of the castle. At the center of the forecourt stands a tiered fountain, its marble carved into the likeness of the god of bounties. The guards at the entrance stand at attention by the front doors, their heads held high but their eyes fixed up on us as we disembark from the carriages.

As I always do when we arrive in a new realm, I search for Dante to measure his well-being. When I find him, I take in his downcast gaze, his weary stance, the slight disarray of his hair. This tour is taking a toll on him. Thankfully, it's our final stop before we can go back to Ivystone.

I'm eager for our gazes to connect, but King Silas suddenly steps between us, clapping Dante on the back before guiding the procession forward toward the front steps of the castle. Silas holds his posture as regally as ever. The people of Mersos might trust no one, but they would be fools not to acknowledge that Hedera is their largest buyer. As long as Silas keeps their coffers full, they'll treat him well. And he knows it.

I wonder if they'll extend even a fraction of the same welcome to me.

 284

The thought tightens my throat. The last communication Delasurvia had with Mersos was a message informing my brother that the trade routes to Delasurvia would be cut off as long as our kingdom continued to shelter refugees from Dulcamar. The memory burns. If not for King Silas arranging to reopen the routes—promising Mersos the Dulcamar refugees would be turned away at the border—my people would be starving.

And as far as Mersos knows, we've upheld our side of that deal. If they were to find out that Delasurvia is still harboring those who slip through the border, it would be seen as deceit. An insult that would completely block Delasurvia from any supplies in the future.

I lift my chin, determined to keep that secret sacred.

A line of officials comes through the front doors, taking their places as the three rulers of Mersos come out to greet us, standing beneath the banners of forest-green emblazoned with the golden sigil of a hammer crossed over a rust-red plow.

I study the two men and one woman who make up the triarchs, thinking back on the lesson I had with Ezra on Mersos and its rulers. Each of them is impeccably dressed in finely woven garments of cotton and silk. Their clothing is precise and practical, like everything else about this place.

The woman, positioned slightly forward, is Queen Shaylin. She wears a tailored ivory coat over a pale-green gown. Her sleek, black hair is twisted into a coiled bun at the nape of her long neck, and the rings on her fingers gleam with the cold glint of wealth. Her face is unreadable—a mask of composed indifference—but there's a sharp calculation behind her pale-brown eyes. Below her hooked nose, her thin lips remain in a straight line.

The man to her right is taller, his deep-brown skin accentuated by royal-blue eyes. King Gallor's dark beard is trimmed close to his jaw, and though he stands with the poise of a diplomat, there's something in his shoulders—an edge of tension, like he's always braced for a fight. The second man, King Birchus, is slightly older, a fact only discernable because of the deep crow's feet beside his green eyes. The auburn-haired

man stands with a broad frame and the kind of steady presence that suggests his words carry weight.

The triarchs are a ruling council of three, but they are also married to each other. They govern together, and—according to Ezra— sometimes disagree on politics, but when it comes to protecting their land and their profits, they stand united.

King Silas inclines his head and strides forward, Dante falling into step just behind him. Queen Eleanor keeps a blank face as her hands remain clasped in front of her. When the Mersos queen finds me, I dip my head politely, my mourning veil brushing against my cheeks.

"King Silas," she says, her voice warm but carefully measured. "Welcome back to Mersos. It has been too long."

"Queen Shaylin," he replies, inclining his head. "It is a privilege to be here. Your city flourishes, as ever."

"We do our best," she says lightly, though the pride in her tone is unmistakable. "And we are pleased to welcome your distinguished company."

Her gaze flicks to Dante for a heartbeat—perhaps weighing his worth, as everyone else has—but lingers on me.

Silas, ever the tactician, doesn't give her time to prod. "In gratitude for your hospitality, I bring gifts from Hedera's royal coffers."

"Then let us proceed inside." King Gallor extends his arm to the open doors.

As our entourage makes its way into the grand entry hall of the castle, I remember another detail Ezra told me about during our lesson. Mersos's culture is heavily based on the life cycle. We live, we die, and the next crop always comes along. It explains why they haven't yet extended their condolences for Torbin's death. Or Bennett's. And something tells me they never will.

Once we're situated in the grand hall, the kings and queen take their places behind a long table that faces us. There is no dais, and there are no thrones. I almost feel as if I were attending a council meeting.

The triarchs cast their expectant gazes upon us. With a nod, King Silas turns to the back of the room, where two of his attendants step

forward, carrying an iron-bound trunk. When they flip open the lid, I blink curiously. There are no extravagant silks or perfumes, no goblets or jewelry. It wouldn't make sense to bring goods like those here. Inside the trunk, the gleam of gold coins catches the light, and lying atop it all are the two dragon scales.

Mersos doesn't need any goods made from another realm. They could and do cultivate anything here. But gold is always welcome, and dragon scales are the only thing Silas can give them that they cannot make themselves.

Queen Shaylin's lips curve faintly. She's not surprised. She would've expected nothing less from him. The smile is rooted in satisfaction. Beside her, King Gallor assesses the gold with a glance, his expression giving nothing away.

"Your generosity honors us," Queen Shaylin says smoothly. "Please, you must all be weary and need rest. Our servants will show you to your rooms, and later, we will celebrate your arrival with a feast. Mersos is yours to enjoy."

CHAPTER THIRTY-SIX

zra taps his chin as he paces the small room the triarchs provided for us for my lesson. Nadya sits in a chair, perusing her greataunt's book, while Ezra decides where we should begin.

Though Mersos has mild weather perfect for crops, orchards, and vineyards, I still feel stifled in my mourning dress. I wanted to argue to the king that, since Mersos doesn't acknowledge the mourning period, it might be acceptable for me to wear something other than the thick, black gown. But when I brought up the idea to Indira, she told me that it didn't matter what Mersos believed; I had to uphold the ideologies of Hedera and Delasurvia, and it would be a dishonor to Torbin to disregard the rules of the mourning period.

She didn't bring up these arguments in Bastos, which further convinces me that there was something in the air there that erased inhibitions.

"We've concentrated a lot on energy force," Ezra begins, "but maybe we need to touch upon the other forms of magic that you seem to have access to. And the first one that comes to mind is telepathy."

I stand in the center of the room, surprised at the sudden churn of

my stomach. I know there must be some modicum of telepathic power alive within my fae blood, but any time I've used it has been accidental as well as painful. I can only hope that under Ezra's instruction, I can find a way to control the power without hurting myself. "Let's give it a try. What should I do?"

"Let's start small." Ezra shrugs. "I'd like you to tell Nadya something with your mind, and she will repeat it out loud."

Nadya closes her book and smiles. "Oh, I like this challenge. I'm all ears. Or, I guess, in this case, all brain?"

Ezra chuckles. "However you are able to receive is acceptable." He turns to me. "Celeste, if you would, please try to speak to Nadya."

Nadya smiles at me, waiting for me to speak. It takes me a minute to even come up with something I want to send her way. Being playful, she bats her lashes and crosses one leg over the other. She then tucks some hair behind her ear and cups it as if waiting to hear something.

"Stop being cute," I try to say to her.

She continues to smile, tilting her head.

"Nadya," I begin, wondering if it works better if I use her name, *"stop being cute."*

She narrows her eyes. "Are you saying anything?"

I try again, but she continues to look at me with expectation.

I huff in frustration. "You don't hear anything?"

She purses her lips, as if waiting, and then shakes her head. "Sorry, no."

I let out a defeated breath and turn my head toward Ezra.

"It's all right," he says, his voice calm and reassuring. "You're trying to force something that doesn't react to commands."

"I just thought maybe—since I've done it before—"

"That it would come easily this time?" Ezra smiles, stepping forward. "It's not about ability, Celeste. It's about familiarity. You've been practicing energy force. You've spent time getting to know its shape, the way it moves through you. Telepathy is different. It draws from a quieter place. One that hasn't been given your attention in any real way."

I glance at Nadya, who offers a small, supportive shrug, then back

at Ezra. "So what do I do? Just keep trying until my brain splits open?"

He lets out a soft laugh. "Hopefully not. But yes, you'll need patience. Think of your mind like a corridor with many locked doors. You've only just found the handle to this one. The fact that you've opened it even once—accidentally or not—is significant. Most people go their whole lives without ever even finding the right hallway."

I breathe in deeply, grounding myself with his words.

"You're learning how to listen inward," Ezra continues, his tone gentle but sure. "You're shifting from instinct to intention. That takes time. The goal isn't to shout with your thoughts—it's to thread them like a needle. Delicate, focused, and precise."

I nod slowly. "So, again, start small."

He inclines his head. "And start soft. Magic responds best when we treat it like a partner, not a servant. You're not commanding it. You're inviting it."

It makes sense, but I'm not sure if I can put the theory into practice. "So what were you trying to tell me?" Nadya asks.

I smirk at her. "I was telling you to stop being cute."

A giggle bursts free from her lips. "I don't think that's possible."

Despite trying again, I'm unable to send any message to Nadya's brain, no matter how short the sentence. And although we move on to other forms of magic my body released during Dante's trials, I'm unable to get the water in Ezra's cup to splash or freeze. We resort to practicing my energy-force magic, which gives me no trouble when I use it on things that are small. But when the light outside the windows begins to dim, we decide to call it a day and get ready for dinner.

Indira finishes my braid and takes a step back. "That should do it," she says. "Dinner is taking place outside on the castle's veranda, and I wouldn't want the wind to whip your hair into your face."

"Thank you, Indira."

"If they serve any mulberry beignets, I highly recommend you have some." She looks between me and Nadya. "I've only had them once, but I remember them being the best dessert I've ever had in my life."

"Why have you only had them once?" Nadya asks.

"Because mulberries aren't usually exported from Mersos. They keep them to themselves, I guess." Indira sighs. "What I wouldn't give for another taste."

"We'll keep our eye out for them," Nadya promises. "Maybe even bring some to you, if we're able."

Indira shakes her head, but there's a hint of a smile on her lips. "Don't go getting in trouble because of me. I'm supposed to be keeping you two *out* of trouble."

Sir Holden escorts Nadya and me down the well-crafted staircase and through the maze of hallways that lead to the castle's veranda. The scent of roasted meat and sweet herbs drifts through the warm, evening air as we step outside. The veranda is massive—an expanse of polished wood stretching along the cliffside, open to the sky. The setting sun casts a golden haze over the fields in the valley below, painting the crops in hues of amber and crimson. Neatly divided patches of farmland stretch toward the horizon, where rows of wheat, corn, and barley ripple in the breeze. Closer to the southern sea, towering stone warehouses loom— no doubt filled to the brim with goods destined for the rest of the realms.

Long tables gleam beneath silk awnings, the fabric fluttering lazily in the breeze. No extravagance is spared. Crystal goblets catch the fading sunlight, glittering like scattered stars. Platters overflow with fresh fruit—figs and blood oranges sliced open to reveal their glistening flesh—while baskets spill with golden bread braided intricately into knots. Pitchers of honeyed wine glint in the firelight from the torch-lit sconces positioned around the deck, flickering against the approaching dusk. Servants carry plates of food I've never seen before in my life, and I wonder if I'll have room in my belly to try them all.

I'm led to my seat near the center of the table, and as I settle into the carved, wooden chair, my eyes immediately find Dante. He sits

directly across from me, and though his posture composed, I sense him relax a bit when he notices me. The evening breeze stirs his black hair, and the fading light sharpens the angles of his jaw. When his storm-grey eyes lock with mine, the rest of the world falls away for a breath, until the scrape of a chair pulls me back to reality.

Queen Shaylin takes her seat at the head of the table, flanked by her kings, Gallor, the tall and brooding one, and Birchus, the auburn-haired man whose smile never quite reaches his eyes. King Silas sits to their right, already deep in conversation with them, no doubt reinforcing Hedera's position as their most generous patron. Queen Eleanor sits beside him, her face pale and drawn, but she holds herself with quiet dignity.

Dante sits two seats away from the king—close enough to remind everyone that he is ready to become the newly legitimized prince, but far enough to maintain the unspoken distance that still lingers between them. I know he's being tested every moment he's here. The triarchs wouldn't let this opportunity pass without gauging his ability to follow in his father's footsteps, and more importantly, to ensure he understands where Mersos's interests lie.

In his pockets, to be precise.

The man beside Dante turns toward us with a warm smile, his dark-brown hair swept back in loose waves and his beard trimmed short to frame his strong jaw. His deep-set eyes are the color of roasted chestnuts.

"I don't believe I've had the pleasure," he says with an accent I can't quite place. "Lord Pedro of Southmere Valley, Mersos. My family oversees the garnet mines east of the Alvean cliffs. You are Princess Celeste, I believe."

"Yes," I say with a polite smile. "And this is Lady Nadya."

Nadya gives a little wave, mid-sip of her wine, and lowers her glass with a grin. "Nice to meet you, my lord."

Lord Pedro's gaze lingers a little longer on her. Not leering, but curious. Admiring. "Nadya," he repeats, as if tasting the syllables. "A rare name. Fitting."

Nadya blushes, just barely, and I exchange a look with Dante,

holding back a smirk.

Pedro turns his attention momentarily to Dante. "Lord Dante, I understand Mersos will be the last stop on your tour. You must be looking forward to finalizing the legitimization."

Dante raises his goblet in quiet acknowledgment. "While it will be nice to return home, I'm making it a point to enjoy the fascinating realm of Mersos. It certainly is filled with rare delights."

Lord Pedro nods, his gaze returning to Nadya. "Yes, you are right. I find that rare delights appear unexpectedly at times, and one must seize the opportunity to cherish them."

Nadya's eyes widen slightly, and I swear I feel her toes nudge mine under the table, probably checking to see if I'm hearing this right.

Pedro gestures to a small pin at his collar—a deep-red garnet nestled in a gold setting. "These stones come from my family's valley. We mine them by hand. They're stubborn to shape, but when they catch the sun just right, they burn like fire. I believe they'd suit you."

"Me?" Nadya blinks, clearly caught off guard.

"You," he says with a slow smile. "Your coloring, your energy... garnet would adore you. If I may, I'd like to have a pair of earrings made in your honor."

Nadya blinks again, then glances at me with what I can only perceive as alarmed delight. "Oh. That's very... generous."

"Not generosity," Pedro says smoothly, "just appreciation. Some beauty deserves to have some light cast upon it."

Nadya sputters something in response—I can't quite make it out over the clatter of silver and the rise of music—but I'm already grinning behind my goblet.

Across the table, Dante arches one brow at me, and I can see he's biting back a laugh.

I sense a shift of movement, and everyone's heads seem to turn. Following their gazes, I find six people of various ages entering, each of them finding places to sit. Two of them, a man who is the spitting image of King Gallor and a woman with bright-red hair and freckled skin, come to our table and take the empty seats near us.

 293

Lord Pedro nods his head at the woman. "Princess Rosemary." He then nods to the man. "Prince Lief. How wonderful of you to join us."

"Lord Pedro, I wanted to thank you for the lovely garnet-encrusted mirror," Princess Rosemary says. "It was a delightful gift." She then shifts her gaze to Dante. "You must be Lord Stregasi."

Dante inclines his head. "Princess Rosemary, it's a pleasure to meet you."

One of my lessons with Ezra comes back to me, sparking the memory of learning that the triarchs have six children. The two who joined us at our table are obviously the oldest two of the six, with Princess Rosemary appearing to be around my age.

"I'm glad to see the new royal prospect is a virile man," Princess Rosemary says, scrutinizing him thoroughly. "Fertility is important to the people of Mersos."

Dante nearly chokes on his drink but recovers with a graceful nod. "Yes, I've heard."

The first course arrives, and even after everything we've seen so far, I can't help but marvel. Silver trays gleam under the torchlight—freshly grilled swordfish drizzled with lemon and herbs, soft cheeses wrapped in fig leaves, roasted pheasant glazed with spiced honey. There are bowls of sugared plums and spiced nuts, and an entire roast lamb with fragrant rosemary still adorning the skin. Everything is local, everything is of the highest quality.

The conversation is civil at first. Safe. The triarchs ask polite questions about the journey and the Hederan court. But I see where it's leading. Dante is the prize curiosity of the evening, and they intend to weigh his worth.

Gallor leans forward, his hands folded neatly on the table. "Lord Stregasi," he says, his voice smooth but probing, "it must be quite the adjustment, stepping from the shadows into the light. How does it feel to bear the weight of a kingdom's future on your shoulders?"

Dante's smile is easy enough to fool those who don't know him. "I'm fortunate to have my father's guidance to ensure I meet the kingdom's expectations."

Shaylin tilts her head slightly. "A wise sentiment. We value stability in Mersos—especially in those who hold the power to shape trade agreements." Her words are pleasant enough, but there's no mistaking the message beneath them: play by our rules or the flow of goods stops.

Dante meets her gaze, but I catch the flicker of strain beneath the polished façade. He hates this, being treated like a commodity to be measured and controlled. And even as proud as I am of how he holds himself, my stomach twists at the thought of them dissecting his every word and gesture.

"Of course," Birchus adds, his tone just a shade too casual, "it's no secret that Hedera relies heavily on our exports. I assume you share your father's commitment to ensuring that arrangement remains as... mutually beneficial as it's always been? I understand that you are part siren, which is something we will need to take into consideration. If you were to use your powers in a way that would manipulate any contracts we have in place, it would destroy more than just our alliance."

The pressure they're putting on him is subtle but relentless. My fingers curl into my lap beneath the table, the warmth of the evening suddenly stifling. I know Dante won't falter, but I also feel like they're ambushing him.

I set my goblet down softly, drawing their attention as I speak. "Lord Stregasi is a man of his word," I say, my voice clear and steady. "Siren or not, he is loyal, not only to the integrity of Hedera, but also to the union King Silas has procured with Delasurvia. I've never met anyone more trustworthy than him."

Silence falls over the table. For a breath, no one speaks. Least of all the king, whose rigid posture suggests I've overstepped. But I don't care. Let them be shocked. Let them hear the truth.

King Gallor's eyes narrow slightly as he studies me, but Queen Shaylin only smiles with a slow, assessing curve of her lips. "It seems your future prince has a fierce defender," she says, lifting her goblet. "A crucial thing, loyalty. We admire it here."

King Silas clears his throat, the sound crisp and cutting. His expression is unreadable, but I can feel his disapproval from across the

 295

table. I've spoken out of turn—and perhaps given too much of myself away.

Dante's eyes find mine again, gratitude flickering behind the quiet storm there. But beneath it is something deeper—something only I can see. My words have touched him, my declaration of my trust in him reaching his heart.

I tear my gaze away, forcing my attention back to my plate. I'm supposed to be in mourning. I'm supposed to be a shadow at these gatherings. But for him, I'd speak a thousand truths, no matter who's listening.

CHAPTER THIRTY-SEVEN

I stare in awe at the trial Mersos has constructed for Dante. The labyrinth sprawls beneath us, carved deep into the raw earth like an open wound. From the covered, elevated platform where the court is seated, I can see every snaking corridor, every moss-covered stone wall, every twisting passage that coils back on itself. It's a maze designed not to test memory or logic—but endurance. Sheer, punishing endurance.

The sky overhead is thick with storm clouds, bloated and bruised. Lightning dances across the horizon, illuminating the maze in brief flashes of silver. The air hums with tension, heavy with the scent of damp soil and the storm that threatens to strike.

Dante stands at the mouth of the labyrinth. Alone. At his feet lies a massive sack, bound in rope. I don't know what's inside—stones, iron, potatoes—but it drags his shoulders low the moment he lifts it onto his back. The muscles beneath his tunic tighten, his jaw clenched with the effort.

At the maze's center, a monstrous bull paces. Its hide is dark and gnarled like scorched bark, rippling with raw muscle. Curved horns gleam in the growing storm light. It snorts, breath steaming like fog, ears flicking toward every sound. It stands behind a weak-looking wooden barrier, and it knows Dante is coming.

King Birchus stands, his broad silhouette outlined against the storm. "In Mersos," he says, his voice a deep, gravelly rumble, "we do not measure a man by the blood he spills, but by the burdens he carries and his perseverance to get the job done. You must bring the sack to the finish line of the labyrinth intact. Let the weight break your back or prove your worth beneath it."

Beside him, a fae dressed in green and brown leathers steps forward. He's tall, wiry, his long fingers wrapped in vine-woven gloves. He lifts one hand, palm to the sky. And the vines around the maze stir like snakes waking from slumber.

I go still. My eyes snap to the creeping edges of the labyrinth—roots, vines, and thorned tendrils winding tighter, coiling like a trap.

I'm not sure if Dante has seen them or if he has a plan on how to avoid getting trapped.

A bell tolls, signaling the start.

He hauls the sack onto his back with a grunt and steps into the maze.

The bull lifts its head.

And the vines move.

Dante walks steadily at first, carefully, his boots landing in the shallow indentations of the path. The sack sways with each step, dragging at him, threatening to throw him off-balance. A trickling of rain begins, and the dirt flanking the stone paths turns quickly into mud. The vines twitch at the corners of each junction, reaching out, ready.

From above, I can see what he cannot. A wall of thorns curls toward his right. If he turns that way, they'll tear into him.

My hands curl into fists against the railing.

"*Dante, you must go left.*"

The magic hesitates inside me, thick and sluggish. I push harder, the thought forming sharper in my mind.

"*Left. Now.*"

A spike of pain drives behind my right eye. My vision blurs with a sudden white-hot bloom. But that familiar hum pulses through me that

 298

tells me my magic has found him. Then he veers left.

My breath stutters. But we're far from safe.

Beside me, Nadya takes my hand.

A thunderclap echoes through the space, loud and aggressive. The bull bellows and crashes through the wooden barrier at the maze's center, hooves kicking up clumps of dirt and mud as the creature barrels forward. Dante spots it and falters, shifting the sack's weight. He bends, regaining his footing, and begins to run. But the vines have begun to lash out, writhing across the path.

One curls around his ankle.

"No." I stand and throw out my hand, and this time, the magic erupts like a lightning strike. It slams into the vines—not gently, not delicately, but violently. With a *crack*, they snap, and he wrenches free.

The recoil hits me harder. As Nadya urges me back to sitting in my chair, a stabbing pain jolts through my stomach like something sharp twisting inside. I double forward, gasping, one hand pressed to my abdomen.

"Celeste!" Nadya puts an arm around me, steadying me.

I shake my head, unable to answer. A hot sting burns my nostrils so much that it makes me pinch my nose. My vision flickers again, and when I blink, I see blood on my fingertips.

The bull reaches the turn, its hooves scrambling for purchase, and charges.

Dante can't outrun it.

I don't know if I can stop the creature, but I don't have time to think. I shove sideways with every ounce of strength I can muster. The energy barrels through the maze, catching the beast just enough to make it skid off-balance. Its horn scrapes stone inches from Dante's shoulder.

He stumbles—then pushes forward.

And the storm breaks.

Rain lashes at the world, transforming the dirt into thick sludge. The walls of the labyrinth glisten, rainwater pouring down like the earth were weeping. Lightning splits the sky overhead, followed by the angry crack of thunder. The crowd gasps and mumbles—whether for the storm

or the show, I don't know.

The final wall looms ahead.

Ten feet high. No ladders. No handholds. And completely drenched, falling apart in the downpour.

Dante braces and hurls the sack upward. It slams onto the ledge, just barely catching.

He jumps.

Slips.

Crashes into the mud.

The bull, now recovered, charges toward him.

Dante jumps again. And again. The sack begins to slide.

Fuck!

I raise both hands, ignoring the scream inside my skull. The magic splits from me, part of it coiling upward, reaching into the clouds themselves, the other part reaching for the path in front of the bull. The pressure builds behind my ribs, behind my eyes, threatening to tear me open.

I stare at the sky. *Clear. Just enough. Please.*

A patch of light breaks through the clouds, streaming above the far wall. The rain dissipates. Sunlight spills like a blessing onto the upper stones. Just enough for purchase.

Dante leaps again, his hands catching on dry stone. He pulls.

I focus on the tendrils of thorns between the bull and Dante. They shudder as they move away from the wall, just enough to block his path. The bull bellows, its hooves digging into wet ground, but it isn't able to stop in time. It lets out a loud groan of pain as it crashes into the thorns.

My eyes go back to Dante. The vines by Dante's feet coil again, snaking up now, sharp with thorns. They tear at his boots, his calves.

I grunt to myself, pushing again.

The burst is white-hot agony. My stomach knots, and I fall back, clutching my side. It feels like something inside me is splitting apart.

But the vines fracture, falling away from Dante's legs.

Dante scrambles over the wall. He grabs the sack and pulls it with him.

Then he collapses beside it, gasping.

The Mersosian court explodes in applause. King Birchus rises. For a moment, I think he might actually smile. His movement is followed by King Gallor and Queen Shaylin.

King Silas stands, a proud smile on his reddened face. Dante has just passed the final test, and Silas is clearly pleased with his son's accomplishments. If I know Silas, he'll be taking full credit for it.

I sag into my seat, shaking. Nadya presses a cloth into my hand so I can wipe the blood from my nose. My head pounds like a war drum.

But he made it. Dante is safe.

Even if I feel like I'm falling to pieces.

CHAPTER THIRTY-EIGHT

The next moments are a blur. Nadya helps me back to my room, with Sir Holden escorting us. I strip myself of my suffocating mourning dress and fall onto the bed in my chemise, clutching my stomach as Nadya runs small hand towels under cool water to serve as cold compresses for my head.

It takes an hour until my healing magic relaxes me enough to fall asleep. When I wake, I'm finally feeling like myself again, and Nadya stays by my side the entire time. She sits next to me on the bed, stroking my head as it rests on the pillow, humming a soft tune.

"Thanks, Nadya. I'm feeling better."

"Are you sure?" She sweeps some hair away from my cheek. "Because Lord Pedro said something about some special celebration Mersos has planned in honor of the tour ending. I think he said they were going to set the sky ablaze, whatever that means."

I smile up at her. "And you have plans to enjoy the celebration with him?"

"Only if you're okay," she says. "You're my priority."

I sit up. "You've more than fulfilled your duties as my best friend."

She lets out a laugh, but it gets interrupted by a *thud* that resonates from the balcony.

Nadya's eyes widen, as do mine, and in the next moment, we jump up from the bed and run to the balcony doors. When I tear them open, I find Dante standing there, straightening his clothes.

"How did you get there?" I ask him. I look up above the balcony's overhang. "Where did you come from?"

Nadya eyes him. "Did you jump down here... or up?"

Dante chuckles. "My room is one floor above yours," he tells me.

I grab his hand and pull him into my room.

"That's so romantic." Nadya heads toward the door. "I'm going to give you two some privacy."

Before she reaches for the door, someone pounds on the other side.

"Your Highness?" Indira's voice calls out, strained with urgency.

Instinctively, I stand in front of Dante, as if to hide him. Or protect him.

We scramble to figure out what to do, each of us apparently with a different idea, when the door suddenly bursts open.

I stand stiffly, while Nadya swallows hard. She mumbles something I can't make out, and a second later, she adopts a casual stance, twirling a finger in her hair. "Oh, hello, Indira. Why do you look so flushed?"

My heart is in my throat, but when I turn around, Dante is not there. I wrinkle my brow. The balcony doors are still closed, and I don't think Dante can fit under the bed.

"I saw Lord Stregasi jump over his balcony," Indira exclaims. She looks flustered, spewing sounds of uncertainty. "I could have sworn he came in here."

"Jumped over his balcony?" Nadya scoffs. "That sounds ridiculous. Indira, you must be weary from traveling and imagining things. No one is here except Celeste and me."

I'm still awestruck, trying to figure out how Dante could just vanish. Until I remember Nadya's cloaking magic.

Indira brushes past us, checking the balcony to no avail. She then throws my armoire open. "I could have sworn..."

Although I'm thoroughly impressed with Nadya's ability, I also

remember she said it doesn't last very long. Panic crawls back up my throat. "Maybe you can't handle the Mersos wine," I put in.

Indira runs a hand over the back of her neck, her brows scrunched together. "I didn't drink any of the wine."

"Oh, well, you're missing out," Nadya says, placing her hands on Indira's shoulders. "You know, I was talking to one of the kitchen servants, who said she would gladly whip up a plate of delectable mulberry beignets if I wanted."

That gets Indira's attention. "Really? Just because you asked?"

"Well, no." Nadya steers Indira toward the door. "As an exchange."

Indira looks over her shoulder at Nadya. "In exchange for what? Oh! Oh, never mind. I don't want to know."

Nadya gives me a wink, closing the door behind them.

I let out a sigh of relief, whirling around to where Dante was standing, but I still don't see him. I dart to the balcony doors, but before I can open them, Dante's voice sounds out from behind me.

"What the fuck just happened?"

I turn to see him sitting on the bed, and my breath catches in my throat. "Oh. Hi."

His black shirt is unbuttoned at the collar, sleeves pushed up to his forearms, revealing the lean muscle beneath. His hair falls in loose waves around his face, but it's his eyes—stormy and intent—that hold me captive. "Is Indira losing her vision or something?"

"Right. That." I clear my throat. "Nadya has been practicing some... magic."

He looks... wrecked. Beautifully, achingly wrecked. He rakes a hand through his disheveled hair, his shoulders slumped. "Magic? What do you mean?"

I move forward and sit beside him on the bed. "There are witches from Bastos in her bloodline. When we were there, we visited her great-aunt, and she gave Nadya a book of spells to practice. In Messanya, Nadya made an apple disappear. It only lasted a minute, but it was completely cloaked. Invisible to the eye." I watch his reaction. "I guess she's getting better."

304

He searches my face, as if waiting for the punchline of a joke. Then his brows come together. "I was invisible?"

"I turned around, and you were gone." I let out a soft chuckle and shake my head. "And it's a good thing because Indira would have either kicked you out herself or reported you to your father."

He nods, but then his gaze drops to his hands.

"What?" I tilt my head to see his face better. "What is it?"

His eyes find mine. "I don't know what it's going to take to get you to stop risking your life for me."

Oh. This is about me using my magic at the trial. "First of all, when I was active as commander of my regiment, I was risking my life almost every day. Second, we don't know that using my magic is necessarily risking my life. It causes pain, yes. But as you can see, I'm perfectly fine now. It's just a temporary cost to an extremely important cause."

He looks like he's about to argue, but I touch my finger to his lips.

"And thirdly," I continue, "that was the last trial. You're finished. I won't have to risk it anymore."

A beat passes between us, and then the tension fractures. His hand lifts, fingers brushing my jaw, tucking a strand of hair behind my ear. "You don't know what it does to me, knowing you're willing to tear yourself apart for me. Willing to speak up for me. Celeste, you're my everything. Don't you see that?"

It feels like my heart is swelling inside my chest, filling me with a comforting warmth that makes my body hum.

He leans closer, his forehead touching mine, and I let my eyes fall shut. I tilt my face up just as his mouth meets mine.

The kiss is slow at first—sweet, unhurried, as if he's savoring every brush of my lips. But when I thread my fingers through his hair, tugging him closer, something in him snaps. His hands slide down to my waist, pulling me flush against his body as the kiss deepens, hunger coiling between us.

I curl my hands into the front of his shirt and pull him to me as I lean back on the bed, answering him with another kiss, fierce and full of the longing I've kept locked away when watchful eyes are around.

 305

A sharp crack splits the air. I jolt, breaking our kiss, my heart hammering against my ribs as I reach instinctively for the dagger tucked beneath my pillow.

Dante's head snaps toward the balcony doors. "What in the—"

Another explosion thunders through the night, followed by a cascade of light flaring against the walls. My pulse spikes, and without another word, we move. I slip off the bed with dagger in hand as Dante jumps to his feet. We reach the balcony together, shoulders brushing as I push open the doors and step into the cool, night air.

The sky is ablaze, just like Nadya said.

Brilliant bursts of color bloom across the heavens—scarlet, gold, violet—each one brighter than the last. Trails of shimmering sparks rain down like falling stars before vanishing into the dark. Another blast follows, louder, shaking the stones beneath my bare feet.

I loosen my grip on the dagger, exhaling softly. "Gods," I whisper. "I thought we were under attack."

Dante chuckles low beside me, but there's a note of wonder in his voice. "So did I." His forearms rest against the balcony's stone ledge as his gaze follows the next eruption, a silver fountain spilling across the sky. "I've never seen anything like this before."

"Neither have I." I lean forward, captivated as the sky lights up again in a dazzling spray of emerald and gold. "I suppose Mersos keeps a few secrets of its own."

The scent riding on the breeze is sharp and metallic, tinged with sulfur and smoke. It carries the acrid tang of burned chemicals—like spent matches or a lightning strike. After each burst of color in the sky, a faint sweetness lingers, like scorched sugar or singed paper, as the powdery haze settles in the air.

For a while, we both watch in silence. Just the two of us beneath the brilliant display of flashing stars. The distant booms echo through the night, but the warmth of Dante's presence beside me softens the sharp edges of my tension.

I feel his gaze shift.

I don't turn right away, still spellbound by the display. "You're

missing the show," I tease softly.

"I'm looking exactly where I'm meant to be looking," he murmurs.

The heat of his words sweeps over me before his touch does. His hands find my waist, palms warm as they trace along the silk of my chemise. He moves closer behind me, his breath teasing the curve of my neck. My pulse quickens when his lips brush against the sensitive spot just beneath my ear.

"You have no control, do you?" My voice is breathier than I intend.

"Mm." His mouth curves into a smile against my skin. "Can you blame me? You're breathtaking. Besides, you started it."

"Oh, did I?" I hold back a shiver as he nuzzles the nape of my neck. "You're the one who jumped onto my balcony."

"Who am I to say that wasn't one of the powers you possess in your ever-expanding magical arsenal?"

I close my eyes as his kisses trail down the side of my neck—soft at first, then more insistent. His grip tightens slightly at my hips as he draws me back against him, the solid warmth of his body and the unmistakable hardness of his cock making my head spin.

A tremor shivers down my spine as his hands move forward, greedily cupping my breasts before drifting lower to the curve of my ass. His fingers trace the edge of my chemise at the back of my legs. I bite my lip when I feel the delicate brush of his knuckles against my bare thigh. And when his hands start to lift the hem with feather-light movements, I can't hold back a whimper.

"Lean forward. Rest your forearms on the balustrade," Dante whispers.

"Wh—?"

"Do as you're told, little pirate." He places a warm kiss on my shoulder blade before urging my upper body forward.

I comply, biting my lip as his hot breath travels down my back, leaving steaming kisses in its wake. I let out a small breath of a moan, settling my weight on my forearms as Dante continues his descent until he's kneeling behind me. The material of my chemise lifts, and in the next moment, Dante drags the material of my underwear down my legs. His

fingers trail along my thighs, his breath dancing across my flesh, sending shivers of pleasure through my body that mimic the flickering lights painting the night sky.

When he presses a kiss to my upper thigh, I arch my back, pushing back into him. His lips graze closer to my pussy, and my breath hitches in my throat. His hands slide up my legs and grab hold of my hips, pulling me back until my folds meet his mouth.

"Dante," I moan into the cool, night air. "More."

He drags his tongue through my center, and when he releases a growl, I almost come undone.

"So wet," he says. "You're dripping for me, aren't you?"

I whimper again, my hands clenching. "Yes. Please."

His tongue laps at my core, up and down, up and down, and then his nose is pressed between my ass cheeks as he plunges his tongue inside my pussy.

My body is instantly on fire, my hips rolling as he spreads my arousal around with his tongue and lips. Shockwaves pulse through me, and the little gasps I let out drift into the open air.

"You taste so good," Dante says, his voice low and husky. "You don't understand what your taste and smell do to me."

I can't even respond because his tongue is inside me again, hitting that spot that makes me see spots, and his hand is holding me in place, his fingers circling my clit. He fucks me with his mouth, unrelenting, unapologetically pushing me to the edge of my mounting desire. My whimpers grow more urgent with each lash of his tongue.

My orgasm explodes just as the sky bursts with light, and I'm sure the moan I let out can be heard above the *bang* that rips through the sky.

My head drops as my ragged breaths compete with the spasms of pleasure that ripple through my body, but I lift it again when I feel Dante's hands on my hips.

He's standing now, still behind me, and I gasp as the hot head of his cock slides along the wet folds of my sensitive pussy. The fire inside me ignites again, and I writhe against him.

"Fuck, Celeste. I can't get enough of you."

"Then take," I say, my voice raspy. "Because I need you. I need you to fill me."

One hand leaves my hip, and I glance over my shoulder to see him lining up the head of his cock. My jaw drops open as he slides into my pussy, inch by inch. I impatiently shove my hips back until he's fully seated.

I hear his breath shudder before he releases a long, growly "Fuuuuck!"

We stay like that for a moment, the heat pulsing between us, and then he slowly begins to thrust. His motions are steady at first, but as our bodies slap together, growing hotter and sweatier, his strokes become more erratic.

"Gods, Celeste, you take my cock so well." His hands are tight on my hips, his fingers digging into my flesh. "Touch yourself," he demands. "Play with that gorgeous, swollen clit."

I do as he says, sliding my fingers down and rubbing frantic circles into my clit, causing even more pressure to build inside my core. Gods, what this man does to me. My head swims as the ecstasy vibrates within me. Our moans and grunts grow louder, and his throbbing cock seems to thicken inside me.

I feel my pussy clenching around him, the heat engulfing me in a deluge of rapture. I'm so close. I'm so close.

"Cum with me, Highness. Cum all over my cock. I want to be covered with your juices."

His last words are stunted as his hips shudder against my ass, and my orgasm pulses out of me. My whole body tingles as aftershocks surge through me. He leans over me, his arms wrapping around my body as his heavy breaths slow.

I don't know how many minutes it takes before he finally pulls out of me. He pulls me to stand and immediately turns me against his chest. His stormy eyes take in my features as he strokes my dampened hair out of my face. He looks as if he's going to say something, and I wait, my heart pounding so hard, I think it's going to break my ribs.

Instead of saying anything, he gently rubs his nose along mine, and

then his lips descend to claim my mouth. It isn't urgent or rough, but gentle, lingering. I can feel his heartbeat. When the kiss ends, I press my forehead against his chest, and he breathes into my hair as he strokes the strands.

I feel like I know what he was going to say, but I'm not going to push him. I feel it. I want to say it, too. But it remains an unspoken claim between us. Not because we don't mean it, and not because we are afraid. But because we are uncertain of what awaits us, of what fate has in store.

CHAPTER
THIRTY-NINE

Ivystone rises from the mist like a fortress out of a dream—sharp spires piercing the low clouds, the silver-grey stone darkened by the drizzle in the air, vines of dark-green ivy clinging to the walls as if the land is cradling the castle in its delicate hands. The familiar sight should feel cold, imposing. And yet, as our carriage rumbles over the bridge, I find an unexpected warmth running through me.

Despite everything, this place has become a home.

The closer we come to the main gates, the more ease I feel, as I managed to sleep a lot during our long journey back. Since there were no more urgent situations where I needed to use copious amounts of my power, the break gave me time to reenergize, but I engaged in little magical exercises Ezra had instructed me to practice to ensure I was learning control. Nadya also practiced, as she spent most of the trip with her nose buried in her great-aunt's spell book.

There were a few nights as we traveled through the mountains near the border that I caught sight of glowing, yellow dots in the woods we passed. I somehow could feel the presence of wolves watching the caravan, as if guarding me in case anything were to threaten my journey.

311

The tour is finally over. No more endless halls glittering with pretense. No more silk-clad princesses fluttering their lashes at Dante while I stand silently in the background, veiled and voiceless. Here, behind Ivystone's towering walls, the weight of the kingdom's scrutiny lifts—if only a little.

The rain drizzles against the window beside me, soft and constant, blurring the courtyard as the carriage approaches. Our convoy got separated halfway back from Mersos, leaving our carriage and one other with Indira and some other servants to arrive much later than the others.

The official mourning period is nearly over, and I smile at the thought of finally ridding myself of this exasperating gown.

Nadya shifts beside me, stretching her legs with a groan. "Finally back. Feels like a dream."

"I never thought I'd say this, but I can't wait to just blockade myself in my room and lie in my bed for a few days."

My body feels stiff as we disembark, and I make a mental note to jump back into my training routine after I get some much-needed rest. Sir Holden walks alongside me and Nadya as we make our way into the castle. The familiar high ceilings and plush furnishings somehow make me feel like I'm seeing an old friend.

A flash of movement catches my eye as we approach the grand staircase. Dante appears as if he's already settled in, freshly bathed and wearing crisp, new clothes.

His broad shoulders seem less tense, though there's still a hint of a shadow beneath his eyes. I wish I could rush over to him and make sure he's all right, to ask him how he's holding up under the pressure of the legitimization.

He hasn't looked my way, and I don't have a minute to try to catch his attention because Indira appears before me and Nadya, immediately urging us up the stairs to our rooms.

I tear my gaze from him, deciding what I really need is to get out of my traveling ensemble and soak myself in a hot bath. Sir Holden leads us up the grand staircase, and as we reach the upper floor, I spot Queen Eleanor heading down the opposite wing. When she glances my way,

there's no mistaking the gloom in her eyes, a weight that no crown can lighten. She carries herself with the same grace she always does, but the grief is still apparent in her expression

I wonder if she feels more trapped here than anywhere else. Her son is gone, and her husband gives her no comfort. In fact, he gives her quite the opposite, and since he has control over the entire kingdom, she must feel she has no one on her side.

I can't imagine what it would be like to live a life where you're never truly free—not even in your own home. I may be subjected to an arranged marriage for the sake of my kingdom, but Dante would never oppress me like his father does to Eleanor.

And unlike the king's marriage, my union with Dante would not be devoid of love.

My cheeks warm. I haven't said it. Neither of us have. But I know that's what this feeling must be. I would do anything for him, even risk my own life, and something tells me he would do the same.

For a moment, her gaze drifts toward me. Her fingers twitch, curling briefly against the folds of her skirt before she lifts her chin and continues toward her chambers. Whatever thoughts linger behind her calm façade, she does not speak them aloud.

By the time Nadya and I reach our connected chambers, my body is heavy with exhaustion, my skin sticky from travel. The weight of mourning—of duty, of expectation—has settled deep in my bones, pressing against me like an ill-fitted corset.

The moment the door clicks shut behind us, Nadya groans, kicking off her boots with little care for where they land. "I'd very much like to strip myself naked, climb under my covers, and remain like that for the foreseeable future."

I laugh. "What about dinner?"

"I'm sure Indira could bring me a tray of food."

"She'll probably make you beg first."

"Celeste, I may have reached the point of begging," she says as she undoes the ties of her dress.

I shake my head, but the amusement fades as I glance down at my

 313

clothes—the black silks, the suffocating weight of my mourning attire. The fabric smells of horse and sweat, of weeks spent wrapped in veils and expectations.

I unfasten the outer tunic first, peeling it from my arms and tossing it to the floor, resisting the urge to set the wretched thing on fire. If I never have to wear black again, it will be too soon.

I pull off my boots, wiggling my toes. "I think I may have to agree. We're getting a night's rest, no matter who tries to stop us."

As if the gods were laughing at my plans, a sharp knock sounds at the door.

Nadya groans. "You spoke too soon."

I sigh, dragging my fingers through my loose hair before crossing the room. When I pull the door open, Indira stands on the other side, looking as exasperated as I feel, with a deep frown and a wrinkled forehead.

"Another summons?" I guess.

Indira shakes her head. "No. Just this." She lifts a small parchment, sealed with dark wax. "The new tower master asked me to bring it to you. Said it arrived a couple of days ago."

I frown, taking the letter. The wax is unmarked, the parchment slightly crinkled from being stored. "For me?"

Indira shrugs. "Also, dinner has been pushed back until eight tonight. King's order."

"I guess we're not the only ones who need to catch up on rest," Nadya comments from my bed, where's she's flopped herself down.

A strange unease prickles over my skin. Who would send me a message by nightfeather now, of all times?

Indira gives me a tired nod. "I'll be back later to help you get ready."

I nod, offering a quiet thanks before closing the door.

Nadya props herself up on her elbows, eyeing the parchment in my hands. "Mysterious messages already? I thought we'd at least get an evening to breathe."

I move toward the candlelight, slipping my nail beneath the wax seal. The parchment unfolds easily, the ink dark and precise.

Celeste,
I have urgent business to discuss with you. Come as soon as you are able.

I recognize my uncle's handwriting, but why would he send a nightfeather to get in touch with me? Why wouldn't he use his telepathic powers to contact me? I get a sudden sour feeling in my stomach, worried that he hasn't truly recovered from his abduction and that something horrible has happened to his power.

I stare at the words, my exhaustion momentarily forgotten. *'Urgent business.'*

It could be a trap. It could be something insignificant.

But my gut tells me otherwise.

I exhale, rolling my shoulders. "My uncle wants to see me. I'll... go tomorrow." There's no way I would survive on horseback tonight. I'd never even make it halfway there without collapsing.

For now, I allow myself one moment of peace.

Because I know it won't last.

The bath was a welcome relief, washing away the dust of travel and the weight of exhaustion from my limbs. My muscles still ache, but it's a dull, manageable discomfort now, soothed by warm water and the lingering scent of lavender oil.

Now, dressed in a loose, pale-blue gown, I walk beside Sir Holden as he leads me through the corridors toward the dining hall. I never thought I'd be so happy to wear a dress like this. The fabric is light, flowing, a welcome change from the stifling weight of mourning clothes, and the color gives me a sense of hope, instead of instilling within me a state of foreboding and dread.

Sir Holden walks a measured pace beside me, his steps silent against the castle floors. As we near the dining hall, I brace myself for the usual formality—an announcement, a procession of servants, the king's scrutinizing gaze from the head of the table. But the moment I enter, the state of the room surprises me.

The long table is crammed with its usual overabundance of food, but the chairs surrounding it are mostly empty.

Only Dante remains, seated at the center with a goblet of wine in hand and a faint crease in his brow. He glances up the moment I arrive, and whatever tension lingers in his shoulders melts just a little. No king. No queen. No Nadya, either.

"Where is everyone?" I ask softly as I approach.

Dante stands, pulling out the seat beside him. "The queen begged off for the evening. Headache, they said." He offers a half-smile, but there's no humor in it. "And my father is holed up in his war chamber, waiting for the nightfeathers."

I sit slowly, trying not to let my surprise show. "Already?"

He nods. "He's convinced the realm's decisions are moments away. Keeps checking the skies, as if willing the birds to arrive faster will make the other rulers approve faster."

"Will they send them all at once?"

"Depends if they're still following the old ways. If they are, each realm will vote—then deliver their decision through a single, marked bird. That's how it was done over a century ago, anyway. At least, that's what Farvis says."

I glance at the flickering candlelight between us, the quiet clink of dishes echoing faintly from the far end of the room, where two servants bring in more dishes—roasted vegetables, pheasant with juniper berries, a loaf of buttered rye.

Dante leans closer, his voice softer now. "What about you? You've got that look in your eye."

I shift in my seat, not even bothering to deal with the fact that he can read me like a book. "I wasn't planning on saying anything yet. But... I received a note from my uncle."

His eyes lock on mine. "'A note'?"

I nod. "A nightfeather reached Ivystone before we returned. He wants to see me. Said it was urgent."

The warmth in his eyes dims. "Are you going?"

"Yes. In the morning."

"I could come with you."

The words are instinctual—his loyalty always so quick, so certain—but I shake my head.

"You should stay. If you're gone when the realms' responses arrive, your father will find someone to blame. And we both know he won't hesitate to point that finger at me."

He leans back in his chair, exhaling. "I hate that you're right."

I offer a small smile. "Sir Holden will come with me. I'll be fine."

He's quiet a moment, then nods. "Still. Be careful."

I reach across the table, brushing his fingers with mine. "I will."

We fall into an easy rhythm, eating beneath the low-lit chandelier and the soft patter of rain tapping at the windows, the quiet between us no longer weighted but comfortable, like a breath finally let out.

I glance at Dante over the rim of my goblet. "Do you think this is what it'll be like when we're king and queen?"

He raises a brow. "Which part? The roast or the lack of other company?"

I smile. "The quiet. The peace. Just the two of us, eating dinner after a long day of meetings and state business. The realm safe, everything as it should be."

He leans back in his chair, eyes glinting. "I imagine most of those meetings will be about what kind of mischief Nadya's gotten into. Again."

I laugh. "And I'll defend her at every turn. Valiantly. Passionately. Even if she's accidentally set the castle on fire."

"Much to Indira's everlasting chagrin."

"She'll have permanent frown lines."

His grin is boyish and warm, but then something shifts. His gaze drops briefly to my lips before meeting my eyes again, darker now. "Every

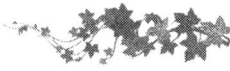 

night," he murmurs, "I'd sit at this table, pretending to care about roast and spiced figs, when really, I'd be thinking about feasting on something else entirely."

My cheeks heat instantly. "Let me guess..." I toy with the edge of my plate. "You'd sweep all the dishes onto the floor just so you could have me right here on the tabletop."

His smirk deepens, a crooked, wicked thing. "Gods, you're dangerous."

I pop a grape into my mouth, biting down with deliberate slowness. "Only to men who underestimate me."

He's still watching me when the door creaks open, and we both turn to see Sir Donovan stepping inside.

"My lord," he says, bowing slightly, "your father would like to see you in the council chamber."

Just like that, the moment fades.

But not entirely.

Because when Dante rises, he still looks at me like I'm a secret worth savoring—and a storm worth braving.

When I'm done with dinner, I take the long hallway toward my chambers, the corridors quieter than usual, the castle hushed beneath the weight of waiting. As I round the corner near the queen's private sitting room, I stop short.

Queen Eleanor steps out of her doors, her arms loosely crossed, her gown a deep shade of plum that dulls beneath the candlelight. She looks thinner than I remember. Tired. Hollow, in a way that grief carves from the inside.

I hesitate for only a second. "Your Majesty?"

Her gaze lifts, and she seems slightly startled at finding me. "Celeste."

Her voice is as poised as ever, but there's a flicker of something softer in it. Something I might dare to call *vulnerability*.

"Are you feeling better? I heard you have a headache." I step closer. "Is there anything I can do for you?"

She shakes her head faintly. "No. But thank you."

The silence between us stretches, gentle and heavy.

"When I was a child," I say, quietly, "I used to think my mother had all the answers. But there were times I would go to her—when something had gone terribly wrong, or when I didn't understand the world—and she would just listen. She wouldn't fix it. She wouldn't give me rules or riddles. She'd just sit with me. And somehow, that made it bearable."

Queen Eleanor's mouth tightens. Her eyes glisten faintly, though no tears fall. She lifts a gloved hand, touches her chest briefly, and then nods.

"I miss having someone listen," she whispers.

"You know, the hurting doesn't really go away. You just have to make room for it." Tentatively, I step forward—not too close, just enough that my voice can be softer. "You do so much for this kingdom. You tolerate... so much. But I hope you know you don't have to carry it all alone."

Her eyes find mine, and something changes in them. A quiet thawing. "You're not what I expected," she murmurs. "The day you came to Ivystone, I thought you were just another pawn in his game."

I meet her gaze. "I'm no one's pawn."

"No," she agrees. "You're not. Maybe I should pay more attention. I might have something to learn."

She adjusts her gloves and turns, walking away without another word.

For a moment, I stand there, watching her retreat. I can't be sure, but I feel as if something has shifted.

CHAPTER FORTY

The Garrison is just as I remember it: loud, bustling, alive with the clamor of soldiers and the scent of sweat and iron. But as I move through its familiar corridors, my focus is only on one thing.

My uncle's summons makes me anxious, but the thing that's clawing at my skin is the concern that he didn't call me with his telepathy. I need to find out the reason behind the alteration in routine.

I quicken my pace, my boots scuffing against the stone as I push through the last archway leading to his quarters. My fae speed makes me quick, and Sir Holden is soon far behind me, unable to keep up. And the only reason I've made it this far so quickly is because my squad isn't here at the moment to slow me down with their greetings.

The wooden door to his office stands ajar, candlelight flickering within.

I step inside to find Uncle Kormak standing behind his heavy, wooden desk, poring over a spread of parchment and maps. He looks up as I enter, and for a moment, the breath catches in my throat.

He looks better. His skin is no longer ashen, his movements steady as he sets down the quill. The sharp lines of his face, once gaunt with illness, have regained their strength. And yet—there is something in his eyes, something distant, as if a shadow still lingers.

Relief floods me so suddenly, I barely know what to do with it. "You're okay." I cross the room, throwing my arms around him like I used to when I was younger.

He hugs me in return without any pretenses of formality.

When we separate, he straightens his uniform and motions to a chair. "You must be exhausted, Celeste. Have a seat."

I don't sit. I feel like I could jump out of my skin. "Your message has me concerned, Uncle. What's going on?"

He lets out a breath, his gaze dropping as he turns and drops into the chair behind his desk. "I needed to see you because I've remembered some things."

My breath gets stuck in my throat. "About your abduction?"

"Yes."

"But why did you send a nightfeather? I haven't heard your voice in my head in months."

He takes a long breath and lets it out. "It has to do with my abduction, what they did to me."

I swallow hard. "What... did they do?" I'm afraid to ask it, but I feel as if I need to know what happened.

The room stills. For a long moment, the only sound is the distant clash of training blades in the courtyard below.

I want to know everything, but I know I shouldn't push him, so I force myself to remain calm and patient. "Okay," I say, finally taking a seat. "Tell me what you remember."

He reaches for a mug that sits on his desk and takes a swig. "The only thing I remember about the actual abduction is the smell."

"The smell?"

"I was searching the area Lord Stregasi informed us about—the pit. The squad I took with me spread out. The area seemed to be abandoned, but there were traces of things. Spikes. Chains. And the ground was stained with what had to be blood. One minute, I was inspecting the bloodstained ground, and the next minute, my nose and mouth were

covered. A chemical smell filled my head, and that was it." He shakes his head.

"So you didn't see who it was?"

"No." He sighs. "And when I awoke, I was chained to a wall in a very cold dungeon."

Oh, gods. I wrap my arms around my middle, waiting for him to continue.

"They were... cruel." He averts his eyes again. "I won't go into that, though. But I remember there was a woman in a hooded, red cloak. Her face was masked, so I don't know what she looked like. But all she had to do was lay her hands on me, and the pain was inconceivable."

"What?" I clench my hands into fists. "Who was she?"

"She was his seer. I never heard her name... or at least I don't remember. But she made it clear she was loyal to the tsar. She's also the reason I wasn't able to use my powers. Why I haven't used them since."

"She stopped you from using telepathy?" I shake my head. "But why? And... how did she stop you? How did she know you were using it?"

"She's very powerful. It's as if she has a sense, like she can feel the energy behind the magic. If I tried to contact you, contact *anyone*, she would punish me. I can still feel the pain, even if I just *think* about using my magic."

"That's... That's horrible." I blink, trying to comprehend what he's telling me. "What did she want from you?"

"She said the tsar wanted me to give you a message. In person. The seer's prophecy foretells of an unchallenged dominion, and she believes the person who will rule this dominion is the tsar. I can't recall all the words from the prophecy, but there were parts that stuck in my mind. The prophecy told of seizing power by using 'the magic gifted by the gods to a powerful descendant.' And she made it clear that the tsar wants you."

"'Magic gifted by the gods.' So fae or siren powers, but why me?" My eyes widen. *To a powerful descendant.* Could that mean...? "Is that why you think the tsar is my father?"

He keeps his eyes on me, inhaling deeply before a long exhale. "She

didn't say it was him, but she was clear that he wanted you. It seemed like an obsession. I believe Torbin was supposed to bring you to him. Not to kill you. Not to break you. He needs you to help him fulfill the prophecy."

I furrow my brow, grasping the arms of the chair while my mind reels. "But 'a powerful descendant' doesn't necessarily mean *his* descendant, does it? Maybe it just means someone who comes from a line of powerful fae or sirens."

"You may be right. But that doesn't change the fact that the tsar has targeted you, and I can only assume that he's done so because of the way the seer has interpreted the prophecy."

I feel sick. I don't know what to believe. I don't know much about the accuracy of prophecies or even of seers, but I feel like something is off. If only my uncle could remember the entire prophecy, I might be able to pick it apart.

"That's not all," he says, bracing himself on the desk as he stands. "The other part of the prophecy that stands out is the whole reason for the carnoraxis attacks."

I lift my chin. "You mean the third-born fae?"

"Yes. It was something like, 'one of fae blood, third-born of kin, shall rise as the harbinger of ruin.'"

"Meaning...?"

"Essentially, a third-born fae could destroy the tsar's plan to take over the world."

"Okay," I say, shaking my head. "But we knew he was after the those fae."

What is he not saying? My mind races, piecing together what little I know. The tsar's campaign against fae-blooded third-borns, the way he has hunted them mercilessly. The way he has torn through entire bloodlines to root them out.

"The attacks had always seemed random," Uncle Kormak says. "Which didn't make sense to me, unless the seer doesn't know who this special third-born is. She somehow is able to detect third-born in specific towns, and she must be using some kind of witchcraft to put the images

or essences or something of the third-borns she sees into the heads of the carnoraxis so that they know who they're targeting. But I was starting to suspect something, and I couldn't understand why she couldn't see certain third-borns. It took me a while to figure it out, but I believe I have a theory."

I'm completely confused, but I let him go on.

"I think she can only see third-borns whose powers have manifested," he explains.

"Okay."

"I think her powers reach out and grab hold of images of third-borns, and she sends the creatures out to attack those fae. That doesn't stop the townspeople from sacrificing every third-born they know, just to cover their bases."

I blink in confusion. "Right. Okay. But... I'm sorry, I'm not following."

"I was trying to figure out why the seer wasn't seeing... you."

"But... what does that part of it have to do with me?" I ask, frowning. "I'm not third-born."

Kormak doesn't speak. He presses his lips together, something unreadable passing over his features.

"What?" I ask. "What is it you aren't telling me?"

Kormak shifts, running a hand down his face. "There's more you need to know." His voice is quieter now but no less heavy. "Before she met your father, your mother lived in Alphemra, among the fae." His voice is careful, measured, but there's something raw beneath it. "She was young. Naïve, perhaps. And she fell in love."

I say nothing, my hands coming together to clasp tightly in my lap. My neck suddenly feels hot, as if he's about to say something that is going to change my world.

Kormak's gaze flickers to me before he continues. "The man she loved died tragically in an accident, but when she lost him, she was already with child."

A sharp breath presses against my ribs, but I don't let it out. My head swims.

"She was meant for nobility, Celeste. Our family had ambitions for her, plans for her future. A child out of wedlock would have destroyed all of that." He shakes his head slightly. "So her parents—my aunt and uncle—they kept it a secret. And your mother had no choice but to leave the child behind."

The world tilts.

My mother. The woman who sang to me, who pressed kisses to my forehead, who stroked my hair when I cried. The woman who never once made me feel like I wasn't enough.

She'd had a child before Bennett and me. A whole other life.

I clear my throat, my voice hoarse. "And then?"

"She traveled to Delasurvia, a young, eligible debutante. And then she met Axel."

I flinch at my father's name.

Kormak exhales slowly. "She fell in love again. Or perhaps she convinced herself she had. He courted her, made promises. He was a prince. A future king. Here was the promise of a secure life. When he asked for her hand, she said *yes*. But she never told him about the boy."

My stomach twists violently. This is too much. Too big. It changes everything I thought I knew. And it means that I *am* a third-born fae.

I force my voice to stay steady. "Is he still alive? My... brother?"

Kormak meets my gaze, unflinching. "As far as I know, he is."

My breath shudders out of me. A brother. I have a brother.

The thought crashes into me, ice and fire at once, setting my pulse into a spiral. I press a hand to my chest, as if that might stop the unsteady thudding beneath my ribs.

"Did Bennett know?" I ask, barely above a whisper.

Kormak shakes his head. "No. Your mother intended to tell you both when the time was right. But then..." His voice trails off. He doesn't have to say it.

She never got the chance. She died.

Something inside me cracks.

I blink rapidly, but the tears spill over, anyway, slipping hot down my cheeks. I don't sob, but my breathing becomes uneven, my fingers

trembling against my lap.

Kormak moves before I can retreat into myself, reaching across the space between us. He crouches down and takes my hand, his grip steady, grounding. "I'm sorry," he murmurs. "I was sworn to secrecy. I couldn't tell you."

I swallow hard, squeezing my eyes shut for a moment, trying to gather the broken pieces of my world into something recognizable. But nothing looks the same anymore.

Kormak exhales slowly, his fingers still curled around mine, as if afraid I might slip through his grasp.

"This is extremely sensitive, Celeste," he says, voice low, edged with something grim. "No one else can know. If the tsar were to find out that you are third-born—" He stops, his jaw tightening. "The target already on your back would change dramatically."

A bitter laugh slips from me, quiet but sharp. "Because I could be the one to end him?" I swipe the dampness from my cheeks, inhaling through the knot in my throat.

Could the prophecy really be about me? Not only as the one the tsar needs to rule the world, but also as the one who could destroy him? It does seem like a sardonic paradox.

"Well, then I can end the slaughter." I straighten my shoulders. "I'll march into Dulcamar and tell the Shadow Tsar that I'm the one he's looking for, that the prophecy is about me and he can call off his fucking monsters and stop terrorizing the realms. It can all end."

"No, Celeste." He rubs at his neck. "That's not how prophecies work. He can't know, because—father or not—he will kill you if he finds out. And if he kills *you*—the one who is supposed to end his reign—then our hope is lost. And the precious realms will die, anyway."

Frustration boils within me. It feels like the right thing to do, a simple way to end the massacres. No more attacks. No more sacrifices. But my uncle is right. If the prophecy is about me, if I'm the one who is supposed to end the tsar's reign, then I can't just march up there emptyhanded. He's got a whole realm protecting him. He's manufactured an entire species of creature to do his bidding. I need to have a plan. An army. I need to figure out how to destroy his whole undertaking, and I won't be able to do that on my own.

"The thing is," my uncle continues, "it wouldn't surprise me if your father turns out to be the tsar, because he showed signs of desiring power, spoke of expanding his reign, even before your mother died." He stands and starts to pace. "It's part of the reason he was against the sirens. Their mind manipulation would have been a problem if he'd ever wanted to take Messanya."

He lets out a deep breath, as if he's not done turning my world upside down yet.

"Your mother was always a wise woman. I don't know what they discussed privately, but in the months before her death, she seemed more worried, maybe even... scared. Looking back now, I think she knew what he had planned, and I think she knew he needed fae powers. I believe she took precaution, because she knew she wouldn't be able to stop him outright. I think she hid your powers—and Bennett's—so Axel couldn't get a hold of them."

The words strike something deep inside me.

My mother always told me magic was a gift, but one that came at a price. Bennett's magic should have manifested before mine. But it didn't.

Maybe because of my mother. Maybe it had been stolen from him before it ever had the chance to bloom. Just like mine.

I grip the arms of my chair as a sickening thought takes root. "She hid them in the dagger."

"The dagger she gave you?" he asks.

"I think so." I don't go into my powers manifesting, no matter how messily. There's already too much to process, and it's not all sitting in my stomach well.

The reoccurring nightmare enters my mind. My mother coming into my room at night, bleeding. The dagger in her hand. *"I'm sorry. I can't let him take it from you."* It makes so much sense now. A sharp chill washes over me. Flashbacks of my mother's frightened face enter my mind. Tidbits of muffled voices, fights I wasn't supposed to hear.

Wait. She was bleeding when she came into my room.

"You said she was scared," I say to my uncle. "Were they fighting?"

"They never fought in front of me," he answers. "But I could see the tension between them."

"I don't think it was only Bennett's and my powers she hid in the dagger," I tell him. "I think she put hers in there, too."

If my mother took such drastic measures—it means she feared him. Not just as a ruler. As a man.

I struggle to breathe past the tightness in my chest. "Uncle, do you think she fell down those stairs by accident?"

Kormak's gaze darkens. "The servants and guards confirmed that he was in another wing of the castle when it happened."

When she died.

But a king can get his people to say what he wants them to.

A part of me finds it hard to believe that not one of them would speak up if it weren't true. But something about the situation nags at me.

Oh, gods.

I don't want to say it out loud, but I see it in my uncle's eyes. He has the same suspicion.

"Uncle Kormak," I start, a slow, creeping dread crawling up my spine, "what do you think really happened?"

The room is engulfed in silence. A silence that tells me everything before he even says the words.

He exhales sharply. "Celeste... I can't prove it to be true. But I believe your father killed your mother."

Something inside me shatters.

CHAPTER
FORTY-ONE

The stone walls of Ivystone loom ahead, their familiar presence both a comfort and a weight pressing against my ribs. The gates are already open for us, the flickering torchlight catching on the damp edges of the courtyard as Sir Holden and I dismount, the clatter of hooves fading behind us.

The journey back from Delasurvia was swift, the road a blur beneath my horse's hooves. But my mind was not still. It was a storm—a relentless, churning force of thoughts too tangled to unravel.

Sir Holden walks beside me as we step into the castle, his gloved hands resting lightly against his belt. He's quiet for a moment before he finally speaks.

"Are you all right, Your Highness?"

I inhale slowly, steadying myself. "I'd like to find Dante," I say, already turning toward the hall that leads to his quarters.

"Yes, Your Highness." He steps back, giving me space. The mourning period is over, so there should be no reason for him to stop me, but I can feel his gaze linger as I move forward.

Because he knows there's something wrong, but he doesn't know

 329

what. I've had the theories clashing in my head the whole ride back from Delasurvia, and I'm nowhere near ready to talk about them.

At least not with anyone except Dante.

I tighten my grip on my cloak, my fingers cold despite the warmth lingering in the air. A sharp breath catches in my throat, and I force my feet to keep moving, pushing past the uncertainty coiling around me.

Because right now, I need something steady. Something real.

I reach Dante's door and raise a fist, knocking twice.

It feels like it takes forever before he opens the door.

Dante's eyes lock with mine as he stands in the warm glow of candlelight, his tunic undone at the collar, his dark hair tousled from sleep or thought—I don't know which.

His expression shifts, a flicker of concern threading through the sharp lines of his face. "Something's wrong," he guesses.

Of course he sees it.

I hesitate, my throat suddenly tight. Then, finally, I speak. "May I come in?"

His lips part slightly before he steps aside, holding the door open wider. "Of course."

I step inside, past the threshold, past the weight of everything I don't know how to say yet.

But I will. Because if I don't tell him, I fear the thoughts will cause my brain to cave in on itself.

I walk past Dante and head right for a chair near the hearth. I sink into it, grateful for the solid weight beneath me. My body feels stretched too thin, my thoughts even more so.

For a moment, neither of us speaks. The only sound is the quiet crackling of the fire, its glow casting shifting shadows along the stone walls.

Dante remains standing, one hand braced against the mantel, his other rubbing at the back of his neck. His eyes never leave me.

I inhale slowly, steadying myself. *Just tell him.*

"There are some things I've learned," I begin, my voice quieter than I expected. "Some crazy, unbelievable things."

 330

Dante's brows knit together, but he doesn't interrupt.

I wet my lips, exhaling slowly before diving in.

I tell him everything. From my mother having a son before she married my father to my connection to the prophesy. I tell him my uncle's theory about the tsar being my father and how he may have been the one who pushed my mother down the stairs to her death—or ordered it done.

When I tell him how my uncle shut down my idea to march into Dulcamar and confront the tsar to end the carnoraxis attacks, Dante doesn't move, but I can see the subtle flex of his fingers, the way his jaw tightens as he processes it all.

Silence stretches between us, thick and suffocating.

Dante stares at me, his mouth slightly parted, but no words come. For the first time since I stepped into this room, I think he is at a loss for what to say.

I let my head fall back against the chair, pressing my fingers against my temples. The weight of everything crashes over me at once—my mother's secrets, my unknown brother, my father's betrayal, the prophecy that names me as the tsar's undoing.

The fire crackles, its warmth brushing against my skin, but I feel nothing. I'm raw. I'm broken.

Then, finally, Dante moves. He crouches before me, resting his arms on the sides of my chair. His expression is softer now, less rigid with strategy, more *him*.

"What do you need?" His voice is quiet, steady, grounding.

I inhale slowly, the words sitting heavily in my chest. "Could you... hold me?"

At that, Dante reaches for me, his fingers curling around my wrist as he pulls me gently to my feet.

He doesn't say anything.

He just holds me.

I exhale against his shoulder, my fingers hesitating for only a second before I grip the back of his tunic, letting his warmth sink into me. His arms tighten around me—not desperate, not demanding. Just there.

"I'll help you," he murmurs into my hair. "We will figure this out."

I close my eyes, pressing my forehead to the curve of his neck. "I know."

Dante shifts slightly, his hands sliding up my back, and when I pull back just enough to look at him, he kisses me.

It's slow, deep, not rushed. A reassurance.

My fingers tighten against his chest, my breath tangling with his as he lingers, as if neither of us wants to step away first.

When we do part, he studies me for a moment longer before murmuring, "You look exhausted."

I let out a breathless laugh. "That's because I *am* exhausted."

His lips twitch. "Stay."

I blink up at him.

He tucks a strand of hair behind my ear. "You don't have to go anywhere tonight."

And gods, I want to stay.

But I shake my head gently. "I think I need to find Nadya." My throat tightens slightly. "She's my best friend. I need to tell her what I found out."

Dante exhales, nodding once in understanding.

He walks me to the door, lingering there as if reluctant to let me go. I glance up at him, and just before I step away, he cups my face, kissing me again—soft and slow, like a tether, like a reason to come back.

When he pulls away, his thumb grazes my cheek.

"I'm here if you need me," he murmurs.

I nod.

With the ghost of his touch still warm on my skin, I slip into the corridor to find Nadya.

CHAPTER FORTY-TWO

zra's lesson room is warm when Nadya and I arrive, the scent of old paper and melted candlewax thick in the air. The temperature is a welcome change from the chill that lingers around the castle grounds. The days are getting shorter and colder, and Nadya and I have had to grab our shawls more often.

Ezra looks up from his desk as we enter, his expression alert, as though he's been waiting for us all morning. "You're just in time," he says, standing. A thick, worn book rests in his hands, the leather cover cracked and faded, like it's been passed through too many hands to count. "The Magister of Podrosa came through for me."

I eye the book. "He sent you something?"

Ezra nods. "He said he would send anything he came across that might prove useful. This arrived yesterday morning by horse messenger. I spent most of the night reading it."

Nadya steps beside me, leaning closer to the desk. "What is it?"

"A collection of lesser-known accounts—oral histories, personal recollections, and disputed reports." Ezra lifts the book slightly, his fingers brushing the edges like he's holding something sacred. "But one story stood out."

 333

We settle into the chairs facing his desk, the fire at the side of the lesson room crackling low. Nadya crosses her legs, already engrossed. I lean forward, bracing my elbows on my knees.

Ezra opens the book and begins. "Centuries ago, there was a female fae born with a rare gift—she could pass through solid matter. Stone, iron, even glass. A magic that rendered most walls and locks meaningless."

"I've never heard of such a power," Nadya murmurs.

Ezra nods. "She was careful with her ability. Her family taught her to keep it hidden, especially once the kingdoms started tracking magical bloodlines. But she was eventually discovered by a male fae who had his own ability. One that allowed him to siphon magic from others and use it himself."

I straighten. "A siphon fae. That's rare."

Ezra gives a tight nod. "Yes. It is. But this fae wasn't content with power for the sake of order. He was greedy. He wanted gold, dominion. He learned of the treasure vault in Hedera—one that held the ancient king's personal fortune. It had been sealed with warding magic so complex, in lieu of entering in the conventional manner, only someone with the ability to pass through solid matter could reach it."

"He tried to steal her power," I say, already guessing the rest.

"He abducted her," Ezra confirms. "Commandeered a ship and took off to Hedera from Alphemra. He would siphon from her every so often during their journey so she couldn't escape. But she devised a plan. Before he took her to the vault, she hid her magic."

Nadya nods. "Clever thinking."

"Where did she hide it?" I ask.

"In a necklace she wore. An amulet," Ezra says. "She channeled her magic into it. It meant rendering herself powerless, but it was a chance she was willing to take. She dropped it where he wouldn't notice, just before they reached the vault."

I glance down at my dagger, where my mother hid our magic.

"When they arrived at the vault, he tried to siphon the power as he'd done before—but it was gone. Useless. Without it, he couldn't pass

through the wards. And when he realized she'd tricked him, he turned on her."

Nadya's eyes widen. "What happened?"

"They fought, but she escaped," Ezra says. "Ran all the way to the castle and begged the guards for help. Told them everything. The male fae was arrested on charges of trespassing and attempted theft from the crown."

"And her magic?" I ask.

"She searched for the necklace and found it again. Then she returned home to Alphemra." Ezra closes the book, but gently, like he's trying not to break the spell his story has cast. "She performed a ritual to draw the magic back into her. At first, her body rejected it. It caused sickness, imbalance. Her magic came back in bursts. Wild and painful."

"Like me," I whisper.

He gives me a steady look. "Yes. It was as if the magic wasn't settling in where it was supposed to. Like it was a puzzle piece that wasn't turned in the right direction. But the ancient fae performed a ritual that was able to direct the magic, to get it to shift in the correct way that wouldn't hurt her."

Nadya leans forward. "What's the ritual?"

Ezra sighs. "That's the part I'm still working through. The account gives some details, but not everything. There are pieces missing, because it's a recounting of what happened, not a recipe book."

My fingers curl against the arm of the chair. "Do you think you'll be able to figure it out?"

Ezra's expression softens. "I wouldn't have told you this story if I didn't believe there was a chance."

Nadya's face lights up. "That sounds hopeful."

Ezra smiles faintly. "I may have to reach out to Alphemra. There's no guarantee they will cooperate, but maybe they'll take it into consideration in order to help one of their own."

I breathe deeply, giving him a nod.

He turns to Nadya. "In the meantime, we should work on training your magic as well. You might have to share your knowledge from your

great-aunt's book. If that's all right with you."

"Sure," Nadya says. "If there's anyone I trust with helping me out with this, it's you."

A knock sounds at the door, interrupting us. It swings open, and Sir Holden steps inside, his cheeks slightly red from the cold air outside.

"Forgive the interruption," he says, shoulders squared. "But, Princess Celeste—the king requests your presence in the council chamber."

I blink. "The council chamber?"

Holden nods once. "Yes. He said to bring you there directly."

Ezra's brow lifts, his mouth parting slightly. "He's never allowed you inside before."

"No," I murmur, rising to my feet. "He hasn't."

Not officially. Not like this.

The only time I've stood within that chamber was the day Dante and I forced our way in—an intrusion Farvis made very clear would not be tolerated again. Every other time, when I asked for entry, I was turned away.

Whatever this is... it isn't ordinary.

I stand and lift my chin. "Well. Let's see what's changed."

"Good luck," Nadya says. "I'll see you later."

"I really hope so," I murmur.

Sir Holden waits just outside the lesson room, offering a polite incline of his head before turning to lead me through the quiet, echoing halls of Ivystone.

With every step, I feel apprehension settling deeper into my chest. My boots tap softly against the stone floors, and I force myself to breathe slowly. I don't know why I've been summoned, only that the council chamber isn't a place I'm normally permitted to enter. I've spent months cloaked in mourning and forced obedience, passed over like a shadow in the corner of every conversation.

But I am the heir to the Delasurvian throne. I am commander of the royal regiment—even if I'm currently on hiatus. I have faced carnivorous monsters with jagged teeth and claws, and I've walked away

breathing. So whatever this is, I will not let them see me small.

My spine straightens as we near the double doors carved with curling vines and old kingdom sigils, the bronze handles gleaming despite the grey light that filters through the tall windows overhead. Two guards push the doors open without a word. They've been expecting me.

It's been so long since I've been in the council chambers that I've forgotten what the place looked like. The space is cool and bright. Arched windows line the far wall, casting thin lines of pale light across the long marble table in the center of the room. Maps are unfurled in places, flanked by scrolls, inkpots, and quills. A low fire crackles behind the king's seat.

King Silas sits at the head of the table, his posture severe and immovable, as always. Farvis stands just behind him with a roll of parchment in one hand and a quill in the other, face pinched with duty. And to the king's right is Dante. His arms rest on the table, fingers laced, his expression unreadable until his gaze meets mine.

"Celeste," the king says, not rising. "You're aware of why you've been summoned?"

I step closer to the table, clasping my hands behind my back. "No, Your Majesty."

"We've received word from the realms." His voice is brusque, every syllable sharpened by power. "Each of the courts we visited during our tour has responded."

I glance toward Dante, and his mouth lifts—just barely, a flicker of something quiet and proud. My heart thuds, a breath catching in my throat.

"Every realm," the king continues, "has accepted Dante's claim to legitimacy."

My gaze snaps back to him. "Then congratulations are in order," I say, a hint of a smile tugging at my lips despite myself. "That's incredible news."

But the king shakes his head once, lifting a hand, as if to halt the celebration. "Not yet. You see, there is one realm left whose approval is required to make the claim official."

Farvis steps forward with parchment and quill, the motion practiced, precise.

I look between him and the king.

"Delasurvia is the final vote we need. And the laws, though ancient, remain clear. Majority must be achieved, and your kingdom's voice tips the scale."

Dante looks at me, and I catch the rise and fall of his chest as his storm-grey eyes flash.

I draw a steady breath, then take a step toward the table, letting my stance reflect the gravitas of my title. "Then I accept," I say, keeping my tone even. "Delasurvia supports Lord Stregasi's claim."

Farvis lays the parchment on the table and offers the quill. I skim the words, making sure there's nothing hidden in the ink, before signing my name with careful, clean strokes.

As I place the quill down, the king speaks again. "The queen is already arranging a celebration ball to honor Dante's new title. The other monarchs will be invited back for the event, and I expect they'll attend. The realms will want to congratulate the new prince in person."

My eyes flick to Dante again, and he gives the faintest nod, as if thanking me—not just for the approval, but for everything else. For standing by him. For always coming through. For trusting him.

But the king isn't finished.

"And during this celebration," he says, settling deeper into his chair, "once the guests have arrived, I will formally announce your betrothal."

My breath catches. I didn't expect the announcement to come so soon.

"We've waited long enough," the king continues. "If I don't make it public soon, you'll likely do something stupid and risky and get yourself killed."

The comment is sharp but not entirely cruel—more matter-of-fact than mocking.

"I understand," I say quietly.

I glance toward Dante again. There's pride in his look. A flicker of gratitude. A thousand emotions tangled between us.

 338

This is happening.

"I appreciate your swift cooperation," the king says. "You're dismissed. We men have preparations to tend to."

Farvis begins collecting the parchment, and the king turns his attention to something else already being laid out on the table. It's clear the moment is over.

I promptly turn to leave.

But as I step back into the corridor, the weight of what just transpired hits me.

Dante is a prince now.

And I'm going to be his bride.

Not just in whispers or private moments—but in the eyes of every kingdom in Terre Ferique.

Everything has shifted.

And this time, no one can stand in our way.

 339

CHAPTER

FORTY-THREE

The halls hum with distant music as Sir Holden leads Nadya and me toward the ballroom. The soft rustle of silk accompanies our steps, the air thick with the scent of candlewax and distant perfume.

I take a slow breath, my fingers skimming the smooth, emerald fabric of my gown. The deep green catches the light with every movement, the gold embroidery at the bodice shimmering like ivy bathed in sunlight. Next to me, Nadya wears a paler shade—a delicate green kissed by silver thread, airy and soft, whereas mine feels heavier, richer, a queen's color.

A symbol of what I am becoming. What I am stepping into.

Beyond the arched doors, laughter and music weave through the grand hall, the familiar melody of strings and flutes swirling through the air. I have seen this ballroom before, walked these very steps during the welcome ball when I first arrived in Hedera.

That night, I had been a foreign princess, a guest in a court that did not yet belong to me.

Tonight, it is different.

Tonight marks the beginning of forever.

A forever with Dante.

My stomach twists. Not with dread, but with something softer, something uncertain. This was not a marriage we chose. Not one we sat beside each other and planned, whispering promises of a future we'd shaped ourselves. It was decided for us. A fate woven by duty and politics, not love.

And yet... I'm not going into it with any regrets. Except for the fact that it's all happening so quickly, it doesn't feel forced.

I brace myself at the threshold. The king has kept Dante busy nearly every hour for the past week. I haven't seen him on his balcony, and there were no secret nights spent together in his room or mine. But he has to be here, in the ballroom, because this is *his* celebration. There's a fluttering in my stomach from the thought of finally seeing him after what seems like forever.

The moment I step through the doors, the moment my eyes find him, the rest of the world fades away, and something fills my soul. Something that's been missing all this time away from him. I feel... complete.

"Somehow," Nadya whispers beside me, "he looks like an actual prince."

I can't help but grin. "Yes. It suits him."

Dante stands beside the king, his dark tunic edged with gold patterns of ivy, his falchion strapped at his side. His presence is effortless, commanding, his posture one of quiet strength. His smile seems to come easily, and I can imagine it's because the hard part is over. He survived the trials, and he won the acceptance of the other realms.

Still, I know he hates these gatherings. I know he'd much rather be hidden in the shadows, not forced to talk to anyone.

I'd love to be sitting somewhere in the shadows with him, hidden away from prying eyes. Just him and me and the warmth of our bodies...

As if sensing me before even turning, his head lifts—his gaze sweeping the ballroom—until it locks on to mine.

A slow breath fills my lungs, but it's not enough to steady me against the force of what rushes through me.

It is not a flicker of warmth. It is not a soft, budding feeling.

It is breathtaking.

A surge of something bright, something overwhelming, something I cannot name but do not need to.

Because in that moment, I know.

I know that, chosen or not, planned or not—this is where I belong.

The moment I step toward Dante, the king's gaze shifts to me. His expression remains composed, his smile carefully set in place for the watching courtiers. A ruler at ease. A father welcoming his future daughter-in-law.

A ruse.

A lie.

I lower my chin in deference, the proper display of respect, even as every muscle in my body tenses at the sight of him.

"Your Majesty," I say smoothly. "Prince Dante."

Prince.

I smile at the sound of the word.

Dante's eyes are still on me, something unreadable flickering in their depths, before he inclines his head. "Princess Celeste."

King Silas steps closer, just enough that the words he speaks next are meant only for the two of us. "You've done well, Celeste." His voice is low, measured. "I trust you will continue to do so."

I keep my posture straight, my expression neutral. *Do not react. Do not let him see what he does to you.* "Of course, Your Majesty."

His smile remains, his eyes never leaving mine. "You must understand, my dear, that your standing—your entire future—is a gift. And gifts can be taken away."

The meaning coils between us like a snake ready to strike.

"I have been generous to Delasurvia," he continues, his voice barely above the hum of the ballroom. "Your people enjoy the benefits of my rule, the security of my alliance. And Dante—" He glances at his son, then back to me, his smile sharpening. "His love for you is apparent. But love, as you know, is not indestructible. If you are to remain in my good graces, Princess, if you are to keep the luxury of the life I have allowed you, you will be loyal. To Hedera. To me."

 342

I want to tear the smugness from his face.

I want to spit the truth back at him, that I do not belong to him, that my life, my future, my heart are not things he can manipulate.

But I cannot.

Not here.

I must swallow my hate, let it burn quietly in the hollow of my chest, because this is the best way to keep Delasurvia safe.

I meet his gaze, steel beneath my carefully controlled features. "Of course, Your Majesty."

The king smiles wider. A perfect performance for any watching eyes.

Beside me, Dante exhales softly through his nose.

"Look sharp," King Silas says. "Our guests are arriving."

Music hums from a small ensemble tucked in the corner, the melody airy yet charged, as if the strings themselves sense the shift tonight carries. The king ushers Dante over to a distinct area near the entrance, and the queen follows along, eventually taking her place beside her husband.

I had been so transfixed by seeing Dante that I hadn't really taken a moment to admire the ballroom. It glows under a canopy of chandeliers, their crystals dripping like frozen rain, scattering light across the polished floors and silk-draped walls. Nadya reappears at my side, and it takes me a second to realize that she had momentarily slipped away.

"Where did you go?" I nudge her with my elbow.

"Lady Stacia told me the other realms' rulers had arrived, so I had to take a peek. You should see how many carriages are lined up outside of the castle."

The doors at the opposite end of the hall open with ceremony, and all in the Hederan court stare in wonder as the Podrosan delegation strides in. King Harold leads them, towering and as rigid as an iron gate, his crimson cloak clasped at his shoulder with a medallion of the black thorns circling a silver sword. His expression is chiseled from stone, the faintest nod of acknowledgment his only greeting. At his side, Queen Agatha glides forward, her dark-brown hair coiled as tight as wire, her lips pressed into a diplomatic curve that never quite touches her eyes.

Their daughter, Princess Orida, moves just behind them, impeccable as ever in a deep-red gown trimmed with black lace, her golden hair plaited into a long braid down her back. She surveys the room until her eyes land on Dante. I can see her cheeks redden as she inclines her head to him.

It's not jealousy that makes me uneasy. She doesn't yet know that Dante is betrothed to me, but that's about to change with the Silas's announcement. I actually feel compassion for her. I'm not sure if the announcement will cause her heartbreak, but if she has already started making plans based on a future with him, it will surely hit her hard.

Lady Marette follows, a soft smile lighting her face despite the small, swaddled bundle in her arms—her newborn son, no doubt, born since our visit to Podrosa. The lord at her side—whom I presume is her husband—keeps a careful hand at her back.

Then comes Lord Marcos, and I almost wish I hadn't looked. His eyes catch mine across the distance, and his face changes when he sees me. I see the hope in his eyes, especially as he takes in my gown and acknowledges that I'm not in mourning anymore. Again, my stomach twists with sympathy, knowing that I will fundamentally be rejecting him once more. He wears a black doublet embroidered with crimson threads, his clothes matching those of his parents, who walk beside him. I force myself to look away.

A pair of Ironshield soldiers flank the rear of their group, their presence a reminder that Podrosa never arrives without a measure of power on display.

Next, the Bastos queens emerge, a vision of elegance and inscrutability. Queen Ambra, bronze-skinned and draped in shimmering, purple silk, smiles with the ease of a serpent coiled on a warm stone. At her side, Queen Eosla matches her stride, her hair an even brighter blue than it was when we left the Baharat Palace. Their smiles are impeccable, but with them comes the faint sense of secrecy, as if they know something we don't, and they can't wait for us to find out. Or maybe it's simply their torrid desires giving them an air of mystery. I breathe a sigh of relief that at least their nipples aren't on display for everyone to see. This is Dante's day, and he could do without the Bastos queens stealing attention away.

I catch Nadya watching them with keen interest. Her Bastos blood, particularly the sorceress element, has become her new obsession.

Then Queen Verina of Messanya enters, adorned in an elaborate, pearl-white gown, flowing like a cresting wave. She carries herself with the grace of an aria's final note, half of her platinum hair pinned high, the rest hanging in coiling tendrils. When her eyes sweep the room, they land briefly on Dante, and though her expression softens, I can't tell if it's approval or something else entirely.

Finally, the triarchs of Mersos arrive. The two kings and solitary queen wear forest green trimmed in rust red, their eyes keen and assessing. While the other rulers absorb the scene, King Gallor meanders toward the nearest serving tray, lifting a goblet to inspect the vintage like a merchant examining a harvest. Queen Shaylin places a hand on his arm to pull his attention back to the celebration, but King Birchus only chuckles under his breath.

"They're inspecting the food," I murmur to Nadya.

She grins. "Of course they are."

I sweep my gaze across the assembly, feeling the weight of their presence settle. Allies, strangers, potential enemies. A part of me wonders what it would have been like if the fae of Alphemra had come?

The question sneaks unbidden into my thoughts. Although they are known for ignoring invitations to such things, I don't even know if King Silas considered reaching out to them. The fae keep their distance, their mountain-shrouded courts steeped in secrecy. But still... I imagine them shimmering like specters beneath these chandeliers, their beauty otherworldly, their power a palpable hum beneath the music.

I shake the thought away, just as Nadya leans closer. "This is surreal. Almost all the nobles of Terre Ferique in one place."

My eyes go to the king, knowing he's about to make his speech. "Very surreal."

As most of the guests take their places at various tables around the edges of the ballroom, Princess Orida separates from her family, making her way toward Dante. I stiffen, wondering if she's approaching him to flirt and throw her hat in the ring as a potential match. Her smile is modest, but the look in her eyes tells a different story. Dante has always been a handsome man, and his height and build no doubt contribute to his appeal. But now that he's a prince, there's an added quality I'm sure our guests find magnetic.

I've always found him appealing, even without the title. Which makes me question what Princess Orida actually sees in him.

She curtseys before the king and queen, her lids lowered slightly as she gazes at Dante.

"Your Majesties, Your Highness." She straightens. Aside from the way she stares at Dante, there is nothing flirtatious about her posture or movements. She carries herself as a Podrosan princess, not a Bastosi queen. "I wanted to personally offer my heartfelt felicitations, Prince Dante. It is a well-deserved recognition."

Dante inclines his head. "It's very kind of you to say, Princess Orida."

"Perhaps, during the course of the evening, we could find a moment to talk. Or maybe even have a dance." She smiles sweetly, her face full of hope.

Dante hesitates only for a second, but he keeps his expression polite. "I will keep that in mind."

She seems thrilled at his response, nodding before gathering her skirts and heading toward the table where her family sits.

Princess Rosemary is the next to approach. She studies Dante as if inspecting how well her favorite tree has grown. "Prince Dante, you have my congratulations."

"Thank you, Your Highness." He inclines his head, and his fingers twitch at his side.

I recall the conversation she had with him at the feast, how she commented on his fertility, and I wonder if she's thinking about putting her theory to the test as soon as possible.

She turns to the king and queen and curtseys. "Mersos thanks you for your hospitality, Your Majesties."

After she joins her family at their tables, the king leads Dante to our

table. The queen, Nadya, and I follow his lead and take our places.

The hall hums with quiet opulence. Servants move in graceful lines, setting down gleaming platters of roasted game, bowls of jewel-toned fruits, and loaves still steaming from the oven. The scents of sage, citrus, and slow-braised meat drift through the air, mingling with the faint tang of spiced wine. Candlelight glints off polished silver and crystal, scattering golden flickers across the long table. A quartet of musicians plucks a gentle melody on harp, violins, and lute, the notes threading through the warm murmur of voices as the guests settle into their seats.

The clinking of cutlery quiets, the low hum of conversation tapering off as King Silas rises from his seat at the head of the table. A goblet of deep-red wine glints in his hand, catching the golden candlelight as he lifts it slightly.

"My friends," he begins, his voice carrying easily over the long table, "welcome. It is no small thing to travel the lengths of the realms, and I thank each of you for making the journey to Ivystone for this most significant occasion."

He pauses to sweep the room with his gaze, slow and deliberate. "You honor not only our kingdom, but my son, with your presence. You have seen in Dante what I have always seen—strength, capability, and the will to lead—and you have returned home to speak in his favor, granting him your acceptance. For that, you have my deepest gratitude."

The guests raise their goblets in polite acknowledgment. I keep my hands in my lap, my eyes on the polished table, because I can already feel the queen across the way stiffen.

The king's gaze turns to Dante, pride swelling in his voice. "Dante, you have proven yourself in more ways than one. You have fought for the safety of this kingdom, you have endured trials most men would not survive, and you have done so without complaint, without hesitation. You have earned your place beside me, and I know you will carry forward my legacy with honor."

Out of the corner of my eye, I catch Queen Eleanor's faint wince, the subtle downward twitch of her mouth. He speaks the words '*my son*' so easily, so warmly, and yet Torbin's name hasn't left his lips in weeks.

 347

It's as though the memory of her child has already been brushed aside, replaced. Even knowing what Torbin became, I sympathize with the queen, because her maternal feelings are still valid.

"I have no doubt," the king continues, "that Dante will go on to accomplish even greater things than I have. And with that in mind"—he straightens, his voice sharpening with a note of formality—"I have another announcement."

A ripple of curiosity moves through the guests.

"It is my pleasure to share that Dante will take Princess Celeste of Delasurvia as his betrothed."

My heart stutters. The words hang in the air, their weight settling over the room. All eyes shift toward us. I notice how Princess Orida's face falls and how Princess Rosemary grinds her teeth.

The king's expression softens by a fraction. "The late King Axel was my friend. I know he would have been glad to see our kingdoms joined in such a way. His daughter has proven herself a formidable protector of her people, a capable commander, and a worthy future queen."

Even if I doubt he believes half of what he's saying, the words still land with their intended weight.

"I am confident their union will stand as a symbol of lasting alliance between Hedera and Delasurvia—a unification of strength, prosperity, and peace."

He raises his goblet high. "To Dante and Celeste."

The hall echoes with voices repeating the toast, goblets lifted, wine swirling like blood in crystal. I know not everyone is pleased to hear this announcement, but in this moment, I don't really care. Dante glances at me from across the table, and for a heartbeat, the noise fades to nothing but the sound of my own pulse.

He's not with me because it's the king's wish. He's with me because he wants to be.

Halfway through our meal, King Harold of Podrosa and King Gallor of Mersos approach, their smiles polite but measured. They offer their congratulations—first to the king, then to Dante, and, finally, to me—but there's a glint in the Podrosan king's eye that makes my skin

tighten.

"It is a fine match," King Harold says, his voice smooth, almost friendly. "I only wonder if the... *arrangements* could have been open to discussion. A union with Podrosa, for example, might have been of equal benefit. Perhaps more so, given our similar leadership."

He knows I can hear him, but this is not a man who cares what women think, so I'm not surprised he is so blatant with his thoughts in front of me.

The air sharpens. King Silas's smile holds, but the faint tick in his jaw betrays him.

I school my features, keeping my voice light. "It's true that alliances with Podrosa have always been strong. I'm sure they will remain so."

Dante's jaw remains hardened, but his tone stays pleasant. "Indeed. And with the realms' approval of my claim, I believe all our kingdoms will only grow stronger together."

The Mersos king murmurs his agreement, but the Podrosan king's lingering glance makes it clear he's not entirely mollified.

Before the tension can stretch thinner, the musicians shift into a livelier song, strings swelling beneath a bright cascade of flute.

"If Your Majesties will excuse us," Dante says smoothly, as if the conversation had been nothing but cordial. "I believe my bride-to-be could use a dance."

Without waiting for anyone's reply, his hand finds the small of my back, warm and steady, and he guides me away from the cluster of royals.

I clench my teeth, pushing down my anger, forcing my breaths to remain even.

Because no one will ruin this night for me.

My pulse stirs as Dante leads me into the center of the floor, the sweep of his arm wrapping around my waist in a way that feels both protective and possessive. The open display of affection causes my breath to hitch. We don't have to hide anymore. This is not only allowed, it also shows the kingdom that their prince accepts me as his betrothed. The orchestra swells around us, the lilting melody threading through the air, a song meant for lovers.

 349

All eyes are on us, but for a heartbeat, I can almost forget the watching crowd.

Because Dante and I have never danced before. I've never seen him at a ball. Even during the ball the queen threw when I first arrived, Dante didn't step foot in the ballroom.

"I didn't know you could dance," I tease, feeling at ease in his arms.

The corner of his lips quirks up. "With all the moves I've shown you, did you doubt me?"

We move in time with the music, his steps sure and confident, mine following as though I've been dancing with him for years. He spins me, and I catch the faintest smirk curving his mouth.

"This isn't just a dance," I murmur.

"No," he says, drawing me close enough that I can feel the steady beat of his heart against mine. "It's us, showing them."

"You might enjoy showing me off a little too much." I raise a brow.

"Of course I do," he replies with no hesitation. "They should know exactly who my first choice is. Or rather, my *only* choice."

My cheeks warm. "Careful, Dante. You're going to make me forget we're making a political statement."

His fingers flex at my waist, a subtle pull that draws me half an inch closer. "I can think of worse things than you forgetting yourself."

I swallow hard, the weight of his words settling deep in my chest. And yet, as I look at him—at how poised he is, how effortlessly he moves through this world he always swore he wanted nothing to do with—I can't help but wonder.

"How are you handling this so well?" I ask, searching his face. "I thought you despised court life."

His lips twitch, though there's something deeper behind his expression. "I do."

"Then why—"

"Because I've already decided where my loyalties belong." His voice is softer now, but no less certain.

Something in my breath stutters.

His fingers flex against my waist as he pulls me slightly closer, his

 350

next words slipping between us like a vow.

"There is only one person in this world I would ever kneel to." His gaze locks on to mine, unwavering. "And she's in my arms right now."

Warmth spreads through me, and. I bite back a smile. "Your Highness, if you're trying to make me swoon, it might be working."

CHAPTER FORTY-FOUR

By the time the musicians trade their lively reels for softer melodies, the night has settled into its steady rhythm. Servants sweep in and out with practiced grace, refilling goblets, exchanging empty platters for trays piled high with sugared fruit and delicate pastries. Dante and the king have made their rounds, exchanging pleasantries with nobles from every corner of the realms, while I've been passed from conversation to conversation like a particularly intriguing trinket.

The royals from the other courts have begun to loosen in their seats, the rigid formality of the evening giving way to easier smiles and low, comfortable chatter. Even those who eyed me with cool curiosity at the start now seem more inclined toward warmth, their nods carrying less scrutiny and more familiarity. I can only hope it means they've accepted the engagement—or at least decided it's not worth challenging.

Out of curiosity, I glance at Princess Orida. She is holding Lady Marette's baby, deep in conversation with her cousin. She doesn't look upset anymore, and I can imagine that it isn't in her manner to have an emotional reaction. Maybe she had envisioned a future where a prince like Dante would be her partner, but it isn't as if she is in love with him.

When I find the spot where Princess Rosemary is, I find her speaking with one of the lords from the Messanyan court. I bite back a laugh, wondering if she chose him to talk to because she considers him a fertile man.

Across the room, I spot a cluster of all the kings gathered near the far hearth, laughing over something shared between them, their jeweled goblets catching the firelight. It's the perfect moment to slip away and look for Nadya, who mysteriously disappeared after dessert.

I'm a little surprised to find her perched on a velvet settee in the corridor just outside the ballroom. I thought she might have snuck off with one of the courtiers. Instead, she sits alone with her half-finished wine in hand. She perks up when she sees me, eyes bright despite the late hour.

"I wondered where you disappeared to. Are you all right?" I ask, taking the seat beside her.

"Don't worry about me, my friend. I'm a survivor. I learn to adapt."

"That is true. You're the most adaptable person I know." I give her hand a squeeze. "Still, you're my best friend, and I want to be sure you're fine."

She swirls her wine, gazing into the liquid. "Do you think we'll stay here? In Hedera? Or..." She lets the word linger. "Do you think there's a chance to go back to Delasurvia?"

I blink at her. "What do you mean?"

"Well, technically," she says, leaning in, "you could be coronated. Queen of Delasurvia in your own right. Especially now that the union is sealed. Dante would be king regent there, and Hedera would be... someone else's problem."

I laugh at her blatancy. "I've thought about it, but we went through the entire tour to declare him legitimate for *Hedera*, not to simply be a king consort. Plus, it's a little complicated at the moment, with the whispers of war, and the carnoraxis attacks spreading." My voice drops. "We need peace first. We need to make sure these other realms stand with us against the tsar. Then I'll think about what comes next."

Nadya studies me for a moment, her expression softening. "Peace

 353

first," she repeats, as if storing the promise away. Then her gaze shifts to something behind me.

When I follow her gaze, I find Dante leaning against the door frame, his arms crossed over his chest as he watches me.

"I wondered why the ballroom grew dimmer," he says.

Nadya gasps, holding a hand to her heart. "Oh, gods, normally, I would gag at such terms of endearment, but I have to admit that was unexpectedly sweet."

"Don't be so sure," I joke. "I suspect he's pretending to be nice because he wants something."

"Oh, he definitely wants something," Nadya says under her breath.

I give a small laugh as I stand. "How may I help you, my prince?"

"If I have to endure another minute of small talk," he begins, pushing off from the frame and taking a step toward me, "I'll willingly throw myself into a hoard of attacking carnoraxis, just to escape."

I laugh and shake my head. "And they say *women* overreact."

He smiles, and I can't help but notice how charming he looks.

"You want to get out of here?" His voice is low and husky, the timber making my stomach flutter.

"Won't the king be upset to find you've disappeared?" I ask.

He takes my hand. "He's probably on his twelfth helping of wine. He probably wouldn't notice if I walked in there naked."

I close the distance and interlock our fingers. "I highly doubt anyone could miss such a display. The other princesses, for example, would surely find it hard to look away."

"Well, they'd be out of luck," he says, running a thumb over the back of my hand, "since I reserve displays like that for one person alone."

"And that's my cue," Nadya says, jumping to her feet. She raises her glass, backing into the ballroom. "Enjoy the rest of your evening, Highnesses."

I giggle as Dante takes off down the corridor, pulling me along.

We rush by Sir Holden and Sir Donovan, and I give them a wave. There's nothing forbidding us from being together anymore, and no one can stop us.

By the time we reach my room, I can barely catch my breath.

"Did you see Indira's face?" I hold my belly, speaking through my laughter.

He pulls me into his arms, letting out a chuckle. "She's too young to have a heart attack, but she did clutch her chest and go pale."

I look up at Dante as the last of my laughter subsides.

He reaches up and cups my cheek, then brushes his thumb across my bottom lip.

"Are you really okay with all of this?" I ask. "Or am I ruining your life?"

"Celeste," he says softly, shaking his head. "You *are* my life."

A sharp, aching warmth rushes through me, catching me completely off guard. Dante's gaze remains locked on mine, the warmth of it an anchor, steady, certain, unwavering, and my throat tightens.

"I would go to the ends of the earth for you," he says.

The words settle deep in my chest, breaking something loose inside me. My breath shudders slightly. He says it so easily, so surely, as if it were the most obvious truth in the world.

I do not speak. Instead, I let my body lean into his, let my fingers slide up to grab the material of his shirt, pulling his body against mine. His focus drops to my tongue as I run it along my upper lip, and the hard length of his cock pressing up against me through our clothes tells me he wants the same thing I do.

Our lips press together, gentle, careful, but then my body reacts to him on its own. The yearning makes my skin hot, desire pooling between my thighs. His fingers tangle through my hair as a small growl forms in his throat and his lips grow hungry.

As his kisses pull me in, his hands move down from my waist to cup my ass. The feel of it sends goosebumps over my body. His mouth moves to my cheek, my neck, my collarbone, and his hands glide up my sides until his thumbs graze my pebbled nipples though my dress.

"Dante," I whisper, his name a plea I can't hold back.

We haven't been together since that night in Mersos, and the heat from wanting him is building so intensely that I feel as if I were about to

explode.

His palm spreads across my skin, and when he lifts his head, his stormy gaze locks with mine. I let my hands drift lower, dragging the smooth, black linen of his shirt free from his trousers. My fingers brush over the taut muscles of his abdomen, and I feel the shudder that runs through him.

His mouth crashes back to mine, his tongue sliding along mine. The kiss deepens—hot, consuming—and then his lips trail along my jaw, each kiss slower, like he's savoring every touch. My breath hitches as his lips find the sensitive spot just beneath my ear, but my hands don't stop, unbuckling his belt and undoing the button of his trousers.

He unties the back of my dress with lightning speed before pushing the material from my shoulders. I shake off the dress, letting it fall to pool at my feet. As soon as it does, he turns me around, devouring my neck while his hands greedily cup my breasts through my chemise.

I bite back a sigh as his fingers glide down my body. With a breathy sigh, I press my ass back into him, until I feel his erection on my lower back. Gods, I need him. He lifts my chemise, and then his fingertips skim over my underwear, circling my swollen nub. I rock my hips forward, grinding into his hand. But it's not enough. I need more.

He must sense it, because he guides his hand under the material and slips two fingers through the hot folds of my wetness, his thumb caressing my clit.

"So fucking wet," Dante says, nipping at my earlobe.

I can only moan in response. He teases me with his fingers, gliding up and down my slick center before finally pushing a finger inside. I cry out when he adds another, stroking in and out of me, the sound of it filling the room.

I reach behind me as he fucks me with his fingers, and I slip my hand inside his open trousers and grip his length. He grows even harder in my fist, and when I circle his crown, he sucks in a harsh breath.

"I want to taste you again," I say breathlessly.

His body seems to go rigid at my words, his fingers pumping faster. "Cum for me first, little pirate," he says, his voice a low growl. "Show

me what a good girl you are."

I melt against his chest as his fingers plunge into me, in and out, in and out, curling to hit that spot that makes my head spin. I stroke him at the same time, but the ecstasy of his touch is making me lose focus. Small whimpers escape my lips as waves of pleasure build and build, until finally my release rips through me, making me cry out.

Before I can register what's happening, he strips me of my chemise and underwear, and then he's lifting me. As the fog of my release clears, I find myself on the bed.

"Get on your hands and knees," he commands, removing his tunic, exposing his beautiful tattoo, and then pushing down his pants.

His cock springs free, and I wet my lips, doing as he says.

"Stay like that." He strokes himself as his eyes roam over my naked flesh. "Gods, you're perfect."

He comes forward, his erection mere inches from my face. One hand smooths over my hair, and the other glides up and down his cock as he gets nearer.

"You want to taste this, Highness?"

I bite my lip. "Yes, please, *Highness*," I say back to him.

I reach out and guide the head to my mouth, licking the tip, already slick with precum. He inhales sharply, his fingers tangling in my hair as I wrap my mouth around him and slide my tongue along his shaft.

"Fuck, Celeste." He hisses through his teeth, guiding me as I begin to bob my head. I swirl my tongue around his swollen head, letting out a moan of my own as he rolls his hips forward.

I stroke him with my hand as my mouth releases him, and I stare up at him, the need growing low in my belly. "I want you to taste me, too," I say, lapping at him once more.

He smirks, then shifts until he's sitting on the bed. I'm still on my hands and knees when he crawls underneath me, his head under my pussy, my head hovering over his erection. He grabs my hips, lowering me until my core is met with his hot mouth.

I cry out as his tongue lashes out.

"That's it, Celeste. I want you to fuck my face. I want my mouth

dripping with your cum."

I buck as he drags his flat tongue from my clit to my ass. Then he takes my clit between his lips and sucks, making my body shake.

But I open my eyes, taking in the sight of his twitching cock, and I can't resist. I take it in one hand and massage his balls with the other, then I descend on his thick length, coating it with my saliva as I devour him in the same delicious rhythm he's devouring me.

He comes up for air long enough to let out a long "Fuuuck!" His thumb comes up to rub over my bundle of nerves, and then he pulls my ass down so he can cover my pussy with his hot, wet mouth again. I'm falling apart from the blissful pleasure, and I don't know how much longer I can hold out.

Like a man possessed, he fucks me with his tongue as he thrust his hips up to meet my strokes, and I relax my throat so I can take him deeper. Our moans and grunts fill the room, combining with the sound of our wet mouths devouring each other.

He continues to lap at me as he pushes his fingers into my pussy, making me whimper with pleasure. Oh, gods, it's almost too much. He pumps in and out, his tongue and lips still licking and sucking and dragging through my folds, and his face is so wet as I grind all over it, needing more, needing another release. He grabs my hips and growls against my core, the vibrations on my soaked flesh sending waves of pleasure crashing over me.

"Yes, Celeste," he says between licks. "Fuck, I'm going to cum."

I suck his cock harder, my hands desperately stroking him at the same time. I'm writhing, rolling my hips in a frenzied desire. And my core pulses as I'm pushed over the edge. He floods my mouth at the same time, his hot seed filling my throat. I swallow, still whimpering from my release, and when every drop of his desire is lapped up, I drop my head to his side. My heart is thundering, and I fight to catch my breath.

He rolls me so that I'm on my side and crawls around so that he's face to face with me. His hands travel over my sweaty body, his heavy breaths covering me. I reach out and caress his skin, running my palms over his biceps, down his ribs, and over his hips. He captures my lips with his, the taste of our arousals mixing on my tongue.

"You are incredible," he whispers. "Fucking perfect."

I reach for him on instinct and find he's already hard again. Heavy lidded, I gaze at him and stroke his cock. He drags his teeth over his bottom lip, and I twist my body, gliding my leg over his torso until I'm straddling him. He stares up at me, his hands on my hips, his fingers digging into my skin. I slide along his length, slickening it with my wet pussy. It stokes the fire of my desire, and my body is thrumming with heat.

I arch my back, looking down at him, claiming him as I slide back and forth, and his hands come up to squeeze my breasts. His thumbs graze my nipples, making me throw my head back.

"Gods, you're beautiful. I need to be inside you, Celeste."

He grabs his shaft and lines himself up with my soaked entrance. When he finally pushes into me, my breath catches. He sinks inside, inch by inch. My mouth falls open as I stretch around him, the burn of it so tantalizing, I have to let out a small sigh. I lift my ass, my pussy squeezing around his length as I slide up and then down, the sensation of our slickness driving me into another frenzy. He grunts as I ride him, my small gasps and whimpers mixing with the sound of our skin slapping against each other.

His fingers squeeze into the flesh at my hips as he drives himself into me, and my heart is once again thundering in my chest. A groan rips from his throat, and he flips me so that I'm under him, my legs wrapped around his waist. He thrusts into me, deep and hard, his entire length filling me. His lips capture mine again—hot and demanding. His teeth graze my bottom lip, sending a fresh wave of heat through me, and then his hand slips between us so he can reach my clit. He rubs furious circles as he buries his thickness into me again and again, and I find myself unraveling with each push and pull, every rhapsodic stroke.

"Such a good girl," Dante says between grunts. "You take my cock so well."

I arch into him as his lips trail lower, down the column of my throat. My head tips back against the bed as his pace quickens.

"Look at me," he says, his voice softer now, filled with something deeper than lust. "I want to see your eyes when I make you cum."

I meet his gaze, and the intensity in his expression steals what little breath I have left. His control snaps, and his body moves with a desperate, aching need that mirrors my own. Every stroke sets my nerves on fire, driving me higher and higher until the world blurs around the edges.

Heat courses through my body, and I dig my fingers into the muscles of his back, rolling my hips in time with every pump of his cock until I'm forced to go hurtling over the edge. His body spasms as he finds his release, spilling into me. I cling to him, letting the sensation pull me under—deeper, sweeter—until nothing exists but the heat of his body, the roughness of his breath in my ear, the sound of my name on his lips.

His forehead rests against mine as he stills, his chest rising and falling against my body. The air between us is warm and heavy, filled with the fading echoes of our pleasure. He rolls until he's lying next to me but turns my face by my chin so he can kiss me. Dante's body still molds to mine, his arm draped across my waist as if he can't bear to let me go, and I press my cheek into his shoulder, where his tattoo is. My heart thuds softly against his chest, and I feel the steady rhythm of his heartbeat beneath my palm—strong, sure, and entirely him.

The night is deep and quiet, the echoes of the ball nothing more than a memory now.

Moonlight spills through the open window, painting silver streaks across the sheets, across him—the sharp angles of his face softened by the glow, the tan tones of his skin catching where the light brushes over muscle and scar.

We lie tangled in the quiet, his fingers moving idly along my bare arm, tracing slow, thoughtful patterns across my skin. I shiver, though not from the cold.

For a long moment, neither of us speaks.

Then, softly, Dante exhales. "I need to ask you something."

"How can your brain possibly be working already?" I ask. "My head's still spinning."

He lets out a slow chuckle and presses a kiss into my temple. "It's

important."

I let out a slow breath. "Okay."

He strokes my hair gently, and I let my fingertips wander over his chest.

"I know neither of us truly had a choice in this," he murmurs, his voice a low thread in the stillness.

I glance at him, at the way his brows draw together slightly, his gaze fixed somewhere distant, lost in thought.

His fingers don't stop moving. Up and down, featherlight over my wrist, my forearm. Like he's drawing a map, committing me to memory.

"I can't control what my father does," he continues. "But I can control myself. And if nothing else, I want to be fair to you."

I shift slightly, turning toward him, my heart pressing tighter against my ribs. "Dante, what is it?"

"I belong by your side." His voice is steadier now, more certain. He finally looks at me, really looks at me, his dark eyes burning with something I can't name. "I know my place. As your betrothed. As your husband. Your partner in all things. That's where I belong."

My lips part, my breath thin, but I don't interrupt.

He watches me for a moment longer, then drags a hand through his hair, exhaling slowly. "I love you, Celeste. And I want nothing more than to marry you."

My breath hitches at his words.

His fingers trail back down my arm, pausing just below my wrist. "But I need you to be sure it's what you want. Not something arranged. Not something you have to do for anyone else. Not for my father, not for Hedera, not even for Delasurvia."

His thumb brushes over my knuckles, slow and deliberate. "For you."

A lump rises in my throat.

I already know my answer.

I know it in my bones, in the way my soul steadies when I'm near him.

I open my mouth to say it. To tell him that I love him, too.

But before I can speak, Dante reaches up, pressing a single finger against my lips.

"Not yet," he murmurs. "I want you to really think about it. Sleep on it."

My heart stutters.

He holds my gaze, his expression unreadable, though there's something tender beneath the quiet restraint. "I don't ever want you to feel like the queen does," he says softly. "Like you're trapped. Like you have no escape." His jaw tightens slightly. "Even if I would never be like my father, I don't want you to feel even a *shadow* of what she does. No regrets. I want you to enter this marriage because *you* want it."

His hand slips from my lips, and for a moment, I think he might say more.

But he doesn't.

Instead, he leans in, his mouth brushing over mine—a slow, deliberate kiss, lingering just long enough to leave warmth behind.

Then, before I can even think to pull him back, he shifts, slipping from the bed, the sheets rustling as he reaches for his clothes.

I watch him from where I lie, my body still tingling from his touch, my mind swirling with his words. I don't want him to go, but he knows I won't be able to think clearly with him in my bed.

He doesn't wait for me to speak again.

Because he doesn't want my answer yet.

For a single second, something flashes in his expression. Worry? Doubt? I remember that look, and it pains me. It's the same way his face looked when Torbin forced me to lie to Dante, when he told me I had to send him away and tell him he meant nothing to me.

Dante has to know I never meant that. I want to reassure him, but he speaks first.

"Tomorrow," he says, as if reading my thoughts. "Tell me tomorrow."

The door clicks softly behind him, leaving me alone with my thoughts. I don't need a night to think about it. There's no need to wait until tomorrow. Because I already know.

Of course I love him.

CHAPTER

FORTY-FIVE

A soft sound stirs me from sleep.

I blink against the darkness, my body sluggish with exhaustion. The room is still, save for the faint flicker of moonlight coming in through the window.

A whisper of movement makes my ears perk.

My pulse kicks up as I push up onto my elbows. My eyes scan the room, searching, and then I spot something on the floor. A slip of parchment, just beneath my door.

Frowning, I throw off the covers and move toward it, the cool air raising goosebumps on my skin. I pick up the note, my breath catching as I unfold it.

Meet me at the stables.

I blink at the familiar slant of Dante's handwriting, and a rush of warmth floods my chest.

I chew my lip, glancing toward the window. It's still dark outside, not an ideal time to head to the stables. But perhaps Dante can't wait until tomorrow for my answer. Maybe he is desperate to know what I'm

 363

going to say, just as desperately as I want to say it.

Technically, it is tomorrow already—past midnight, at least.

Excitement flutters in my stomach as I pull on my clothes, my hands clumsy in my haste. I know my answer. I want to tell him. I want to say it aloud. I don't want anything more to stand in the way of us being together. It's taken months just to get to this point.

I reach for my boots, but I'm still a little groggy and end up dropping one. As I slip one on, the adjoining door creaks open, and I look up to find Nadya watching me sleepily.

"Celeste," she mumbles, rubbing her eyes. "What are you doing?"

"Nothing," I say quickly, stuffing the note into my pocket. "Sorry I was loud. Go back to bed."

Her gaze sharpens slightly as she looks me over. "Did you take Ezra's powder? To make sure you won't wander?"

I sigh. "I'm not wandering, Nadya." I shove my foot into the last boot, lacing it quickly. "I'm meeting Dante."

Nadya's brow furrows, her sleepiness fading. "At this hour?"

I shrug. "He asked me something last night, and I guess he's too impatient to wait for my answer."

Before I can move past her, the note falls from my pocket.

She bends down and picks it up, but as her fingers grasp the paper, she freezes.

"Nadya—"

"Celeste, don't go." Her fingers twitch against the parchment, her lips parting slightly.

I frown. "What? What's wrong?"

She doesn't answer right away. Her grip tightens around the note, like it's suddenly something dangerous. "I don't know," she mutters, a crease forming between her brows. "I just—" She shakes her head. "It doesn't feel right."

"It doesn't *feel* right?"

"I'm getting a bad feeling from it. I've been reading about malevolent energy and how it can flow from sources—"

"Nadya!" I exhale sharply, snatching it back. "You're taking this

witch thing too seriously."

She doesn't laugh.

I shake my head, tucking the note into my blouse. "I'll be fine. I'm allowed to be seen with Dante now. It's okay. Go back to bed."

She looks stunned but doesn't stop me as I slip out the door.

The courtyard is empty, silent save for the distant rustle of leaves and the occasional hoot of an owl. I move quickly, keeping to the shadows as I cross the stone path toward the stables, my heart pounding—not with fear, but with anticipation.

I know what I'm going to say. Dante is the only person in this world I would choose. And I want him to know it. I don't know how he doesn't already know it. I can't believe he would doubt it. He must feel it. But maybe he just wants to hear the words.

The stables come into view, dimly lit, the scent of hay and damp earth filling my senses as I step inside. It's empty. I frown, my breath misting in the cool air. Maybe I got here first.

A rustling noise echoes from deeper inside.

I smile. "Dante?"

But when I step forward, Nadya emerges from the shadows behind me. I frown.

I open my mouth, but she beats me to it. "Celeste," she hisses. "Something is wrong."

Frustration flares in me. "Why did you follow me?"

She glares at me, folding her arms. "Because I don't trust—" Then her expression changes. Her breath hitches, her lips parting slightly.

"Nadya?" I whisper, but she doesn't answer.

She's staring at something just behind me.

A wolf howls in the distance. Dread slithers down my spine.

Slowly, I turn.

A figure steps forward from the shadows, his mouth curling into a sneer.

"Hello, Princess."

The last thing I hear is Nadya screaming my name, just as a sharp scent fills my nose. Then everything goes dark.

 365

CHAPTER FORTY-SIX

Dante

The corridors of Ivystone are unusually still as I make my way toward Celeste's rooms, the echoes of my boots lost against the thick tapestries that line the stone walls. Early sunlight filters through the arched windows, slanting long, golden beams across the floor, but even the light feels subdued this morning. Another sign that winter is on its way.

I run a hand through my hair, trying to smooth the nerves that have coiled tight in my chest since I woke. Last night was amazing. Like every time with Celeste is. If someone were to have told me a year ago that I would be in love with this woman, that I would be betrothed to her and fated to spend the rest of my life able to hold her, I would have thought that person had lost their mind. But now, I can't imagine my life without her.

Still, I had to give her the choice. Though I feel like I know what her

answer will be, I need to be completely sure it's what she wants. I can't just assume because of the way she kisses me, the way she looks at me, the way she melts into my arms, the way her body responds to me.

I told her to take her time. I know I said I didn't need an answer right away.

But gods, I want her answer now.

I need to hear it from her own lips, see it in her own eyes. I need to know she's choosing me—not because duty demands it, but because she wants to.

I almost went to her last night. I went to my room after our night of incredible passion, only to pace it for an hour, wondering if I was being stupid.

I went as far as stepping outside my door, the urge to return to her room so strong, it was pressing in on my heart, but I couldn't do that to her. I told her she could sleep on it, and it would have been unfair if I went back on my word. That's not how a successful marriage works.

But now, it's the next day, and hopefully, she'll have had plenty of time to think it over. My heart races, hope swelling in my chest as I head to her room.

I reach her door and knock once, twice, lightly enough not to wake her if she's still sleeping. I wonder for a moment if she slept soundly or if she tossed and turned all night like I did. I wait, shifting from one foot to the other, but there is no answer.

I frown and knock again, a little harder this time. Still no answer.

And Sir Holden is not at his post. Is it even his post anymore?

Perhaps Celeste has already gone down to breakfast. Perhaps she hadn't been able to sleep and was up with the dawn, starving.

I force myself to turn away, unwilling to start the day by acting like a desperate fool. I'm a prince now, and I'll be expected to act like one. Especially while the nobles from the other realms are still in Ivystone Citadel. The thought makes me square my shoulders as I head to the dining hall.

Celeste is probably halfway through her breakfast, gossiping with Nadya about which of the kings was the most misogynistic. Hopefully

not in front of Silas, though Celeste is brave enough to do just that without batting an eye. I love that about her. She's not afraid to stand up to him.

Is she waiting for me to arrive? Is she constantly looking at the door, wondering when I'll step through it? Is she anxious for my arrival so she can give me her answer?

Or is the answer I'm expecting not the one she's ready to give me?

Maybe she's avoiding me because she wants to delay crushing my heart.

Unease prickles beneath my skin as I make my way through the corridors. Each step echoes louder than it should. Each turn feels too empty.

When I reach the grand dining hall, the tension in my spine unspools just slightly at the smell of roasted meats and fresh bread drifting through the air.

She's here. She must be.

I step inside—and immediately scan the room.

Some of the kings and queens from the other realms are seated at the long table, already helping themselves to the fresh fruit, eggs, and sausages. I put on my princely face, steel myself for empty pleasantries. But as my gaze passes over the faces gathered, I don't see Celeste.

The queen sits at her place, her back rigid, her gaze lowered to the goblet in her hands when she isn't conversing with Queen Shaylin. Across from her, King Silas eats methodically, his knife carving into a slab of meat with mechanical precision as he nods along to something King Birchus is saying. The coldness between my father and the queen is palpable, an invisible wall erected between them, thick enough to suffocate the entire hall.

Celeste's chair remains empty.

My stomach knots.

The present royals greet me, wishing me a pleasant good morning, but I can only nod in response. My mind is reeling, my fingers itching to do something, anything that will help me figure out where Celeste is.

King Gallor lifts his goblet, his tone carrying easily over the table.

"You disappeared last night, right in the middle of the lovely ball," he says with a knowing gleam in his eye.

Before I can form a response, Queen Nemesia adds lightly, "Princess Celeste was also nowhere to be found." She arches a brow, her jeweled fingers drumming against the table, as though she's amused at the implication.

"Ah," Gallor says, his smile sharp as he leans back in his chair, "young love. To be able to find each other after so much sorrow... it is one of life's great gifts."

Laughter ripples down the table, a few heads nodding in agreement.

I force the corners of my mouth upward, a shallow echo of their amusement, but inside, my chest is tight. My pulse hammers in my ears.

"Sit," King Silas says, looking up at me.

I reluctantly obey, settling stiffly into the seat to his right. The air feels heavy around us, weighted with things unspoken. I tear a hunk of bread from the basket in front of me and chew without tasting it, my eyes flicking to the door with every sound.

She's just late.

She'll come sweeping in, slightly breathless, cheeks flushed from sleep or from hurrying, the usual sparkle in her eyes when our gazes meet. That confident stride that always has me buckling to her will. We'll exchange longing looks, and she'll lick those luscious lips of hers, getting me instantly hard and making me think about how her greedy mouth was wrapped around my cock last night.

I clear my throat, pouring myself some steaming kahva to sip on until she gets here.

Any moment now.

Silas glances at me. "Something troubling you, boy?"

I school my features into neutrality, swallowing down the tightness in my throat. "Nothing, Your Majesty."

His eyes narrow slightly, but he doesn't push. He simply grunts and returns to his meal, carving another bloody piece of meat with a flick of his wrist.

I force myself to sit through it, each passing second scraping against

my nerves. Every moment that ticks by without her arrival feels like another stone piling on my chest. My stomach is too taut with nerves for me to eat. I pour myself another cup of kahva and tap my finger on the rim as I wait.

The door opens, and Princess Orida enters the room. My shoulders slump. She's not Celeste. She will never be Celeste. I don't even bother offering a polite smile because the truth is I don't give a fuck about any of these people. Not really. The only person I care about is not here.

After what feels like an eternity, I push my chair back and march out of the room. To hell with civil conventions.

My strides are quicker now, carrying me back through the corridors. A bead of sweat trails down my back despite the chill. I shove it away. Overthinking it will only make it worse.

Maybe she's with Nadya.

I reach her rooms again and let out a sigh of relief when I see Sir Holden approaching.

"Good morning," I greet him.

He inclines his head. "Your Highness."

I'm still not used to the title. "I'm looking for Princess Celeste. Is she—?" I point to the door, not finishing my question.

"She should be," he answers. "I only stepped away for a moment to relieve myself. If she's not here, she's probably at breakfast."

I shake my head. "I just came from the dining hall. She wasn't there."

I don't wait for him to respond; I knock on her door, hoping she's just sleeping heavily. Still nothing.

Heart hammering, I turn to Sir Holden.

He gives me a nod and raps on the door quickly before twisting the handle and pushing the door open. "Your Highness?" he calls out.

I step past him, but the room is empty.

The bed is untouched, the covers neatly folded at the corners. Her brush lies on the vanity, a few strands of dark hair still caught in its bristles.

I move to the adjoining door, the one that connects her chambers to Nadya's. I knock once, then push through.

Also empty.

My brows scrunch together, and a strange feeling coils in my stomach.

I try not to panic. I asked her to think about whether she really wanted to be betrothed to me, and what if her answer wasn't just *no*, but a definitive *never*? What if she left because she would rather be alone in Delasurvia than be with me?

And of course Nadya would go with her.

Is that what happened?

Fuck!

A small piece of my heart crumples at the thought.

I turn back to Celeste's room, taking in the sight of all her things. Strange. If they fled, they left everything behind.

Which means either they left in a hurry, or they didn't leave of their own accord.

A sour twist writhes in my gut.

No. No, she wouldn't. She wouldn't run—not like this. Not without a word. Not after everything.

Still, the seeds of doubt root deep.

Maybe she couldn't bear it. Maybe she decided marrying into this damned court was too high a price. Maybe she—

No.

I slam the thought down.

"Should I be worried?" Sir Holden asks me, scanning the room.

For a moment, I'm not sure what to say. Fear of embarrassment— and fear of facing that truth—keeps me from telling him she might have left, that she might have rejected me.

But there's still one more place to check.

"I'll check with the magister. She might be at an early lesson."

He nods, his hand on the hilt of his sword. "I'll ask the other guards if they've seen her."

"Thank you, Sir Holden." I turn on my heel and storm through the halls, ignoring the curious glances of passing guards. The corridors blur past as I make my way toward the eastern wing, to the narrow staircase

that leads to the tower classrooms.

Ezra. If Celeste needed counsel—or comfort—that's where she would have gone.

I take the steps two at a time, the rough stone scraping beneath my boots.

When I reach the top landing, the door to the classroom stands ajar. I push it open but find no one.

The desks sit empty. The hearth has burned low, faint embers casting a weak glow against the stone floor. Shelves sag under the weight of ancient tomes, untouched.

No Ezra.

No Celeste.

No Nadya.

The ache in my chest turns jagged, sharp enough to steal my breath.

Where are you, Celeste?

I brace my hands against the doorframe, bowing my head, fighting the sudden roar in my ears. The fear I've tried so hard to keep at bay now rips free, uncoiling through me like a fucking storm.

She's gone.

And I don't know if I will ever get her back.

I lean against the cold, stone doorframe, staring into the empty classroom, as if by sheer will, I could summon her.

A shuffle of footfalls behind me jerks me upright, my hand instinctively flying to the hilt of my falchion. I whirl around—hope, stupid and reckless, roaring to life inside me.

But it's not Celeste.

Ezra halts mid-step, lifting his hands in a calming gesture. "My apologies," he says quietly, his sharp eyes missing nothing. "I didn't mean to startle you."

I curse under my breath. My heart pounds against my ribs, an erratic drumbeat I can't seem to quiet. "I'm sorry, Magister Kadmiel. I've been looking everywhere for Celeste." I force my jaw to unclench. "She's not in her room. Not in the dining hall. Not here."

"Perhaps she went for a ride. She's very fond of her horse."

The tightness in my gut loosens a bit. "The stables. Of course."

"You could also ask the coach master if she took a carriage into town."

Now that he says it, I feel even more the fool. There are a number of places she could have gone. For all I know, her uncle could have summoned her for something important, and she left for Delasurvia in the middle of the night.

But she normally has Sir Holden as an escort, if she were to leave. I can only hope she and Nadya went for a ride on horseback, just so Celeste could clear her head to give me a well-thought-out answer to whether or not she truly wants to spend the rest of her life with me.

I thank Ezra and head to the stables, trying my damnedest not to run in a panic. But when I get there and find Thora in her stall, my stomach drops, and my throat closes up. She didn't go for a ride. Where the fuck is she?

I make my way to the coach master to inquire if she left via carriage, but the coach master tells me no carriage has left the premises. Not even one of the carriages from the visiting kingdoms.

Fuck!

Something is wrong. I can feel it in my bones.

I rush back to Ezra, whom I find cleaning out vials at his desk. He peers up at me as I enter the room, and he must see the alarm on my face because he stands immediately.

"No one has seen her." I swallow hard between heavy breaths. "Her horse is still in the stables, and the coach master said no carriages have left."

His brow creases. "What do you think happened?"

I rake a hand through my hair. "Last night, I asked her to think about marrying me, to give me a truthful answer regarding what she wants. I told her to sleep on it and tell me in the morning." I shake my head, unable to communicate the intrusive thoughts harrowing me.

But Ezra sees it on my face.

He steps closer, his voice low enough not to carry. "Dante. I've seen the way she looks at you. She didn't run." His certainty slices through

some of the rising panic, but not enough to banish it completely. "Maybe she needed more time. Maybe she took another horse to Delasurvia to clear her head, to speak with her uncle."

I want to believe him. I need to.

But I know her. She would never leave Thora behind.

I rake a hand through my hair, turning to the window, where the morning light spills in. "If she needs time... I'll give it to her. But I need to know she's all right."

And if she chose something else—someone else—at least I'll know.

I clasp his shoulder briefly in thanks, then turn on my heel.

I spend the next moments gathering provisions for my ride. I hurry through the corridor, my riding cloak fastened at my neck, and I'm almost through the front doors when a voice stops me.

"Dante."

I freeze.

It's the king.

I turn slowly, every instinct telling me to keep moving, but there's no ignoring him.

My father strides toward me, Farvis trailing two steps behind. The king's cloak billows behind him, the polished hilt of his sword gleaming at his hip. His expression is as sharp as a blade.

"You're in quite a hurry," he observes, his voice cold and cutting.

"I have something I need to attend to," I answer, careful to keep my tone even.

He narrows his eyes, stepping into my path. "You can't leave now. We have guests. Guests who have traveled from afar to see the new prince."

I stiffen. "Father, it's important. I have to go."

He studies me for a moment, his thick brows plunging down over narrowed eyes. Then he scoffs, a humorless sound. "She left, didn't she?"

My stomach twists, but I say nothing. Silence is answer enough.

The king's face darkens, thunderclouds gathering in his expression. His voice is a low, dangerous growl. "I knew she would betray us. I've always found her a conniving bitch."

"Father, no," I say quickly, forcing myself to meet his gaze, "I don't know that she has. Let me find her. Let me bring her back."

"'Back'?" He laughs bitterly. "You still think she wants to return? Foolish boy. She was agreeable when it came to marrying Torbin, but perhaps she couldn't stomach being stuck with the spare. She's spat in your face—and mine. She broke our agreement."

No. That's not what happened. But how can I convince him?

Farvis shifts slightly, but he doesn't speak.

"If she's broken the deal," my father says, his voice rising, "then Delasurvia belongs to Hedera by right."

"No," I say, stepping forward before I can stop myself. "Please. Give me time. Give her a chance to explain. It doesn't make sense. Her horse is here. She knows what would happen to Delasurvia if she left. She wouldn't do that to her people." *She wouldn't abandon me.*

The king sneers. "You think you know her? You think a few kisses and doe-eyed glances mean you know the heart of a woman?" His lip curls. "They are all the same. Selfish. Deceitful. And weak."

My fists clench at my sides. I want to strike him, but I hold myself back by the barest thread.

"Farvis," Silas snaps, turning away from me. "Come. We will convene the council. It's time to discuss how best to take Delasurvia before the vultures circle."

"No," I say again, more quietly. More desperately.

The king doesn't even spare me a glance. "She betrayed us. She lied, as all women do. And now she will pay for her treachery."

The words echo down the corridor long after he's gone, a poisonous brand searing into my skull.

I stand there for a long, aching moment, the fire inside me threatening to consume everything.

She didn't break the deal. She didn't abandon her people. She didn't leave me.

Something is very wrong.

And I need to find out what happened, to make sure she's safe.

I stride back toward the stables, cutting through the castle corridors

like a man possessed. My boots strike hard against the flagstones, and a few servants scatter from my path, their faces flickering with wary glances.

I barely care.

I need answers.

The stablehands barely have time to react before I'm saddling my horse, tightening the straps with fingers that shake from more than adrenaline. The cold bite of the morning air slices through my clothes, but I barely feel it.

Celeste is out there.

And I'm going to find her.

Or gods help me—I'll burn the world down trying.

CHAPTER FORTY-SEVEN

Celeste

I wake to silence.

Not the familiar stillness of Ivystone, where the distant murmur of guards and the occasional hoot of an owl drift through the night. Not the shuffling of feet as the servants prepare the castle for the day. This silence is thicker, weighted, like the air itself is pressing in around me.

My body is sluggish, my limbs aching in a way that doesn't feel like simple exhaustion. My head throbs, a dull, pulsing ache at the base of my skull. I reach up, inspecting my scalp, to find a swollen bump that's sensitive to the touch. My throat is raw, my limbs as heavy as stone. For a moment, I can't remember where I am. The bed beneath me is too stiff, the air too cold. Not Ivystone. Not Delasurvia.

Not... safe.

I blink against the dim light filtering through a small window, my vision sharpening slowly. Despite the panic building in my chest, I sit up

with a groan, the blankets stiff with embroidery and the chill biting through to my bones. The chamber is unfamiliar, vast and grim, stone walls slick with moisture, the windows tall and narrow like arrow slits. Frost grips the corners of the glass, a pale shimmer that makes everything feel... dead.

The bed beneath me is simple but not unpleasant. The sheets are soft, the wool blanket heavy against my legs. The walls are stone, adorned with a delicate woven tapestry depicting a winter landscape. A wooden table sits near the hearth, a single chair tucked beneath it. A small basin rests on a side table, a cloth neatly folded beside it.

Everything is pretty, comfortable—but wrong.

Because this is not Ivystone.

And I don't know how I got here.

I'm still wearing the clothes I pulled on when—

A shudder runs through me as the memories come flooding back.

The note. The stables. Nadya's warning. And then the fear in her eyes.

The chemical smell.

Torbin.

My stomach knots so violently I think I might retch. I was right. Torbin lives. And it was his hands that dragged me from the stables. My chest tightens, breath coming too fast, and I clutch the bed frame to steady myself. Of course it was him. Of course.

The door creaks open. I flinch, instinctively reaching for a dagger that isn't there. I sit up too quickly, my head swimming as a figure steps inside. I immediately jump to the opposite side of the bed and take a defensive stance.

A woman enters—middle-aged, small in stature, sharp cheekbones, and a long braid falling over one shoulder. She's bundled in layers of dark wool with the skirt of her grey dress scraping the floor. She's holding a tray, steam curling from a delicate porcelain teacup.

She meets my gaze, her expression calm, unreadable.

"Who are you?" I rasp. "Where am I?"

She says something softly, but the words are garbled, alien. A

 378

strange, sharp rhythm to them. It's not the common language, but I've heard this dialect before. From the refugees we rescued. It's Dulcamaran.

I shake my head. "I don't—I don't understand you."

She responds again in the same language, her voice gentle, but I can't make sense of a single word. I try to interpret her signals as she gestures toward the tea.

I shake my head. "No. What is it? What do you want from me?"

Again, she says something, her tone insistent but not unkind. She places the tray on a nearby table, points to her ears, and then lifts the cup, holding it out to me with both hands.

The steam carries something earthy, almost metallic. My lips are cracked, my throat parched, and her eyes carry a kindness that doesn't match the coldness of the room.

"Fine," I mutter, my hand trembling as I take the cup. "But if this is poison..."

She gives me a tight, amused smile that I don't need translated.

The tea burns on the way down—bitter, thick, with a strange mineral aftertaste. My tongue tingles. I finish the tea, not because of the taste, but because my throat is thick and dry. For a moment, I feel lightheaded, and then my ears pop.

"My name is Staja," the woman says. As clear as day.

I freeze. "I... I understand you."

Staja nods. "The tea. Brewed by our court sorceress. It allows your mind to receive our tongue. It will last a day. Perhaps two, if your fae blood doesn't fight it."

I lower the cup slowly. "You work for Prince Torbin?"

"He has commanded that I see to your comfort." She pauses. "He will want to speak with you soon."

My stomach sinks.

Of course he will. My blood turns to ice, and a chill slides down my spine, colder than the northern air seeping through the window. My mind is spinning—not from the tea, but from the reality of where I am and why. Slowly, I step toward the bed and sit on the edge.

He's abducted me. Taken me against my will.

My breath catches.

Nadya.

I lurch forward, grabbing Staja's arm. "My friend. Where is she?"

She doesn't flinch, but her voice remains calm. "She's unharmed. In a room much like this one. She's not been touched. The prince said she won't be harmed, so long as you cooperate."

Nadya is here. He has her. Trapped like me.

My knees nearly give out, and I stumble backward until I hit the edge of the bed.

I should fight. I should find her.

The thought strikes me with sudden clarity. My strength hasn't fully returned, but I still have power—power that I haven't yet mastered, but power nonetheless. If I concentrated hard enough, I could overtake Staja and escape this room. Then I could search for Nadya, find her somehow, and try to escape.

No. The soldier in me knows the risk is too great.

I don't know how many guards are stationed beyond that door, how many people Staja could call with a single shout. I have no idea how big this castle is or where to begin looking for Nadya. And I don't know how involved this woman before me is. Just because she works for him does not mean she's loyal to him.

Staja watches me carefully, her posture too poised to give anything away. She takes the teacup from me, setting it down with a quiet clink, then folds her hands in front of her. "The prince is expecting you for dinner."

Dinner? What time is it?

My mind spins, not just from my confusion, but from the lingering ache in my head.

Staja crosses to a tall, iron-handled dresser and opens it with a groan of hinges. From within, she draws out a dress.

If it can even be called that.

The fabric is sheer and flows like mist between her fingers—a slip of dark-blue chiffon with a neckline that plunges far too low and sleeves that fall off the shoulders in diaphanous drapes. The bodice is boned but

narrow, the skirt split up the sides, meant to reveal rather than conceal.

"That's it?" I ask, my voice raw. "It's freezing in here."

Staja doesn't answer. She simply holds the dress out to me with quiet resignation.

I square my shoulders. "I'm not going," I say.

Her gaze flicks to the closed door, then back to me. She takes a hesitant step forward. "Please... it would be better—for both of us—if you do what he says."

I frown. "'Both of us'? Did Torbin threaten you?"

She shakes her head, eyes tight with something like fear. "He didn't need to. I've seen what happens to those who don't obey. I'd like to keep my position... and my skin." She swallows, her voice softer now. "And if you want to keep your friend safe—"

The walls feel closer now, like they're pressing in, heavy and damp. I can taste salt on my tongue, and my clothes suddenly feel thick with dirt and dried sweat. Despite the chill in the air, my chest tightens with a sick heat that makes it hard to breathe. My ears ring with the sharp thrum of my pulse.

He has Nadya.

And I don't have a choice but to do as he says, for her sake.

And maybe, I can trick him into telling me where she is.

I nod slowly, tasting the bitterness of surrender on my tongue. "Fine."

Relief washes over Staja's features. She sets the dress gently across the bed, smoothing the folds like it's something sacred.

"I'll prepare the bath," she says, walking toward a second door—this one carved with curling floral motifs that feel out of place in such a cold place.

As the sound of running water reaches my ears, I stand and go to the window. I rub the condensation from the glass, but all I can see outside are snow-covered mountains. Flurries drift down at a steady pace, but otherwise, there is absolutely no movement to be seen.

After a few minutes, Staja emerges from the bathing chamber, and steam rolls out with her. "Your bath is ready, Your Highness."

The warmth of the room envelops me as soon as I step inside. The air is thick with the scent of lavender and pine. A copper tub sits in the center, filled with steaming water that ripples with my reflection. Dozens of small candles line the stone shelves, their flames soft and flickering.

"The prince instructed me that you be made pristine," Staja says gently. "That I use the finest soaps and oils. For your body. Your hair. He said he doesn't want any scents from... before... clinging to you. He wants you perfect for him."

Her voice doesn't betray emotion, but her hands wring together nervously.

'Scents from before'? What does she mean?

I stare at the water, the fragrant oils already glimmering on its surface like a lure. I grit my teeth and step toward the bath.

I have to admit that the hot water makes me feel better. It warms my chilled bones and loosens my muscles. I only stay in long enough to ensure I'm clean, and when I step from the bath, Staja is ready with a thick towel.

Though I could manage alone, Staja helps me slip into the thin dress. The bodice molds tightly to my skin, cinching just beneath my ribs, and the sheer skirt offers no warmth, brushing like breath against my thighs. I shiver, arms prickling with gooseflesh, and not just from the cold.

She doesn't meet my eyes as she opens a small jar of glittering lotion, the scent of vanilla and clove thick in the air. "He likes when the light catches," she murmurs, smoothing it onto my bare shoulders, down my arms, across the tops of my breasts. "Says it makes the skin look like starlight."

My stomach roils. I clench my jaw, my breath catching in my throat. I couldn't care less what he fucking likes. But I don't argue with her. It's not Staja's fault I'm in this mess.

As she moves behind me, gathering my hair and combing it out with quick, practiced strokes, a wave of helplessness crashes over me.

I shouldn't be here.

I should be back at Ivystone. I should be with—

Dante.

Oh, gods!

I close my eyes, willing the memory to surface. The last moment I saw him. That look in his eyes—part challenge, part promise—as he asked me to decide what I really wanted. To choose him.

And I did.

I was going to tell him. I was ready to—

My chest seizes, the air sucked from my lungs like I've been punched. My blood feels like lead, like I'm being weighed down despite my urgency to run.

He must've gone to find me. To hear my answer. Only to find nothing but silence.

What if he thinks I left because my answer was *no*? That I ran away instead of choosing him?

The thought slices clean through me.

No. Please, no. Not after everything. Not after all we've been through.

I bite down on the inside of my cheek and press trembling fingers to my temples.

"Dante."

The name echoes inside me—not spoken aloud but hurled like a stone into the icy air. My telepathic magic has always been unpredictable. I don't even know how to control it. It didn't work when I tried it on Nadya. I don't know if it's bound by distance, or by the chaos of my emotions. But I have to try.

"Dante, please. Hear me. I didn't leave you. I didn't run. I was taken. Torbin has me—and Nadya too."

I wait. I pray. I don't even care if it hurts me; the pain will be worth it if he hears me. I open my senses, hoping to feel that familiar buzz I felt when Dante heard me before. But there's nothing.

Only the creak of the floorboards as Staja shifts behind me, weaving delicate braids into my hair.

"I was going to say yes*, Dante. I was ready to say* yes*. Please don't think otherwise."*

 383

Still nothing.

Tears burn behind my eyes, but I blink them back. I can't cry now. Not with Torbin waiting. Not with Nadya's life tangled in the knot of mine.

A shiver travels up my spine, and I feel as if I could jump out of my skin. I just hope that Dante is confident enough in our love to know I would never abandon him and to have the resolve to come find me.

CHAPTER FORTY-EIGHT

S taja finishes twisting my hair into a loose, elegant braid and fastens it with a clasp that gleams like polished bone. She gives me a onceover, then nods. "It will do," she whispers.

She opens the door, and I step out of the room.

The hallway beyond is dim, the stone floor slick beneath my bare feet. Iron sconces cast long, flickering shadows, and every ten steps, another Dulcamaran guard stands sentry. Their armor is matte black, with jagged pauldrons that catch the candlelight like teeth. They watch me with eyes like slate—unfeeling, unreadable.

Then another figure approaches, and I feel a chill run up my spine.

"Finally awake, I see." Osrem, Torbin's advisor and spy, scrutinizes me. This is the man King Silas mistakenly sent to search for Torbin, not understanding fully how loyal he was to the monster his son has become. "Let's not keep Prince Torbin waiting."

With Osrem leading the way, and the guards following behind me, we make our way down the hall. Each step I take, flanked by Staja, feels like walking into an elaborate trap. My skin glitters with a shimmer that doesn't feel like mine. My stomach clenches with fear that Nadya may be

harmed. And my heart aches with words that may never reach the one person I need to hear them.

"Please, Dante. Hear me. I'm still yours."

And I pray with everything I have left that the bond between us is stronger than the darkness rising around me.

The wind cuts sharp against my skin as Osrem leads me through a room and continues toward glass doors that lead out to a balcony. As I step outside, the cold, northern air coils around me like unseen chains. The sheer curtains behind me flutter in the freezing wind.

I keep my spine straight, my chin lifted, refusing to shiver, even as the thin silk of my gown offers little protection. The fabric grips me, shimmering like frost-kissed water, the delicate embroidery of silver vines trailing over my arms. The slits in the skirt expose far too much of my legs, and every movement makes the cool silk whisper against my skin like a ghost's breath. The dress is beautiful, elegant—but impractical, meant for display rather than warmth.

Perhaps that was Torbin's intent.

Heat. I imagine heat.

I inhale slowly, steadying my breath against the bitter air. I should be freezing.

But I'm not.

A strange warmth lingers beneath my skin, spreading through my veins, pulsing from somewhere deep inside me. I will my body to stay warm, and it does.

I don't understand it, but I expect it's the battle of mixed magic in my body. Instinctively, I check my nose and my ears, but there doesn't seem to be any blood, and I don't sense any pain other than the lingering ache from the bump on my head.

But I don't have time to question it right now, as Staja leads me farther onto the balcony.

It stretches wide, its white marble railing etched with intricate carvings of winter birds. Beyond it, the kingdom of Dulcamar sprawls in shades of grey and light blue, mist curling between the distant spires, snowy mountains standing like jagged shadows against the evening sky.

 386

At the center of it all, waiting for me, is the man who betrayed my trust.

Torbin stands beside an ornate dining table, draped in deep-red silk, the silverware gleaming under the soft glow of hanging lanterns. A feast has been prepared, featuring roasted meats, spiced wines, platters of fresh winter berries. It feels like an illusion of civility. The air is thick with the scent of charred fat and cinnamon, but beneath it all, something darker simmers—coppery, metallic.

Torbin is dressed like a prince, his navy doublet adorned with silver embroidery, a fur-lined cloak draped over his shoulders. But his eyes betray him.

There is something wrong in them. A gleam that doesn't belong to the boy I once knew. But it is not his gaze that holds me captive. It is his scars. A burn mark mars one side of his face, just along the edge of his jaw—the exact place where my hand seared his skin when I pushed him off the balustrade at Ivystone. And at his temple, a thin, jagged scar disrupts his otherwise-flawless features, a reminder of the antler crown that pierced him when he fell. A reminder that I threw him to his death.

Yet here he stands. Whole. Alive. Smiling. The sight of it sends something sharp through me, like a splinter driven beneath my ribs— revulsion and guilt twisted into one.

Torbin's lips curl at the edges as he takes a step forward, hands outstretched in mock welcome. His eyes move slowly over the length of my body. "You look ravishing, Celeste. As always."

I instinctively rub at my arms, uncomfortable with his gaze, especially since this dress is so revealing.

"I was beginning to think you wouldn't come," he muses. "That would have been... unfortunate." His head tilts slightly. "For Nadya."

I try to disclose my tight swallow. I turn my head to where Staja was, but she is gone. Osrem has also disappeared into the shadows, leaving us alone.

"You won't hurt her." I try to minimize the grinding of my teeth as I speak to him.

He cants his chin. "You're awfully confident."

"If you kill her, you'll lose your leverage."

"Is that something you're willing to bet her life on?" He smirks, his eyes traveling the length of me. "Then again, maybe it was simply hunger that brought you here."

"What I'm doing here is exactly what I'd like to find out. What do you want from me?"

Torbin gestures toward the elegantly set table, his smile smooth, practiced. "Please, sit."

I don't move. "I have no appetite."

His expression flickers—a tightening of his jaw, a brief narrowing of his eyes—before he exhales through his nose, as if forcing patience. "You could join me for dinner," he says, his voice light, conversational. Then, with a casual shrug, he adds, "Or I could give one of my carnoraxis access to Nadya's room, where it may or may not jump at the chance to claw her insides out."

Ice floods my veins, and my vision pulses at the edges. For a split second, I forget how to breathe.

"The choice is yours." He waits, his brow lifted.

A sharp retort burns at the back of my throat, but I swallow it down, biting hard against the inside of my cheek. I won't give him the satisfaction of my anger. Instead, I lower myself into the chair he gestures to, keeping my movements slow, controlled, as if this is my choice and not his command.

Torbin watches me as he takes his own seat across the table, the soft scrape of his chair against the stone unnervingly loud in the silence between us.

I do not look at him. Instead, I turn my head, letting my gaze drift over the landscape beyond the balcony, the endless, frozen sprawl of Dulcamar stretching before me.

Mountains rise in jagged peaks, their icy slopes cutting into the sky, swallowed by the thick, swirling haze that floats on the valley below. The snow-covered ground is vast, untouched, except for the winding, treacherous paths carved into the cliffsides, the only roads leading in or out of this place.

I shiver, though not from the cold.

I am so far from home. How long did it take for him to bring me here? I don't remember any of it. Whatever he used to incapacitate me, to make me lose consciousness, must have been strong. It must have been the same thing the tsar's men used on my uncle.

The weight of it presses deep into my chest, settling like a stone in my ribs.

It must have taken days. If anyone were to come looking for me, it would take just as long. What if no one finds me before the tsar uses me for his malicious scheme? What if I am already lost?

I press my nails into my palm beneath the table, grounding myself against the creeping dread.

I am not lost.

I will not let him win.

Finally, I shift my gaze back to Torbin, my face carefully blank. "You still haven't answered my question. What do you want from me?"

His smirk deepens. "My dear, in case you've forgotten, you promised yourself to me."

"What?" I spit out.

"We are betrothed."

He smiles, and I flinch in shock. His canines are longer than the rest of his teeth. Sharper. He's becoming more like the monsters he creates.

I stiffen my jaw, my muscles going taut. I bring my hands to rest upon the tabletop, and the glint of the silverware catches my eye. I'm overcome by the instinct to grab the knife, but as my fingers inch toward it, Torbin clicks his tongue.

"It would be foolish of you to think you're stronger than I am," he says.

I press my lips together in frustration and retract my hand.

"Besides, that knife wouldn't do any damage I couldn't overcome." He leans slightly back in his chair, as if we were simply talking about the weather. "Have you forgotten what strength the carnoraxis potion has given me?"

I fix my focus on the burn mark on his jaw. "Doesn't look like it's

any good at erasing scars."

His smirk is laced with venom. "Ordinary scars are not a problem. But the ones infused with fae magic appear to be... trickier."

"Good to know." I tilt my head and allow myself a cocky smile.

He scrutinizes me for a moment, and then he laughs. "I've always admired your spirit, Celeste. I can see why you've risen in the ranks of the regiment. It will make you a worthy match in our inevitable marriage."

"In case you didn't get the message when I threw you from the tower, our engagement has been called off."

His laugh is heartier this time. "Hunger always did make you grumpy." He gestures to the plates between us. "Let's eat."

Torbin leans forward, grabbing his silverware and cutting into the slab of meat in front of him.

I wrinkle my nose and frown. I assumed the bloody meat was a rare, thick steak of some sort, but my mind starts processing where I am and what that could mean. The carnoraxis feed on human flesh and blood. Torbin has been ingesting carnoraxis potion, giving him their strength and rage. He has fangs that resemble their teeth. Who's to say the transformation doesn't also give him their hunger? Does he crave what they do?

My breath is trapped in my throat as repulsion churns my stomach. I inch back in my seat, trying to pull oxygen in past the bile rising in my throat. He wouldn't serve me human flesh, would he? My tongue turns dry. My stomach coils, and I brace myself against the rising nausea.

"Celeste."

I shoot my gaze at him, my nails clawing into my palms while I attempt to control my heartbeat.

His voice softens. "If I make you uncomfortable, that's not my intension."

"Liar."

"It's beef, Celeste."

"But you *do* feed humans to your creatures. You kill them for food or for sport or to get ahead in some political plot." My face grows hot

390

with anger. "How can you do that to innocent people?"

He sets down his silverware and folds his hands under his chin. "You say that as if it should matter to me."

"What?" I shake my head. "It *should* matter. Torbin, I know you. The real you. You have a heart. I've seen it in you."

His jaw tightens and he drops his hands, fingers splayed on the table. "I'm no longer that naïve child you befriended long ago, Celeste. I know now what gives a man power in this world. And it's not compassion."

"I disagree," I say, my voice steady, though the fire beneath my skin is threatening to break loose.

He sighs, his gaze traveling over my features. "Celeste, there is only one person I'm compassionate about. Only one person I want by my side as I rise to power. Only one person I want to share it all with."

"I don't care what you want."

He tilts his head. "You know, the tsar is convinced that your power is the key to ultimate control. Even if you are unwilling to give it to him, he will take it. But you don't have to be cast aside, Celeste. I will take care of you. I will shelter you, protect you. You could live a long life at my side, as my wife."

I retreat into my chair, prickles stabbing my skin. "That's not going to happen, Torbin."

"The tsar thinks differently, Your Highness." He takes a sip of his wine. "It was always your father's wish. After all, it was his idea. It was Axel who suggested the match to Silas. Wouldn't you want to carry through with your father's wishes?"

I inhale deeply, a sour feeling in my gut telling me Torbin is trying to reveal the truth to me.

I stand abruptly, the chair's legs scraping against stone.

Torbin's dark brows lift in faint amusement, but his grip on his goblet remains lax, unconcerned. The candlelight casts sharp lines across his face, accentuating the shadows beneath his eyes.

"I'm tired of this," I say. "You've alluded to the fact that the tsar is my father, but I want to see him face to face."

 391

Torbin exhales through his nose, swirling the dark liquid in his cup. The deep red stains the sides like something thicker than wine.

"Why?" he muses. "You don't trust my word?"

"No," I say bluntly. "You've sworn your loyalty to this man, but the man you describe doesn't sound like my father. I need proof."

The words are bold, but my stomach churns. I cannot believe my own father would want to use my power for his own greed.

Torbin taps a slow rhythm against the rim of his goblet, watching me. His eyes gleam in the dim light—calculating, searching for something in me.

Then, with a sigh, he pushes back his chair and rises. "If proof is what you require, then so be it."

The tension in the room coils tighter.

Torbin strides toward the balcony doors, his dark cloak sweeping behind him. He doesn't wait for me to follow.

I glance around once—at the untouched food, at the flickering candlelight, at the snowy land beyond the walls. Then I go.

The halls of Dulcamar's fortress breathe ice. Whatever magic I may have manifested to keep me warm has vanished. Each breath I take is a puff of frost in the air, my lungs burning with the cold. The stone corridors stretch endlessly ahead, silent and stifling. Two of his guards follow closely behind, ensuring I don't flee.

The deeper we go, the more warmth is swallowed whole, devoured by the ancient rock around us. The walls are rough-hewn, damp to the touch, veins of frost crawling across their surface like silver roots. Torches flicker dimly in iron sconces, their flames too weak to chase the chill.

My boots strike the stone floor with a hollow rhythm, each step echoing through the narrow halls, a metronome of dread. Torbin walks ahead of me, his pace unhurried, his back straight, hands clasped behind him. He doesn't speak—he doesn't need to. His confidence tells me this path is one he knows intimately.

My nerves feel grated. I need to get out of this trap. I try calling out again with my mind.

"Dante, please find me." The words pulse from my mind like a

whisper sent on the wind. *"Can you hear me?"*

Nothing.

No answering warmth. No flicker of connection.

Only silence.

"Please. Hear me. I'm still trying. I'm still fighting."

We round a final bend, and the corridor narrows. I stop when Torbin does, facing a tall, iron-banded door. Its surface is pitted with rust and age, frost masking its hinges.

I don't realize I've stopped breathing until I'm forced to draw in a sharp gasp.

This is it.

My fingers twitch at my sides. My body wants to turn around, to flee. But my mind won't let me.

My father could be alive.

He could be something worse.

The chamber beyond is wide but feels close, as if the walls themselves lean in to listen. Heavy drapes of deep-wine and moss-green velvet spill from the high windows, their fringes brushing warped floorboards the color of old blood. The air is thick—humid and sweet—with the scent of decaying roses and beeswax clogging to the back of my throat. Candles crowd every surface, balanced in iron candelabras, cradled in glass hurricane lamps, clustered on warped tables, each flame swaying in the sluggish draft, painting the room in swaths of molten gold and deep shadow. The walls disappear into darkness above, where the glimmer of a chandelier's crystal teardrops hangs like captured rain. Somewhere, faint and almost hidden, the slow drip of water marks the silence.

And in the center, a cloaked figure stands, facing away from me. As the figure turns, my breath hitches.

CHAPTER FORTY-NINE

This was not whom I expected. A woman stands before me, still as carved stone. A deep-red cloak pools at her feet, its hood casting her face in shadow. When she lifts her chin, candlelight skims over an intricate silver mask that hides everything from her brow to the tip of her nose, leaving only her mouth bare. Below it, full lips are painted the shade of fresh blood. Her presence is a tangible weight in the air, confident, deliberate, as if every movement has already been decided before she makes it.

"You're the seer," I say.

It feels as if her gaze were piercing straight through me.

"You can call me 'Ella.' We've been expecting you, Princess." Her voice is smooth, certain, and threaded with something that makes the fine hairs on my arms lift.

The words don't settle *over* me as much as they settle *into* me, making them impossible to shake off.

"Have you?" I manage, though my voice sounds smaller than I'd like it to.

The corner of her mouth lifts, not quite a smile, not quite a sneer.

"You've taken your time getting here."

I straighten my shoulders. "I've been busy."

A low, lilting hum slips past her lips—barely audible, but it slides under my skin like warm oil, coaxing my pulse into a slower rhythm. "The things you've been occupying yourself with are trivial. You are a special being with special purpose. And you belong here."

"I belong at the head of my regiment, protecting Terre Ferique from your monsters."

And I belong with Dante. At his side. Forever.

She doesn't answer right away, simply staring, as if measuring me. "The prophecy speaks of one with great power—power to change the tides of fate itself. I see that power in you. And I am going to help you use it... to change the world."

A chill ripples through me, not from fear of her words, but from the certainty that her idea of change is twisted. "Then it seems," I say evenly, "that our visions of the world are vastly different."

Her smile deepens, slow and knowing. "Perhaps. Or perhaps you simply haven't seen clearly yet."

"Or maybe you're not as good a seer as the rumors say you are. Because if you were any good at it, you would *see* I'm not going to cooperate."

The corner of her lips quirks upward. "Though you are a clever girl, there are some things you simply don't understand."

Before I can retort, footfalls echo behind me, measured and purposeful.

The seer glances over my shoulder, clasping her hands together and straightening her shoulders.

I swallow hard, steeling myself before turning around.

The man in the black-hooded cloak raises his head. Just a fraction. Enough for the candlelight to catch his bearded jaw, the line of his mouth.

My throat closes.

He lifts his hand in a single, smooth motion, grabbing the black fabric of his hood and pulling it back.

My knees nearly give out.

"No..." I whisper, but the word barely escapes.

He's older, shadows etched beneath his eyes. But it's unmistakably him.

My father.

Alive.

And in his eyes, there is no warmth. Only calculation and power and something that cuts deep.

Like betrayal.

I stagger back a step, my eyes welling with tears.

He is alive.

And he is the tsar.

I can't feel my hands. My pulse thunders in my ears, drowning out the hiss of the candles and the cold that bites at my skin.

My father is alive. Not a ghost or a myth. Not some charlatan in disguise. He stands before me, the same jawline that appears in dusty portraits hung in Delasurvia's castle halls. The same presence from my childhood that once made me feel safe.

But now, there's a coldness behind those eyes that makes me feel sick.

I shake my head slowly, as if I could dislodge the truth and make it untrue again. "I thought you were dead."

The words are so quiet, I'm not even sure I truly said them.

He regards me for what feels like forever before he finally speaks. "I was. In all the ways that mattered."

My breath stutters. "No," I say louder now. "No. You—" I step back, the stone floor solid beneath my boots, anchoring me before I fall. "You let the world believe you were gone. You let *me* believe it. And instead, you—" I gesture around at the fortress, the frozen rot of this place. "You became this."

He doesn't flinch.

"How could you be here all this time?" My voice trembles with anger. "Living all this time as the Shadow Tsar. I wanted to believe the tsar was just some monster. That it couldn't be you. Because that was

easier than thinking my father would ever become something so... so—
" I choke on the word. "Cruel."

His expression barely shifts. A twitch of his mouth. Not quite a smile. "I became what was necessary."

I stare at him, heart splintering, trying to reconcile the man I remember—golden and fierce and jovial—with the one in front of me now.

Torbin watches this exchange with thinly veiled satisfaction, clearly pleased with the drama unfolding—but I doubt he could understand the magnitude of this moment. How it's breaking me. His gaze flicks between us, hungry for the next words.

I steady my breath, forcing steel into my spine. "What exactly do you need me for?"

The question falls like a gauntlet at his feet.

He steps closer, slow and deliberate. The candles flare as he moves past, catching glints of silver at his sleeves, the hint of a blade at his side.

"You carry something precious," he says softly. "A power inside you that I need to access."

My stomach knots. Does he know that my mother hid our power? Does he know it's trying to break free?

My fingers curl into fists. "You think I'll help you?" I snap. "That I'll stand beside someone who slaughters villages and creates monsters? So you can make everyone bend the knee?"

A grim smile twists across his face, a look of conviction.

"You think too small, Celeste. I don't care about thrones. I care about reshaping the world."

"Well, I care about the people who live in it," I bite out. "And I will never support someone so callous, so malicious, so twisted as to become what you've become."

There's a beat of silence.

Then he says, almost gently, "You will."

My breath catches.

"Not because I ask," he continues. "But because there will come a day when you'll have no other choice."

A chill wraps around my spine—not from the room, but from the certainty in his voice.

I grit my teeth hard enough to ache. The pulse in my neck pounds, furious.

I could kill him.

Or at least hurt him enough to incapacitate him.

The thought doesn't come as a whisper this time; it hits like a blade unsheathed, bright and cold. I see it in my mind as clearly as if I've already done it: my energy ripping through him, his body crumpling, the tyranny ending with one, clean strike.

The memory of Mersos rises like a tide—the vines snapping under my command, their sharp recoil. I could snap him just the same. Bone instead of wood.

The buzzing inside me swells, sharp and electric, racing through my chest, into my fingertips. It's eager. Hungry. My hands twitch with the need to aim, to release.

I lock my eyes on him, already imagining the way he'll stagger when the force hits, the silence that will follow. The world would be free of him. Dante would be free. *I* would be free.

One heartbeat. That's all it would take. One heartbeat and—

Movement cuts through the air.

Ella glides forward from the shadows, her deep-red hood catching the light, silver mask gleaming. She tilts her head, like she's reading every thought in my skull, and then... she hums.

The sound is low, almost intimate, curling into my ears like smoke. At first, it's nothing—just a note hanging in the air—but then the melody snakes through me, winding into my ribs, my spine, my skull.

The fury dulls. The hunger fades. The buzzing sputters and dies, leaving only emptiness.

My legs weaken. My breath comes shallow, as if the hum has stolen the air itself. My limbs go heavy, sluggish, like they've been packed with wet sand.

A siren. My uncle warned me about a siren.

The thought barely forms before my knees buckle. Torbin's grip

 398

closes around my arms, catching me, keeping me upright.

The humming stops, but the silence she leaves behind feels worse—like she's carved my power out with a surgeon's precision and locked it away, just out of reach.

The tsar lifts a hand and gives a dismissive wave. "She's tired. Take her back to her chamber."

Torbin bows slightly, his hand still at my elbow.

Despite the weakness pulling me down, I jerk away. "I can walk," I snap.

The tsar doesn't watch me leave. He's already turning back toward the center of the chamber, the flickering light swallowing him once again.

The seer watches me intently as I make my way out of the room.

As the door shuts behind me, my head drops. I don't know if I'm mourning the man he was, or the one I wanted him to be. But either way, something inside me cracks.

Torbin leads me back through the frozen halls in silence, though I feel the weight of his gaze on me every few steps.

When we reach the door to my chamber, I stop short, planting my feet.

"I want to see Nadya," I say, my voice low but firm. "Where is she?"

He turns to face me, brow arching slightly. "You're in no position to make demands."

"She's my friend," I snap. "She's done nothing wrong—"

"She is fine," he cuts in smoothly, stepping closer. "You, on the other hand, have bigger things to worry about."

His smirk widens, and he turns the iron key in the lock. The door creaks open, and I take two steps inside.

When he follows, I stop short and whirl to face him. "What are you doing?"

His gloved hand rises—slowly, deliberately—and brushes a lock of hair behind my ear. The gesture is almost tender. Almost.

It takes every ounce of control I have not to flinch.

His eyes flick to mine, and something dark and possessive stirs

 399

there. He chuckles softly, seeing through my tough façade. "Everything is falling into place, Celeste. You'll see that soon enough. All you have to do is stop fighting it."

"You'll have to excuse me if I don't agree with you."

His eyes flit over my features as he clicks his tongue. "Be smart, my dear. You've already seen what happens when you go up against the seer. You wouldn't want to test my patience. Things could get rather... ugly."

I shake my head. "I'll take my chances. You've had a chance to kill me, but you haven't. So unless you're going to kill me right now, why don't you get the hell out of my room?"

For a moment, he simply stares at me, his expression unreadable. Then he leans in before I can pull away, his lips brushing my cheek in a mockery of affection. The touch curdles in my stomach.

I dip my head and recoil.

He lets out a small chuckle. "Sleep well, Celeste. We have lots to discuss in the morning." He steps back, watching me as he pulls the door closed.

After the sound of his footsteps diminish, I check the handle.

Locked.

Of course.

I stand frozen in the dim room, the silence pressing down on me like a second skin. The fire in the hearth has burned low, throwing soft, twitching shadows against the stone walls. I press a hand to my cheek, wiping away the ghost of Torbin's kiss as if it were filth. Then I walk to the small window, needing air I can't reach.

He's alive.

My father is alive.

The thought circles my mind like a vulture. It doesn't feel real. It can't be. And yet—I saw him. I heard his voice. I felt the gravity of his presence in my very bones.

He's not a rumor or a myth or a nightmare conjured by others. He's real. And he has become something I don't recognize.

Something I want no part of.

I think of what my uncle said. *"I can't prove it to be true. But I*

 400

believe your father killed your mother."

I hadn't wanted to believe him. Not then. Not even now.

But after tonight... how can I not?

I sink down to the cold, stone floor, pressing my back to the bedframe. My hands are trembling, rage and sorrow warping every breath I take.

Hot tears streak down my cheeks, leaving me with the last ounce of hope I had that my father was not some wicked fiend. I close my eyes and reach out—not with my hands, but with the quiet ache that lives deep beneath my ribs.

"Dante."

I don't know if he'll hear me, but I reach, anyway.

"Can you hear me?"

I picture his face, his hands, the warmth I felt when he held me. That quiet certainty that, even if no one else could save me, he would try.

"Dante, please."

Nothing.

Just the crackle of embers in the hearth and the howling wind outside.

Still... I wait.

Because some part of me—irrational and fragile and impossibly stubborn—believes he might hear it. Might feel it.

That somewhere, across the miles, his pulse has stuttered.

That the same ache I feel in my chest might echo in his.

 401

CHAPTER

FIFTY

Dante

I push my horse hard, Sir Holden and Sir Donovan riding close behind. It didn't take much convincing to get them to accompany me. Once they realized Celeste was truly missing, they threw themselves into the mission. My knuckles are raw against the reins, my jaw locked tight. By the time the Garrison's stone walls rise ahead, the wind has frozen my face, but it's nothing compared to the cold sinking deeper in my chest with every mile.

She's not at Ivystone.

She's not anywhere she should be.

The moment we pass through the gates, soldiers straighten, some bowing in surprise, others stepping aside as I swing down from the saddle. I don't waste time with pleasantries.

"Where's General Kormak?" I demand.

One of the guards nods toward the far end of the training yard, where Kormak stands with his arms folded, watching two of Celeste's squad members trade blows in the sparring ring. Mylo is there too, leaning against the railing with his usual quiet watchfulness, while Aila, Isaac, Giorgi, and Lorne linger nearby, their attention shifting as soon as they hear my tone.

Kormak's posture changes the second he sees my expression. He steps forward, boots crunching over the packed dirt, and the rest of the squad falls in behind him like a shadow.

"Prince Dante." His voice is even, but his eyes narrow. "What brings you here?"

"It's Celeste," I say, closing the distance. "She's gone."

The air around us seems to tighten. Mylo straightens, his jaw hardening.

"'Gone'?" Kormak asks.

"Her horse is still in the stables," I tell them, sweeping my gaze over each of their faces. "You know she would never leave Thora behind. She would never leave without telling me. Without informing any of you. This isn't her."

Kormak studies me, weighing the words. "Are you certain she didn't head out on some errand?"

I shake my head. "She wouldn't without letting someone know. And not for so long. We've just become—" I stop for half a second, making sure my next words land. "She's my betrothed. And I am honored beyond measure that she's to be my queen. But none of that will happen if she's dead."

Kormak's jaw tightens, the briefest crack in his composure. Concern, yes, but edged with something sharper.

"I think the tsar has her," I continue. "Even if it was Torbin who took her, he'd have taken her straight to the Shadow Tsar."

The name alone makes Kormak flinch, his gaze darkening as if shadows from another place have reached for him.

Isaac exchanges a look with Giorgi and mutters a curse under his breath.

Aila crosses her arms, her expression tight. "Last time you came to

us with something that sounded far-fetched, you turned out to be right. About Torbin. About the pit."

Mylo nods once, decisive. "If you say she's in danger, then we believe you. What do you need from us?"

"As many soldiers as the general can spare," I say without hesitation. "You. All of you. I want the entire squad. And anyone else willing to ride to Dulcamar with me. If you're willing."

Kormak's jaw flexes.

"You're fucking right, we're willing," Isaac says. "There is no Delasurvia without Celeste. It's our duty to rescue our queen."

"But there's more," I add, my voice hardening. "King Silas believes Celeste has broken our agreement. He told me that if she leaves Hedera, he will take Delasurvia by force. Which means if I'm right, and she's been abducted, he'll use her absence as an excuse to invade."

The squad exchanges grim looks. Mylo's jaw tightens, and Aila's brows draw together in a deep frown.

"You told him she might have been taken?" Mylo asks.

"I did," I say, bitter heat rising in my chest. "He won't hear it. He's convinced she acted against him, and nothing I say will change his mind."

Aila shakes her head sharply. "So we're fighting on two fronts—rescuing her and holding the king back from seizing her kingdom."

"Exactly." My gaze sweeps across them. "If we march into Dulcamar, the soldiers who stay behind will need to be ready to defend the castle, the Garrison—everything. Silas will see an opportunity and take it."

Lorne's voice is low but steady. "Then we make sure he doesn't get the chance."

Kormak nods once, the steel in his eyes matching my own. "I'll ready the soldiers. Some will march with us into Dulcamar. The rest will remain here to defend the capital if the king makes his move."

"I'll get the supplies," Giorgi shouts before scrambling off.

Kormak steps closer, his voice lowering so it's for me alone. "Are you sure about this?"

I meet his gaze without hesitation. "I *heard* her," I say, the words

rough in my throat.

It's faint—always faint—as though she were calling my name from the far end of a long, dark hall. Sometimes I almost think I've imagined it, that I'm chasing shadows in my own head. But it's there. And I can feel her. It's weak but so real. That tug. That thread that winds through my chest and pulls, ever so slightly, toward her.

Her voice is never clear. Never steady. Not like it was during the trials. And it kills me because if it's unclear, that means she's far. Farther than I can reach.

But distance doesn't matter. I would follow that pull to the ends of Terre Ferique, to the edge of the world, if it meant finding her. I'd ride until my body broke, search until my last breath, if that's what it takes to see her safe again.

"She's calling to me," I tell him. "She's in danger."

Something shifts in his expression—part recognition, part something darker. He studies me for a long moment before speaking.

"I know what it's like to be taken," he says quietly. "I know what waits on the other side of that darkness." His jaw hardens, his voice like tempered steel. "And I won't let what happened to me happen to her."

I nod and clap him on the back.

Relief cuts through me, but it's edged in fire.

Dulcamar has her. And we're going to tear the place apart until she's free.

CHAPTER

FIFTY-ONE

Celeste

My mother is bleeding.

The room is dark when the door is thrown open. My mother stands there, panting, holding a hand to her side as blood seeps through her fingers. She has a dagger in her grip as she sweeps her deep-brown hair out of her face.

I sit up, unable to slow the thrashing of my heart. "Mother?" My voice is from my past, when I was a child.

My mother slams the door and presses her back against it, panic twisting her features. Moonlight illuminates the tears running down her face.

She hurries closer in the darkness. "I'm sorry." She reaches out to me. "I'm sorry."

I think she means to embrace me, but I flinch from the sight of the blood on her hands.

The dagger is firm in her grasp. "I'm sorry. I can't let him take it from you."

"Mother, no!"

The dagger pierces my chest, and I let out a scream. I clutch the hilt, but my mother's hand is still holding it firm. Blood pools around the blade, and I'm in so much pain, I cannot move. I look up at my mother to see her eyes closed. She mumbles something in whispers too quiet to hear.

A vibration moves through me, pulling from every part of my body and compressing to the place where the dagger is embedded. I feel my veins tremble as if I'm being drained of my blood. My sobs are silent as I continue to stare at my mother.

Her red-rimmed eyes open, tears continuing to spill. She places a hand over my wound, her fingers flanking the blade as she slips it out of my chest. My jaw hangs open as a warm, tingling sensation fills my chest.

"He's dangerous," my mother whispers. "You don't know what he's capable of. He's already betrayed me."

My pain dissipates, but my mother's hand is still flush against my chest. "Mother?"

"I don't want to leave you without your powers, Celeste. But if he finds a way to take them, it would have dire consequences."

"Dahlia!" My father's voice roars through the castle, making my mother flinch.

"Quickly," she whispers to me, "change into a fresh nightgown. Hide this one. Go back to bed, and forget this ever happened."

She hurries from the room.

When the door slams behind her, I jerk forward and call for her. "Mother!"

But I'm no longer in my room. It takes a moment for my eyes to adjust to the darkness I find myself in.

The walls curve around me, smooth, damp, and glistening in the dim light. I blink, trying to force my eyes to adjust. I'm in... a tunnel.

The air bites at my lungs, thick with the scent of wet stone and something sharper, stranger, beneath it. Every inhale feels weighted,

every exhale a pale ribbon in the darkness.

Somewhere ahead, water drips in slow, deliberate intervals.

Drip.

Drip.

Drip.

Each sound ricochets off the stone like the echo of a clock, counting down to something unseen.

I hug my arms to my body, panic scraping at the edges of my mind. My pulse lurches. How far from my chamber have I wandered in my sleep? How far from safety?

The tunnel slopes downward, a jagged vein plunging into the earth. The stones beneath my feet form uneven steps. A faint draft stirs against my skin, carrying a chill that cuts deeper than the damp air before it. The hair along my arms lifts.

I turn, searching for the way back, but the shadows behind me are heavy and seamless, swallowing any sign of the path I came from.

My heartbeat hammers in my ears. I take a careful step forward, the stone beneath my boots slick with moisture.

The air shifts again. Growing warmer.

Too warm.

I frown, slowing my steps. How did I even get here? Torbin locked my chamber—I checked the door myself before bed. Did I...? The thought catches in my throat. Did I use my power without knowing? Could I have slipped through the lock in my sleep?

A shiver coils through me that has nothing to do with the temperature. If I can leave my room without realizing it, what else might I do?

Another step, and the warmth becomes oppressive. The scent changes—less like stone and more like something raw, something ancient.

I glance behind me, thinking of the way back to the castle. If I could find a way out, would I even survive the night air? Dulcamar's winter would slice right through a nightgown. My bare feet would freeze before I made it past the gates.

The temperature rises too quickly. For a moment, I think I'm making it happen, like the way I kept warm when Torbin made me come to his balcony dinner. But no, this feels different. My skin prickles; sweat gathers at my spine, my collarbone, the hollow of my throat. My breath catches, the thickened air scraping against it like grit.

The tunnel yawns into a cavern. The walls drip with condensation, but the floor—

I stop dead.

The stone beneath my feet is fractured, blackened as though fire once claimed it.

A faint, pulsing glow spills from the far end of the cavern, casting long, quivering shadows. My gaze locks on it.

Then I hear a sound that isn't the drip of water or the crackle of heat. Low. Deep. Resonant.

Like thunder rolling beneath the earth.

I draw a sharp breath. Something stirs within the glow—a slow, deliberate shift, the movement of something vast, a shimmer that doesn't move like flame. Two round shapes, each as large as my head, gleam from the shadows. At first, I think they're lanterns hung in some strange, high place, casting their silver light into the cavern. But they hover too still... and too alive.

The glow deepens, shifting like molten moonlight. Then they blink.

The motion is slow, deliberate. Not mechanical. Not human. A chill slices through the oppressive heat as the truth sinks in.

They're not lanterns. They're eyes. Silver. Serpentile. Luminous. Fixed on me.

My lungs forget their rhythm. My blood surges so fast, I can hear it rushing in my ears. Whatever it is, it doesn't feel like it's happy to see me.

I step back, my boot scraping over loose stone. The sound echoes, sharp in the stillness.

A heavy, growling exhale follows, dragging through the cavern like a rasp, bringing with it the scent of brimstone and sulfur.

Shouts ring out. "She's here!"

Torches flare, flooding the edges of the cavern with light. I whirl, but before I can run, hands clamp around my arms, iron-tight, dragging me back into the tunnel's darkness.

A gasp tears from me, my feet stumbling over slick stone as the cavern recedes.

I turn my head to find Osrem glaring at me beside the Dulcamaran guards who hold me tightly.

"Going somewhere, Your Highness?" His voice is laced with bitter cruelty.

I'm not given a chance to answer. The guards drag me through the tunnel, back to where I came from. The last thing I hear—over the pounding of my heart—is the slow, deliberate scrape of something massive shifting in the shadows behind me.

CHAPTER FIFTY TWO

A pale-grey light filters through the narrow window, casting long shadows across the stone floor. The fire has long since died out, and the air in the room is thick with cold. I sit on the edge of the bed, wrapped in the same gauzy blanket they gave me days ago. Soft but thin. Decorative. Like everything here, comfort is an illusion.

I haven't slept. Not really. My thoughts have spun too fast to catch. My father is the tsar. The man I once imagined was brave and noble and dead. It turns out he's none of those things. And he's keeping something monstrous in the caves beneath the fortress.

A secret weapon?

He's created carnoraxis, so I wouldn't put it past him to have another beast to terrorize Terre Ferique.

My thoughts keep drifting back to the night before. To the way the cold stone seeped through the thin soles of my feet in that tunnel, the heat blooming at the end of it, the silver eyes blinking in the dark. And the fact that I wasn't even meant to be there.

I've only ever sleepwalked when I've gone without Ezra's powder. I've been without it for days now. Here, there's no familiar jar tucked into my satchel, no chalky bitterness on my tongue before bed to keep me anchored. No one to shake me awake before I wander somewhere dangerous.

And in Dulcamar, *everywhere* is dangerous.

The thought makes my skin prickle. If it happened once, it could happen again. And next time... I might not make it back to this room. Or worse, they might find me before I wake.

I try to imagine finding my way out of this place in a half-dream state, but I've never seen the fortress from the outside—only the blinding white drifts through the arrow-slit windows. Even if I did somehow stumble past Torbin's locks and guards, I wouldn't get far in the freezing night. Not barefoot. Not in a nightgown thin enough for the wind to cut through.

A soft knock at the door jerks me upright.

For a moment, I'm afraid it's Torbin. But it's Staja who slips inside, a bundle of fabric in her arms.

She closes the door quickly behind her, her eyes flicking to the corners, like she's being watched—even though we're alone.

"Good morning," she says gently. "Can you still understand me?"

"Yes."

She smiles and nods, then crosses the room and sets the clothes down on the chair beside the hearth. My gaze catches on the deep-green wool of the tunic; the sturdy, brown trousers; the thick, grey shawl lined with fur. Not silk. Not sheer. Not a dress meant to humiliate or seduce. Real clothes, thank the gods.

"You're letting me dress like a person today," I murmur.

She doesn't look at me. "He gave no orders on what you should wear this morning. I took the liberty."

My brows lift. "And that's allowed?"

She pauses just slightly, her back still turned. "Not usually."

I rise from the bed and step closer to the clothes, letting my fingers ghost over the fabric. It's soft, warm. Meant for travel. Meant for someone who might need to run.

I glance at her again.

She stands with her hands folded in front of her, shoulders stiff, face carefully neutral. But something flickers there—beneath the surface. Something that makes me choose my next words more carefully.

"I appreciate it," I say, quiet but sincere.

Her gaze flicks to me briefly, and in it, I see something unexpected. Kindness.

I sit slowly in the chair and begin to pull on the new clothes. She waits, respectfully turning her back.

"Staja," I say after a long silence. "Why are you here?"

She stiffens.

I keep my tone casual. Gentle. "Yesterday, you said that it would be better for *both* of us if I listened. Which tells me you're not here by choice."

For a moment, I think she won't answer.

Then, softly, she says, "My husband and son serve the tsar. But they serve him under threat." She turns her head, just enough for me to see her profile. "If I disobey any orders... if I help anyone defy him... he said he will turn them into beasts."

I freeze. He'll turn them into carnoraxis if she dares step out of line. A bitter weight settles in my stomach.

"I'm sorry," I say, and I mean it. "I didn't realize—"

"No one does. No one realizes the extremes he's taken to force others into obedience. That's how he keeps control."

I take in the tension in her shoulders, the faint tremble of her hands. "How long have you been here?"

Her gaze is fixed on the fire. "Longer than I ever meant to be."

"You were taken?"

"No," she says. "Not taken. Trapped."

She draws in a slow breath and exhales it just as quietly.

"I used to live in Bastos," she adds, almost wistfully. "It was always warm there. The heat soaked into your bones, stayed with you. The food was better. The people laughed more. I miss it... Not just the freedom, but the heat. The cold here never leaves you."

My eyes widen. "Bastos?"

She nods again. "My husband and I had a market stall in the old capital. Spices, mostly. That was before."

"Before what?"

Her lips press together. "Before the tsar's men came. They were in Bastos to have an audience with the queens. But some of them were making the rounds, growing their army. They took us, promising my husband and son 'positions of value.' But things changed when we got here, and I became the tsar's servant, whether I wanted to or not."

There's bitterness in her voice now. Quiet, but real.

"Wait." I shake my head. "If you're from Bastos, why can't you speak the common language?"

"We are forbidden." She swallows hard. "The seer... She is a siren, and she used her magic to make our tongues forget. We can't physically form the words."

"But why?"

"Just another way of controlling us."

I blink, my gaze dropping to the floor as I try to wrap my head around this. Was this so the people trapped here couldn't get word out to their families outside of Dulcamar? "You were here when she arrived?"

"She came with him," Staja says, glancing at the door before lowering her voice further. "When the Shadow Tsar took the throne from the old ruler, the seer was already at his side. They arrived in Dulcamar together."

The words land oddly in my chest. My father... and a siren? It's a pairing that shouldn't exist. He never trusted sirens, so why bring one here? Why keep her close?

The thought turns over in my mind like a jagged stone. Could she be controlling him? Steering his war, his hunger for power, his... interest in me?

I can almost hear her voice from the chamber where we first met— low, certain, brimming with confidence. *"We've been expecting you."*

A chill runs over my arms that has nothing to do with the cold.

"Do you think the prophecy is true?" I ask.

Staja exhales slowly. "Prophecies tend to hold truth, yes. But often, there is a chance for someone special to change them. But she believes it, and she's convinced the tsar it's true. She's why he believes he's destined to rule everything. Why he's doing all this. The war. The blood. You."

"I don't even know what the full prophecy says," I admit. "Only fragments."

Her voice takes on a rhythmic cadence, like she's speaking something memorized long ago. *"Power taken by force in the heart of Dulcamar shall shape the world anew. He who wields it shall stand above all, unchallenged in dominion, unbroken in will. But to reign eternal, the magic gifted by the gods to a powerful descendant, must be seized, torn from its vessel, and bound anew. Yet beware—one of fae blood, third-born of kin, shall rise as the harbinger of ruin and bring the fall of he who seeks to command the world."*

The words wrap around me like a tightening snare. Third-born of kin. The harbinger of ruin.

Does she not know?

I search Staja's expression for some clue, but she offers none. Could the seer be oblivious to the truth of who I am because my magic is trapped, dormant in ways it shouldn't be? Or is it something simpler? That she's relying on the fact that Axel only had two children, never knowing my mother had a child before she married him, and therefore does not see me as a third-born fae?

But a darker thought stirs, uncoiling in the back of my mind—what if she *does* know, and she's holding it close, biding her time until it serves her? What if Torbin knows, too?

The door swings open without warning.

Torbin steps inside, his presence filling the space like a shadow. He's dressed immaculately in a dark-crimson doublet, his golden hair combed back from his face, every button and thread in place. No sign of a sleepless night. No crease of guilt or weight of a thousand deaths etched into his posture.

His eyes narrow, sweeping over me from head to toe. The weight of his gaze is sharp, assessing—not just my body, but something deeper, like

he's looking for cracks in the mask I wear.

I force myself to meet his stare, my spine straightening even as my pulse spikes. His scrutiny lingers on my face a moment too long, and I can't shake the prickle at the back of my neck—the sense that he's searching for something *he already suspects.*

Finally, his mouth curves, not into a smile, but something colder. "Good morning, Princess." His tone is flat but edged. "I won't bother to ask how you slept. Osrem tells me you wandered from your room last night."

He doesn't know about my night wanderings. He doesn't know about the powder Ezra gave me to keep me from leaving my bed at night. He probably thinks I was trying to escape.

"It goes without saying, Celeste, but you would be a fool to think you could escape from the fortress."

I gather my resolve and square my shoulders. "Did you just come here to reprimand me, or is there something else you needed?"

He lifts his chin, his posture infuriatingly relaxed. "Breakfast is being served. The tsar would like your company."

I suppress a flinch. The tsar. The man who betrayed his family.

"I'll go," I say evenly, "but only if you let me see Nadya."

His jaw tightens subtly. "Fine. But first, you're expected by the tsar."

I narrow my eyes. "Fine."

He offers his arm.

I don't take it.

We walk in silence, Torbin's boots clicking in measured rhythm against the stone. The corridors grow darker as we move deeper into the fortress, the torches spaced wider apart, their flames struggling against the cold draft that snakes through the hall.

The dining hall is cavernous, its vaulted ceiling lost in shadow. Tall, narrow windows line one wall, their black panes rimmed in frost, the morning light leaking through in pale streaks. Iron chandeliers hang above the long table, their candlelight casting jagged shadows across the walls. The scent of smoke and cold steel lingers beneath the richer smells of roasted meat and spiced wine.

The seer is there—Ella—hood drawn low, the silver mask catching a glint of the weak sunlight. She stands apart from the table, gazing out one of the windows as if waiting for something only she can see. Her stillness is eerie, deliberate, as though she were listening to the heartbeat of the world.

At the head of the table sits the tsar. His posture is easy, almost casual, as he cuts into a slab of venison with measured, unhurried strokes. When his eyes meet mine, his mouth lifts into something that could almost be mistaken for warmth.

"Sit," he says, gesturing to the chair on his right. "I trust you slept well, daughter."

I lower myself into the seat, the wood cold beneath me. "Don't call me that."

Torbin moves to the opposite side of the table and takes his place without a word. The scrape of silverware is loud in the silence that follows.

I stare at the table, tracing the carved edges of my plate, but the images from my dream—the truth—burn behind my eyes. My mother's blood on her hands. Her voice, trembling and fierce. "*He's dangerous. He's already betrayed me.*"

The words are out before I can second-guess them. "Did you kill my mother?"

His fork stills. He sets it down with care, the clink of silver against porcelain far too soft for the weight of the moment.

"Nothing," he says slowly, "will get in the way of my destiny, Celeste. Not my wife. Not even my daughter."

A coldness spreads through me, sinking deep into my bones. It's the kind of chill that no fire can touch. Hatred stirs at the edges of it, sharp and certain. Whatever faint hope I might have had—that some part of him could be reasoned with, reached—dies right there between us.

The seer doesn't turn from the window, but I feel her attention like a thread pulled taut. She's listening. Measuring. Torbin lifts his glass, his eyes on me as he takes a sip.

I will not cry in front of them.

But the tears well, anyway, pressing hot against the backs of my eyes—not just for my mother, whose blood I see as vividly as if it were still fresh, but for the hatred taking root in my chest. Hatred for the man who sits before me, eating his breakfast as though he hasn't just admitted to destroying everything that should have bound us as kin.

My gaze drifts to Ella. "Did you do it of your own will," I ask quietly, "or did she make you?"

The tsar's knife hovers above his plate. He doesn't answer.

"I thought you hated sirens," I press, my voice sharpening. "Banned them from setting foot in our land. Imprisoned them. Killed them."

His mouth curves faintly, not in amusement, but in something colder. "Ella is different. She opened my eyes to the truth. Showed me what I am destined to become."

My nails bite into my palms beneath the table. "And how do you know she wasn't manipulating you? That she isn't still?"

His gaze hardens, that faint curl of his lip deepening into disdain. "Because unlike you, I can see beyond the narrow scope of a single lifetime. I see the shape of the ages, the rise and fall of empires. You look at what is and think it will always be. I look at what will be and shape it into reality."

My pulse spikes. "What I see," I say, my voice cutting through the space between us, "is you destroying everything you touch. Creating monsters that feed on humans. Tearing apart villages. Destroying families. Waging war on the realms as if their ruin were your birthright."

His chair scrapes violently against the stone as he shoves it back, the sound shattering the air like a blade drawn. "You are as small-minded as your mother."

I rise too, holding my ground. "And you can't count on your so-called destiny," I snap. "Because I will never help you."

His eyes flash. He doesn't waste breath arguing further. Instead, he calls sharply for his guards.

For a heartbeat, I don't realize what's happening until rough hands seize my arms.

The tsar strides toward the door without looking back. "Bring her along."

Torbin falls into step behind my father.

The guards drag me after them. I twist against their grip, my boots scraping over the cold, stone floor. "Get off me!"

The seer turns then, finally pulling her gaze from the window. Her steps are soundless as she follows, her head tilting the slightest degree.

A hum slips from her lips—low, resonant, and impossibly smooth.

The sound slides into my skin like warm water, pooling in my bones, winding through my veins. My power, which had been simmering hot and wild beneath my ribs, ebbs away in an instant.

My knees weaken. My resistance falters.

CHAPTER FIFTY-THREE

The guards jerk me forward, hands tight on my arms, dragging me through the endless marble halls. My feet scrape against the cold stone, the echoes of our steps bouncing off the high ceilings. Every ornate carving, every gilded frame, every flickering torch seems to mock me, like the tsar designed these halls to remind me I'm already trapped.

"Where are you taking me?" I demand, my voice trembling more from fury than fear. My question hangs in the air, unanswered.

The tsar glances back, lips curling in that infuriatingly calm smile. "Somewhere you will understand the weight of your choices," he says, his tone silk over steel.

I bite back a sharp retort, forcing my mind to reel with possibilities. My chest tightens, a coil of dread and rage twisting in my stomach. I have to survive. I have to make it through this.

He steps closer, his presence dominating the narrow hallway. "With your gift—your energy, your potential—I could be unstoppable. I could rule without challenge. Unite the fractured realms under one banner."

I look past him at Torbin, but he doesn't seem to oppose my father's plan. Of course not. He's banking on being part of it.

The guards jerk my arms again, and I stumble, catching myself just in time. I glare at the tsar, trying to hide the heat of my anger.

"And in exchange for you giving me your gift," he continues, "you will be allowed to live—with Torbin as your mate. You would be given lands of your own. Freedom. Status. The wealth of ten kingdoms. You could have more than Delasurvia ever gave you."

I let out a slow, measured breath, forcing my hands to stop trembling. My blood is a fire I cannot release here, not while the guards hold me like a prize. Not when the seer can stop me with one breath. Freedom, status, wealth... all of it is worthless if I'm not myself. If my power is gone.

And of course, with Torbin bonded to me as my husband, the tsar would be assured that I remember my place. That I don't step out of line.

"You want to rip the magic out of me," I say, the words razor-sharp, "and you think *you're* doing *me* a favor?"

He inclines his head, almost kindly. "I think I'm giving you a choice."

"No," I spit, the cold truth lancing from my tongue. "You're giving me a fucking ultimatum."

The tsar's eyes sharpen, but his composure remains eerily calm. "I had hoped you'd see reason. But my seer is a master of her craft. She has told me your power can be removed with or without your consent."

A tremor ripples through my chest, but I press my lips together, forcing my jaw rigid. *Without my consent...* He would take it, anyway. But he underestimates me if he thinks that frightens me.

His gaze hardens further. "Let's see how far your resolve carries you if you refuse, dear daughter."

The guards drag me to a set of massive double doors. They swing open to reveal a balcony high above a vast arena. My stomach drops as they shove me forward to the balustrade. I grasp the stone, looking down over the expanse below.

The arena sprawls like an amphitheater, ringed with iron cages, each one holding a snarling carnoraxis. Their eyes gleam in the dim torchlight, their claws scraping against the bars with an almost musical rhythm of

menace.

My gaze sweeps the empty ground below. Why here? What does he want me to see?

Then, with a sudden clang, the gates at the far end of the arena swing open. A dozen—no, more than a dozen—Dulcamaran citizens are shoved forward, herded by guards with long spears. Some stumble; some cling to each other in panic. Tears streak faces already pale with fear. I see a small child pressing her face against her mother's chest, shaking. Others huddle together, whispering prayers or sobbing outright.

My heart hammers against my ribs. My chest tightens so sharply, I can barely draw a breath.

Oh, fuck! No!

My stomach twists with dread. I glance across the arena again, taking in the terrified citizens pressed together in the center.

Torbin stands at the edge of the balcony, his posture rigid, expression unreadable—but there's no fear in his eyes. Only cold calculation. He watches the chaos with a detached interest, as if he belongs here, as if he agrees with the tsar's methods.

I could stop this. I could end the bloodshed now, if I just tell him that I'm the third-born fae he's been searching for. Just one sentence could change the fate of these people. But I have to choose: the fate of the few versus the fate of the many.

No. My uncle's words echo: *"He will kill you if he finds out. And if he kills you—the one who is supposed to end his reign—then our hope is lost. And the precious realms will die, anyway."*

My chest tightens. I can't do it. I can't give him that power. I have to survive. I have to find another way.

I glance down, trying to muster the fire inside me. I can feel it, coiled, ready to surge—but the tsar's seer, standing a few paces behind him, watches me closely. If I try anything, she'll use her siren magic to stop me.

Then the iron gates of the carnoraxis' cages clang open, and a low, growling roar fills the space. The beasts leap forward, claws scraping the stone, teeth bared. Panic erupts among the citizens. Mothers scream,

children cry, people scatter and hold fast to each other.

I launch my hands forward, trying to channel energy, to create a shield, to throw the beasts back—but the seer releases a low hum, blocking my magic instantly. It's like hitting a wall of ice, and for a moment, I can't even breathe.

"No!" I cry out, but the sound is swallowed by the din of screams. My stomach twists.

The carnoraxis surge, teeth snapping, tearing flesh, splattering blood, ripping body parts to shreds. I cannot stop them. I cannot fucking stop them. A mother holds her child's hands tightly, shrieking at the top of her lungs as one of the beasts tears the panicked child away from her with its claws. Her bellowing stops when another creature rips out her throat. The citizens' faces are etched with pure terror—and my hands tremble.

I can't—

I can't—

I can't do anything. And I can't look.

I close my eyes and turn my head, a reflex born of helplessness, of desperation to avoid seeing the slaughter I cannot prevent.

The tsar's voice cuts through my panic, smooth, merciless, as he nears until he's close to my ear. "Think carefully, my dear. Refuse to give me your powers, and the terror will continue. I would hate to see poor Nadya brought here as a consequence."

My stomach drops again. My mind freezes on the thought of her face, the innocence she carries, and I can feel my resolve waver—not in giving in to him, but in how I can survive to protect her.

Torbin's calm footfalls sound behind me, steady and deliberate. My eyes flutter open to glare at him. He makes no move to intervene; no flicker of doubt crosses his features. He stands with the tsar, a quiet reminder that some of those I thought I could count on are part of this trap.

"I think I've made my point," the tsar says. "Take her away."

 423

CHAPTER FIFTY-FOUR

'm barely aware of Torbin stomping down the corridor behind us until he speaks.

"I'll take it from here." His hand grasps my bicep and yanks me away from the guards.

Tears are streaming down my face, and my body is shaking. My heart is breaking for the people in the arena. I can only hope their deaths were quick, their suffering cut short.

But heartbreak is quickly overshadowed by the absolute rage ablaze inside my blood. Rage surging because of the tsar's heartlessness. Rage boiling because of the seer manipulating him. And because of Torbin betraying me.

I try to pull away from him, but he's too strong. "You promised me I could see Nadya."

He lets out a humorless laugh. "You're in no position to be making demands, Princess."

I wipe away the tears I'm unable to stop from flowing. "Why are you doing this? What can you possibly gain? The tsar will destroy everything. You're only making enemies. If you think the realms are going to let him get away with this... You'll be on the wrong side of a world-changing war."

His eyes are cold when he glares at me. "You're mistaken. I'll be on the victorious side. And I don't fucking care what the other realms think of me, because I will be the one with power, not them."

I sniff back the last of my tears. "Gods, Torbin. What happened to you? How did you become this way? What happened to the Torbin I used to know? He's in there somewhere, isn't he?"

For a fraction of a second, he stiffens. "Nice try, Princess. That boy you befriended was the weakest part of me. If you're looking for redeeming qualities in me, there's only one that should concern you."

"And what's that?"

"There's a place in my heart for you, a part of me that longs to keep you by my side. Our friendship turned into something more when you came to Hedera."

"And you think I should overlook everything else because of that? You think I could love the monster you've become?"

"This is the better version of me."

I gnash my teeth. "It seems the only version of you that would be best is the dead version."

His nostrils flare. In one swift motion, he seizes my arms and yanks me toward him, his grip bruising. I twist, thrash, trying to wrench free, but his fingers dig deeper.

"I'm stronger than you, Princess."

I bare my teeth, rage rising like a tide in my throat. "But I'm more pissed."

I slam my elbow into his ribs, but he only grunts, shoving me back until my shoulders crash against the wall. The cold stone bites into my spine. His breath ghosts hot across my cheek as he leans close, inhaling.

"Stop—" My voice catches as he lowers his face to the curve of my neck, breathing me in like some starving beast. I push at his chest, nails scraping, but his body is solid, immovable.

"You reek of power," he whispers, his lips brushing my skin. "Gods, you always have."

Revulsion twists my stomach. His mouth grazes my throat, trailing

 425

down until his lips press to my skin in a rough, claiming kiss. I thrash harder, panic sparking with every second of his touch.

"Don't—" My cry rips into a snarl as his hands roam, pressing against me, trying to pin every frantic movement.

One of his hands snake around to cup my ass as the other holds my jaw. His mouth crashes against mine, lips untamed.

Fury surges. I squirm away enough to break the unwanted kiss, then reel back and slap him, the crack sharp, echoing between us. His head jerks to the side, his cheek reddening, but instead of retreating, his eyes darken, hunger flaring.

"You shouldn't have done that," he growls.

His mouth opens, his fangs sharp and merciless as they sink into my neck.

I scream, the sound raw, strangled. Fire shoots through my veins, hot and sharp, the sting of betrayal and pain colliding all at once. My knees buckle, but fury keeps me upright. With everything in me, I summon the smallest spark of power, just enough to blast him back.

A wave of energy bursts from my palms, snapping against his chest. He stumbles, hissing, my blood still wet on his lips. My breath comes in ragged gasps, my hands trembling as I grab the burning wound at my neck.

For a heartbeat, he just stares at me—his chest heaving, lips curled back. His eyes dart across my face, as if he can't comprehend that I dared strike him. Then the disbelief curdles into monstrous anger, his expression twisting, every muscle in his face taut with rage and hunger.

"Unlock her room," he snarls at a nearby guard, his voice guttural, shaking with restraint.

I'm unsure of what he means until the guard obeys, fumbling for the keys and sliding it into the lock of the nearby door.

Nadya's room! I hold on to the hope that I will be able to see my friend.

Torbin's eyes cut back to me, feral and starving, his lips curling into something between a warning and a promise. "Go ahead and see your friend," he says, his voice low, dangerous. "But whatever you do... you should step away from me. I don't know how much longer I can resist the smell of your blood."

The door creaks open, and I force my legs to move, every step swaying under the pull of blood loss. My neck throbs, warm liquid seeping down my collar, staining the fabric. The hallway blurs, walls tilting, until at last, I stumble through the threshold.

"Celeste?" Nadya's voice breaks on my name. She's on her feet in an instant, skirts rustling as she rushes to me.

I collapse against her, the last of my strength draining away. My head finds her shoulder, her hands clutching my arms tight to keep me from crumpling to the floor. I lift my gaze with effort, the world hazy, her face the only thing that stays clear.

"You're alive," I whisper, the words slipping from my lips with what little breath I can manage. Relief burns through the pain, a fragile comfort. "Gods... you're alive. Oh, Nadya, I'm so sorry I didn't listen to you about the note."

She gently shushes me, her arms wrapping around me. My knees buckle, and Nadya lowers us both, cradling me as if I were made of glass. Her hand presses against my neck, trying to stem the flow, her body trembling beneath me.

"Stay with me, Celeste," she mumbles, her voice thick with panic, breaking into fragments as she rocks me in her arms. "Don't you dare leave me."

She mumbles something more. I can't understand it, but it's rhythmic and somehow filled with a hum. The sound of her voice fades, swallowed by the darkness closing in. I let go, sinking into it, into a consuming darkness.

Someone is stroking my hair as my eyes flutter open. For a second, I flinch, not knowing where I am or who's touching me. But then I realize it's Nadya, and my shoulders relax.

"Nadya?"

Her voice wavers as she helps me sit up. "Celeste...what happened to you? Gods, you're covered in blood. Did someone—did they use a dagger on you?"

I shake my head faintly, fingers trembling as they rise to my neck. The skin is closed, smooth now—only tender bruising left beneath Nadya's touch. "No. It wasn't a blade." I swallow, the taste of iron still permeating my tongue. "It was Torbin. He has fangs, Nadya. Like the carnoraxis."

Her hand freezes in my hair, her eyes wide with horror. "Fangs? But... how—"

"The elixir," I rasp. "He... He's gone feral. Wasn't even himself. He fought me, and then he bit me. Tore into my neck like—" My voice falters, heavy with the memory.

Nadya presses her lips together, as if to swallow down her own revulsion. "Oh, Celeste."

"How am I healed? Did you...?" My words stumble out raw, my throat aching.

She nods.

"But how were you able to? Even with fae magic, it shouldn't be possible. Not that fast. That bite—he nearly..." The sentence trails into silence, my chest too tight to finish it.

Nadya offers me a shaky smile, though her hands don't stop smoothing over my hair, as if reassuring herself I'm really here. "I've been practicing. I don't know why, but lately, it feels like my magic listens to me better than it used to. It's stronger, sharper. And I've been thinking that if I can use it on you, maybe I can use it to get us out of here."

My heart lurches. "You think it's enough to escape?"

Her gaze falters, the briefest waver in her face before resolve hardens it again. "It has to be. I can't just sit here waiting for them to hurt you again."

I push myself up slowly, ignoring the dizziness that swirls around me. "We have to have a concrete plan."

She nods, her eyes far away, as if she's already summoning ideas.

"Nadya—there's more. There's a seer, and she's working with the tsar. They're preparing some kind of ritual to take my magic. Rip it out of me. Can it even be done like that?"

Nadya's brow furrows. "Stealing magic like that...it shouldn't be possible. But there's so much about magic I have yet to learn. It would take a very powerful sorceress."

"I think she must be powerful. It would make sense that a seer like that would be working with the tsar." I swallow hard, and this time, the metallic taste has subsided. "There might be more to this than we thought, though."

"What do you mean?"

I shift to face her fully and tell her about the cavern, about the massive shape I saw beneath stone and ice. The eyes glowing in the darkness. "At first, I didn't know what it was. Something buried. Something alive. But then I remembered the old stories—about the sleeping dragons."

Her breath catches. "The sun dragon and the moon dragon? Gods. Celeste, if that's true..."

"I think the tsar means to wake it. That has to be his ultimate weapon. He doesn't just want to rule the world; he wants everyone in Terre Ferique to fear him. And with a dragon—"

"He could do that," Nadya whispers, horrified. She leans closer, gripping my arm. "But I remember reading about dragons, and they need someone magical to bond with, someone they'll choose. They don't just...obey."

A shiver runs down my spine. "So you're saying he can't control it. Not without someone like me."

Her silence is answer enough.

My stomach knots. "Does he know? Does the seer know? Or Torbin? Is that why they want my magic so badly—because they think they can bend a dragon to their will if they steal my magic?"

Nadya shakes her head, fear and fire mingling in her gaze. "Maybe. Or maybe they're desperate enough to try, even if it kills you. But if they succeed... Celeste, imagine what the tsar could do with a dragon bound to him."

I can imagine it all too well—and the thought threatens to unravel me.

CHAPTER FIFTY-FIVE

The air smells of frost and iron, so cold, it burns the inside of my nose when I breathe. I sit on the edge of the bed, the chipped porcelain cup cradled in my hands, steam curling from the dark liquid within. The translation tea is bitter on my tongue, but it warms me, warding off the chill that forever saturates this cursed keep. My mind keeps circling the night that Torbin bit me.

When I had told Nadya what the tsar and seer had planned, she insisted we try something—anything—before they came for me. Her hands trembled as she traced symbols into the air above my chest, her voice low and steady despite the uncertainty in her eyes. *"It's a protection spell,"* she said. *"I don't know if it will work. I've never done one before. But maybe...maybe it will make a barrier. Keep the seer from stealing your magic."*

I agreed, because what else was there to do? We had no way of knowing if it worked, no visible sign, no spark or shimmer of light. Just the quiet of her magic settling over me like a second skin. Exhaustion claimed us soon after, and we drifted into uneasy sleep side by side.

In the morning, rough hands tore me from Nadya's room. My heart lurched, certain they were dragging me to the tsar himself, to the ritual we both feared. But instead, they shoved me into my own chambers and locked the door.

Days have passed since then. I've not been allowed to leave. Staja would bring trays of food and tea, but otherwise, I had no contact with the outside. No summons, no explanations. Only silence. I tried time and again to call out to Dante telepathically, but the sensation of him hearing me never came. I feel utterly alone. The walls are starting to feel like a tomb, and my thoughts rattle endlessly inside it.

Only Staja's whispered visit offered me a clue. "The tsar is planning something," she murmured, eyes darting nervously toward the guards. "But no one knows what. It's being kept very secret."

That was enough. Enough for me to imagine the worst. Enough for me to picture dark circles of salt and blood, words of binding, power torn from my veins whether Nadya's spell held or not.

And now I wait. I set aside the tea and walk to the window, pressing my palms against the cold glass and wracking my brain for some way to break free before it's too late.

"Dante, please, hear me. Find me."

Beyond the barred window, dusk settles heavy and low, casting the snow-blanketed landscape in bruised hues of violet and grey. Nothing here feels alive, just frostbitten stone and the skeletal remains of trees, their branches clawing at the sky like brittle fingers begging for mercy.

The muffled clatter of wheels grinding over ice and gravel breaks the silence. Hooves crunching frost. Voices carried thin on the wind, low and somber. I stand on my tiptoes and strain to see where the noise is coming from. When I peer between the bars, I spot them.

A procession of shadowed figures, cloaked in thick, black wool, moving in tight formation as they disembark from a line of carriages so dark, they seem carved from onyx. There's no music, no laughter—only the methodical cadence of boots meeting frozen earth. They move like mourners on their way to a grave, not guests arriving for a celebration.

A prickle runs down the back of my neck.

I'm still straining to make sense of it when the door creaks open behind me. I whirl, heart stammering in my chest.

Staja enters, carrying a bundle of folded fabric draped over her arms, her expression drawn tight with unease.

"What is it?" I demand, stepping away from the window. "What's going on?"

She hesitates, gaze flitting nervously to the door, as if she expects someone to be listening. "I've been sent to help you prepare, Your Highness."

"Prepare for what?"

A flicker of pity crosses her face, but she doesn't answer. She simply steps forward and lays the garments on the bed with reverent care. The dress is finer than anything I've been given since arriving here—black velvet trimmed in deep crimson, the bodice stitched with gleaming thread that shimmers like garnet in the low light. A matching mask sits atop the fabric, glossy and shaped like the delicate bones of a raven's face, with crimson ribbon meant to tie it at the back.

"Why?" I press. "What is all this for?"

"I don't know," she murmurs. "I'm just doing as I was told."

My hands curl into fists, frustration tightening my jaw. "Right. Of course." I pick up the dress, the heavy velvet cold to the touch. "And Nadya? Have you seen her? Is she all right?"

"She's fine," Staja says, her voice soft but certain. "She'll be joining you this evening."

I blink. "Joining me for what? Is that why all those people are arriving? Some kind of event?"

The servant nods faintly. "I think so. The kitchens have been working all day, and we've been told to ready the ballroom."

I swallow hard. Maybe this is part of it. The tsar wants to put on a show when the seer steals my power and gives it to him. He wants Dulcamar to witness his transformation.

I dress without Staja's help, though she moves to assist me with the back lacing. The velvet embraces my body, molding to my curves, the crimson threading gleaming like spilled wine. I set the mask aside, unwilling to wear it just yet—it feels too much like a trap disguised as finery.

As Staja smooths the folds of the skirt, I glance toward the barred

 433

window again, listening to the procession still filing into the keep. They seemed like they were attending a celebration, but no part of this feels like a celebration. It feels like a noose tightening, one loop at a time.

As Staja draws the last tie on my bodice and begins pinning up my hair, I close my eyes and reach for that familiar thread of connection— the one that hums faintly beneath my skin, somewhere deeper than blood, deeper than bone.

"Dante."

I whisper his name in my mind, like I have been for the past week. Whatever magic stirs in me, I try to summon it now.

"Dante, please. Find me."

But there is nothing. No pull, no whisper, no answering warmth in my chest. Just the aching cold and the sensation of emptiness where he should be.

A sharp rap at the door jolts me from the attempt. Staja startles, and before I can ask her to wait, she's already crossing the room and pulling it open.

Two guards stand in the hall, their figures tall and grim, eyes obscured by the shadows of their helms. And between them, as if conjured from a half-forgotten memory, stands Nadya.

Relief unfurls in my chest. She's still alive. Stiff with dark circles beneath her eyes, but alive.

She wears a high-collared gown of ash grey, the fabric smooth and heavy, the sleeves snug from shoulder to wrist, where they disappear into silver-threaded gloves. Her dark curls have been twisted and pinned in a simple coil at the nape of her neck, and in her gloved hands, she holds a delicate mask of silver lace, as intricate as frost on a windowpane.

"Nadya," I breathe, stepping forward.

The guards say nothing. They only motion for us to follow.

Staja hands me my mask and then gives us a parting nod before heading down the opposite way. Without hesitation, we're urged forward, hemmed in on either side, the corridor narrowing around us like the throat of a beast.

We walk in silence for a few paces before I risk a glance at Nadya.

She keeps her gaze forward, her expression unreadable.

"Do you know what this is?" I murmur, keeping my voice low.

She shakes her head. "Only that I was warned. If I didn't dress and cooperate, they'd hurt us both."

A hot spike of anger prickles beneath my skin, but there's no time to answer before we reach a spiral staircase, its stone steps slick with frost. My gloved hand trails the frozen iron rail as we descend, each step colder than the last. Narrow windows slit the walls here and there, each one clouded with frost so thick, the outside world is little more than a blur of grey and white.

As we descend, the faint strains of music drift up to meet us. Not lively or bright, but slow and somber, like a dirge dressed up in velvet and lace.

When we reach the bottom of the staircase, the guards lead us down another corridor, darker than the last, until they halt before a towering set of iron doors, filigreed with twisting patterns of thorns and skulls. Without a word, one of the guards heaves the doors open.

The sound of the ballroom swells around us—the hollow echo of strings, the low, heavy pulse of a drum like a heartbeat slowed to near death.

The ballroom itself is a cathedral of stone and shadow. The walls are lined with columns of grey marble, each etched with grotesque reliefs of vultures and serpents twining together. Frost coats the windows high above, muting the scant moonlight that filters through. A vast chandelier of black iron hangs from the ceiling, dripping with glass pendants that catch what little light there is and scatter it in muted, ghostly reflections across the floor.

The guests stand or waltz in slow, gliding circles, all cloaked in dark fabrics—deep reds, bruised purples, storm-cloud greys—every neck high, every sleeve long, every gloved hand pristine. Their masks gleam in shades of tarnished gold, bone-white porcelain, silver, or black lacquer, each one resembling an animal's face. No one smiles. Even in dance, their movements are stiff, mechanical, as though they were marionettes strung from the rafters.

I try to see their eyes through the masks, but I can only sense it. That

 435

palpable weight of their stares, each one heavy with judgment. As if I'm some curiosity on display. An exhibit in a gallery of cruelty.

Who are these people? Were they once courtiers of the last tsar? Were they forced to stay, their loyalty bound by fear? Or did they adapt easily, shifting their allegiance from one tyrant to the next as easily as changing a mask?

I wouldn't be surprised. Dulcamar has always had a taste for rot beneath the silk.

The music slows, taking on a darker timbre, as a ripple passes through the masked crowd.

My eyes land across the room on Torbin, who steps forward from the shadows near the far archway, his golden hair slicked back from his sharp, familiar features. His mask is a grotesque imitation of a vulture's face— hooked beak, angular cheekbones, deep hollows around the eyes. The dull red of the painted feathers around the edges makes the resemblance unmistakable: the red griffon vulture of Dulcamar. An omen of death.

His glacial-blue eyes are unchanged. Barely hidden behind the hollow sockets of the mask and still piercing enough to chill my blood.

He moves with easy grace, parting the crowd like a knife through silk, until he stops before me and extends a gloved hand.

I stare at it. The urge to refuse, to spit a rejection in his face, rises sharp and wild in my throat. But my gaze flicks to Nadya, standing silent and pale near the doors, and the memory of her saying she was threatened rings too loudly in my head.

I have no weapon. No dagger tucked at my thigh. No hidden blade to pierce his heart.

Only the hope that Nadya's spell worked.

So I place my hand in his.

His fingers close around mine—firm, sure, possessive—and he leads me to the center of the floor. The masked courtiers part to make way, their hollow stares following us.

When he pulls me into the dance, I expect roughness, some cruel assertion of control. But his grip is steady, almost reverent, his other hand pressing lightly to my waist, the heat of him bleeding through layers of silk and velvet.

"You look beautiful," he murmurs, his gaze sweeping over me. "I always imagined you in our colors."

He means Dulcamar's colors, and it's unnerving how easily he's let go of his loyalty to Hedera.

He tilts his head, a smile just curling at the corners of his mouth. "Black and red suit you, Celeste. Just as ruling by my side will suit you."

His words grate against my ears. "What is this? A charade of politeness after you practically tore a hole in my neck? What game are you playing?"

"No game," he says, spinning me gently, his steps precise, as smooth as water. "I'm presenting you to the court. Their future queen. *My* queen. As it was always meant to be."

I scoff under my breath, but the sound feels weak. His presence is suffocating, his body solid and strong beneath his tailored jacket, every movement calculated, measured. I can feel the ridges of muscle through the fabric where his arm supports my back. There was a time when I loved how strong he was, when that strength felt like safety.

But now, it feels like a cage.

His gaze locks on mine, those piercing eyes catching in the low candlelight. I remember being young, watching the sun catch the pale blue of his irises, feeling enchanted by the rare clarity of that color.

Now all I see is the cold behind them.

I glance sideways, my heart thudding, and find Nadya standing near the edge of the room, still guarded, still quiet. My stomach knots tighter.

Torbin guides me into another turn, bringing me closer. His voice drops low, conspiratorial. "Imagine it, Celeste. You and I, ruling together. Power unmatched, under the tsar's watchful guidance. The lands united, the old kingdoms brought to heel. No more squabbling, no more feigned peace. We could shape the world."

"I have no interest in your fantasies," I snap under my breath.

Especially because that is not how this would play out. With my power drained, he would keep me under lock and key. I would not be ruling by his side. I would be his prisoner, his plaything. I wouldn't put

it past him to keep me tied to his bed while he terrorizes the world.

"You will," he says softly, eyes crinkling with something too close to fondness. "Given time."

The song begins to slow, the notes drawing out like a dying breath, and the masked courtiers pivot in place, creating an opening.

From the far end of the ballroom, a new presence enters.

The tsar.

Clad in dark furs and silver-threaded robes, his imposing figure cuts through the gathered crowd. His hood is up, his mask a simple dark leather piece covering the upper half of his face, but the effect is no less unnerving. Beside him, half a step behind, moves the seer. Cloaked, masked, silent, like a shadow trailing after its master.

On the other side of the tsar stands Osrem, and I'm beginning to see that he never really worked for Torbin. He was always working for my father.

The air shifts. Every guest stills, lowering their heads in respect, like a kingdom bowing to its god.

My pulse pounds against my ribs.

The tsar raises a hand, and the musicians cut off mid-note, the last tremble of strings vibrating into silence. The murmurs of the crowd dissolve just as swiftly, as if the cold itself has commanded their obedience.

"Welcome," the tsar says, his voice deep and cutting, no warmth to soften its weight. "I have gathered you here tonight not simply to feast, but to witness the beginning of a future—one forged in strength, bound by power."

The masked faces around us remain still, heads tipped just enough to show deference. Their eyes glint like shards of ice behind their painted disguises.

The tsar's gaze sweeps the hall, his posture unyielding, his presence coiled like a serpent waiting to strike. "Dulcamar will rise, greater than before. With this union"—he gestures to Torbin and me, his lip curling faintly—"we secure the force necessary to conquer whatever dares defy us."

Torbin's grip tightens ever so slightly at my waist, possessive, as though I were a jewel he was polishing for display.

The seer steps forward. Behind her, two guards hold Nadya tightly in their grips. It's a warning. I need to do as they say, or she will be harmed.

Torbin moves, guiding me forward, his hand firm at the small of my back. I glance up at him sharply, but his expression is carved from marble. No explanation, no hint of pity. Just certainty.

My feet stumble, my pulse galloping in my chest.

Wait. The tsar said *union*. What is this? What's happening?

The seer stops just shy of us, her arms lifting. The gesture is ceremonial, deliberate.

My breath knots tightly in my throat.

This isn't a ball. This is something else. Something worse.

My gaze darts to Nadya. Her eyes are as wide as mine must be.

The air thickens, and the courtiers press in closer, their hunger for spectacle palpable. I catch their stares—cold, eager. They know what this is.

A wedding.

A union I didn't consent to.

The seer begins to murmur, low and rhythmic, words I don't recognize but feel all the same—like nails dragging along my spine. My skin prickles, my mind screaming for some way out, some means of stopping this before the noose tightens around my neck for good.

No, no, no. This can't be happening.

"Torbin, no." I whisper, but I should be screaming it.

"I told you, Celeste." He smirks, the hand on my waist cinching me closer. "You are still my betrothed."

Fuck! No. I can't let this happen.

The seer continues. The tsar stares with fascination. The guests are rapt with attention.

Something sparks inside me. A coil pulled taut—energy thrumming beneath my skin, rising from the pit of my stomach, through my chest, coalescing in the center of my ribs. My muscles tense, my heart

hammering faster, like it knows what's coming.

The seer pauses, her eyes settling on me. She knows I'm trying to use my powers, and it's apparent she's not happy about it. A soft hum escapes her lips, a low melody that weaves its way to my ears.

But that's as far as it gets.

Somehow, her siren power hasn't snuffed out the buzzing in my blood. Instead, the sound only sharpens me, a taunt rather than a leash. My veins feel molten, like lightning is crawling just beneath my skin, begging for release. Every inhale makes the pressure swell higher in my chest, every exhale shakes with the effort of containing it. The air around me hums, prickling against my arms, strands of hair lifting as though the storm inside me is pulling the world closer. Nadya's spell holds—the siren can't reach me—and the realization feeds my fury. I stop resisting. I let the energy climb, let it coil tighter, denser, until my bones ache with it, until the windows themselves seem to shiver in anticipation.

I don't hold back any more; I let it loose. Every single window shatters as one. A violent, ear-splitting symphony of glass bursting inward, jagged shards raining down like knives from the sky. The entire hall ducks, cries erupting, masks flying askew as the courtiers throw up their arms to shield themselves.

Torbin shouts, but I don't stay to hear what.

I throw my hand out, pushing an energy force to knock back Torbin, Osrem, the tsar, and the seer.

I whip my head toward Nadya. She's already moving, her hand outstretched. I grab it without hesitation, the heat of her fingers grounding me, and together, we sprint toward the nearest corridor, boots slipping on the glass-littered floor.

The music is gone. The revelry shattered with the glass.

I risk a glance over my shoulder.

Torbin stands amid the chaos, his mask half-cracked, his pale hair gleaming in the torchlight. His jaw is set, his gaze locked on me—not with shock, but promise. A vow made without words.

He will come for me.

I tear my eyes away, breath burning in my lungs, and run harder.

CHAPTER FIFTY-SIX

Dante

The valley lies before us like a graveyard of twisted hemlock, gnarled and blackened by the relentless cold. Mist hovers low to the ground, swirling in ghostly tendrils around the horses' hooves. Every breath clouds the air in front of my face, the chill sinking past my cloak and numbing my skin beneath the layers.

We've been on the move for days, the world narrowing to a rhythm of hooves, creaking saddles, and the rasp of weary lungs. Sleep comes in fragments, stolen in shifts against hard earth and colder stone, and even then, it never holds. When we move, we move with precision, and every mile closer knots the tension tighter between my shoulders.

At dawn, we made the choice to split our forces—an old gamble but a necessary one. A column of soldiers peeled north, tasked with circling wide and cutting off any retreat. Another squad veered east, skirting the ridges to find higher ground. And now the rest ride with me: Celeste's squad keeping close, Sir Holden and Sir Donovan grim-faced and watchful, and General Kormak out ahead, clearing the way with the efficiency of a man who's lived half his life in the wild.

The silence among us is telling. No one dares waste words when the wrong sound might carry. The soldiers glance at the trees as though eyes hide within the twisted bark, as though the forest itself resents our intrusion. I catch the same unease in my companions—the stiffness of their posture, the way hands linger near sword hilts. We're enveloping a predator's den, and every instinct screams that it already knows we're here.

We move slowly, each step a struggle. The thick carpet of hemlock grabs at our boots and the horses' legs, making the beasts snort and toss their heads in protest. Mylo rides ahead, his hatchet flashing now and then as he hacks a path through the thickest snarls. The sound of it— *thwack, thwack*—echoes eerily through the valley, swallowed almost instantly by the heavy fog.

I tighten my grip on the reins, my knuckles white against the leather. I can feel my horse's unease—hear it in the restless stamping of his hooves. As if even the animals know we are deep in enemy territory.

Giorgi rides to my left, their sharp eyes scanning the broken terrain ahead, even as the mist thickens around us. Their presence is a steady reassurance. If anyone can guide us through this cursed valley without getting us killed, it's Giorgi.

But even their skill doesn't ease the knot in my gut.

I lean forward slightly in the saddle, my heart hammering in my ears, as if somehow, I can will myself to hear her voice across this cursed wasteland.

"Celeste. I hear you." I know she can't hear me, but I send the thought anyway, fierce and desperate. *"Hold on. I'm coming."*

There is a faint shift in the air. So faint, I almost miss it, but a whisper brushes against the edge of my mind. Not words, not fully, but something. A feeling. A flicker of fear... and hope.

I stiffen, jerking my gaze upward.

"Did you feel that?" I rasp, barely above a whisper.

Mylo glances back at me, frowning. Giorgi shakes their head once, scanning the mist. No one else felt it.

But I know I did.

I clench my jaw, urging my horse forward, heart thrumming painfully against my ribs. She's alive. She's fighting.

And he has her.

The thought of Torbin—of my deceitful brother—touching her, threatening her, sends a white-hot surge of rage through my chest. My hands tighten so hard around the reins that the leather cuts into my palms, but I don't care. I won't care until she's safe in my arms again.

A low branch snaps against my shoulder as we push through another thicket of hemlock. I barely feel it. My mind is a tunnel of single-minded fury now, aimed straight at the heart of Dulcamar.

Torbin will pay for this.

I swear it on every breath I have left.

Ahead, Giorgi raises a hand, signaling for us to slow. The mist parts just enough for me to make out the outline of a crumbling wall—stone, ancient and weatherworn, cloaked in the same ghostly vines that infest the valley.

Beyond it, shrouded in shadow and fog, looms the fortress of Dulcamar.

My pulse pounds harder, my breath frosting in the air.

"There's a side entrance," Giorgi murmurs, barely audible over the creaking of leather and the distant moan of the wind. "Northwest corner. Looks like it's fallen into disrepair. If we're careful, we can get through without being seen."

I nod once, sharp and decisive. "Let's move."

We dismount near a crag of broken stone half-hidden by the mist. The fortress looms above, its black towers dissolving into the clouds, walls crusted with frost and lichen. The air is sharp enough to cut skin, and as I fumble with the reins, my fingers ache with the cold, stiff and clumsy inside my gloves.

Mylo ties off the horses quickly, whispering soothing words to them as they shudder against the icy ground. Kormak checks the straps twice, ever methodical, even as the wind bites at us with each passing second.

Aila comes up beside me, tugging her cloak tighter around her shoulders. Her breath billows white into the air as she glances toward the fortress.

"You've literally gone to the ends of the earth for her. She must mean a lot to you," she says, her voice low but not accusing.

I tighten the knot on my horse's reins and stare up at the monstrous silhouette of Dulcamar.

"She is my life," I say, the words scraping raw against my throat. "Without her... there's nothing left worth living for."

Aila watches me for a moment, her dark hair plastered against her cheeks from the damp wind. Then she nods once, firm and sure. "Good. Then you'll fight like hell to bring her home."

I meet her gaze. "Nothing will stop me."

Not the tsar.

Not Torbin.

Not even the gods themselves.

Giorgi finishes securing the last of the horses and signals that they're ready.

We fall into a crouch, moving low across the frozen earth toward the crumbled breach in the wall. The wind tears at us, carrying the smell of smoke and cold stone. Each step feels heavier, not just from the thick hemlock tangling at our boots, but from the weight of what lies ahead.

The fortress waits, silent and watching.

My blood thrums in my ears as we slip into its shadow, ready to tear it apart stone by stone if that's what it takes to bring her back.

All at once, the sky seems to crack open.

A thunderous boom echoes across the grounds, as sharp and sudden as a war drum. I jerk my head up just in time to see the glass windows of the fortress explode in a hail of shimmering shards, like frozen stars flung from the sky.

The squad drops lower by instinct, shields half-raised, but there are no arrows—only the echo of shattering glass and the sharp, startled shouts that follow.

Then a voice carries over the courtyard. Cold, commanding,

unmistakable.

"Seal the halls! Find them! I want them alive!"

Torbin. His bark of authority reverberates off the stone, snapping the guards to attention.

Lorne stills beside me, head tilted just slightly, like a wolf catching a scent.

"That him?" he asks under his breath.

I nod, pulse thudding. "That's him."

Lorne grins, teeth flashing in the dark. "Good. I can work with that."

He means his voice magic. I smirk in return. He'll have what he needs when we breach deeper.

We slip into the fortress through a gap in the crumbling outer wall, the stones slick with ice, the mortar between them cracked and blackened with age. The cold wraps around us like a second skin, repressing every breath, numbing every movement.

But the fire in my chest burns hotter than ever.

Inside, the air is worse—stagnant and metallic, heavy with the scent of burning wood and something fouler beneath it. I grind my teeth as I creep forward, my hand brushing the hilt of my sword to steady myself.

Aila moves like a shadow beside me, her crossbow drawn and ready. Mylo's boots make almost no sound despite his massive frame, and Giorgi leads us with quick, sharp gestures, their navigation senses tuned sharper than any of ours. Isaac brings up the rear, his hand tight around the grip of his crossbow.

We weave through abandoned corridors and service tunnels, the stones beneath our boots slick with frost. The only light comes from the occasional torch sputtering weakly on the walls, casting warped shadows that lurch and stretch across the uneven ground.

Giorgi halts us at an intersection, their hand shooting up in a clenched fist. We press to the wall, holding our breath.

Footfalls.

Two guards, cloaked in Dulcamar's black and red, their breath misting visibly in the freezing air, round the corner ahead. Their hands

rest lazily on the hilts of their weapons, unaware.

Kormak signals something to the squad. Giorgi flicks two fingers to Isaac, who nods, slipping into the darkness.

The moment the guards pass, Isaac moves. As swift and silent as a striking viper, he takes one down with a quick arrow to the throat. Giorgi disables the second with a brutal strike to the temple, catching the man's body before it can hit the ground.

No noise. No alarm.

We move again.

Every step draws us deeper into the beast's belly, where the cold seems to seep into our bones, where even our own heartbeats feel too loud.

The floor suddenly begins to tremble, and we freeze. The disturbance lingers, and I swear I hear a low, grumbling growl. We exchange glances until the sound dissipates.

I tighten my grip on my sword, my jaw clenching so hard, it aches. Every instinct in me howls to run ahead, to tear apart every stone until I have Celeste in my arms again. But I force myself to stay with the others, to move carefully, methodically.

If I get reckless now, I'll never reach her.

As we climb a flight of stone stairs, heavy footfalls echo from the hall ahead—guards shouting to one another, their voices bouncing off the stone like sharp blades.

"Seal the main floor!" one of the guards shouts. "No one gets past— by order of the prince!"

We press ourselves into the shadows of an alcove, backs against the cold stone, breath low and shallow. The clatter of boots grows louder. Too many of them. We'll be cornered if we don't act fast.

Lorne creeps forward, his hand cupped around his mouth, eyes glinting with anticipation.

"Hold," Dante murmurs.

Lorne's calls out, clear and sharp—but it's not his voice. "All of you—back to the east wing! Double the guard there, now!" Torbin's voice. Commanding. Absolute.

The guards stumble to a halt mid-stride. For a heartbeat, there's confusion—then swift obedience. They turn on their heels, boots hammering the floor as they rush in the opposite direction.

When their footsteps fade, Lorne turns back to us, a smug glimmer in his eye. "That'll buy us a bit of time."

I flash him a nod. We push deeper into the dark, the path ahead clearer, though the stakes only grow heavier with each step.

We climb a narrow, stone stairwell, the steps slick with frozen dew, and Giorgi motions to a heavy, wooden door up ahead.

Aila gives me a look, fierce and certain, as she readies her sword. Mylo hefts his hatchet, Isaac holds up his crossbow, and Giorgi readies a short, wicked blade.

Kormak looks back at us with a nod before throwing open the door.

We mean to barge in and strike fast, but for a heartbeat, the world stills.

The corridor is filled with chained carnoraxis. They surge from the shadows—hulking beasts of twisted flesh and sinew, their black claws gleaming under the guttering torchlight. Their snarls are low and guttural, their eyes burning red as they lunge toward us with terrifying speed. Their collars are connected to chains bolted to the brick walls, but they can still reach us.

"Hold the line!" Kormak roars, his sword already singing from its sheath.

The first carnoraxis slams into me, claws raking out. I pivot, driving my sword clean through its throat, but not before its jagged claw tears a deep gash across my forearm. The blood splatters warm and fast against the icy stone before I even feel the sting of pain. I grit my teeth and swing my falchion, slicing it through before shoving the creature's body aside.

I continue to slash through the horde, but I take in the battle in my periphery. A beast barrels toward Isaac, who twists just in time, but not fast enough. A curved claw scores a brutal line across his cheek, blood spilling bright against the pale stretch of his skin. Isaac staggers but doesn't fall. His crossbow releases a bolt, and the creature crumples at his feet.

 447

Aila looses an arrow at another beast, striking it clean between the eyes—but the recoil jolts her injured arm, and she hisses in pain, clutching it against her chest.

"Mylo!" she snarls, backing toward him. "You better be ready to cover my ass!"

Mylo swings his hatchet in a vicious arc, cleaving through another carnoraxis with a roar. "I was born ready, lieutenant."

But in the chaos, he doesn't see the creature lunging at him from the blind spot behind his shoulder.

Aila does.

Battered arm and all, she steps in, wielding her sword one-handed. It hits home, the beast collapsing mid-lunge.

"You owe me." She pants, flashing him a wild grin.

"Buy you a whole tavern if we survive this!" Mylo growls, swinging again.

A stairway comes into view, and everything inside of me is telling me I need to climb up. Celeste is near. I can feel her presence like a pulse beneath my skin, a frantic drumbeat calling me home.

"Go!" Aila shouts to me, planting her boot into a carnoraxis's chest and slamming her sword into its throat. "We'll hold them!"

I bolt through the chaos, boots pounding up the narrow, stone stairway sodden with ice and blood. My lungs burn with each breath, the wound on my forearm slick and seeping, but I don't slow.

Nothing matters but getting to her.

CHAPTER FIFTY-SEVEN

Celeste

Nadya and I tear down the corridor, the cold gnawing at my legs despite the heavy fabric of my gown. Our boots barely make a sound on the stone, but the thundering footsteps behind us grow louder. We take a sharp turn, reaching for the handle of a heavy door—locked. Another door—locked.

Nadya curses under her breath. "It's like they knew we'd try to hide."

"We just need one." I pant. "One that isn't bolted."

We round another corner, nearly skidding on a patch of frost-slick stone, and finally a door gives way under my shove. We stumble inside, slamming it behind us, my heart beating so loudly, it drowns out everything else. The room is dim, dust suspended in the cold air like motes of ash. Shelves of forgotten ledgers and tarnished candelabras line the walls, but only thin slits for windows, not big enough for a body to fit through. No other exit.

Nadya presses her back to the door, both of us heaving, the damp air stinging my throat. "What now?" she whispers, frantic. "We can't stay here."

I pace, my pulse thrashing in my ears. "Can you use your magic—cloak us?"

Nadya shakes her head, her eyes wild. "Maybe. I don't know how long it'll hold. I don't know how far we'll get."

"We have to try." I search the room, looking for something to keep us warm if we make it outside. "Please."

"And then what?"

I shake my head. "I don't know, but this can't be it. We have to at least *try* to get out of here."

She takes a deep breath, then nods as she releases it. I bite into my bottom lip, trying to stop the pounding in my ears as I hold out for hope.

Nadya closes her eyes, bracing herself, and I watch her hands tremble as she mouths the spell.

But before she can even murmur a word, the door crashes open with a brutal crack.

Fuck!

Torbin storms in, eyes blazing, his breath fogging in the frigid air. Before either of us can react, he strikes Nadya hard with the hilt of his sabre. The sound of it—bone meeting steel—makes me flinch. She collapses like a ragdoll, crumpling to the floor with a soft gasp.

"Nadya!" I drop to my knees, but Torbin shoves me back with one arm, his boots thudding closer.

I scramble to my feet, blood roaring in my ears. He kicks the door closed, locking it with a decisive smack of the bolt. The sabre hangs at his side, but his fury is far sharper.

"You are an ungrateful wretch," he spits. His voice is low, trembling with the effort to control himself. "I offered you everything. Power. Wealth. A fucking place beside me."

He stomps closer, but I throw my hands out and he flies backward, his back hitting the wall. He recovers quickly, sneering at me. I faintly feel the blood seeping from my nose.

"You offered me ruin," I snap. My chest heaves, my fists clenching. "You offered me the end of the world. You're too deluded to see it."

"You would've been queen!" His shout echoes off the stone, venomous and raw. "You would've been everything."

His hand lunges, grabbing for my arm, but I twist away. My gown catches under his grip, the sleeve tearing with an ugly sound. The bodice strains, ripping jaggedly across my chest. I throw a punch—fingers stinging as they connect weakly with his jaw—but it does nothing to stop him. He's too strong. He snarls, seizing my waist. My dress rips more as he drags me closer to him. We're face to face as he glares at me.

The door bursts open with a deafening crack.

I gasp, stumbling back as Torbin whirls around, his sabre halfway raised.

And there, framed in the doorway, breath misting in the cold, stands Dante. His falchion gleams in the low light, and the look on his face is a raging storm.

For a breathless moment, his eyes meet mine. There's a faint flash of relief as neither of us moves.

The cold air is thick with smoke from the torches, the walls seeming to close in around us. My heart thunders against my ribs, my wrists raw where Torbin has grabbed me.

I feel Nadya shift on the floor. Thank the gods, she's conscious! She looks between the two brothers before glancing at me. Swallowing hard, she winces, her fingers trembling as they stretch out.

"Well, if it isn't my dear brother," Torbin drawls, turning slightly to face Dante, keeping one hand resting possessively on the back of my chair. His eyes gleam, full of mockery. "I was wondering when you'd come crawling."

Dante's voice is a low, lethal growl. "Step away from her."

Torbin chuckles. A lazy, cold sound. "Still so noble. So predictable." His gaze flickers down to me, then back to Dante, and something dark flickers in his eyes. "You think you're here to save her, little brother? That's charming."

Dante moves forward, each step deliberate. His sword glints under

the weak light, the muscles in his arms flexing with restrained fury.

Nadya slowly gets to her feet to stand next to me. Blood stains her hair on the side of her head. She winces again as she sways, and I grab a hold of her arm to steady her.

"You have no idea what you've unleashed," Dante says. His voice is low, but it vibrates through the room, setting every nerve in my body alight.

Nadya shifts again beside me. I feel her tug subtly at my sleeve, trying to inch us backward, little by little, toward the door.

I glance at her out of the corner of my eye and catch the tension humming in her body, the way her fingers twitch like she's gathering something unseen.

Magic.

I keep my face carefully blank, hiding the surge of hope—and fear—that pulses through me.

Torbin only laughs. "You always were sentimental, Dante. Still desperately hanging on to scraps of loyalty. Still fighting for people who would fucking *spit* on you if given the chance." His gaze sharpens. "You don't belong with them. You belong here—with me. With us."

Dante shakes his head once. Slowly. "You made your choice. Don't pretend this was ever about loyalty."

Torbin's expression hardens, the false humor draining from his face.

"You're weak," he spits. "Just like our father always said. A bastard prince playing the hero. You have no idea what it means to actually have a backbone and take what you want."

"I'll never trade my honor for false glory," Dante retorts, circling Torbin with measured steps.

Torbin cants his chin. "Perhaps you are a lost cause. But there's still hope for Celeste."

Dante scoffs. "Is that what you want? For her to be like you?"

"No. I want her to be *with* me."

Dante shakes his head. "How's that working out for you? You think you can make her love you if you fall into power? Think again, Brother."

"Power is everything, and if you think any differently, then you're a

fool."

Dante's jaw tightens. The muscle ticks in his cheek.

But he doesn't move, doesn't lash out.

Because despite everything, he loves his brother. And I know it's tearing him apart to confront him like this.

Torbin prowls closer to Dante, his hand straying toward the dagger at his belt. "You're not leaving here with her. You're not leaving at all."

Torbin pounces, his blade swinging.

Without warning, Nadya strikes.

A sudden *whoosh* of heat blasts through the room as the tapestries along the far wall burst into flames. The fire spreads fast, devouring the heavy velvet, smoke billowing in thick, black coils toward the ceiling.

Torbin staggers back, cursing, shielding his eyes from the sudden blaze. The fire dances chin-high between him and Dante, trapping Torbin against the wall.

"Now!" Nadya hisses at me, grabbing my hand.

A muscle jumps in Dante's jaw, the flicker of relief fierce and wild—but he hesitates..

"Come on!" Nadya shouts over the crackling fire, dragging me toward the door.

Dante stands frozen, staring at Torbin through the growing inferno.

Torbin stumbles against a table, coughing as smoke engulfs him, his silhouette framed by the roaring flames.

And I see it.

The war inside Dante—the grief, the fury, the heartbreak.

Torbin is his brother. Twisted, broken, monstrous. But still his brother.

Dante's hand trembles on the hilt of his sword.

Nadya pulls harder at me, trying to get us through the doorway. The smoke is choking now, blinding.

As I back up toward the door, I pull Dante with me. "We have to go!" I shout, my throat raw. "Dante!"

He stumbles into the hall with me, but he turns his head, and his grey eyes meet mine. There's a heartbreak in them that shatters

 453

something inside me.

"I can't let him die," he says hoarsely.

"Dante, don't!"

"He's my brother, Celeste. I can't let him go. Not like this."

And before I can stop him, before I can scream for him to come back, Dante plunges into the fire.

Fuck!

Flames beat at the door. A layer of smoke conceals the ceiling, thick and black, writhing like a living thing. It leaks into the hallway, advancing on me and Nadya.

I cough, my lungs burning, eyes stinging. The fire is everywhere, devouring the wood, the stone, the air itself.

Dante is barely a silhouette ahead of me, his body carving a path through the inferno. He throws his arm up to shield his face, trying to reach Torbin, who stumbles, half-choking, deeper inside the collapsing room.

He won't make it.

Oh, gods!

A raw, desperate instinct rises in me—something deeper than fear, deeper than reason.

I thrust my hand forward, feeling the power coiling inside me, reckless and volatile. I barely think. I just will it forward, shoving the flames aside, parting them with a surge of force that tears at my skull.

Pain explodes behind my eyes, bright and sharp, but I push harder, carving a clear path through the searing heat.

"Dante!" I scream through the roaring fire. "Go!"

Through the opening I've made, Dante lunges, grabbing Torbin's arm and hauling him up just before a flaming beam crashes where Torbin was just standing.

Dante staggers, smoke curling around him like a shroud, but he keeps going, dragging his brother through the gap, toward us, toward freedom.

The fire snaps at their heels, furious and wild, but Dante doesn't slow.

He bursts through the doorway, coughing, Torbin slumped half-conscious in his arms.

I let the magic fall away, leaning against Nadya, my body trembling, blood trickling from my nose.

For one glorious, aching moment, we're free.

Until the Dulcamaran guards swarm from the shadows.

Steel flashes. Rough hands grab us. Soldiers throw water on the fire.

A shout splits the air, boots thundering across the stone floor. Dante drops Torbin in a defensive stance, his blade flashing up, but there are too many.

I twist, elbowing a guard in the ribs, but another grabs my arm, yanking it behind me. Nadya screams, kicking at the men dragging her back.

Dante's hand goes immediately for his falchion, eyes widening when he doesn't find it at his side. He whips his head toward the guards and releases a humming sound but stops immediately, wincing and reaching for his throat.

It's then that Torbin staggers to his feet.

For a heartbeat, I think he'll say something. *Thank you*, maybe. Some flicker of remorse. Some acknowledgment that Dante just pulled him from the fire.

Instead—his lips twist into a cruel smile. "Maybe that will shut you up, Brother."

I stare in disbelief at Dante's neck. The gleam of the enchanted collar bites into his skin, its pendant glimmering from the light of the dying flames. My breath lodges in my throat, the world tilting as the truth claws at me: while Dante was pulling Torbin from the fire, while he was saving his life, Torbin slipped the shackle onto him.

Dante claws at the collar, but it doesn't budge.

Torbin squares his shoulders. "Take them to the dungeon," he rasps, voice thick with smoke and venom.

My blood ices. "What?"

Dante goes rigid.

Torbin just laughs—a wet, ugly sound. His face is soot-smeared, his

455

clothes singed, but the hatred in his eyes is untouched.

"You didn't think saving me would change anything, did you?" He sneers, lifting Dante's falchion and gazing upon it as if it were a newly acquired treasure. "You're a fool, Brother."

The betrayal slices through the air, as jagged and cruel as any blade. He didn't just bind Dante's power, he bound his trust, twisting his mercy into a weapon against him.

I see it—see it in the way Dante stares at him, as if Torbin's words gut him deeper than any wound.

Torbin turns, grabbing Nadya roughly by the arm. She lets out a startled gasp, struggling, but he clamps a hand tightly around her wrist. "She's coming with me," he growls. "Can't have you getting any bright ideas."

Dante lunges forward, fury breaking through the soot and blood marking him. "Get your hands off her!"

A guard slams an elbow into his ribs. Dante folds with a grunt, falling to one knee. My own cry tears free as I reach for him, but hands clamp around my arms, yanking me back.

"Don't!" I shout. "Let her go!"

Torbin doesn't look back. He drags Nadya down the corridor, her feet slipping on the blackened stone, her wide eyes meeting mine one last time before they vanish around the corner.

The ache in my chest expands, sharp and hot. Dante and I are pulled away.

We're taken through narrow halls, the smell of ash and smoke lingering. My muscles scream with each step, exhaustion dragging at my limbs, but I don't stop. I can't. Not while Nadya's still in Torbin's grip.

Not while I'm being dragged toward gods-know-what.

CHAPTER FIFTY-EIGHT

We reach the lower levels—a damp, dark corridor where the air turns colder and wetter with each step. Moisture drips from the ceiling. The walls here are carved from rough rock, jagged and damp with moss. The only light comes from rusted iron sconces set too far apart, leaving long stretches of darkness that swallow the floor.

The guards throw Dante and me into a cell without ceremony. Iron bars clang shut behind us with a teeth-rattling slam. Chains rattle. A heavy lock clicks into place.

I stumble and catch myself against the wall, panting, my wrists scraped and aching.

Dante is already on his knees, head bowed, one hand pressed to his shoulder.

I crawl to him, heart hammering. "Oh, gods, you're hurt."

"I'm fine," he mutters, teeth clenched. But I can see the blood soaking through the fabric of his tunic, the torn skin along his shoulder where a carnoraxis must've gotten him. "Just bruised."

I place my hand gently over the wound. Power swells between my fingers, flowing through to heal him. The ache inside me is constant now,

 457

like something trying to claw its way out. I press harder, pushing the energy through my palm. The bleeding slows. The angry red of the wound begins to pale.

He watches me with something quiet and terrible in his eyes. Then his expression changes. He draws me in suddenly, fingers curling around my face, calloused thumb brushing the curve of my cheek. His eyes search mine, as though he's still not entirely convinced I'm real.

"I thought I'd lost you," he breathes. "When I went to your rooms and you weren't there—when no one knew where you'd gone—I thought maybe... maybe you'd run."

I shake my head. "No. I would never."

"I didn't believe it. Not really. But the king—he did. He said you'd betrayed us. He wanted to take Delasurvia by force. I fought him. I left the capital without permission, rode to your uncle, to the Garrison, hoping you were there. But you weren't. And I... I couldn't breathe." His voice cracks. "I couldn't breathe knowing you might be gone."

I press my forehead to his, both our chests heaving. "I didn't run. I would never run from you."

His lips find mine, the motion slow and reverent. As though kissing me might stitch the pieces of him back together.

"I swear," he whispers against my mouth, "I'll make them pay for this. For touching you. For taking her. For everything."

I back up enough to look him over, and my gaze lands on the collar gripping his throat. I search for the clasp, but I can't open it. Frustration builds as I try to slip my fingers beneath it somehow to pry it free, but it's simply stuck.

Dante gently grasps my hand. "It can only be removed by the one who bound it."

He looks down at my ripped dress, then stands to remove his jacket. After pulling me to my feet, he wraps the jacket around me. I slip my arms through the sleeves, and then Dante pulls me into his embrace.

"I thought... I thought maybe there was hope for him."

My arms squeeze him tighter. "Dante, he's unhinged."

He lets out a soft, mirthless laugh. "I noticed." His mouth pulls down into a frown. "I didn't want it to be like this. I don't want him to be my enemy. He's my brother. I don't know if I can bring myself to... hate him."

I don't know how to respond to that, because I can feel his struggle. Dante's biggest weakness is his heart and what he would do for the ones he loves. Even though Torbin has become something other than himself, Dante is still holding on to the brother he opened his heart to.

"Did you hear me calling you?" I ask softly, deciding to change the subject.

"I felt you," he says, brushing a strand of hair away from my face. "Your voice was faint, but I could feel you calling for me."

My heart thrums with the knowledge that our connection is strong enough for him to hear me, feel me, even over such a long distance.

He runs a thumb over my cheek before softly kissing me. I pull him closer, wishing our reunion didn't have to take place in this dank, smelly cell.

His fingers brush over the bite mark on my neck, and he stiffens. "What's this? Who did this to you?"

"He... Torbin bit me."

His jaw hardens, his eyes narrowing. "'Bit' you?"

"He has fangs, Dante. The serum he takes, it's changing him." I place my hand on top of his.

He stares in horror at the mark, which has healed a lot quicker since Nadya used her magic. I can see the fury burning behind his glare.

Then his eyes meet mine and his gaze softens. "I won't let him hurt you anymore. I promise."

For a while, we simply hold each other, wondering what's going to happen next. But my thoughts don't slow down.

"What do you think he's going to do to Nadya?"

"I'm not sure." His arms tighten around me. "But we'll find her."

I close my eyes for a moment and let myself relax deeper in his embrace. The feel of him gives me hope. Relief floods through me in waves so fierce, it nearly buckles my knees. For a moment, it doesn't matter that the dungeon stinks of mildew and blood, or that the stone

beneath my feet is ice. I'm not alone. Dante found me. He's here, holding me together when I feel like I should be falling apart. I bury my face against his chest, drawing strength from the steady beat of his heart, but the terror coils just as tightly inside me.

I'm sure the tsar still means to rip the magic from my veins. Something tells me this is only a pause before the ritual begins. My stomach twists at the thought of Nadya suffering somewhere above us, of Dante shackled by that cursed collar, of myself, powerless to stop what's coming.

Footsteps echo outside, making us jump. We both turn toward the door as a key turns in the lock and the door groans open. Large guards stomp in, and in the next moment, rough hands seize us again, wrenching us forward.

"Where are you taking us?" I demand, struggling against their grip. "Where's my friend?"

One of the guards sneers down at me, breath sour and eyes hard. "The tsar awaits you," he says, dragging us into the hall. "In the arena."

The sky is a muted indigo, barely touched by morning light, but the interior of the fortress pulses with a terrible glow—torches lining the corridor like burning eyes. Their flickering light throws our shadows long and twisted across the walls. Our wrists are bound. Dante walks beside me, silent, his head high despite the bruises and dried blood that mar his jaw and shoulder. His hand brushes mine as we turn a corner, and though the contact is brief, it's enough to steady me.

We emerge into the cold.

The air cuts like knives. It sinks into my lungs and curls icy fingers around my ribs. My boots crunch over gravel and broken bone. We're led into the massive, open space ringed by jagged walls and towering iron torches. The space I looked down on when the tsar made me watch the

carnoraxis attack the Dulcamaran citizens.

Now that I'm down in the arena, the full impact of the place hits me. Designed for spectacle. For horror. The ground is packed dirt, but it's stained—dark, ugly patches in the soil where blood has seeped in so deeply, it will never be clean again. Cages line the outer ring, each one bristling with bars and rust. From inside, the carnoraxis cry out—high, warbling whistles that fray at my nerves. They snarl and claw at the metal, saliva stringing from their jaws, red eyes catching the firelight like coals. The sound is unbearable.

I flinch as one throws itself at the bars closest to me. They rattle under the force of it, and one of the guards lets out a harsh laugh behind me.

Dante shifts closer, muscles flexed, his body half in front of mine.

I swallow the bile rising in my throat.

At the far end of the arena, a stone, spiral staircase leads up to the balcony I once stood at, black stone, ornately carved. And at its center stands the tsar. His eyes are already on us, glittering in the firelight. There's a coldness in his expression that makes me shiver.

To his left, Ella, the seer. Poised at his right is Osrem, his hands folded in front of his body.

Draped in her deep-crimson cloak, she wears her hood pulled forward to shadow her face. Her silver mask gleams over her eyes, delicate and sharp, like a masquerade piece forged from blades. She doesn't speak. Doesn't move. My magic recoils the moment my eyes land on her, like it remembers what she can do.

Near the cages, with spears in their hands, are the tsar's guards. They stand beside the levers that release the cage doors, awaiting the tsar's command.

Dante swallows hard beneath the enchanted collar, his fingers twitching at his sides. His wide eyes find mine, and his jaw hardens. He's as unprepared for this as I am.

The tsar raises his arms, and his voice rolls out across the arena like thunder.

A hush falls over the arena. Even the growls and snarls of the

carnoraxis grow quieter.

The tsar's gaze cuts past me, settling on Dante. His lips curl. "So. This is the boy who dares to break into my fortress. Who dares steal from me—take my daughter, my prisoner, my prize." His voice slams through the chamber like a hammer blow. "You thought yourself clever, slipping past my guards. Thought you could drag her from my grasp. But here you are, collared, captured. Every thief pays a price."

My stomach drops. The room feels colder, tighter, like the walls themselves are pressing inward.

"I believed she was the key," the tsar continues, his eyes gleaming like fire on ice. "The gods' gift. My weapon to wield. And perhaps she is. But perhaps..." His hand drifts through the air, pointing at Dante like he's already marked him for sacrifice. "Perhaps there is more than one key."

The words slam into me like a blade. My chest cinches tightly, my breath shattering in my lungs. *No, no, no.* Not him. Not Dante. The thought of his life twisted into the tsar's hands makes my stomach heave. He already took Torbin, but I'll be damned if he takes Dante too. Desperation claws up my throat, hot and suffocating, drowning out reason. I can't let this happen—I *won't* let this happen.

"No," I blurt out, the word tearing raw from my throat. "Please! He doesn't deserve this. Let him go. I'll do whatever you ask, I swear it."

Dante tenses beside me.

The tsar chuckles, a sound so mirthless, it scrapes like broken glass. "You will do whatever I ask regardless."

"Then take me!" My voice cracks. My chest burns. "I'll marry Torbin. I'll bind myself to him, give you my power—just release Dante!"

The tsar's grin spreads slowly, like ink bleeding across parchment. "It appears I've found your weakness." He takes a step forward and raises a brow. "It is far too late for bargains, daughter. I make the rules now. And here is what I've decided."

My heart lurches violently against my ribs.

Dante doesn't move. Doesn't even blink.

The tsar lifts one arm, gesturing to the shadowed tunnel across the

 462

pit.

Torbin emerges. Stripped to the waist, his skin wrapped in fresh bandages, his sabre gleaming at his hip. His eyes burn with something unrecognizable, something feral. Twisted. My stomach knots so tightly, it hurts.

"You've participated in trials throughout most of the realms, Dante. But you've yet to endure mine," the tsar proclaims, his voice reverberating through the arena. "Here is your trial. Dante and Torbin. Blade against blade. Strength against strength. The gods themselves will decide who is worthy."

My breath stutters. My lips shape a frantic whisper. "No... no, no, no."

"If Dante prevails," the tsar goes on, ignoring me entirely, "Celeste will be freed. She may leave Dulcamar untouched." His gaze slants toward Dante, cold and merciless. "The prophecy speaks of power descending through blood. 'Magic gifted by the gods, to a powerful descendant, must be seized.' My seer believes *you*, boy, could be that descendant as well. She believes I could take you in Celeste's place. Your strength will serve my throne."

A chill tears down my spine. Dante's shoulders go rigid beside me, and I can't tell if he's breathing at all.

"And if Torbin triumphs," the tsar continues, his mouth twisting into a blade-sharp smile, "Celeste will remain here and become his bride. Her power will be mine to claim. If she is the chosen one, she will fulfill her destiny under my hand—whether she wills it or not."

The ground tilts beneath me. My knees weaken. My stomach pitches. My body wants to scream, but the sound catches in my throat, jagged and raw.

"And if I refuse?" Dante calls, his voice clear, slicing through the night air.

The tsar doesn't even blink. "Then her friend dies."

I blink, holding my breath, and then my gaze is yanked to the left, where guards drag Nadya forward, tying her to a post driven into the ground near the carnoraxis cages. Her eyes are wide with fear, her curls

wild, her movements frantic as she tries to break free.

I lurch forward. "Nadya!"

A guard grabs me, yanking me back, and I thrash in his grip. "Don't touch her! Don't—"

The tsar tilts his head, studying Dante the way a predator studies prey that's already snared. Slowly, almost lazily, a smile spreads across his face—cold, deliberate, cruel. His hands clasp behind his back as he begins to pace the balcony, every step echoing like a drumbeat in the vast chamber. He stops, his gaze dropping to Nadya's trembling form lashed to the post, and then back to Dante, his eyes glittering with satisfaction.

"Celeste's beloved friend," the tsar says to Dante, "will be left to the carnoraxis if you forfeit the fight. Choose, boy."

My breath leaves me, and I fear my legs are going to give out.

CHAPTER
FIFTY-NINE

I look to Dante. His jaw is so firm, it could be carved from stone, but I see the storm behind his eyes. His fists clench. His chest rises, then falls. His eyes flick to me—holding, grounding. Apologetic.

He glares, not at the tsar, but at Torbin. "I'll fight."

"Perhaps you're not as foolish as I believed," the tsar says.

But then the tsar stills as the seer leans toward him. She whispers something, and the tsar nods. I can't help but wonder if it's a conversation or if she's manipulating his mind. There's a subtle shift in her jaw, the delicate curl of her fingers at her side. The tsar's expression sharpens as he darts his focus between Torbin and Dante.

Osrem leans in to hear the whispered words, his brow creased. Even Torbin looks confused, glancing toward her with a slight tilt of his head.

As the seer takes a step back, the tsar straightens, spreading his arms wide.

"Our dear seer has reminded me of something crucial." The tsar's eyes gleam as they land on Dante. "It would not do for this fight to be unbalanced."

I exchange a look with Dante, neither of us unclear of what to

 465

expect.

"Torbin is not the mere human he used to be. He has had the benefit of our seer's alchemy skills to make him stronger."

He means the carnoraxis potion, which gave him superhuman strength. I wasn't aware that it was the seer's concoction.

"So, let us give both of our challengers equal advantage." The tsar's grin is laced with malice as he nods to Osrem.

Fuck! No!

My heart stutters. He can't mean—

Osrem disappears from view for a moment, then appears again, descending the stairs. In his hands he holds a pair of glass vials. The serum inside is thick, metallic orange, swirling sluggishly as though it were alive.

There's no way he was coincidentally carrying the potion with him to the arena. Those vials were already prepared. This was the seer's plan all along. And she means for Dante to consume one of them. Which means he will become what Torbin is.

"No," I breathe. "No, no—don't."

The tsar gestures casually, as if he were suggesting a game, not sentencing a man to corruption. "Drink," he commands. "Both of you."

I twist in the guard's grip. "You can't! That serum—what it's done to Torbin—Dante, it will change you!"

"If he doesn't drink," the tsar shouts, his hands planted on the balustrade, "then he forfeits the challenge."

Oh, gods. Oh, gods!

Dante doesn't speak. He only watches the vial handed to him, expression unreadable, but his movements are stiff and there's a quick rise and fall of his chest.

Torbin, for his part, doesn't hesitate. He takes his and downs it in one long, defiant swallow, then throws the vial to the ground. His muscles flex, his nostrils flare—and for a second, I swear his pupils narrow like a beast's.

The carnoraxis release high-pitched whistles and screeches from their cages, as if they can feel what the serum is doing to Torbin. As if they feel he has their power.

Dante lifts his vial slowly, eyes meeting mine. The muscles in his jaw tighten for a heartbeat, until resolve slams down like an iron door.

After releasing a long breath, he swigs the potion.

I flinch as the serum disappears down his throat. For a moment, nothing happens. Then his shoulders twitch—once, twice—and he drops the vial. His breath hitches once before he emits a series of coughs. I feel like screaming, but I can't find the breath to do it. Dante bends forward, one hand on his knee, as though grounding himself against the sudden tremor racing through his bones.

"Dante," I whisper, tears threatening.

At first, he squeezes his eyes shut, his teeth gnashed together. Then he straightens slowly, his chest heaving, gaze locked on me. His throat bobs as he swallows. He looks as though he can't speak, but he gives me one curt nod, as if to tell me he's all right.

But I don't believe it.

With a mocking flourish, Torbin unsheathes his sabre, raising it high, then points the tip at Dante. "You came all this way just to be sliced to ribbons."

A guard marches out, carrying Dante's falchion. I see my dagger strapped to the guard's belt, the sapphire embedded in the weapon's hilt catching my eyes.

The guard hands Torbin the falchion before retreating. I keep my eye on where he is because if I can find an opportunity to get my blade back, I'm going to take it.

Torbin paces, a weapon in each hand. For a moment, I think he's going to keep them both, but then he tosses the falchion, hilt first, to Dante.

"Wouldn't want you to accuse me of not being fair, Brother." Torbin swings his sabre in a half-circle before adjusting his grip.

"We're far beyond that." Dante doesn't flinch. He takes one slow step forward, dragging his falchion through the dirt before lifting it into ready position. "And you can stop calling me that. From this moment, you are no longer my brother. You are nothing to me."

467

I can't tell if he really means it, or if the serum has shifted something inside him. Is it clarity, or has the potion made him crueler?

Torbin moves to the center without hesitation, his boots leaving prints in the damp soil. "You think she holds your heart? I can't wait to rip it out and hand it to her."

Dante sneers at him. "You can fucking try."

Torbin bares his teeth in something like a smile as they circle each other. His sabre glints as he moves, boots crunching over the blood-soaked earth. "I made them scrub her raw when she got here. Not that it helped much. I can still smell you all over her."

It's a lie—at least the scrubbing part. Though she did say Torbin wanted the 'scents from before' washed away, Staja left me to bathe on my own. Torbin is just trying to provoke Dante. Taunting him so he'll make the first move.

Dante's jaw ticks, but he doesn't rise to the bait.

They strike at the same time. The sound of steel clashing against steel is deafening. Their movements are brutal and fast, each blow meant to injure, to weaken, to end.

I can barely breathe.

The tsar and seer watch with pointed focus. The carnoraxis growl and shriek from their cages, agitated from the ruckus of the fight.

Torbin lunges, Dante blocks. Dante swings wide, Torbin ducks beneath it, his sabre flashing as it cuts across Dante's arm. The fabric tears. Blood seeps into the sleeve.

Dante doesn't pay it any attention.

Torbin chuckles, backing up but keeping his sabre ready. "I have the feeling you already know, Brother, but I have to say this—she is delicious."

My stomach turns. I rub my neck where the pain from his bite still lingers, like a brand of violation etched into my skin.

"Then again," Torbin says, orbiting Dante with the easy arrogance of a predator, "you may have been tasting from a different part of her than I. But if I win, I'll be sure to make my own comparisons."

Dante lets out a vicious growl. His next swing is aimed at Torbin's

neck.

Torbin deflects it at the last moment, the blades scraping so hard, it sends a shock up my spine. He spins and slashes at Dante's ribs—barely missing.

They regroup and start circling again.

"You're afraid," Torbin taunts, breathing heavier now.

Dante grits out, "Afraid of *you*? You've grown delusional."

Torbin's grin sharpens. "No. You're afraid that Celeste knows what I am and still might want to be with me."

"Like I said," Dante replies, eyes burning, "delusional."

They clash again, blades screaming against each other. Torbin ducks under Dante's guard and slams a fist into his ribs. Dante staggers back but recovers, driving his shoulder into Torbin's chest, forcing him off-balance. Dante takes the opportunity to swipe low, slicing a gash in Torbin's side.

For a moment, Torbin backs up, pressing his hand against the wound and then staring at the blood as if he doesn't believe Dante landed a strike. But then he grits his teeth and raises his sabre again.

Their blades clash a final time—locked. They press into each other, each trying to get the upper hand, but neither is willing to back off.

Then, as if by mutual agreement, they throw their swords aside. The falchion clatters near the edge of the arena, the sabre skidding to a halt against a blood-streaked stone.

They attack each other, hand to hand now. It's raw and ruthless, with Torbin landing the first punch. It's a clean hook to Dante's jaw that snaps his head sideways. Blood sprays from his mouth. But Dante retaliates instantly with a brutal knee to Torbin's gut, doubling him over.

The crowd roars. I want to scream at them to shut up.

Sweat glistens on their skin. Blood drips from both their wounds, their noses, their lips.

Torbin swings his fist again. Dante blocks it, then slams his elbow into Torbin's sternum. They grapple, dust rising around them.

I want to help Dante, like I did during the trials, but I feel the seer's gaze land on me. It's almost as if she can read my mind. It's almost as if

she's daring me. Like she will see to it that Dante fails if I make a move.

"Why are you holding back?" Torbin growls at Dante, spitting blood onto the ground.

Dante pants, chest heaving. "Maybe there's part of me that doesn't want to believe you're a lost cause. That there's still a part of you that's human enough to save."

"Now who's delusional? I don't need saving, Brother," Torbin shouts. "What I need is for you to let me go." Then he throws his forehead forward, cracking it against Dante's head.

Dante stumbles, knees buckling, but he doesn't fall. He lunges, punching Torbin in the temple.

Torbin's snarl curls through the air like coiling, venomous smoke. His chest heaves. But his eyes burn with that same twisted hunger that's haunted me since the day I found him in the pit.

He staggers upright, swaying slightly. When he straightens, there's a manic gleam in his eye. "You don't think I'll hurt you?" he rasps, his voice rough as gravel. "I'll do far worse than that. I will rip you limb from limb, shred your insides, and then, when you're a useless heap of blood and flesh, I will finally revel in tearing out your heart with my bare hands."

Torbin surges forward like a bolt loosed from a crossbow, driving his fist straight into Dante's face. The sound is sickening—a dull, wet crack that echoes through the pit.

Dante staggers. His knees give. Blood pours from a fresh gash across his brow, dark and gleaming in the firelight. He sways, breath ragged, hands twitching, like he's barely holding on. He almost falters as he gets to his feet, still hunched over.

Torbin circles behind Dante, arm raised, ready to bring his elbow down in a finishing blow.

No.

I push forward, heart slamming into my ribs, ready to throw my magic out despite the seer's glare. "Dante!"

In the final instant, Dante pivots. Faster than he should be able to, fueled not by strength, but fury.

He catches Torbin's arm mid-swing and yanks hard, using the

momentum to haul him across his hip. For a heartbeat, they're locked—Torbin midair, Dante twisting beneath him—and then Dante slams him into the earth with a force that shakes the entire arena. The air is filled with the echoes of a deafening crack.

Beneath Torbin's head is a jagged rock, piercing him. A grunt rips from his chest. His body seizes once and then goes frighteningly still.

Dante collapses beside him, gasping, one hand pressed to his ribs where blood pulses through his tunic. He doesn't rise. Doesn't move save for the rise and fall of his chest.

Dust hangs in the air. Smoke curls from the torchlight. My body is frozen as the silence stretches.

"Dante, please. Get up."

Dante's still breathing. I can see it—just barely. It's the only thing I'm holding on to.

In my peripheral vision, the seer moves. She leaves the tsar's side, her red cloak pooling behind her as she descends the stone steps into the arena, the silk whispering like smoke across the dirt.

"What is she doing?" I whisper, but no one answers.

The air around her seems to pulse as she approaches the two challengers lying flat on the arena floor. She kneels—graceful, deliberate—between the two broken bodies.

Dante stirs beside Torbin, barely lifting his head, the movement labored, strained. His bloodied face turns toward her, and something in him tightens. Like he's steeling himself for whatever she's about to do.

She lifts her hands, and my insides are screaming again. What is she doing? Is she checking if Torbin is dead? Is she about to declare Dante the winner?

Slowly, with a precision that feels like a ritual, she pushes back her hood. A cascade of dark curls falls loose around her face. Then, with steady fingers, she slides the silver mask from her eyes.

The air grows still.

Even from here, I can see her face. The high cheekbones, the set of her jaw. Her storm-grey eyes.

Dante goes rigid, his breath hitching. "M-Mother?"

I reel backward, blinking hard, trying to piece together what I heard.

He said *Mother.*

But there's no time for questions. No time to react.

Her expression doesn't change. There is no smile, no acknowledgment. She simply lowers her hands again. One to Dante's chest. The other to Torbin's.

Dante winces, his head falling back to the ground.

What the fuck is she doing?

I summon the buzzing in my bones, ready to throw her back off him, but the instant her palms touch the two men, the world shifts.

Everyone stumbles back. My head swims.

Power surges outward from her body—an unseen force that sweeps through the pit like a wave of heat before a wildfire. The torch flames whip sideways, gutters of wind spiraling around her. The dust kicks up in a swirling cyclone, lifting in blinding sheets.

The magic is not like the magic I know. Mine is like instinct, raw but alive, wild but pulsing with purpose.

Hers feels cold and piercing. Like blades. Like the spiked horns of a dragon. Like something that was once living and isn't anymore. It doesn't bloom—it *consumes.* It doesn't ask—it *takes.*

"Stop," I choke out, reaching toward the bars, toward her. Toward Dante. I push for my magic, scrape together the broken shards inside me, and try to summon something—any modicum of magic—to stop this. But it dies in my chest like a flame smothered beneath snow. My magic can't get out because hers is taking up all the air in the space.

The seer leans into the connection, her hands still pressed to them both. And suddenly, Torbin's body jerks. A faint glow forms, outlining Torbin's body. It grows denser. Thicker. Then it moves, like a current traveling, like a lifeforce is being dragged from one body into the other.

What is she doing? What the fuck is she doing?

Dante groans once. His head rolls to the side, then goes still. His eyes flutter shut.

Fuck! Did she just save him or kill him? *Please, no. Please, no!*

 472

A scream lodges in my throat, but I can't let it out. I'm frozen, my fingers curled so tightly, they burn.

The dust begins to settle, and the torchlight dims.

The seer rises without a single word, her mask once again veiling her face, her hood falling over her curls like a shroud. With an eerie grace, she walks away. As if nothing has happened. As if she hasn't just taken something from me I'll never get back.

A thunderous *crack* suddenly fills the air. The far gates to the arena explode inward. Stone flies. Shouts erupt. Chaos descends.

But I remain still.

Because Dante isn't moving.

CHAPTER SIXTY

It takes me a moment to realize what's happening. Splinters fly, dust kicks up, and shadows pour in like a tide.

Not guards. Not the tsar's men.

My squad? *How—?*

Aila bursts through first, blade gleaming as she charges forward with a feral snarl. Isaac follows, loosing arrows with deadly precision. One sinks into the throat of a guard, but it's too late. His dying hand jerks the lever next to him.

The cages slam open. The carnoraxis break free.

Giorgi slips through the chaos like smoke, already sprinting toward the far gates, eyes flicking as they map escape routes in a heartbeat.

"Mylo!" The word rips out of me, raw and breaking. "Get to Dante!"

He barrels through the wreckage, blood streaking his temple, eyes burning with fury and relief when they find mine. He charges forward, sword swinging as he tries to reach for Dante.

For a heartbeat, I can't move, can't breathe. My squad is here. We have a chance.

Behind Mylo, Sir Holden and Sir Donovan fight like men possessed. Sir Holden's sword cleaves through a guard with ruthless precision, while Donovan plants himself as a wall between me and the swarm, shield raised, shouting orders like we're still drilling on the training grounds.

I stagger forward, lungs heaving, and go for the guard with my dagger strapped at his belt. The side of my hand slams into his throat—hard. He chokes, stumbles. I rip my blade free and drive my boot into his stomach.

I need to get to Dante.

I don't think. I run.

A guard lunges to intercept, but Mylo slams into him from the side, knocking him flat with a roar. "Go!" he snarls.

Behind me, Nadya cries out, her palms blazing with fire. She flings it wide—an arc of searing flame that forces a pack of carnoraxis back. The magic flickers and spits, wild and unrefined, but it buys us precious seconds.

Mylo crouches beside Dante, pressing trembling fingers to his throat. "He's alive," he breathes, relief cracking his voice. "But I'll have to carry him."

I release a shaking breath. He's alive! Thank the gods!

Mylo hauls Dante over his shoulder, staggering under the weight but refusing to falter. My heart lodges in my throat at the sight of Dante limp and unmoving.

"Go, go, go!" Aila shouts, parrying a sword strike with her good hand. One arm dangles uselessly, bruised and bloodied, yet she still drives forward.

A guard barrels toward Mylo's unprotected side, blade raised for the killing blow. Aila intercepts, steel flashing as she hacks clean through the man's leg. The guard collapses with a howl, and Aila limps past, eyes blazing.

"Saving your ass again, Commander," she calls hoarsely.

"About time," Mylo grunts, adjusting his hold on Dante's slack body.

A bolt whistles past my ear—Isaac, calm as ever amid the chaos, reloading in a blink before dropping another carnoraxis mid-charge. Beside him, Lorne plows through two guards at once, his sword cleaving a brutal arc that sends them sprawling in a spray of blood. Their violence clears just enough space for us to breathe.

Across the arena, my uncle's eyes find mine. Just a flicker—his face as hard as granite, his sword dripping red—but the weight of that look roots me to the ground. Fierce. Proud. As if reminding me I'm not alone, even here.

Giorgi plants themself in the gap, blade flashing, blood streaking their cheek. "This way," they bark. "But it won't stay clear for long. Move."

I glance up at the balcony in time to see the seer's red cloak vanish into shadow. The tsar is already gone.

Fucking cowards.

A carnoraxis lunges at me, its claws slashing across my arm and ribs. Pain explodes hot and sharp. I stagger, blood soaking my dress. Desperate, I shove my magic out, and the creature is hurled back by a crackling force. But another pounces before I can recover, its jaws snapping for my face, its weight crushing me to the ground.

Sir Donovan's blade flashes, carving into its side. He shoves his shield between me and the beast, teeth bared. "Run!" he roars.

I scramble free, but he stays, holding the line. The carnoraxis pile onto him. He fights like a storm—shield smashing, blade cutting, blood flying—until one sinks its teeth into his throat.

"No!" My scream tears my chest raw. Power surges uncontrolled, bursting from me in a shockwave that blasts every carnoraxis back. The pit trembles with it. But it's too late.

Sir Donovan shudders, blood pulsing from his throat, and then lies still.

My body shakes violently, blood dripping from my wounds, fury and grief warring in me. There's no time. There's no time.

I grab Nadya's wrist and pull her, dragging her along as we run. Firelight catches her curls, streaking her smoke-stained skin. Her mouth is set, eyes wild.

"Are you okay?" I shout.

She nods, panting. "I think so."

She lifts a trembling hand, magic rippling over us like a veil. The world blurs. Sound is muffled. Shadows press in tighter around us. She's cloaking us, but I know it won't hold for long.

The squad pushes through the exit, Mylo carrying Dante's dead weight, Aila staggering with her blade, Giorgi carving a path. Sir Holden covers our rear, blade flashing as he snarls at the beasts snapping at his heels.

We bolt through the corridors beyond the arena, feet pounding cold stone, and as expected, Nadya's cloaking spell gives out. The din of battle grows behind us—distant now, dulled by walls, smoke, blood.

We're not safe yet, but we're moving. And we're alive.

Through the chaos, I haven't had a chance to let it sink in—my uncle is here. The sight of him hits me all at once, a rush of fierce relief that he's all right, that he came for me... tangled with a sharp edge of fear. He shouldn't be here, not after what happened to him. He looks too pale in the moonlight, too worn, and yet he stands unyielding, as if nothing could break him. My chest tightens until it aches. He's here, and I don't know whether to weep with gratitude or beg him to turn back before it's too late.

"You're here," I breathe.

Uncle Kormak wastes no time in answering—just pulls me into a crushing hug.

For a second, I forget to breathe.

"I had to come," he says quietly, his voice rough. "Dante said you were taken." His hand cups the back of my head. "I couldn't let him hurt you."

I lean into him for one breath, one heartbeat. "You shouldn't be here," I whisper. "Not after what he did to you."

"I'm still standing," he replies, stepping back. "Now, let's get out of here."

The cold hits us the moment we break free from the fortress. It slams into my lungs like stone, stealing the air from my chest. Snow whips

 477

through the darkness in thick, biting flurries, swirling around our heads and coating the already-treacherous ground in a fresh, deceptive sheen. Behind us, the fortress burns, torches flaring in confusion, the distant din of shouts growing louder by the second.

We won't have long.

Even if the guards aren't fast on their feet, the carnoraxis will be rushing out at breakneck speed.

We stumble down the slope, boots slipping on ice, then crest a low hill. For a heartbeat, I think we've gained ground—but the snarling erupts behind us. Shadows streak forward, hulking and too fast, their claws tearing through the snow. The carnoraxis are closing in. My chest seizes with dread—until a blur explodes from the treeline.

Wolves. Dozens of them. They hurl themselves at the beasts, silver pelts flashing, fangs snapping into scaled flesh. The night splits with shrieks of pain and fury as wolves and carnoraxis collide, blood spraying across the drifts. A few of the creatures are dragged down, but others barrel past, relentless, the pounding of their pursuit vibrating through the ground beneath us. And over it all—shouts. The guards are closing in too.

Nadya's hand slips into mine, fingers trembling with adrenaline and cold. "I can do it again," she murmurs beside me, her breath fogging in the air. "Just—Just stay close."

I nod, squeezing her hand. "We trust you."

Around us, the others gather—Aila nursing her injured arm, Mylo still hauling Dante's unconscious form across his shoulders. Sir Holden trudges grimly beside him, his sword dripping with blood, his face ashen but determined. Lorne, still gripping his sword, looks like a mountain torn from the earth, blood streaking his cheek but his shoulders unyielding. Isaac's bow is slung across his back, the string frosted with ice.

Giorgi glances up at the keep behind us, then toward the twisted sprawl of woods ahead. "We'll take the western ridge," they say, already mapping a path in their mind. "Snow's thicker there. Should cover our tracks if the wind keeps."

Uncle Kormak steps closer, his presence like a wall of stone against the storm. "Giorgi says there's a way out," he says. "There's a river—hidden underground, near the cliffs."

"The Schierling River," Giorgi adds quickly, urgency in their tone. "If we reach it, we can vanish. It's the only way out."

"If my soldiers followed my orders correctly," Uncle Kormak continues, "there should be a ship waiting for us where the river meets the sea."

My heart hammers. The shouts are closer now. The snarls too.

"Ready?" Nadya whispers beside me.

Her free hand lifts, fingers tracing invisible symbols through the air. Her eyes flutter shut, her lips moving in a whisper I can barely hear. The wind seems to hush for a moment—just a moment—and then the air thickens around us. A shimmer curls like heat off a summer stone, then vanishes. I send up a silent prayer that Nadya's magic is working.

"I can't promise it'll hold if we stray too far," she whispers, sweat beading on her brow despite the cold. "Stay close. No sudden moves."

We begin to move—one cautious step at a time, boots crunching softly in the snow. The castle falls away behind us, swallowed by the storm. No one speaks. The only sound is the wind, howling low like wolves in mourning.

I glance at Dante's unconscious form over Mylo's shoulders, his face slack and pale, lashes dusted with frost. Fear claws at my chest. "*Survive this,*" I beg silently. "*Please survive whatever the seer did to you.*"

The snow covers our tracks almost as fast as we make them, but I glance back, anyway—just to be sure.

The glow of torches wavers through the trees, distant but searching.

We push deeper into the woods.

Nadya stumbles. The veil ripples, like gauze torn by a knife.

"Hold!" Giorgi hisses.

We freeze. Footfalls crunch through the snow. A patrol approaches, their faces stern. I don't breathe. None of us do.

The guards pass within arm's reach. One glances to the side, eyes narrowing, as if he senses something just beyond his reach. My heart seizes in my throat. I swear he's looking right at me.

"Over here!" a voice shouts through the storm.

The guards jolt, heads snapping toward the sound. Without hesitation, they take off after it, crunching through the snow in the opposite direction.

I turn my head toward Lorne—his jaw set, one hand half-raised, his power flung into the night like a lifeline. He doesn't even look at me, but I know the strain it takes, know he just saved us all.

The relief lasts only a heartbeat.

A low growl rumbles through the trees, and I spot the gleaming, yellow eyes. The carnoraxis are here.

Around us, the veil shatters.

Nadya gasps, stumbling to her knees. The cloak collapses around us like smoke torn apart. The beasts scent us instantly, their snarls splitting the storm.

"Run!" Giorgi barks.

I grab Nadya's hand and help her up.

We surge forward, running for our lives—but one shadow stays behind.

Sir Holden holds his stance, a heavy brow lowered.

"No!" I choke out, spinning.

He meets my eyes. For a moment, the battlefield noise falls away. His lips curve, not quite a smile, but something gentler. "It has been my privilege," he says, voice calm even as the beasts prowl nearer, "to serve as your Royal Ward."

My throat burns. "Don't—"

But he's already moving. He charges the carnoraxis with a cry that splits the night, drawing them after him, his blade flashing silver against their dark hides. They swarm, teeth and claws and shadows—but he holds them, buying us seconds. Seconds we can't waste.

I'm being pulled forward. Tears streak my face as we race toward the cliffs. Dante's weight drags heavy on Mylo's shoulders, Aila stumbles beside me, Nadya clutches my hand like a lifeline. We carry on. Because we have to. Because it's the only way to honor the man who stayed behind.

 480

CHAPTER SIXTY-ONE

We follow Giorgi's lead through thickets and frostbitten branches, down an incline where the snow grows deeper and the air heavier. Mylo grunts with every step, Dante limp against his shoulder.

Sir Donovan's death weighs on me, his grim resolve still etched in memory, but it is Sir Holden who breaks me. His face, his voice, the way he met my eyes before turning into the dark, choosing to die so the rest of us might live. He was the steady one, the kind one, the knight who never doubted me, always on my side through everything, even when Torbin lashed out at me. He was my shield long before this night, and now he is gone. The ache claws at my chest until I can barely breathe.

But I cannot let my sorrow claim me. Not in this moment. His sacrifice demands more than my tears; it demands that I keep moving, that I carry his faith in me forward. So I bury the grief deep, force it down with every step, and let it harden into resolve.

I can't lose anyone else.

My eyes go instinctively to Dante. He hasn't stirred once.

I can't stop looking at him—at the pale set of his mouth, the bruises at his throat, the blood dried at his temple, the bloody wounds on his

body. The way his hair clings to his skin, damp with sweat and soot.

He gave everything to save me. He was willing to fight for my freedom.

And now I don't know if he'll ever wake again.

I still don't know what happened in the arena, but I can only guess that the seer—Dante's mother, if I heard him correctly—took the last breaths of Torbin's life and pushed them into Dante. Because he's still alive. But alive doesn't mean awake.

"We're here," Giorgi calls in a low voice.

The cave opening looms ahead, black stone choked in hemlock and frozen moss. It isn't a wide opening, but it's deep and swallowed in shadow. The sound of rushing water echoes within, cold and fast and merciless.

The air is thick with the bitter scent of hemlock—numbing, dizzying. My lungs ache just breathing it in. I cover my mouth with my cloak as the others do the same.

"We need to stay low," my uncle warns. "The air will clear once we're deeper. And mind the water."

He gestures to the small, black boat tied to a wooden post in the tunnel, frost cohering to the edges. There's just enough room for all of us—barely.

As we file in, Nadya and I slide into the rear of the boat, still holding hands.

"I've got you," Nadya whispers.

"I know," I answer.

Isaac helps steady Mylo as he climbs in with Dante, who still hasn't moved.

I make a noise as they settle, and Mylo gives me a nod. He knows what I leave unsaid: *Be careful, please.*

I settle beside Dante, holding on to his arm as his head slumps against Mylo. His skin is cold and clammy, but he's alive and breathing. I force myself to believe he'll be all right.

Lorne keeps a lookout at the cave entrance while we load up. Isaac whistles to let him know we're all aboard. Once Lorne joins us, Giorgi

pushes us off with an oar, and the tunnel swallows us whole. Isaac grabs the other oar, and the two of them steer the boat off toward the Batu Basah Ocean.

Ice drifts in fractured sheets across the surface of the underground river, cracking and shifting with each ripple. The walls of the cavern glimmer faintly, as if lined with countless tiny crystals, catching the faint light and scattering it in fractured beams that dance across the water. Stalactites hang from above like jagged teeth, mirrored by stalagmites thrusting up from the riverbank, forming a cathedral of stone that seems both ancient and watchful. Shadows stretch and twist in the inky darkness, the air damp and heavy, carrying the scent of mineral and cold.

The tunnel curves almost immediately, black as pitch. The boat rocks gently at first, then harder as the current tugs us deeper. The air grows damper, heavier. We all breathe through cloth, and still, the bitter taste of hemlock burns my tongue.

A groan echoes from beneath the surface. Something brushes against the hull—long, slick, and heavy.

Aila curses, gripping the boat's edge. "Tell me that was just the current."

"Not unless the current has scales," Isaac mutters, staring into the water and notching a bolt to his crossbow.

Water slaps the side again—harder.

"We'll be fine," Giorgi says tightly. "Just don't fall in."

We round another bend, and icy droplets rain down from the jagged ceiling. The tunnel narrows. The hemlock glows faintly along the walls, casting everything in a sickly, green hue.

Somewhere ahead, a light glimmers.

The exit.

"Just a little farther," my uncle says.

I cling to Nadya on one side and Dante on the other. I cling to hope, to the soft, steady heartbeat of the man I love, lying limp in the hollow of this boat.

The river current slows, then stills.

I blink against the sudden rush of cold moonlight as the cavern opens into the sea. The Schierling empties into a quiet cove nestled beneath jagged cliffs, where the Batu Basah Ocean glitters in shades of steel and silver. The air is sharper here—wet and biting, the kind of cold that seeps beneath skin and bone.

A ship waits for us in the shallows. Broad-shouldered, low-slung, and cloaked in sails so dark, they disappear against the night sky. Built in Messanya, judging by the look of the iron reinforcements along the hull—but there are no banners flying. No markings. Nothing to give away who we are or where we're going.

Aila is the first to disembark. Mylo follows with Dante's limp body propped on his shoulder. His boots sink into the slushy gravel as he splashes toward the waiting crew, who lower a rope ladder and help guide him up with careful hands. I follow close behind, soaked to the knees, Nadya and the others on my heels.

By the time we all climb aboard, the ship is already lurching forward, breaking through a thin layer of ocean ice. The sound of it cracking beneath the hull is almost deafening. I grasp the rail, boots slipping on slick planks, and feel the cold biting through my gloves and cloak. The wind screams around us, whipping hair into my face, carrying the sharp tang of salt and frozen water. Each sway of the deck sends a shiver through my body.

We move quickly, herding the injured toward the companionway. The wood beneath my fingers is slick and bitter with frost. My heart pounds, not just from exertion, but from a gnawing worry for Dante. Uncle Kormak remains on deck speaking to the crew.

"This way," Mylo says.

Tension coils in my stomach. Every sharp sway of the ship reminds me how fragile we all are, how little separates us from being thrown into

 484

the freezing waters.

The companionway creaks beneath Mylo's weight as he descends, still balancing Dante on his shoulder. I follow, noting how the narrow stairwell smells of damp wood and the faint, oily tang of the ship's lanterns. Each step is cautious; one misstep could send Mylo and Dante tumbling. I keep my hand pressed against the wall, trying to steady myself and my racing thoughts. For a moment, I allow myself a heartbeat of gratitude for this small reprieve from the wind before pushing down the fear gnawing at my chest.

Below deck, the air is still frigid, though there's some small comfort in being out of the wind. The room he lumbers into is small, spare, with nothing more than a single cot and a bucket of half-frozen water in the corner. The cot creaks under Mylo's weight as he gently lowers Dante onto it.

"I think he's fevered," Mylo mutters, wiping his brow with a shaking hand. "He's burning through his shirt."

I kneel beside him immediately. "Dante," I whisper, brushing damp curls from his face. He doesn't stir. His skin is flushed, far too warm. Sweat beads at his temples, adhering to his lashes.

I press my hands gently to his chest and call the power forward.

It comes—hesitant, flickering. But when it touches him, it... falters. Like something inside him pushes back. Like whatever the seer put inside him is resisting my magic.

I recoil slightly, heart hammering. "It's not working," I whisper.

Aila enters quietly, her hair damp with sea spray, a wet cloth in her hand. "Here," she murmurs, passing it to me. "We'll keep his fever down for now. Your uncle wants to speak with you."

I glance down at Dante, then to Aila. "Will you stay with him?"

She nods. "Of course."

I rise on shaking legs and make my way back above deck.

The cold hits me again as soon as I push open the hatch. Snow still falls, soft now, a lazy drift over the ocean. The sails crack mechanically overhead, and the moon throws a path of silver across the waves.

My uncle leans against the railing near the prow, his cloak drawn

485

tightly around his shoulders. His eyes are fixed on the horizon.

I smooth out the skirt of my dress. The dress Torbin made me wear. A macabre wedding dress. My mind spins with how much has happened since he tried to make me his bride.

"You wanted to speak with me?" I ask, approaching.

He turns slowly, his expression unreadable. "I thought I should let you know what was happening. We're headed to Alphemra."

I blink. "Alphemra? Why?"

"We're about a week out. If the weather holds."

"But why?" I ask again, wondering why he's avoiding my question. "I thought we were going back to Delasurvia."

"We can't," he says, gently but firmly. "King Silas took your disappearance as a betrayal. He's trying to take Delasurvia as a result of you breaking the agreement."

"But I didn't—" I shake my head, knowing it doesn't make sense to state my case to my uncle. It's not he who made the decision. "If he's trying to take our land, then that's even more reason to go back there. To fight. To defend what's ours."

"I know, but we can't do that yet. My troops will hold our defenses until we can join them. But first, we need to understand what's happening with your magic. And we need to ask them for help." His eyes meet mine.

I hesitate. "There's more you don't know."

He waits, silent.

"I saw something in the fortress," I say slowly, forcing the words out. "In the lower levels. Something massive. Something the tsar is hiding."

He frowns. "What do you think it is?"

"I don't know what I think," I admit. "But he's created creatures to do his bidding. I can only imagine what something that size will do." I don't mention Nadya's theory that it could be a dragon. Mostly because I don't want to believe it myself. "And the seer. Dante called her '*Mother*.'"

His eyes narrow. "You're sure?"

"I saw his face," I say. "He called her '*Mother*.' And she didn't deny

it."

"Then there may be more at play here than we realize," my uncle mutters.

I glance back toward the hatch, where Dante lies below. "That's what I'm afraid of."

He rests a hand on my shoulder. "Alphemra may have the answers we need."

I nod slowly, the sea wind lashing at my cheeks. "I hope so."

Because if we're wrong—if whatever the seer did to him can't be undone—then I haven't saved Dante.

I've already lost him.

It's been a week since we fled the fortress, but the endless stretch of sea makes it feel longer.

The ship creaks beneath my boots as I lean over the starboard railing, wind tugging at the loose curls that have escaped my braid. In the distance, the jagged outline of Alphemra rises through the mist, its sharp peaks like broken glass slicing the clouds.

The wind shifts, cold and salt-heavy, biting at my skin. I tug my cloak tighter.

I thought I was imagining it at first, but there's no denying it now. The buzzing magic stirs in my veins the closer we draw to the shores of Alphemra, like a tide swelling with each passing breath, carrying whispers of power that prickle along my skin.

Ezra will be able to help me figure it all out. One day into our trip, Uncle Kormak told me he'd sent a nightfeather to summon Ezra to Alphemra. The thought of Ezra at my side steadies me. If anyone knows how to help Dante, it's him.

Still, grief coils sharp in my chest as thoughts of Sir Donovan and Sir Holden haunt me. Two more lives cut short in the tsar's grasping

cruelty. The ache of their absence gnaws at me, but I refuse to let despair hollow me out. I will fight in their honor. I will see this through and ensure their sacrifices were not in vain.

Behind me, Mylo lets out a long, theatrical sigh. "I swear, if I never see another wave after this, it'll be too fucking soon."

Aila snorts. "At least you're not being dramatic and threatening to throw yourself overboard like Isaac."

"He hates ships," Giorgi says. "Or rather, what they do to him."

A loud gagging sound echoes from behind us. We all turn in time to see Isaac lurch to the side of the deck and retch violently over the railing.

Lorne raises a brow. "Well, at least it's keeping him from tormenting me."

"Fuck," Isaac croaks, wiping his mouth. "How is it still moving?"

"It's called sailing," I say, trying not to smile. "You'll live."

"Debatable," he mutters, sinking to sit against a barrel, pale as a bone.

The brief laughter warms my chest. It's the first time since Dulcamar that the weight has lifted, even slightly.

But it's still there—beneath the surface.

Dante hasn't woken.

He groaned once in his sleep yesterday, sweat pouring from his brow. His body burned with fever and magic I couldn't touch. I've tried—gods, I've tried—but even with my hands pressed to his skin, nothing answers.

Whatever the seer did to him... it wasn't to heal him. It's something else entirely.

I glance toward the aft cabin, where he rests. Nadya emerges from the shadows a moment later, her curls wild in the wind, her cheeks flushed.

"He's stirring," she says breathlessly.

My heart lurches.

I'm already running, trying not to trip down the stairs.

Inside the cabin, it's dim and quiet. The cot creaks as I drop to my

 488

knees beside it, reaching for him. Dante's skin is no longer blazing, just warm. His breaths are steady. His brows furrow and his lips part with a low groan.

"Dante," I whisper, brushing damp curls from his temple. "It's me. I'm here. You're safe. Please, just be okay. Don't leave me, not now."

He shifts beneath my hand. His lashes flutter.

When his eyes open, I hold my breath.

His stormy-grey gaze locks on to me, studying my face. "Celeste," he rasps, his voice raw and ragged.

A sound breaks from my chest. I press my hand to his cheek, and he leans into it, his fingers curling over mine. "We're safe," I say quickly. "We escaped Dulcamar. We're on a ship bound for Alphemra. My uncle's here. Nadya's safe. We all made it out."

His brows pull together like he's trying to remember. "How...?"

"I'll tell you everything," I promise. "Later. Right now, I just want to know how you're feeling."

His thumb brushes along my jaw. "Like I was crushed under a mountain and then buried alive," he says with a weak smirk. "But seeing you helps."

I hold his gaze for a minute, then quietly ask, "Do you remember what you said? Before you passed out? The seer, when she touched you... you called her '*Mother.*'"

The smirk vanishes.

His expression changes—eyes tightening, breath catching, as though I've hit something raw and barely healed. "I did," he says hoarsely. "Because it was her."

He looks away for a moment, as if he's bringing himself back to that moment.

I take his hand and squeeze it.

"I know how impossible that sounds, Celeste. I buried her. There's someone in that grave by my manor—someone so mangled, I couldn't really recognize her. They said it was her. I thought..." He swallows hard. "But I *know* what I saw. That woman working with the tsar, that was her. She's alive."

We're silent for a moment. We were both lied to, each of us by a parent we thought was dead. And it seems it was all part of some grand scheme.

"I knew your mother was a siren," I murmur. "But I didn't know she had... seer powers."

"I didn't, either," he says, shaking his head slowly. "She never spoke about it. Never hinted at it. And now—" His jaw tenses. "Whatever she did to me, I don't think it was just to save my life. I feel... strange."

I lean closer. "You scared me," I whisper. "When you collapsed, when you didn't wake up... my heart cracked open. I thought I lost you."

He reaches for me. His arms tremble, but he draws me down, his forehead resting against mine. "I would fight a thousand battles for you, Celeste," he says hoarsely. "I would burn down kingdoms. I would give up my name. My blood. My life."

I close my eyes, letting the words sink deep. "Don't say that. Just... stay with me."

"I'm here," he breathes.

He cups my face, his eyes intense as he takes in my features. And then his lips capture mine. The kiss is soft at first—barely a whisper. But it deepens, his hand sliding behind my neck, drawing me close as his mouth claims mine with growing hunger. My fingers twist in his shirt, clutching the warmth of him, the solidness, the truth.

He's here. He's alive.

I feel his breath stutter against my lips as he murmurs my name. "Celeste—"

He lets out a small gasp.

There's a tingling along my skin, and I pull back, alarmed.

Shadows fall across his face. The lantern above the cot flickers.

His eyes flash. Not storm grey. A silvery blue.

And for the briefest moment, his mouth curls. But it's not a smile; it's a sneer.

My breath catches. The scar that marked Torbin's face, my handprint burned upon his skin, appears faintly on Dante's cheek.

I stare, frozen in place, unable to breathe. The world tilts as I

stumble back, my throat thick.

Gods, no!

Something is wrong. Horribly, deeply wrong.

And it's inside Dante.

The story continues in

A Falchion in the Nightshade

Coming 2026

ACKNOWLEDGMENTS

I have been blown away by all the awards the first book in this series has won, especially because it is the first romantasy book I've ever written. Perhaps I have found my niche. Here's hoping, anyway.

That said, I had so much fun writing book two. I've always been a fan of games-and-trials books, but I was a little unsure about pulling it off. I hope Dante's trials met your expectations.

Also, I hope you enjoyed the extra spice.

I'd like to thank everyone who stood by me and cheered me on for both book one and the release of book two. I couldn't do this properly without the help of the Crimson Fox Publishing team, the support of my agent, my ARC readers, and my amazing editor Amy McNulty. I'd also like to extend my gratitude to the book tour companies who provided gorgeous posts of my books on social media. Heart eyes all the way!

And of course, there needs to be a shout-out to my family for giving me the time and space to let this world come to life, even though some of my own life was set aside or put on hold so I could finish the book.

There is one more book in this series. After that? Well, let's see.

ABOUT THE AUTHOR

Dorothy Dreyer is a Philippine-born American living in Germany with her family. She is an award-winning, USA Today Bestselling Author of fantasy, romance, and horror books that usually have some element of magic or the supernatural in them. Aside from reading, she enjoys movies, binge-watching series, chocolate, take-out, traveling, and having fun with friends and family. She tends to sing sometimes, too, so keep her away from your Karaoke bars.

Connect with Dorothy at www.dorothydreyer.com

Printed in Dunstable, United Kingdom

76394807R00290